The War Apart Part I

By

TJ Johnson

Library of Congress Control Number:
2008910664

ISBN 978-0-9764817-5-1

Published By
Hard Title Publishing

www.ItsFiction.com

The War Apart – Part I

In life, love often has to survive a variety of pitfalls. In this story, love must also overcome the trials of America's Civil War. Thrust into battle on opposite sides by family loyalties, Josh and Zeke must fight for their homeland. In spite of the terrible war, their hearts belong only to each other. The most terrible war on America's soil could not stop their love.

"**The War Apart – Part I** is an enjoyable read spiced with what-if diversions of fantasy, a romantic adventure, but one that is stained with history's blood – of families, friends and foes alike. At a time when men loving men was not considered normal, Josh and Reid avowed their love for each other before allegiances to the Confederacy and the Union could separate them. The horrors of war, the revulsion of slavery and the atrocities of prison life at Andersonville are woven into their story as easily as a drag show in Washington, D.C."
John Deen
Stonewall News Northwest
Spokane, WA

"This story is lots of fun as TJ Johnson mixes a unique twist of historical fact, with historical maybe, and inventive fiction to produce an exciting adventure with the bonus of a heart tugging love story. It is the love of the opposing young solders that transforms the fiction feel from a 'what-if' to a 'perhaps' there were gay soldiers from the North & South who were forced to fight for their homelands while seeking an end of battles and on to the blossoming of their romance. It's a fun story where you'll find yourself cheering for the good guys!"
Alan Anderson

Books by TJ Johnson

The War Apart - Part I

The War Ahead - Part II

The Will

Stranded

The Raceboys

Coming soon:

A Writer's Fantasy
(About His Favorite College Basketball Star)

The Blackfeet Boys

Gay Grifters

The War Beyond - Part III

Forever Alone…Again

Web Site and Release Information:

WWW.ItsFiction.com

This is a story of two men who fell in love in the midst of a country at war. The story weaves history and fiction so well that it leads one to believe these events could be true. It is a romantic adventure, full of the tears of sorrow, stained with the blood of families, friends, and foes. It is a love story between two young men from opposite sides of the country, and yet these differences drew them to each other. It is an enduring love story that takes on all odds. To the boys, who quickly become men, giving up on true happiness is not an option, regardless of public sentiment at the time.

The War Apart – Part I is a story of discoveries. Josh and Zeke discover their love for each other as a friendship is found between military academy cadets from both the North and the South. However, they suffer from jealousy and deceit at the academy, and find themselves forced to fight on opposing sides as the war begins. Nevertheless, they are willing to fight against seemingly hopeless odds to reunite after a long separation.

They also meet John Ericsson, the engineer building ironclad ships, and learn Morse code, see one of America's first drag shows, find a hidden homosexual bar, witness the cruelties of slavery, discover the trust only love can produce, and witness exploding trains, sinking ships, buried treasure, the price of past mistakes, and the human sacrifices that war inevitably requires.

Josh and Zeke are forced to become men quickly, but they survive what war and revenge can impose upon them so that their love can be reunited.

Dedication

This is booked is dedicated to the three most loyal friends I'll ever have—my dogs: Beeper, Megan, & J-Henry. They loved me no matter what – as long as I did not run out of Milk-Bones!

ONE

The fifteen hundred acre Johnson plantation was just over forty years old, established by Samuel Johnson, a ship's captain who saved his money for more than ten years to buy the land. With the deed secure in his pocket, he decided to make one last ocean voyage to bring to the States another cargo of African slaves. Unlike the other slave cargoes he hauled to the States, these would be different. This time Captain Johnson personally inspected and selected these plantation workers.

Most sailors of the ocean spent their silver and gold on liquor and women, but Johnson always knew his duties, as a captain, remained temporary. He was always fond of saying the slaves were a mere stepping-stone—a means to an end as. In his well-worn leather journal, he kept a careful tally of his money, and he always knew exactly how much more he would need to accomplish his goal for his future family. His plan included auctioning part of this last ship of slaves to use the profits to build a house, and develop a plantation on the land he had so carefully selected and secretly purchased.

Upon his arrival at the Carolina coast, he counted the Africans very carefully as they shuffle-walked down the gangplank wearing chafing shackles, and felt pleased so many survived the voyage, instantly making him one of South Carolina's largest slave owners. Many of the captains were cruel and harsh to the confused seasick slaves, but Johnson looked upon them as valuable investments, and he always took good care of everything he owned. He forbade his men to beat or mistreat the slaves, and warned the men to stay away from the women. You could depend on his word, and in return, he treated everyone fairly. When he gave an order, none of the crew second-guessed his decisions, and no one dared challenge him. His stoic facial features betrayed no hint of cowardice, but rather the traits of an autonomous leader.

He sold off over fifty of his top-of-the-line slaves to raise the capital for developing his plantation. His white workers grouped the remaining slaves in a line, and marched the darkies to the future Johnson plantation, where immediately they began clearing land, building cabins, digging rice fields, and planting corn, as well as a new cotton crop. With a careful eye to the calendar and attention to the weather, they worked without a day of rest. The captain never wasted a day. Later, he would allow the slaves to rest on the Sabbath, but not until they built the houses, cabins, and barns, filled the lofts with hay and the root cellars with fruits and vegetables.

Charleston became the most popular landing spot for Europeans discovering the New World. It almost never snowed, and the climate remained mild most of the year. The Europeans were tired of the windy, cold winters, and the bone chilling dampness they endured for centuries. They liked the heat and the sunshine that warmed their faces in Charleston. Since the South bought slaves in far greater quantity than the North, commerce grew quickly, and shipping flourished in spite of the occasional hurricane born in the eastern Atlantic. Charleston became a cultural town with plays, musical concerts in the park, dancing in the ballrooms of the larger homes, and fancy teas in the gardens.

Charleston possessed a captivating view of the harbor. The shipping companies that used its harbor were successful because they followed a simple formula. They arrived with a full cargo load of slaves, and shipped out with a cargo full of goods. Thus, they made money whenever their ships set sail. The big sailing vessels carried cargoes of cotton, rice, and indigo while bringing in thousands of slaves sold at the market right alongside the crops from the local farmers. Slave auctions became so large and important that soon the farmer's market became known simply as the Slave Market. In the first century of the American Republic, more slaves entered America through Charleston than any other port on the continent. Slavery became an accepted way of life, even to those who detested the practice. A person's status and way of life totally relied on a household of slaves to carry out menial tasks.

Even the most gentle of Christian wives found themselves dependent on the help of their slave maidens to empty their stool pots, and dress her with the extraordinary tight custom corsets, along with hoops and gowns that were the fashion of the day. Pride overcame sympathy in all the owners of a true working plantation. They emulated the lifestyle of the queen they left behind in Europe. The number of slaves owned was in itself a measure of their wealth. One could estimate the worth of any plantation not by the goods produced, but by their number of slaves. They even believed they were doing the Christian thing by taking such good care of their slaves who would have been lost in this big new world of America.

There were two large flowing, freshwater rivers, the Cooper and the Ashley that emptied into the ocean on each side of the point of land called Charleston. The river waters quickly mixed with the saltwater just as the numerous cultures landing in Charleston soon became the homogenous blend that made up the South.

Charleston was also a fortified city, at least from the prospective of attackers arriving from the ocean with Fort Moultrie on one bank and Fort Johnson on the other. Both kept a watchful eye over all vessels entering the harbor. For even more protection, they established Fort Sumter in the very center of the harbor entrance, maintaining a security level that had not been challenged in many years.

The Johnson plantation was just fifteen miles east of Charleston near a little village called Goose Creek, which was really nothing more than a tavern and an Episcopal church. It was a place where travelers from Columbia, South Carolina stopped off on their way to and from Charleston. The flatlands of the low country were a combination of swamps and pine forests. The pines stayed on high ground while giant oak trees grew in the swamps. Their branches were covered with a gray, sponge-like moss, pretty by day with their soft greenish gray glow, but dark, damp, and eerie at night.

It was a rich fertile land with many opportunities for growth and development. Samuel Johnson knew that as he had selected his property with great care. Before purchasing the land, he had spent an entire week riding over every square foot, acre by acre, while constantly checking and double-checking the quality of the soil. He had refused to close the deal on the property until it rained, so he could watch how the water naturally drained from the high ground and into the creeks and rivers. He had agonized about purchasing the swampland that bordered his property, but the more he studied the lay of the land, the more he realized that the swamp provided a natural boundary to protect his plantation. It was like a giant moat surrounding his American castle. He knew he would also enjoy the hunt of the plentiful game that fed off the swamp. There were deer, rabbits, and wild boar to be hunted for his family's table. Satisfied he found the perfect spot, he bought it without further indecision.

The Johnson property backed up to the Cooper River, which Samuel used for shipping his products to Charleston. It took several months to construct, but he managed to build a fifty-foot long dock so the bigger barges could get to him, and at twenty-feet wide, his wagons could delivery their goods all the way to the ship. Even some of the other plantation owners brought their crops to his dock for export—for a small fee, of course. In two years time, the small fees more than paid for the cost of building the dock.

He married a pretty girl from Holland he met while transporting her entire family over the Atlantic to the New World. She was barely eighteen years old when he asked her father for her hand. They were married on February 15, 1820 in the church at the four corners of law in Charleston so named for the buildings located on each corner of the intersection. They were the City Hall, State Office, Federal Post Office, and the church that represented God's law.

After a one-night honeymoon, he loaded up his new wife and moved her inland to the budding plantation in Moncks Corner so he could continue overseeing of the construction of their new house. The new bride was forced to live in a small wooden shack for almost a year while he built her a magnificent home. The house soon became a four-column, two-story home with a huge dining room and large kitchen in the back. He added a barn and stable to the farm, along with numerous slave cabins to accommodate his personally picked breeding stock of slaves.

Captain Johnson played matchmaker by often putting a selected couple together in the same cabin until they grew fond of each other and fell in love. Each couple that produced an offspring earned a new pair of work boots for the family. He cleverly had fathers and mothers encouraging their sons and daughters to find a mate so they could get their boots as well. His efforts paid off and almost every month a new slave baby was born, securing the growth of his slave population. Each new slave was purchased, in effect, for the mere sum of a pair of new work boots. Visitors would remark about how well dressed the Johnson slaves were and even more impressed that each slave had on a pair of boots. They thought Johnson was a generous soul while in fact he was a shrewd businessman. After all, a slave with a cut in his foot produced nothing.

Maintaining his slave numbers was a crucial undertaking as each year a dozen or more died, most commonly from mosquito fever, but sometimes from the bite of a water moccasin or a rattler. Two men had been attacked by an alligator sleeping in the dry grass on the edge of the swamp. One of the poor men lost a leg and an arm then bled to death before a doctor could be secured. The other man had been seen screaming and clawing at the ground while a large crocodile dragged him into the swamp and below the black, stagnant water. His body was never found.

An outbreak of smallpox killed six slaves in just a month's time, but Johnson kept increasing the quantity of his slaves through breeding. He was fairer than most and so far, not one slave escaped. He fed and clothed them, but still they were slaves—his slaves. He never mistreated a slave and thus never felt threatened, but he still carried a pistol everywhere he went. Once or twice, a year the **News & Courier** ran an article about a plantation owner killed or wounded by an uprising of his slaves. The remaining slaves and family members would not forget the article ended by stating the offending slaves were all hanged, and the limp, grotesque bodies were left hanging for a full week, instilling fear in the remaining slaves.

In two short years, the Johnson plantation had grown and prospered while so many others went bankrupt. Samuel Johnson was an astute manager of all his assets. He was also a tough disciplinarian, but chose to verbally chastise rather than use his fists or a weapon to make his point. All admired him. There was even talk of him running for governor, but he declined the offer saying he had spent too much time away from home as a ship's captain. For now, his intentions were to begin building his own family, and spend as much time as he could on his beloved Johnson Plantation.

Samuel's only failure was planting Indigo. He soon discovered it was just too complicated and too fickle to work with. Water levels had to be kept in perfect balance and that was nearly impossible. Rains came in the summer in the form of fast arriving thunderstorms and downpours, or there would be weeks of no rain at all. The consistency wasn't there for their primitive farming methods. Cotton, corn, and rice were easy for the slaves to handle so he dropped indigo from his production and chalked the loss up to his continuing personal education.

After a few years of hard work, his crops began to multiply and soon filled his bank account with more money than he ever dreamed possible. One of his favorite passions was riding and raising horses, and he used some of the money from the crops and bought top quality horses whenever he could. In just over five years, with careful attention to breeding and buying, his herd grew to over a hundred horses. He enjoyed breeding and training the horses, but not nearly as much as he enjoyed racing them. As with the slaves, he handpicked the matches, constantly striving for a better and stronger horse. Soon his horses were multiplying as well, increasing the value of the Johnson properties even more. He built a larger stable and purchased best tack, along with new carriages, wagons, and buckboards, along with uniforms for the drivers and grooms. He also hired two blacksmiths to make and install horseshoes, as well as various iron hinges and locks, and other metal works required for the rapidly growing plantation.

Samuel Johnson was neither tall nor short, but his stocky frame remained tough and lean. He declined gorging himself as so many sailors did, and now as a land based captain, he refused becoming lazy and fat. He saved his money and his health by eating lightly. His blond hair was not just sun-streaked, but natural and clear as if daylight could be seen through the strains of his fine strands of hair. Elizabeth thought he was handsome, even from a distance, but when she gazed into his ocean blue eyes, she quickly began falling in love with the captain.

Early on, he and his wife Elizabeth also began raising a family, and even though their first child had been stillborn, they were determined to try again. A year later the entire plantation took a holiday and celebrated with a huge barbecue feast when Richard Samuel Johnson, Jr. was born February 8, 1822. A year later, his sister Colleen was born on February 2, 1823.

Samuel was a good father and a great teacher. He taught his son to treat the slaves not as property, but rather as living assets. By that, he meant they needed doctoring, good food and rest, and a limited education. He didn't teach them how to read and write, but rather how to do a task, and to do it well. He made them practice even the simplest job over and over again until they got it right. They were never made to just do a chore, but rather to do it well and with pride. He congratulated them on a task well done, and encouraged little Richard to do the same.

As a young boy, Richard became confused as he watched how his father treated his horses and his slaves. To him it appeared that they were treated the same except that the slaves could talk, and some could cook very well. He laughed about his confusion later, but the point of his father's teachings stayed with him for life. He too learned that he could get far more from his investments if he treated his property with great care and concern.

Samuel carried a whip over his saddle horn, but never once had Richard seen his father use it on a slave or a horse. About the only time, he saw his dad use the whip was to kill a water moccasin. He always marveled at how his dad could snap the head right off the snake with just one lighting stroke of the whip. The slaves noted his skill as well. They heard of other masters who constantly beat their slaves with just such a whip. They were thankful Master Johnson was not like that, but they always shuddered at the sound of the crack of his whip.

Richard was a tall handsome man. This trait he got from his mother's side of the family. He had blond hair and deep blue eyes that came from his father's genes. He married Rachel Stewart, a mill worker's daughter he met on a trip to Charleston, on February 14, 1844. They met quite simply because he accidentally knocked her to the ground, a feat she never let him forget. Whenever her back ached, the accidental introduction was recalled as a mere sympathy induced tactic to get Richard to massage her back. She had long dark brown hair that flowed softly down to her waist. She almost always kept her beautiful hair pulled back with a bright red ribbon, which became a personal trademark. It only came off when they were making love, as she longed for him to stroke her soft, lovely hair. He delighted in doing so.

Even without the traditional corset, she had a tiny waist. She had a captivating smile that betrayed a sneaky, mysterious side while at the same time illuminating a deep sense of contentment that just seemed to glow from within. It was love at first sight for Richard, perhaps even the same for Rachel, though she never admitted it. After all, she was supposed to be mad at him for knocking her down on their first meeting.

As was the custom of many large plantation owners, Rachel simply moved into the family home with Richard after the wedding and helped his mother oversee the house and the planning of parties and other such social and charitable events. Mrs. Johnson spent lots of time teaching young Rachel the way to properly set a table, how to eat politely, and most importantly, how to be charitable.

Rachel learned that Elizabeth also knew how to get more work out of a slave by encouraging rather than scolding. Many of the households in

Charleston chose the cruel methods of their ancestors. Rachel helped Mrs. Johnson tend to the sick slaves, and even assisted with the birthing of a new baby slave. The whole plantation always took part in celebrating a new birth. She was also a big help in the planning of Elizabeth and Samuel's only daughter's wedding. Colleen married Bob Brown of the Piedmont region. The wedding was a happy occasion that ended sadly as Colleen left the plantation for her new home in the mill town called Greenville South Carolina.

On February 15, 1845, Richard and Rachel's first child was born. They named him Joshua Jeremiah Johnson, and naturally assumed that his birth would secure the family name for yet another generation of Johnsons. He was the first grandchild to be born on the new plantation. Two years later, his sister Mary was born on February 20, 1847, and almost three years to the day, Elijah Samuel Johnson was born on February 18, 1850, improving the odds for the continuation of the family name. There were now three grandchildren for Samuel and Colleen to cherish and love. Many of household servants loved the Johnson children, but they were especially dear to their beloved nursemaid, Sally.

Everyone called Joshua by his biblical name until he turned thirteen years old. He then simply told everyone to call him Josh. He thought this was an act of manhood. Everyone either obeyed his wish or got their ears boxed, except his mother who, in spite of his pleas, still called him Joshua. His dad called him Josh unless he was angry with his son, which was quite often. He then called him by his full name, Joshua Jeremiah Johnson, and usually loud enough for the entire plantation to hear, while hoping young Master Josh wasn't about to get yet another whipping.

Josh was an impatient, easily bored rascal who found adventure with every opportunity. He was curious about everything. He delighted in aggravating his sister by threatening to put his latest capture of a bug, frog, or garden snake on her lap. His brother, Elijah, was the youngest, and Josh detested the fuss made over him by his sister, his mother, and even his grandmother. He often felt he got off on the wrong foot with young Eli simply because of the adoration these three women bestowed upon poor Elijah.

In his short thirteen years, Josh grew tall and lean, almost six feet in height. He possessed deep blue eyes like his father and golden blond hair. Rachel claimed the genes for the hair came all the way from Holland. Richard reminded her that he had blond streaks in his hair as well.

Josh's tiny ears grew close to his head, which was the very reason his grandfather Samuel thought his grandchild could ride faster than anyone he knew. He taught his grandson all he could about horses, especially how to care for them. Josh knew how to tell a blacksmith what was wrong with a horse's hoof or shoe. By watching a horse walk, he could easily judge how well it would run. He recently made his grandfather howl with laughter after watching him stand up on the back of the trotting horse as if he was some kind of a circus acrobat. Only Josh failed to see the approaching tree limb that caught him right in the stomach, doubled him over and dropped him to the ground.

Grandpa loved his two other grandchildren very much, spending all the time he could with them on forays around the plantation, but Josh, his roustabout, easily became his favorite. Josh's sense of humor as well as his love for adventure was attributes that his grandfather could easily have said were his own. For his grandfather, the years at sea had been his adventure, while the plantation had been his dream. He and Josh were close pals.

Grandpa taught him how to hunt and to fish conservatively, never killing more than he could eat, and especially taught him how to bet on a horse. Josh loved his grandfather very much. From a very early age, he could be found trotting behind him like a shadow or stray cat. Josh looked up to him, and wanted very much to be like him.

Life for a plantation boy was really a lot of fun—or so Josh thought. He had almost no chores, as there were plenty of slaves, so he spent most of his days avoiding the schooling his mom tried to give him. He preferred to spend his time hunting or fishing or both, if he could manage it. The nearest neighboring plantation was fifteen miles down the road. They had two daughters, but no boys for Josh to play with. His friends became a slave boy called Knobby, so named because of his coconut shaped knee caps, as well as his reddish horse named Buck, and his dog Junior, a coon dog of very little intelligence but lovable nonetheless. Josh once watched his dog track a fox right into an old fallen log only to run his nose into a hornet's nest. The dog was immediately stung and took off yelping back to the plantation. He laid low for a few days until the suffering and swelling went away.

Having grown up around the plantation and the barn, Josh became aware of sex at an early age. He had seen horses do it many times. Quite often, he would menacingly fire his slingshot at mating chickens trying to knock the poor old rooster off his perch, so to speak.

One late summer afternoon, Josh and Knobby were hunting for rabbit deep in the woods on the western side of the plantation. They were having no luck, and Junior was growing quite tired of sniffing the ground. The dog gradually began walking slower and slower.

"Let's go back. My legs are tired," complained Knobby. Though he was and always would be a slave, in private he talked like a friend to Josh.

"We're almost to the road to Columbia. If we haven't found anything by then, we'll turn back and go swimming or something," replied Josh.

Knobby complied even though he was two years older than Josh. He knew that he was a darkie and Josh a white boy, and that was that, at least as far as he was concerned. Born a Negro and slave was all he had ever known. He had been bred carefully thanks to Josh's grandfather. He was lean and strong, and his muscles were well defined even for his young fifteen years. He had jet black eyes, and his hair was kept almost shaved on his head, to avoid the harboring of lice. He had a huge mouth full of yellow crooked teeth. Whenever Knobby broke into a grin, Josh would bust out laughing by just looking at him.

Knobby's mammy had been glad when Josh picked him as a friend because she knew that Knobby would be spared hard labor at his young age and would eat better too. She hoped that with luck, he might even get an education.

They had just leaped over a small creek, when suddenly they heard a yelp from just over a hill. Knobby's eyes went wide. Josh often accused him of being afraid of his own shadow. Josh put a finger to his lips to silence Knobby, and then waved his hand for the slave boy to follow him. Together, they cautiously crept over the hill on their bellies. Junior crawled up beside the boys, anxiously enjoying an opportunity to lie on his belly and rest. In spite of the noise, the dog was sound asleep in less than minute. They were just below the top of the hill. Suddenly, they heard a high-pitched scream, which caused Knobby to immediately start shaking with fear. The white of his eyes seemed to expand as if air had been pumped into his head like a balloon.

Knobby whispered through chattering teeth, "Let's go, Master Josh. Surely someone is being hanged! Let's go before we get kilt, too!"

"Shh!" ordered Josh. "Lay still and hush up, you liver belly chicken," he added with a grin, enjoying Knobby's trepidation as well as the adventure of the moment.

Josh slid up the hill a bit further and quietly pulled a briar limb out of his way so he could see. He spotted two ugly, bearded white men standing beside a beat up old wagon full of freight they must have been hauling to Columbia. One of the men had his pants around his ankles, and Josh could see the man's lily-white butt as the sun beat down on them. The peculiar sight almost made Josh burst into a big chuckle, but Knobby nailed such a thought with a quick unexpected statement.

"De's fucking!" exclaimed Knobby.

"Shh!" whispered Josh once more by placing his index finger to his lips, and frowning sternly at Knobby. However, his mind was already replaying what his friend had said, and so he looked back at the two men as comprehension of what he saw taking place took hold.

Sure enough, the half naked white man was pumping someone on the ground just like Josh had seen their old bull do out behind the barn. The other man was holding an old rusted muzzle-loading musket to the downed person's head. After about ten minutes, the scraggy looking white man, groaned loudly, became quiet for a few seconds, then stepped back and laughed heartily.

"Your turn, Fred, it's a good piece of ass!" he said as he jerked his pants up.

Just as the man stepped back, the person bent over the fallen log stood up as if planning to run. Josh and Knobby's eyes went wide when they realized the victim was not a woman as they had assumed, but rather a young man. His pants had been stripped off him and his penis swung loosely as he spun around.

Knobby exclaimed, "Oh, my gosh!"

Josh reached over and put his hand over Knobby's mouth to keep the frightened slave from screaming aloud.

Before the young man could run, Fred slammed the barrel of the musket across the poor boy's head then shoved the dazed naked boy back over the log.

His friend snapped his suspenders up, grabbed the rifle, and took aim at the boy, "Go at it, Fred, before I kill this son of a bitch."

Fred straightened the man over the log, spread his legs with a kick to the boy's heels, dropped his pants, leaned into the boy, and quickly began pumping him. Knobby closed his eyes as if hoping the white men couldn't see him if he couldn't see them, but the braver, more curious Josh watched what they were doing very carefully. The young man screamed loudly as the second man worked him, and then when he pulled out, the man stepped back, farted loudly, and laughed.

"Ralphie, I got to pee real bad!"

"Well, don't let me stop you. Hurry it up and let's get back on the road."

The man began urinating right on top of the fallen man. To Josh, it was like the man was marking his territory just as he had seen his dog Junior do many a time.

"That'll cool him off. Should we kill him?" asked Fred.

"Hell, no. Who's he going to tell? If it had been me, I wouldn't tell a soul if my life depended on it." He kicked the poor boy in the groin knocking him over on his back. "He's worthless. Not even worth a bullet. Let's go!"

Josh waited until the wagon had rolled around the bend and out of sight. "Come on, we have to help him," said Josh as stood up.

"I ain't goin' down there," replied Knobby. "I's afraid."

"Go fetch my horse and bring the water bag. Hurry!"

Knobby took off running as Josh began making his way down to the clearing. The man was still lying on his back, his groin exposed. Josh had just seen glimpses of another man's penis when they had to urinate in the woods. He and Knobby had skinny dipped together since they were eight years old, but this was the first time he had seen a grown man's private parts so fully exposed.

Josh knelt down beside him. "Are you all right?" Josh noted the man's bleeding split lip, as well as the blood that dripped from a cut in his scalp. He wasn't much bigger than Josh. The man was about twenty-five, guessed Josh, who was fairly good at guessing a horse's age.

The man groaned and opened his eyes. "Oh, my lord!" He quickly tried to cover himself with his pants.

"It's okay. I won't tell anyone. We should hunt those men down and kill them," said Josh. "You just rest easy. Knobby has gone for my horse and some water for you. I can take you back to the house and get you some clean clothes and a bath. I can't believe they did this to you."

The man managed to stand up though he was still a bit woozy, "I must go. Thanks, but no thanks. Forget you ever saw what they did. I'll get even with them. If it is the last thing I do, I'll kill them."

Josh watched the man dress and then hobbled down the road. Knobby came over the hill with the horse, Josh climbed up, and then pulled Knobby up behind him and quickly spun the horse around and road off in the other direction.

An hour later, with no other adventures to occupy them, the easily bored boys tied off Buck, quickly stripped out of their clothes and then ran as fast they could off the side of a big hill, screaming and crashing into a huge pool of water that had become their own private swimming hole. Josh was pretty sure that no hunter knew of the pools whereabouts, as you had to cross through some of the worst part of the swamp to get to it. Most of the white men stayed clear of the swamps as it was filled with snakes and alligators. Josh wasn't afraid of anything, while Knobby was afraid of almost everything. Josh often took advantage of Knobby's insecurities.

However, Josh wasn't afraid of snakes, and he rarely saw an alligator. He carefully made a hidden trail to the water hole by carving the letter J on the trees. In time, he and Knobby memorized the trail as they came there as often as possible. The two teens swam and played in the water over and over until their arms and legs were exhausted, so they climbed out and walked back to where they had tied off Buck. Josh pulled a blanket from his saddlebag and spread it over the soft grass on the high bank overlooking the swimming hole.

"Let's stretch out and get a tan," said Josh, still naked as he lay down on the clean blanket.

Knobby looked down at his naked body and shook his head, "I don't need to get darker. If I wus to get darker, you wouldn't be able to find me in the dark, now would you," laughed Knobby as he gave Josh one of his teeth filled grins.

Josh chuckled, "I guess not, but come on, let's take a nap."

Knobby lay down on his belly beside Josh who lay on his back. Soon the slave boy was snoring as usual. He was a bit like Josh's dog Junior. Given the opportunity to lie still for more than a minute, he was soon fast asleep sawing logs. Josh's eyes were heavy, but he just couldn't quit thinking about what he had seen earlier. He saw the two men doing it to the poor young man, and then he saw the man's genitals.

The sun and the daydreams awakened his own penis so he reached down to play with it while noting Knobby's smooth brown butt. He rolled over to hide his erection and elbowed Knobby. "Wake up, you lazy rascal. Rub my back."

"Huh? Oh, Geez, do I have to?" asked Knobby. The mere questioning of an order around the other white folks would have gotten Knobby's teeth knocked out, but he and Josh were friends. Josh allowed him to talk freely, rarely ever making him do something he didn't really want to.

"Please, Knobby."

Knobby preferred to sleep, but he sighed, straddled Josh, and began rubbing the white boy's back. Josh's erection increased. "Rub my shoulders," he ordered.

Knobby noted his Master's white ass. He loved to look at the gentle curve of Josh's buns that were like the melons on the farm. He leaned forward, his own naked and now hard penis bounced against Josh's white buns. Knobby became aware of his erection, but was not embarrassed as he and Josh were often naked together, and it was just something that always happened. He didn't know why.

Suddenly, Josh rolled over on to his back leaving Knobby still straddling him. "Play with it."

"What?"

"You heard me. Play with it."

"Master Josh, I don't think I should. I could get a whipping if someone was to find out. You could get a beating from Master Johnson, too."

"Knobby, just a little while, please."

Knobby had been skinning rabbits and chickens since he was five years old. His hands had pulled the intestines out of many a hog, and he had shoveled enough horse shit to last him a lifetime. In his mind, he had already touched the worst life had to offer. At least Master Josh's dick was clean, he thought. He took a hold of it and squeezed.

Josh didn't say a word but put his hand over Knobby's clenched fist, and began moving it up and down while squeezing.

"I feel like I'm milking a cow," laughed Knobby.

Josh didn't respond as he laid back and sighed. Knobby began to get worried that he was hurting young Master Josh, when the white boy's legs began to shake back and forth like he was having some kind of a fit. Josh's head began rolling back and forth, and the boy moaned. Nervously, Knobby looked down at his master's penis in his hand, and pulled up and down faster and faster until they both got a surprise. Josh suddenly ejaculated all over his chest and Knobby's face.

Knobby jumped back. "What in the hell...."

Josh quickly grabbed his tool and pumped out the rest of it. His stomach was now glistening from the sun and the juice that covered him. "Wow that was really something. Whew! What a ride!! Come on, let's wash up."

Josh jumped to his feet and leaped off the hill into the water once more. Knobby soon came running behind him. For the rest of the summer, at least every day or so, they returned to the swamp to play both in the water and on the shore. The swamp became like another world to them, a place where they could do as they wished and milk the cow as they called it.

The following winter nearly drove Josh's hormones wild. He couldn't go to the swimming hole, as it was just too cold and there was nowhere else, he and Knobby could be alone. By spring, he was too horny to wait any longer, so after a few days of warm sun, he and Knobby trotted off on old Buck to the swamp.

They found the water way too cold for a long swim so they quickly made it up the bank, grabbed the blanket, and laid down to allow the sun to warm the goose bumps that covered their soft flesh.

Knobby once again fell asleep on his belly. Josh got an erection and began slowly playing with himself while staring at Knobby's butt. Quietly, he slipped over onto his knees between Knobby's legs. Carefully, he bent down and pushed the tip in.

On an early September day, Josh had just downed his breakfast when he heard a bunch of riders pull up in front of the plantation. Josh leaned out of the dining room window to see his dad approaching the riders as they came down the long straight road that his grandfather built. Josh's grandmother planted fifty trees down each side of the road that lead to the front of the house. The trees, over forty years old, were now tall and their limbs canopied the roadway.

As the riders came to a halt, Josh recognized the man up front as Horace Adams. He didn't like Mister Adams. Neither did the rest of the family.

"Well hello, Horace. What brings you out this hot day?" asked Richard, trying to be as polite as possible, while inwardly detesting the man and the way he treated his slaves.

"Lost the trail of a runaway, you seen him?" replied Horace as he spat chewing tobacco on the ground. Josh laughed when a chunk of the slimy wet tobacco bounced off Mr. Adam's chin and fell off his shirt. "Damn!" said Horace as he brushed his shirt, spreading the tobacco-stained saliva into a large stain.

"Nope, I don't reckon he'd come this way, or he would run into the swamps, and I doubt he would do that. If he did manage to get through the swamps, he would then have to swim the Cooper River and it's too swift. Nope, he wouldn't come this way," hoped Richard. Richard would have done what he could to help the runaway, but it would have also put him in the middle of a dilemma, as he would be forced to return the man to horrible Horace. It was the law. It was the way things were done. He could have bought the slave to rescue him from Horace, but he believed the poor slave would in fact instill a sense of rebellion in his own well-mannered herd.

Horace surveyed the beautiful plantation house and grounds. He had also been jealous of how well things were done around the Johnson farm. He sighed, not wanting to directly accuse his neighbor of harboring a runaway so he took a different tact. "None of your darkies hiding anybody are they?"

Richard frowned, "My slaves are loyal to me and my family because we treat them well. If you but follow my example, you'd be sitting home drinking whiskey instead of chasing runaways."

Josh was proud of his dad's response as he slipped out onto the porch to listen. He knew that in the forty-four years of the plantation, not one slave had run. Josh observed Horace more closely. He noted the man was a bit taller than Richard, sporting both a moustache and chin whiskers. He had an ugly scar on his left cheek, and rumor had it that he had gotten into a knife fight after losing a card game. He had a fat wife who talked almost as fast as she ate. His house was always in disarray. He always wore the same crumpled black suit with a shoe string tie, and scuffed black boots and black hat. He had black eyes and a crooked nose the result of another card game quarrel, or least that was also the rumor. He could easily have played a villain in one of Charleston's famous plays at the Dock Street Theater.

"Yeah, right," stated Horace sarcastically as he swung back into the saddle. "Mind if I search the east pasture?"

Richard hesitated. After all, it was his land, but he didn't want Horace spreading tales that he and his family were uncooperative, so reluctantly he agreed. "Sure, go ahead."

Horace thanked him and kicked his horse, and the gang of twenty men trailed off down the road behind him. Josh came up beside his dad. "They're looking for a runaway?"

Richard glanced at his oldest son and answered, "Yeah." Then he faked walking away before suddenly turning and grabbing Josh in a headlock harshly while playfully rubbing the knuckles of his free hand into his son's scalp.

Rachel leaned out the window from upstairs. "You're hurting my boy," she teased.

"He's tough. All the Johnson boys are tough, aren't you, Josh?" laughed his dad.

"Ow! You're killing me!" screamed Josh as he tried to jerk free.

Richard laughed as he let go and then pointed his finger at Josh as he gently rubbed his head, "Just wanted to give you a sample of what is going to happen to you if you don't finish that book your mother gave you last week. I'm going to scalp you like an Indian," he teased.

Josh laughed. "I'm almost done. It's so boring. Shakespeare should be the name of an Indian fighter, a cowboy, not some turkey in the King's court!"

Richard laughed again as he put an arm over his son's shoulder and turned him toward the house. "Give me an hour of reading, and then you and Knobby can head off to the swamp. Is that fair enough?"

Josh knew the question wasn't really a question, but he appreciated the asking nonetheless. "Sure, Pops. I'll get right on it!"

"Good, now get!" exclaimed Richard as he took a playful kick at his quickly departing son's butt, deliberately missing him by a mile. Josh's sister Mary overhead her father's instructions, and she took it upon herself to add to Josh's directions. "Josh is so stupid. He has to read. He's got to read!" she repeated with a sneer.

"Shut up, goat face," he replied with a laugh while trotting up the steps and into the house. Richard quickly darted around the side of the house. Josh looked sheepishly out the front window. He didn't see his dad so he assumed his father was already off doing some chore. Josh walked quickly through the kitchen, stepped out the back door, and was suddenly tripped and knocked to the ground.

Before he could get up, a man sat down on top of him, pinning his arms beneath him. "And where do you think you're going? I thought we had a deal!" laughed his dad.

"Ow! You're squashing me! Get off!" exclaimed Josh, his face turning red.

"Not until you give me your word. One hour of reading, and not one second less."

"Okay, okay. I promise."

"Good," laughed Richard as he stepped back and pulled his son up to his feet. "Don't ever forget that I'm smarter than you are."

"Not for long," grinned Josh as he leaped up the steps. "I'm getting craftier and faster every day."

"That you are, my son, that you are. Now get going."

Josh's mom stepped up beside him, "What happened to you? You've got dirt in your hair." She began to brush the dirt from Josh's hair and the back of his shirt.

"Dad just knocked me to the ground. He's such a brutal man. I guess he got that way after reading Shakespeare," laughed Josh as he retreated into the house. Richard chuckled.

"Dear, you knocked our oldest son to the ground?" asked Rachel as she came down the steps.

"I caught him sneaking off to the woods instead of reading. I think I got through to him this time."

"I hope so," she said as she took his arm and led him away from the house. "Was that horrible Horace I heard out front?"

"Yes. He's chasing a runaway."

"On our land?" she asked.

"I'm afraid so, I couldn't refuse him, but I wanted to." He pulled her closer and kissed her temple gently. He smiled and winked at her.

She leaned into him. Worry crept across her brow. "I know, dear. I know."

The Johnson plantation library room was bigger than most of Charleston's private libraries. Josh didn't mind looking at some of his grandfather's picture books, but to read something scholarly just bored him silly. He glanced up at the big clock in the corner. Ten mor4e minutes he calculated. He concentrated on reading another page or two.

The hour of reading ticked by ever so slowly, but soon Knobby and Josh were riding Buck across the East pasture to the swamp, quickly forgetting all about Shakespeare and Horace Adams.

Josh and Knobby had been swimming for quite a while, never hearing the man on the horse as he made his way quietly through the swamp. The man stopped here and there to look at the footprints he saw along the trail. He studied them carefully, hoping he had finally found the runaway. He noted Josh's carvings on the trees. His curiosity kept him following the trail.

The two boys crawled out of the water and lay down on the sheet to play. Lately, they no longer waited for the sun to dry them off. Josh had just entered Knobby when they heard a twig snap. Before they could react, a horse pushed through the brush and the rider instantly saw them on the blanket naked and engaged in male sex.

Knobby shrieked, scrambled from beneath Josh, and ran frantically for the woods. Josh cursed and reached for his pants as he looked up at the ugly face of Horace Adams. The face turned into a wicked grin as he spat tobacco juice on the blanket. "I'd be doing your daddy a favor if I was to just go ahead and blow you and your bitch's brains out right now," said Horace coldly as he aimed his rifle across his horse at Josh.

Josh rapidly pulled his pants up. His heart was pounding. He chewed his lower lip, desperately trying to think of something to say. He knew he had been caught red-handed at something so many considered completely and utterly disgusting. It was just fun and secretive, just like what his parents did in the early mornings behind locked bedroom doors, he told himself. He had heard the bed squeak. He knew what they were doing. Everyone did. They just never talked about it. He had never considered being caught. He had no plan and no time to think of one.

"You seen my nigger?" asked Horace.

Josh swallowed hard. His throat was dry. He struggled for the words to come. He finally replied, "No, sir."

"I reckon you didn't have time to, now did you. You are one sick boy, Joshua Johnson. How's it feel to be the lowest form of life on this earth? You should whip that nigger, not fuck him!" Horace spat once more and then turned the horse around and continued through the swamp.

Knobby came out from hiding behind the bushes and grabbed his clothes. He was shaking, and though the sun was hot on his skin, he was shivering with fear. "What happens to us now?"

"Nothing. Nothing happens. Just forget you ever saw him. Just get dressed and let's get out of here, and if anybody asks, you don't know nothing, you hear?"

Josh spoke boldly, hoping every word was true. He silently prayed nothing would happen. He had gotten away with small things before. Perhaps this would slip by, too. At least he hoped it would.

TWO

Josh couldn't comprehend why, but the long silent ride he and Knobby took back to the plantation felt ominous. As they crossed the pasture to the house, Josh felt like the eyes of every slave and overseer were suddenly looking at him differently. It was as if Horace Adams had become a nineteenth-century Paul Revere, and had already ridden from field to field proclaiming what Josh had done. He had many friends among the slaves, but suddenly they seemed to be turning away from him, too busy to throw up a hand and wave. Was he overly suspicious or was it true, he wondered.

In truth, Horace had said nothing to the slaves, but guilt causes one to become apprehensive as well as paranoid, much like a child who hadn't been caught with his hand in the cookie jar, but still had visible crumbs on his shirt. He thinks everyone on the planet can see the crumbs, and the more he brushes the shirt, the more the crumbs seem to multiply and spread. It all suddenly reminded Josh of his Shakespeare. He just wanted to scream.

Josh tried to think positively. He even tried to think about other things. He thought about how beautiful the plantation was, the rich green fields, the order in which his grandfather had organized the planting, the rows of slave cabins, the barn and the blacksmith shop, the fantastic scents floating out of the big kitchen windows, and especially the thousands of flowers his grandmother and mother had planted all around the house. It was a magnificent plantation, and he was almost overwhelmed when he realized how lucky he was that this beautiful place was his home.

Josh and Knobby hadn't said a word to each other since leaving the swamp. They both feared the future, and though they couldn't, they really wanted to blame each other. Their friendship was already being put to the ultimate test, but Knobby knew that it was he that was the slave, and it was bound to be him that would bear the blame. Knobby was literally trembling when he climbed off Buck, and ran quickly into his family's cabin. Josh dropped Buck off at the stable, and gave the reins to a stable hand with instructions on how much to feed him. He turned to walk to the house kicking pebbles along the way, his mind deep in thought and fear.

He leaped over the short white fence surrounding their front yard and began walking through the hedges. However, as he came through the leaves and branches, all hope fell from his thoughts when he recognized that the horse tied up in front of his house belonged to Horace Adams. For the first time in his life, he wanted to really kill another human being, and now wished he had killed Horace Adams back in the swamps. He had just told on him, thought Josh. Adams was a grown up tattletale, he muttered to himself. He would never forget nor forgive Horace Adams.

Josh ran around to the kitchen, washed, and crept up the back stairway and into his room. In a few minutes, he heard Adams ride off. He then heard his father's footsteps coming up the wooden staircase. Josh's heart raced. He could suddenly feel his pulse in his temples. Josh quickly grabbed the Shakespeare book, and sat down on the edge of the bed pretending to read.

Richard opened the door so quickly that it slammed into the plaster wall cracking it. He closed it behind him, and stared intently at his oldest son. His father's chest began to swell much like a human volcano just minutes before explosion. Josh's heart suddenly seemed to beat louder in his head than in his throbbing chest. His palms were cold and clammy. He chewed his lip. Drops of perspiration fell from his forehead to his cheeks. His eyes were wide with fright. He struggled to hold on to the book. Shakespeare became his shield.

Josh didn't want to, but slowly he allowed his eyes to leave the pages of the book he had been pretending to read, and slowly wander across the oak wood floor and upward until he met his father's menacing gaze. Until that very moment, Richard had not fully believed Horace Adams' tale, but one cold hard tooth-grinding look into his son's rich blue eyes told him the tale that Horace had so delightfully described was indeed true.

He took a jerky breath, walked over, snatched the book from Josh's hand, and slapped him hard across the face. Blood spewed from Josh's split lip down onto his white shirt.

"How could you do such a thing? How could you?" yelled Richard with words that came from his mouth like fire from a dragon.

Josh's eyes watered. His brow wrinkled. He sucked in on his bleeding lip. "But Father, we were just..." cried out Josh.

Richard cut him off. "Not a word! Don't say a word! You're just a spoiled rotten kid. You have brought shame and disgrace upon your entire family. I must do something with you before it's too late, but for now, you're confined to this room. Don't leave this room until I say you can. Is that clear?" he yelled, his lips quivering with outrage.

"But father, please."

Richard swung out again and slapped his son across the face once more. "That's the trouble with you! You don't listen and you don't follow orders. You don't even follow God's law. You've done an abominable thing." He took a slow deliberate breath and said the next sentence slowly, while pronouncing each word very carefully in a lower pitch, and in an almost whispered voice, "Don't speak to me. Don't speak to me ever again. I am disgusted at the sight of you. You've broken your mother's heart. She is downstairs right now crying her eyes out. You're the worst thing..." Richard caught himself in mid sentence, sighed heavily, then abruptly turned and left the room slamming the door behind him.

Josh fell onto the bed crying, his head pounding, his heart racing, and the tears bursting from his eyes. By dark, he had fallen asleep where he lay until he heard the blood-curdling scream from out the back window of his room. Hearing the sound once more, Josh leaped up and ran to the window.

Again, he heard the scream and leaned out the big glass window to find a Negro man tied to a tree limb at the entrance to the slave cabins. The man had been stripped naked, a white man was flexing a whip back and forth, and then in a snap he sent the whip streaking through the air, tearing at the soft tender flesh of the Negro man. The poor wounded man let out another loud terrifying scream.

Josh's eyes went wide as he realized the young man being beaten and tortured was his childhood friend Knobby. He heard the white man curse and yell. He recognized the drunken voice as that of his father. He had never seen his father drunk before, and never in the plantation's history had a Negro man been beaten and yet now, his own father was beating the very life out of poor naked Knobby.

Josh watched in horror as the bloody red stripes began forming across the boy's back and more than once, the tip of the whip sailed around the boy's buttocks, tearing at his exposed genitals.

The entire village of slaves stood by helplessly as the boy was beaten over and over again. They counted ten lashes, twenty lashes, and then thirty lashes. Tears rolled down their silent horrified faces. Knobby's mother had to be restrained by his father, as she desperately wanted to rescue her son no matter what he had done. His screams pounded into Josh's ears. Josh quickly covered his ears with his hands but it was too late. The screams replayed over and over in his mind and refused to stop. Josh collapsed into a heaping sob on the floor. It was his fault, not poor Knobby's, he whispered to himself in the dark. It was mine, he wanted to yell, but couldn't.

A week passed when Josh's mother surprisingly entered his room. Josh sat up quickly on the bed. He had not seen his mother's face or anyone in his family throughout the week. His grandfather took his grandmother on an unexpected trip to Charleston. He assumed they didn't want to see him either. Josh knew he had broken their hearts as well. A tray was brought in for his meals and his chamber pot emptied. He had eaten little. His mother saw his pale face and her heart broke, but she stood steadfast and rigid by the door.

"Your father has refused to see you. The chore is left to me," she added as if still preferring not to even see or talk to her own son. "We have decided to send you to Pine Ridge Academy."

He asked in a whisper, "Where?"

"I'd prefer it if you didn't speak. Let me continue," she said coldly. His heart sank. He longed for her smile, her embrace. "Pine Ridge is in Petersburg, Virginia. There you will receive discipline and the academics as well as learn how to be a real gentleman. It's a military school. We will never speak of the idiotic indiscretion of yours ever again. I'm sure it was all Knobby's fault..."

Josh wanted to correct her, but chewed his bruised lip and said nothing.

"You're leaving before sun up. I don't want anyone here to see you off. Samson will take you to the train station." She handed him an envelope. "Here's your train ticket, and tuition for school. Sally will come in and get you cleaned up and packed. Good-bye," she added as she turned and left the room without looking back and without embracing her son.

Slow tears ran down his cheeks as Sally came into his room. Sally had nursed Josh from the day he was born, and looked after him every single day of his life. She was slightly overweight and had a good sense of humor. She also had a very kind and gentle soul. Her heart broke when she saw Josh's tear-streaked face. She quickly stepped into the room with two buckets of hot water. "Let's get your bath water ready, Master Josh. You have a long trip ahead of you. Come on now," she said loudly, as if saying it to someone out in the hall and not to Josh, who was but five feet away. Sally listened carefully until she heard Mistress Johnson heading down the steps.

"Come on, Josh, baby. We have to get your bath. Get undressed now."

Josh just nodded as Sally went over to the corner and filled the galvanized tub with the water. Josh wiped the tears from his face, slipped out of his clothes, and unashamedly walked over to the tub. Sally knew every square inch of his skin, and could tell you blindfolded where every single beauty mark was, so there was nothing he could hide from her.

"You okay?" she asked in a whisper.

"Yes, I guess so," he replied timidly as he sat down into the warm water.

She took a pitcher and poured water over his hair and began washing it gently with some soap.

Josh thought his next question over for several minutes before finally getting the nerve to ask. "What's happened to Knobby?" whispered Josh.

Sally rolled her eyes and sighed. "He was beaten pretty badly, and then Master Johnson had him hauled out of here. I heard he was sold away."

"Sold?" Josh wanted to cry, but no more tears would come. "And all because of me."

"Child, what's happened has happened. We can't take back things we say or do, no matter how hard we try. I'm sure this was just a child thing. But you're a man now and de good book says, 'when a child becomes a man he's puts away childish things.' I guess your pappy put away poor Knobby because he was a childish thing. You have to put away what happened, too. Shut your eyes now. Here come de water." She rinsed his hair with another pitcher of water and then began scrubbing his back.

"What's to become of me?"

"Well, child, as I sees it, you were due some learning anyhow. I'd say make this trip just another one of your adventures. You're going for a train ride, you're going to school, you're going to learn to read and write better, and Samson says you'll even learn how to use a sword properly. Now all that don't sound so bad does it now?" she smiled.

Josh tried to smile back, but he just couldn't. He loved the way Sally could always find something good in any situation. He began to think about what this school might be like, but even though it did sound exciting, it would not be home. It would not be the plantation he so loved.

Sally came for him way before dawn, and together, they silently crept down the stairs. Samson had already loaded a small trunk onto the buckboard. She handed Josh a checkered cloth filled with some of her buttermilk biscuits and another bag full of sandwiches. She gave him a warm hug, and he climbed aboard. Samson snapped the reins and the horse began trotting around the circle in front of the Johnson house, and then just before it turned down the long straight driveway, Josh looked up at the house he had been born in. All but the kitchen candles were out. He spotted no one standing at the window, waving goodbye. His heart sank.

Right up until he climbed aboard the buggy, he hoped that somehow his family would forgive and take him back. They didn't. Their rejection speared his soul as if he had been stabbed in the back with one of Shakespeare's bloody daggers.

Samson left him at the train station without a word. Except for Sally, all the slaves blamed him for the vicious beating that had happened to poor Knobby. Samson was one of Knobby's uncles. He understood Samson's silent accusation. Josh wandered around the empty train station. He read the labels on the wooden crates that apparently arrived in Charleston the night before. He found crates from England and France, and even one from China. He wondered what mysteries were inside the big wooden boxes. He could smell the salt air, and he began to wonder what Virginia smelled like.

He waited three hours for the steam locomotive to arrive. The big engine churned and spewed both smoke and steam as it rolled into the station. Josh waved at the engineer and hoped the man was smarter than the engineer on the infamous Best Friend of Charleston, the first engine built in America. After an exciting inaugural voyage, the engineer had grown tired of hearing the whistle from the steam valve so he wrapped a rag around it tightly to close it off. The boiler blew up and the Best Friend died a quick and sudden death.

Josh counted eight passenger and freight cars as they rolled by. The train came to a slow and jerky halt. A conductor waved him over, snipped his ticket, and Josh climbed aboard. He wandered from car to car and ended up near the end of the train. As the engine began to pull away from the station, Josh stood alone on the porch of the last car with no one to wave goodbye to. He had been on short train trips before, but never to Virginia, and never under such horrid circumstances. He spotted the sign that read Charleston South Carolina, and he wondered when and if he would ever see it again.

He investigated the lunch basket that sweet Sally had fixed him, but it was more out of curiosity than hunger. He had hoped to find a note there as his father often had left him hidden notes in his stuff. However, there was no note, no letter of goodbye, nothing. So he just sat on the well-worn, hardwood seat and stared out the window, wondering what future, if any, he had. For one moment of pleasure, his whole life changed. He knew the Scriptures, and he feared a verse that kept repeating itself in his head, "...the wages of sin is death." He caught himself almost saying it aloud and desperately tried to shake it from his mind as he watched the swamps that he loved go roaring by as the train picked up speed. His nostrils took in a long sniff, sensing that he would not get to smell the salty, musty air for many days to come.

Zeke Robertson just recently celebrated his fifteenth birthday with his family and friends. It had been a happy occasion with all of his favorite foods being served. When it came time for the opening of his gifts, he found the usual assortment—a scarf from his mother, a handkerchief from his grandmother with his initials embroidered on a corner, and a new pocketknife from his father, but it was the white envelope from his grandfather that changed the course of his life. His grandfather had whispered to him before dinner that his gift was indeed a special one, so Zeke politely saved what he had hoped was the best for last.

Zeke glanced up at the green and white sign that was labeled, "Portland, Maine" as the train began to slowly pull out of the station. It had been quite a while since he had left his hometown of Portland, but it was his first train trip, and he was very excited. He quickly turned back to wave at his family as they stood proudly on the platform waving frantically back at him.

He wanted to cry, but his father taught him to keep a good stiff upper lip, to hide his emotions, and so he did.

Zeke spotted his dad as he lifted his baby brother, Timmy, into the air so that he could wave, too. His middle brother James was standing with his mom watching the wheels turn on the newest steam locomotive of the N & B Railroad. Zeke waved anxiously until he could see them no more as the train pulled around a bend and blocked them from sight.

He had been very happy when he opened his grandfather's gift on his last birthday and discovered the letter announcing he was sending his oldest grandson to a fine academy, but now that the event was actually happening, he was not really sure he wanted to go. His father had assured him over and over again, how lucky he was to get such an opportunity, and how he wished he had had the same opportunity when he was a boy. Zeke felt obligated to accept his grandfather's gift. He felt as if the entire family's future depended on him getting a better education.

The Robertson family owned a small fleet of fishing boats. His grandfather started the business some forty-five years ago with just one boat. Now they had twenty. They weren't rich, but they never went to bed hungry. Zeke had been taught to work hard, do a task well, and to proper completion. There were many dangers aboard a fishing vessel, and he had been trained extensively on the proper procedures to insure safety, and followed each one very carefully and to the letter. He could sail any boat anywhere any time. He loved the sea. He had also been taught to save his money, preparing for the possibly of a financial storm, or at least that was the advice his grandfather always gave him. They were a frugal family, never letting on that they had money in the bank. They dressed well, but not too flashy, and they were kind and charitable to all.

Zeke had grown tall rather quickly, but he was also lean and trim, and made his bulging arm muscles appear to be even bigger than they were. He developed the muscles from hauling in the big nets filled with fish. He also had a strong back and wasn't afraid to work. Zeke had dark blue eyes that sometimes changed to gray with the change of weather. His dark thin hair blew gently in the breeze that floated through the train car's opened windows. He could run faster, and out swim any boy in town. He had learned to sail even before he learned how to ride a horse. He had done well in school as the harsh winters in Maine afforded him an opportunity to use and develop his mind. His mom had taught him to read as well as how to study, but now he was off for a formal education. He just hoped he could measure up to the other boys. He very much wanted to make his family proud of him, and to please his grandfather who had been so generous in the gift. He was a determined and handsome young man with a bright future and plenty of promise. Many Portland girls dreamed of being carried off by young Zeke.

Josh's neck and back hurt from trying to sleep in the most uncomfortable wooden booth he had been in since leaving Charleston. The train rolled on all night, stopping here and there to drop off a passenger, pick up a freight car, or load up more water for the boiler. At the Durham Station in North Carolina, they had stopped for a load of wood and for him, a much needed trip to the outhouse.

The conductor had just awakened him as the train began slowing down. Josh stretched and leaned out the window. Suddenly, they rounded a bend and the town of Petersburg, Virginia was before him. As they crossed over the Appomattox River, Josh delighted in looking down as the river flowed beneath the train. He sat up quickly in his seat and let his eyes take in the town. The conductor had told him the town was established in 1748 on the site of Fort Henry, and became famous during the American Revolution. He didn't say why as he continued working his way through the passengers. It wasn't as big as Charleston and somehow that disappointed him. After all, the bigger the town, the more mischief he might find, he thought.

Next to the southern end of the railroad station was a large stockyard, the smell of which nearly doubled him over. He wondered how anyone of any intelligence could live in a town that smelled so strongly of fresh manure.

He noted the small shops for merchandise and barbering and even saw a saloon. The railcar jerked a few times as the brakes were applied as the train slowly rolled to a stop in front of the green and white train station. Josh looked up at the sign and was pleased that it read Petersburg. He had been half afraid he had slept through and was in Pennsylvania instead.

He gathered his belongings, made his way down the crowded aisle, and stepped off the train onto the platform. People were shouting hellos and goodbyes, barking orders at freight haulers, and he could hear dogs barking. The conductor quickly called for all aboard bound for Richmond. To Josh it was chaos, and for a moment, he forgot why he had been sent here in the first place.

He spotted his trunk being pulled out of the freight car and instantly went over to claim it. As he did so, someone tapped him on the shoulder.

"Excuse me, sir. Are you looking for Pine Ridge Academy?"

Josh turned around quickly and was startled by the full-bearded face of an elderly man, in his seventies he judged, with white hair, gold-rimmed spectacles, and a black cane with an ivory handle. The man's intertwined beard instantly reminded Josh of the many bundles of moss he had seen hanging from the trees surrounding his home. The man pulled a gold watch from his vest where it was attached to a beautiful golf chain inserted through a buttonhole. The man checked the time.

"Yes, I'm Joshua Jeremiah Johnson, from South Carolina." Josh politely stuck out his hand.

The man looked over his glasses at young Josh but did not take his hand. Josh slowly let his hand fall to his side. Josh felt chided. "Very well, just follow me and bring your trunk with you. I have a buggy waiting for us over there," he pointed with the cane.

Josh quickly heaved his shipping chest up on his shoulder, grabbed his satchel, and followed the man through the crowd and over to the buggy. Josh gladly put the heavy trunk down in the back of the buggy and climbed aboard. The man just stood beside the buggy and said nothing.

"Aren't we going to the school now?" asked an excited Josh.

"Nope," he stated with no emotion.

"Where are we going?" asked Joshua, impatient though glad to be off the train and standing on firm ground.

"Nowhere, at least not for another hour or so I'm afraid. If you must know, we're waiting on another new student to arrive on a train out of Washington. The damn train is running behind schedule, so just steady your butt for a wait."

Suddenly, Josh remembered he felt the need to pee. "Can I walk around a bit?"

The man frowned. He liked keeping children in their place, but he could think of no harm in wandering about. At least the boy with the thick Southern accent wouldn't be asking him dumb questions, he thought. "Yes, I guess so. Check back here when you hear the train whistles. It'll be dark soon, and I want to get you to your cottage, fed, into bed, and out of my hair."

"Yes, sir."

Josh quickly took off half afraid the man might change his mind if he was to stay within earshot. Josh noted the large tobacco warehouse on the northern part of town where he could hear an auctioneer busily seeking a high price for the local farmers' products. He had seen auctions before, but mostly those held for the slaves at the Slave Market off King Street in Charleston. He didn't feel good about people being sold, but he delighted in the adventure of seeing a new recruit straight from Africa, and wondered if the men with the strange scar marks on the chest and face were once African warriors, tales of which his grandfather had told him of when he was a boy.

He listened to the auctioneer for a while, and then made his way down the street and around the back of the first store he came to, quickly undid his fly, and started to urinate. He had failed to notice the storeowner's big dog tied up nearby. The dog had sniffed the pee, woke up, growled, and leaped at Josh. Josh jumped back with the final stream of urine wetting the dog.

This made the poor dog even angrier. Had it not been for the rope that tied the dog to the fence railing, surely the dog would have leaped on him and ate him alive, or so Josh thought, as he backed up a step or two. Josh was surprised to find he had not wet the front of his pants.

A man suddenly opened the back door and stepped out with a two-foot long wooden club in his hand. He started yelling even before he noticed whom he was yelling at. "I've told you street urchins to keep away from my shop. I told you to leave my dog alone. I told you I would wallop you when I caught..." He stopped in mid sentence when he noticed Josh was not some street urchin all dirty and unkempt, but rather a respectable young gentleman, dressed nicely in his Sunday suit.

He also noticed that Josh's hands were holding his penis, and the boy's eyes were frozen wide with fear. He soon realized the boy had taken a leak and nothing more.

He dropped the club slowly, reached down, and petted his dog. "Calm down, boy. Calm down. Hush your yelping. It's just a visitor, not a criminal." He took another look at Josh and half smiled, "You can zip it up now. The dog won't hurt you, but if you leave your tally whacker out much longer, he might just snap it off. He's pretty hungry, and could eat just about anything," laughed the shopkeeper.

Embarrassed, Josh quickly buttoned himself up and started to retreat.

"Where you from, lad?" asked the man with a strong Irish accent.

"Moncks Corner," replied Josh.

"Monkey's what?" asked the man.

"Moncks Corner—it's near Charleston, South Carolina."

"Oh, I see. Come on in the shop. Don't worry. He won't bite you. You're too clean for him." The man motioned for Josh to come inside so he quickly slid by the dog and stepped in.

"Come on up front, lad. I've a customer waiting on me. We can talk there," urged the man.

Josh pushed through a curtain covering the hallway, and instantly realized he was in a barbershop. There was a man sitting in the barbershop, his face covered in shaving soap. Another man sat in the window, staring out intently.

"Have a seat, young man. Would you like a cup of coffee?" asked the shopkeeper who turned out to be the town's barber. My name's Ike." He picked up his razor and set about sharpening it on the long leather strap attached at one end to the wall behind the barber chair.

"No thanks."

"What's your name, son?" asked Ike, as he placed the razor on the man's neck and slowly pulled upward.

Josh flinched at watching the shiny blade pull at the whiskers on the man's neck. "I'm Joshu..." he caught himself in mid sentence and corrected himself quickly, "I'm Josh Johnson from South Carolina," he added.

"I'm pleased to meet you, Josh. What brings you to town?" asked Ike, as he rinsed the razor in a pan of water and began scraping once more at the whiskers.

"I'm on my way to school at..."

"At Pine Ridge Academy. I should have guessed. Your parents send you here?" asked Ike.

"Yes, sir, they did."

"Well, it's a hard, tough school, but if you hang in there, and take what they dish out, you'll come away a fine man. How about doing me a favor?"

"Sure," replied Josh not quite sure what the favor might be.

"I've already got another customer waiting on me," gesturing at the man sitting in the window, "and the sheriff is due here any moment for his haircut, and I've yet to get a break for lunch. Catch!" he tossed Josh a silver dollar. "Go across the street to Sarah's and tell her I need a lunch plate. You can get one for yourself if you like, and bring mine back here to me. Okay?"

Ike almost sounded like Josh's father. Giving an order and then turning it into a question, but Josh didn't mind. At least it would give him something to do. "Sure. I'll be right back."

Josh pushed out the door and realized there was nothing keeping him from just pocketing the silver dollar. Josh would never have done so, but he wondered why Ike trusted him not to run away with his money. It was refreshing to be in a new town where people talked and trusted you again. He made his way between the wagons up the steps and into the little corner restaurant. Once inside, Josh suddenly realized how hungry he was. The aroma of good food nearly lifted him off his feet.

A pretty lady about forty years old with bright red hair and green eyes came up to the counter and began wiping it with a towel. "May I help you, lad?" she asked in an even thicker Irish accent than Ike's.

"Yes, ma'am, Ike can't break for lunch, and asked if you'd fix him a plate."

"Okay, I'll be right back." She quickly turned to leave.

"Oh, ma'am? Could you fix me a plate as well?" He gave her a hint of a sly smile.

She turned back, gave him a good look, and then slowly smiled and winked at him, "I'd be happy to, child. Sit down, and I'll be right back."

She soon returned with two plates covered with red-checkered napkins. That'll be forty cents," she said as she sat the plates on the counter.

Josh stood quickly and handed her the silver dollar. She gave him his change. "Where you from, boy?" she asked.

"Charleston, South Carolina," replied Josh as he had already realized that no one here had ever heard of Moncks Corner. He picked up the plates.

"I've been there. It's a lovely town with so much to do. Let me get the door for you." She moved around the counter for the door. Josh was suddenly feeling a bit homesick. She smiled at him. "You off to Pine Ridge for school?"

"Yes, ma'am."

"Well, if you need someone to talk to, come see me or your pal Ike. He's my husband, you know."

"He is?" asked a surprised Josh, now wondering why Ike had to pay for his lunch.

"Yep, twenty years now we've been married. He was handsome like you when I married him, but now look at the bloke," she laughed. "Be careful you don't drop those plates as you cross the street, or Big Ike might give you a close shave with his razor." She chuckled as Josh recalled the sharp blade, gulped at the idea, and turned to cross the street.

"Thanks, ma'am, I'll be careful."

"What's your name?" she called.

"Josh. Josh Johnson," he called without looking back.

He hurried to the shop where Ike had already opened the door for him. Ike put his plate on the counter behind the barber chair, took a quick bite, and went back to cutting the man's hair. Josh sat down on the bench, removed the cloth, tucking it in his collar to make a bib and nearly passed out at the sight of fried chicken, beans, and potatoes. He began eating feverously, licking even his fingers clean.

"Josh, there's a professor at school who comes here for his haircut. His name is Frederick Abercrombie. Colonel Frederick Abercrombie. The kids call him Frederick the Great. He teaches battle strategy and history. Stay clear of him if you can. The kids say he's tough."

"I will, sir. I promise. Your wife is a great cook."

Ike patted his stomach. "I know, I know. That's how I got this big and tall," he laughed.

Josh suddenly heard the train whistle. "Whoops, I have to run, because I'm supposed to hurry to the buggy when I hear that whistle."

Ike came around from the barber chair and stuck out his hand. "It's been a pleasure to meet you, lad. Come back to see us."

Josh shook Ike's hand firmly and smiled. "I'll look forward to seeing you, and eating more of Sarah's cooking!" he said with a chuckle. "Thanks for lunch. Bye, now!"

"Bye," called Ike.

Josh turned the corner a bit too quickly and ran straight into a man with a full beard carrying a walking stick. Josh knocked him to the ground.

"Oh, geez! I'm sorry, sir. Let me help you up." Josh reached down to pull the man to his feet.

The angry man responded by striking Josh's forearm with a cane, nearly breaking his arm, and then grumbled as he got to his feet.

"Ow!" screamed Josh at the pain. "What did you go and do a fool thing like that for? It was just an accident. I said I was..."

The man cut him off and hit Josh with the cane across the shoulder. Josh screamed out and jumped back before the man could swing again.

"Take that, you heathen. If you ever cross my path again, I'll whip you good."

Josh didn't know what to make of what the man had said or done. He took a good hard look at the man's face, never wanting to forget it. The man's eyes were light gray, almost white. He wore a military uniform of sort, and his long white hair was pulled back under his hat. Josh then turned and ran down the street toward the station. When he got to the buggy, he found another student loading his trunk onto the back of the buggy.

"Climb aboard, you two. Let's go. I've been waiting here long enough," ordered the man as he climbed up into the seat behind the horses.

Josh nodded at the other student as they both climbed aboard and sat behind the driver's seat facing backwards. The horses pulled off and they quickly made their way through town and into the countryside.

"Hi, my name's Josh. I'm from South Carolina. How about you?" asked Josh as he smiled and stuck out his hand?

The buggy hit a rock and the two boys were knocked into each other. They both chuckled. The stranger took Josh's hand and shook it warmly while looking directly into Josh's eyes. For a moment, neither boy said a word. It was a moment Josh would remember for a long, long time.

"My name is Zeke. Zeke Robertson. I'm from Maine."

"Maine? Wow, that's a long way off," commented Josh, but inwardly he was thinking, my goodness, Zeke's eyes are as blue as mine.

"Yeah, my butt's tired of riding. The train was fun at first, but after a while, well, it just got boring," stated Zeke.

"I know what you mean. I wish we had a swimming hole around here," said Josh.

"A swimming hole?"

Josh gave him a puzzled look. "You've never heard of a swimming hole?"

"No, we swim in the ocean where I come from."

"I've been to the ocean, but the water is so salty and smelly. Me and my friend..." Josh caught himself in mid-sentence; suddenly the memory of poor Knobby invaded his mind like a plague. He struggled to continue, "Huh, well, we used to swim every day in the middle of the swamp."

"The swamp? Wouldn't that be dangerous?"

"Hell, no," shot back Josh. "You see, there's a small river that runs through the center of the swamp, keeping our swimming hole cool and fresh. We jump off a big hill into the water. It's great fun."

Zeke laughed, "It sounds like it. I can't get over your accent."

"What accent?" asked Josh?

"Well, you talk funny."

"I talk funny?" quizzed Josh. "You talk like you got marbles in your mouth!"

The two strangers elbowed each other and talked the whole way to school. When they reached the campus, Josh turned around to survey the school. There were a number of buildings spread out over a green field. The man said the two big buildings were classrooms, and the rest were student cottages. The buggy came to a halt near the fourth cottage on the right.

"Okay, you two, the ride's over. Get your stuff and go in that cottage right there. Take any empty bunk. Then report to the building with the flag hanging from the door. That's the administration building. You pay your fees there, and they'll tell you what to do next. Now get moving," he ordered.

Josh and Zeke scrambled out of the buggy, lifted their belongings, and began walking to the cottage. A cadet in full uniform walked past them, and they both turned to look at him.

Josh asked, "Geez, is that what we're going to become?"

"Yep, soldiers," replied Zeke.

"I can't wait to see what kind of horses they have here," added Josh as they stepped into the cottage.

"Me, neither. I love to ride."

"All right, so do I."

They stopped inside the door and surveyed the twenty-by-twenty foot room. Each of the four corners shared two bunks. The beds were standard army issue with a thin cotton-filled mattress over a board frame. In the center of the room was a small potbelly stove. Above the bunks was a single shelf and there were pegs along the wall by the door for winter coats to be hung. There was also a table with an oil lamp on it. The boys scouted the timber rafters as one by the one they read the names of the boys who had carved them there. Some names and dates were over forty years old.

"Over here by the window," urged Josh. "Let's take these two bunks."

Zeke followed him, "Sure, why not?"

"Let's go get this stuff over with, and then maybe we can check out the horses."

They each retrieved an envelope from their vest pockets and made their way across the parade ground. They spotted a few other cadets as they stepped into the office. A cadet behind the counter quickly stood and came over to them.

"Your name, surname first."

Josh hesitated while he thought about how to say his name backwards, "...Uhh, I'm Johnson, Josh."

"I'm Robertson, Zeke," added Zeke quickly.

The cadet scanned a list, and checked off their names. "Wait here. Do not sit. Stand straight," he ordered as he left the area and knocked at an office door behind him.

"Johnson and Robertson have arrived, sir," said the cadet boldly as he saluted the man inside.

"Very well, show them in," ordered the voice from inside.

Cautiously, Josh and Zeke walked into the commander's office. He stood, walked over, and shook both of their hands firmly. "Gentlemen, welcome to Pine Ridge. My name is Colonel Augustus Lee, commander of this school. I believe you have tuition for me." The boys quickly handed him the envelopes. "Very well. Mister Jones," he called. "Show these two recruits to the supply room. Good luck, gentlemen. Study hard and you'll soon turn into fine soldiers. That's all. You're dismissed." He turned away from them and sat down. Josh was studying the battle pictures mounted on the office walls. The cadet cleared his throat. Zeke quickly pushed Josh out of the room.

"Follow me," said Jones as he led them out of the office across the parade ground and into another building. "Stay here," he ordered as he led them into the entranceway, and then disappeared down aisles packed high with military uniforms and supplies. He soon returned with his arms full of blankets, pants, coats, shirts, and even new boots.

"Take this stuff to your cottage, pack away your civilian clothes and put these on. You'll wear these from now on. You are to address everyone older and certainly of higher rank than you, as sir. Do you understand?" asked Jones in a tone which said to them he had given this speech too many times.

"Yes," replied Josh.

"Aye," replied Zeke.

"Good, now get your butts out of here. When you hear the bugle then come to the building with the blue flag on it and we'll have supper. Get moving!" he ordered.

Josh and Zeke quickly made their way across the field and into the cottage where they dropped the heavy blankets and stuff onto their bunks.

"These outfits sure don't look too comfortable," said Zeke.

"I don't think they care what we think or feel, much less whether we are comfortable or not," replied Josh as he pulled off his coat and began unbuttoning his shirt.

"Yeah, you're probably right," Zeke replied as he unbuttoned his shirt.

Josh slid his shirt off and began unbuttoning his trousers, "What's Maine like?"

Zeke pulled his shirt off. Josh noted the bulging arm muscles and the tight stomach. Josh's tummy was soft and tanned, but he carried no excess weight. "I live on the coast in a town called Portland. My family owns a fleet of boats. We're fisherman, except my granddad wants me to be a soldier. Where do you live?"

Josh had just slipped out of his pants.

"You don't have any long johns on?" asked Zeke as he sheepishly stared at Josh's naked body. He was surprised how smooth and tender the boy's flesh seemed to be. Most of his friends were older fisherman whose skin was wind blown and tanned, giving it a rugged leathery look.

"Long johns?" asked Josh.

Zeke dropped his pants and Josh saw that he was wearing tight fitted white undergarments. "These. They keep you warm."

"It doesn't get that cold in Moncks Corner."

Zeke reached over to Josh's bunk, searched through the pile of clothing, and tossed him a pair. "Here. Put these on first. It'll keep these wool uniforms from itching us to death."

As Josh caught the long johns, Zeke couldn't help but notice Josh's privates. He hadn't seen a naked boy in a long, long time, and Josh's member was rather large. "Thanks," replied Josh as he tried to figure out how to pull them on.

Zeke laughed, "Here, let me show you." Zeke took the long johns and shook them out. "Sit down and put your feet in here and push." Josh did as suggested, but it wasn't easy. The cotton fibers had probably shrunk from a recent washing. Finally, he got his feet through the bottoms. "Now, let's pull them up." Together, they struggled to get them up. Zeke's head bumped Josh's penis, but neither boy said anything or pretended to notice. Josh felt Zeke's soft hair through his most tender organ. It was a gentle bump, but to Josh it was like a bolt of lighting. He quickly pulled the long johns up a bit higher, half afraid an erection might soon embarrass him.

"Now reach down and put your arms through these sleeves and pull it up and over your shoulders." Josh struggled to get them up and over but finally, he did.

"Now stuff your lily in and button up your front and you've got it," grinned Zeke.

"Stuff my what?" laughed Josh.

"You know, your worm, your lily. When my dad's got to pee, he says he's got to go shake the dew off his lily!" exclaimed a grinning Zeke.

Josh chuckled once more as he turned and patted his behind. "And what are these buttons for?"

Zeke laughed, "That's the crapper flap."

"Oh," was all a surprised Josh could say. He hadn't thought of going to the outhouse wearing a pair of long johns.

"Get dressed. Let's get moving."

THREE

They were delightfully surprised to find the stable filled with some great horses, and wondered which ones they would get to ride. The boys were also amazed to find the stable had been kept very clean and tidy by a crew of slaves who seemed to ignore their visit. They were just about to leave when a white man, an overseer, entered the barn and yelled at one of the slaves who had been shoveling manure into a wheel barrow.

"Samuel, I told you to walk that chestnut horse an hour ago. Now get to it," he ordered.

Josh noted the man barking the orders appeared to be in his early thirties, with a long black mustache that hung beneath a nose that had long ago been broken.

`"I is, Master Bell. But you told me to clean out..."

Bell kicked the feet out from under the young slave. The bucket of horse manure he was carrying fell all over the poor boy. "Don't ever talk back to me, you nigger. Now get this mess cleaned up, and do what I told you!"

The slave boy scrambled to his feet and hurried out the door. Josh chewed his lip. He didn't like seeing a slave mistreated. Zeke was appalled. He wasn't accustomed to being around slaves. He made a step forward to say something, or help the boy up, but Josh grabbed his arm.

"And what pray tell are you two recruits doing in my stable?" asked Bell as he noticed them.

"I'm just checking out the horses, sir. You've got quite a fine lot here," began Josh, reluctantly offering a compliment. "Someone here really knows how to take care of a good horse." Josh learned how to compliment a horse manager from his grandfather. He knew that the easiest way to get the proper information before a race was to use honey instead of vinegar, a favorite saying of his grandfather.

Michael Bell enjoyed the accolade, a clever ploy on Josh's part. "Why thank you, sir. We do our best, but boys, it would be best if you didn't come here except when it's time for you to ride. My boys will bring your horse out to you. I'm sure you understand," added the man so cordially that Josh knew it was a polite but direct order.

"I'm sorry we troubled you, sir. We'll be on our way. Thank you," added Josh as he pushed Zeke from the barn, and they began walking across the yard.

"Oh, you were no trouble. We'll see you soon," replied Bell almost too politely, watching them as they left the barn and began walking across the parade ground.

"Why did you let him get away with slapping that kid?" protested Zeke.

"That slave?" quizzed Josh. "I see. You didn't like the way he treated that slave?"

"That boy was barely twelve years old," stated Zeke.

They heard the bugle and began walking toward the dining hall.

Josh took a deep breath, "Zeke, I assume you didn't have slaves way up north like we do here in the south, so let me give you a few pointers. First of all, the man was wrong to treat his slave that way. My grandfather never did. My father never did," he lied. "And I didn't. We treat them well, and they work hard for us. However, and I mean a very big 'but', you don't tell a man how to raise his child, and you don't tell him how to treat his slaves. It is an unwritten but important rule. Do you understand?"

"Yes, I guess so, but I don't think there should be slaves in the first place," stated Zeke as they made their way through the door.

"Can we eat first before we have that long and deep discussion? I'm already starving," winked Josh.

"I guess so," replied Zeke as they got in line behind the other cadets, grabbed a plate and silverware and held their plate out for the slave cooks to serve them.

"May we join you?" asked Josh of two cadets sitting at a table that easily held six.

The cadets looked up from their food. The taller smirked, "Why of course. I enjoy nothing more than eating my fine dinner with a low life freshman who smells of new wool."

The other boy laughed. Reluctantly, Josh and Zeke sat down, already wishing they had picked a different table.

"Where you from?" asked the tall boy.

"I'm from South Carolina," said Josh proudly.

"I'm from Maine," added Zeke as he cut the beef and stuffed a piece in his mouth.

"I can't think of a nice thing to say about either of those places. I'm a senior, and it's my job to make your first year miserable for you. How am I doing so far?" he sneered.

Josh looked at Zeke who was already looking at him as if searching his blue eyes for an answer. Neither boy said a word as other cadets sat down between them and the seniors on the end.

When their meal was about done, a cadet rang a school bell two times and the room fell instantly silent. Commander Lee then stood from the head table. He quietly surveyed the room and smiled slightly, "Gentlemen, you are here for a reason and that reason is simple. We expect you to get a top education while learning how to be an officer and a gentleman. Before you become either, you must learn to be a good soldier and a good student. My staff will push you to work harder and study more than you ever have in your life, and if you survive, and that is a very big if, then you'll be something your family and you can take great pride in.

"But I warn you, every term we lose a dozen or more boys because they simply can't measure up to our standards. Those dropouts are to be pitied, my friends. Your goal is not be one of those quitters. No matter what happens, you must make yourself hang in there and stick to it. Your goal is to graduate with your class.

"As always, should you have a problem that needs my personal attention, my office is always open to you. Good luck, gentlemen. I surrender this time to Lieutenant Jamerson," Lee sat down.

A gruff-looking Lieutenant stood up. "You will have thirty minutes after you are dismissed to take a shit, and get yourself ready for bed. First bugle is at five. Breakfast is at five thirty. Don't be late. That's all."

Suddenly, the older cadets stood and began leaving the room. Josh and Zeke gulped down their last bites of supper, and left the room with the others. The outhouse behind their row of cottages was about fifteen feet long and had twelve holes. Modesty was not part of the construction. The room filled and a line was left standing outside. As one cadet got up and left, another went in. Soon the stench hurt their nostrils.

Zeke and Josh were near the last to go in, a mistake they would not soon want to repeat. Now they understood why everyone rushed out of the dining hall. Finishing the task, they headed for their cottage and received a big surprise. The two boys that were so rude at their table were in bunks on the opposite side of their room. Josh rolled his eyes as he sat down on his bunk. Zeke sat down opposite him.

"Well, looky here. Our friends have become roommates of ours, Eli," said the taller boy.

"Daniel, looks like your boots need a good polishing," snickered Eli, a pale-looking kid whose nose always dripped.

Daniel leaned off his bunk where he had already stripped out of his uniform, now wearing only his long johns. "Yep, you're right. Hey, blond boy, you stupid Southerner. Give a good shine to my boots now, you hear?" he said, rolling a thick Southern accent into his words.

"Not in a million..." shot back an angry Josh, but another older cadet cut him off across the room.

"Sorry, but you're a freshman. Freshmen are supposed to do what their superiors tell them, no matter what. It is meant to teach you how to follow orders, but it is also meant for us older ones to learn how to lead responsibly." The boy shot a look at Daniel. "Look fellows, my name is Thomas, Thomas Booker, and I'm your squad commander. You have to do what Daniel wants, or I'll have to write you up on a report that would mean you get a demerit. If you obtain twenty demerits, you're booted out of school. You'll need every spare one you can get to finish school this year. Don't waste a demerit over something as trivial as polishing an older cadet's boots. It just isn't worth it. Do you understand?"

Josh sighed. He had never even polished his own boots. He always had slaves do it. Zeke never had slaves, and had always taken care of his boots himself. Josh slowly stood and walked over and picked up the boy's boots.

"The polish is in the cubby hole over there. You there, you get Eli's boots and do them," ordered Daniel to Zeke. Daniel suddenly farted. "Oops! Sorry," he laughed again.

Reluctantly, Zeke obeyed. They had finished the task just as the bugle sounded taps, and the lamps throughout the school were blown out. Josh and Zeke slid out of their uniforms and slid beneath the heavy wool blankets. Neither boy could fall asleep right away. Josh, ever the avid hunter, soon picked up a faint groan from across the room. It took a while to put the sounds together, the low moan, the squeak of the bed board, and he soon demised that Daniel was masturbating.

As the realization hit him, Josh tried to pull the blanket up and over his ears to drown out the sound, as the memory of Knobby's soft butt began playing over and over in his mind. He couldn't force it from his mind so he tried to think of other things, the journey up from Charleston, the meeting of Ike and Sarah, and the meeting of Zeke. He finally drifted off as he found himself dreaming about Zeke's incredible blue eyes, as well as the moment his soft hair bumped against his privates. He began to swell.

Zeke didn't know what was going on with the moaning so he just turned his head toward the wall and did his best to fall asleep. He, too, recalled the two-day journey he had taken to Petersburg, and the fun he had had in meeting Josh, and the look of Josh's deep blue eyes. However, just as he fell into a deep sleep, his mind kept replaying the picture of a naked Josh. He saw the boy's soft tanned tummy and wondered why it kept consuming him. He recalled his close look of Josh's privates. He squeezed his erection, turned over on his tummy, and drifted off. He had never thought about anyone, as he was now thinking about Josh. It puzzled him, but he couldn't stop the dream.

It was still dark when they heard the five o'clock reveille. Zeke was up quickly, as he was quite used to rising early and heading for the docks to prepare the boat for the day's catch. However, Josh had been used to sleeping late while the family's slaves did the early work.

Zeke hurriedly slipped on his trousers. Josh hadn't moved. Zeke leaned over to shake him. "Hurry, Josh. Let's take a pee and get ready for breakfast. We don't want any demerits. Get up!"

Reluctantly, Josh forced his eyes opened, and quickly focused on Zeke's blue eyes staring back at him. "Right! I'm up. Here I go." Josh quickly pulled the blanket back and sat up. Zeke looked down and saw Josh's erection poking at his new long johns. It was huge.

"Get dressed. Let's go," urged Zeke as he sat down to pull his boots on and push the thought from his mind.

"Right," a solemn reply from Josh as he pulled on his trousers, stuffed his erection inside and then slid on his boots and buttoned up his coat.

"Ready?" asked Zeke, as they were the last to leave the cottage.

"Yep, I reckon. Just don't let me fall asleep on the way to breakfast, will ya?" Josh grinned.

They ran through the door and saw a line of boys standing at the edge of the woods.

"Geez, it's still dark," grumbled Josh.

"What they doing?" asked Zeke.

"The same that I'm about to do. They're pissing. Come on" laughed Josh as they joined the line, fumbled with their trousers, and began to urinate. Steam began rising from the stream created by a hundred young boys.

Finished, they ran for breakfast. They were told to eat quickly and silently. Josh nearly fell asleep as he chewed on some smoked ham and biscuits. To their sudden surprise, a bugle sounded, and they ran out to the parade ground. They were quickly shown how to line up properly and how to stand at attention. The upper classmen yelled orders at them. "Stand straight, chin tucked in, chest out, stomach in, no smiling!" Josh thought the last order was ridiculous as who could smile while holding everything in at this hour of the morning.

Lieutenant Jamerson explained the rules of the school to everyone. Then a young kid began playing a drum and they all marched around the parade ground for an hour. Josh and Zeke were terrible marchers. They always started off on the wrong foot. Then they were told to go their classroom, building B on the backside of the parade ground.

Josh and Zeke were the last to enter the room and were forced to take the only remaining seats in the front row. They vowed to start walking faster to whenever they went from the outhouse to the dining hall to the classrooms. They had just sat down when the instructor entered a back door. All the cadets immediately leaped to attention. All eyes were straight ahead, except Josh's.

"You may sit," ordered the teacher.

Josh looked straight at the professor and to his astonishment, it was the man he accidentally knocked down the day before, the very man that beat him with the cane. Josh rubbed the bruise on his sore arm. He was about ready to bolt for the door when the man began speaking. He was carrying that menacing cane as he made his way around the room.

"My name is," he paused as he said in perfect, well-pronounced English, "Frederick Abercrombie. Mister Abercrombie to you. It is my job to teach history to you urchins. You will do as I say, or I'll fail you. It's that simple. You will study hard, take good notes, and you will pass my tests or your life is over. Do I make myself clear?"

The room responded with a solemn unison reply, "Yes, sir!"

"Now we will begin our history lesson by talking about where you are right now. We need to build a foundation on which we can grow. We need to..." He suddenly stopped upon recognizing Josh.

"Ah, I see I have a friend among you. What is your name, soldier?" he demanded quickly.

Josh's eyes went wide, "Uhh, Josh. Josh Johnson."

"Don't you dare speak to me like that, you ignorant son of a bitch! Surname first. Weren't you told that? Don't you have any memory capacity in that pitiful grain-filled head of yours?"

"Sorry..." began Josh.

"Sorry what?" demanded the teacher.

"Sorry, I gave it to you wrong..."

"Sorry sir is the correct phrase, you bastard."

Josh's temper began rising. Zeke kept his head down, feeling woefully sorry for his friend.

"Sorry, sir. My name is Johnson. Josh John...I mean, uhh, Johnson, Josh, sir," he finally managed to get out.

"I'm going to remember you. This is going to be the longest year of your life, if you make it that far. Now what great fort was Petersburg settled on?" Abercrombie didn't expect any of the boys to be able to answer, but the truth was, Josh did have good memory cells. If he was told something he remembered it, then he decided whether it was important enough to use or not.

To everyone's amazement, Josh quickly replied, "Fort Henry, uhh, sir."

The answer caught the teacher off guard as he swung around and fired off another question, determined to make Josh falter, "And what was the name of the Great War that made Fort Henry so important?"

Josh again replied, "The American Revolution, sir."

Zeke was delighted and almost shouted aloud, but bit his lip. He was proud that his new friend Josh knew the answers because he certainly did not. Neither did the rest of the class.

Abercrombie turned away from Josh and looked back over the class, "Now listen, boys. Here are the facts and they'll be on the exams. Benedict Arnold and William Phillips captured this dear city in April 1781. It was also the site of the campaign led by General Charles Cornwallis. The campaign began here, but he was soon defeated and forced to surrender at Yorktown. Now that you know what happened here, let's go back in time and talk about European history..."

Josh struggled to stay awake during the two-hour class. At the break he, Zeke, and fifty other boys headed back to the woods for another pee. Then they were stuck in an English class before lunch. After lunch, they were taken to a field behind the barn and each given a long thin sword. The instructor began demonstrating the rudiments of swordsmanship. They paired off and followed his commands for over an hour. This was more fun than history or English, but it was still taught in a slow and boring manner. They really wanted to fight like musketeers.

Josh and Zeke left the field holding their shoulders. The thin but heavy swords wore their arms out. They were taken to a riding ring where each was given instructions on riding horses. Josh and Zeke did not listen very well as they already knew how to ride.

When they mounted up, they were forced to follow precise orders for starting and stopping, mounting and dismounting. Josh wanted to kick the horse, jump the fence, and ride off at full gallop, and Zeke would have been right behind him, but orders were orders so they obeyed. The hardest part of the new riding program was the way a soldier's legs never moved or bounced around, but stayed in close and still against the horse's side. They learned that it was their legs and not their hands that maneuvered a horse, much like the Indians of the West who rode bareback. This was all done so that a soldier's hands might remain free to fire and reload his weapon, or swing his sword in battle. It also kept the rider from being knocked off by catching his leg on an opponent, a piece of equipment, a fence, or even a tree. It was a new skill Josh and Zeke were determined to master.

By supper they were exhausted from the day's work, but when they entered the cottage, Josh and Zeke found Daniel and Eli's dirty boots beside their bunks.

"Clean them," ordered Daniel with a laugh. Eli snickered as he fell back on his bunk and farted.

Josh chewed his lip. Zeke patted his shoulder. "Let's get it over with." Josh agonizingly nodded slowly in agreement.

As they waited for sleep to overtake their tired, worn out bodies, they once again heard the moaning, so they pulled the blankets up over their ears and fell asleep secretively thinking of the other.

Three weeks passed, and slowly but surely Josh, Zeke, and the other freshman were beginning to march a little better. Daniel and Eli became bored so they dreamed up more and more chores for Josh and Zeke to do for them. Josh's temperament had more than reached its limit on many occasions, but Zeke kept him under control by reminding him of the demerit system.

Josh was heading to the outhouse and just as he stepped through the door, Daniel stuck his foot out and tripped him. Josh tumbled face first into the mud near the door. Daniel and Eli started bellowing in laughter and turned to walk off, feeling smug at the success of their prank.

Josh's anger overwhelmed him. His patience and temperament had run out. He leaped to his feet, ran out the door, spun Daniel around, and smashed his fist into the unsuspecting boy's nose. The crack of the bone caught everyone's attention, much like the scratching of fingernails across a blackboard. A crowd of students quickly encircled the two boys.

"I'm bleeding, you bastard. I'll write you up for this. You'll get ten demerits!" threatened Daniel, as he wiped the blood from his nose.

"You could write me up, or you could fight me like a man instead of running off to the Commander like a spoiled brat. Which is it, Daniel?" taunted Josh.

Zeke ran up and began cheering with the crowd for the two to fight, and yet he worried the bigger bully Daniel might beat Josh.

Daniel had been trapped into a fight. If he ran off to give the demerits, he would be branded a coward and traitor. "So, it's a fight you want. Well then, let's just explain the rules of cadet fighting to you so we can begin."

"What rules?" asked Josh, letting his fists relax a bit.

Daniel calmly walked closer to Josh and lifted his right hand slowly with his index finger pointed upward, "Now the FIRST rule is..." he stopped as the hand quickly tightened, became a fist, and he swung hard and hit Josh in the face.

Josh fell back and the crowd booed at the dirty trick.

Daniel laughed, "The first rule is there are no rules!" He swung again, but Josh ducked, and hit Daniel hard in the ribs, doubling him over.

The crowd cheered. Daniel had few supporters, but some of the upperclassmen were yelling for him simply because he was fighting a freshman.

"Finish him!" yelled Zeke.

However, Josh wanted more opportunity from Daniel, and so he gave the boy a chance to regain the wind that had been knocked from him. To Josh's surprise, Daniel faked a right punch, and caught Josh hard on the chin with the left. Zeke yelled encouragement to Josh.

However, the punch to Josh's chin did little damage as Josh spun around and hit Daniel once more in the face, and then landed a hard right to Daniel's gut. The boy dropped to his knees. The crowd cheered. Suddenly Eli ran from the crowd and leaped on Josh's back. Josh thought a huge cat had landed on him. Eli was pelting him from behind while Josh was turning round and round trying to get him off. Daniel saw an opportunity, stood up, and when Josh came around once more, Daniel swung hard and hit Josh in the face, splitting his lip.

Zeke leaped through the crowd and pulled the scratching, screaming Eli from Josh's back. Zeke spun Eli around and hit him with two quick punches to the face. Eli hit the ground—out cold and out of the fight.

Josh had fallen to one knee as the last blow hurt him. Daniel quickly stepped back and swung his right foot in an attempt to kick Josh right in the face. Josh stepped back quickly. Daniel missed and fell hard to the ground, flat on his back. Josh was about to jump on him when suddenly a bugle sounded for them to assemble. They had expected the dinner bell, but this was an emergency assembly.

The boys scattered quickly to the parade field. Josh did not know what to do. Zeke pulled him up. "Come on, there's nothing more to do here. We must hurry!"

Josh gave Daniel's bloody face a hard stare.

Daniel propped up on one elbow, "This isn't over, Johnson. I'll get you yet."

"Yeah, you just try, and I'll wallop you some more!" Josh called back as they rounded the cottage and headed out to the field.

Zeke and Josh quickly found their place in line. They were surprised to find not the usual Lieutenant Jamerson in front of them preparing to give them the orders of the day, but rather Colonel Lee, whom they rarely saw or talked to. Daniel was the last to get in line, wiping the blood from his face as he ran to his spot.

"Gentlemen, stand at ease," ordered Lee. "In the past couple of days some important events have happened not too far from us. As you know, the political debate over the slavery issue has been heating up. It is not a soldier's duty to think politics. It's bad enough we have to talk to the politicians," he added with a slight, mischievous grin. "We are trained fighters, but as part of your education, it is important for you to know what is happening in the world outside this academy. Two days ago, on October 16, 1859," he stated slowly as if he were one of the professors preparing his students for an exam, "a zealot by the name of John Brown, led a group of rebel abolitionists as they seized a federal armory in Harper's Ferry at the junction of the Shenandoah and Potomac rivers. It was Brown's plan to use the weapons to establish a place where runaway slaves could find safe passage.

"My father, Colonel Robert E. Lee, used both State and Federal troops to storm the armory and force surrender." Lee stated the last sentence with great pride. The cadets knew of his father's career and they almost broke into a cheer, but adhered to orders, and stood still and remained quiet.

"Seventeen of Brown's supporters were killed. Two of Brown's own sons were killed. Brown was convicted of treason and hanged. Gentlemen, I bring this historic event to you for two reasons. One, we must be prepared to fight our enemies anytime anywhere. We must make ourselves fit for battle physically and mentally. You must push yourselves to study hard and fast, as we never know when we shall be called to serve with honor. In addition, the battlefield is not a place to decide the issue of slavery. My family has slaves on their farms for decades. We treat them well. Shall one man such as Brown decide for the rest of us how we shall live? Shall he draw up his sword and force me to make that decision? I think not. We are a democratic society. Congress makes those decisions, and not the likes of some hooligan like John Brown."

He paused as if surprised he had said all he had actually said. He added simply, "Remember today. Remember it well."

The lieutenant called for attention, and the cadets snapped to attention and saluted. The colonel returned their salute, then turned and left the field. The boys were dismissed for lunch.

Zeke gave Josh his handkerchief so he could wipe the blood from his face and hands.

"Do I look that bad?" asked Josh as he looked up into Zeke's eyes, and noticed the worry there. Zeke's brow wrinkled as he studied the purple bruises already beginning to swell.

"Nope, not nearly as bad as Daniel. You know, we haven't seen or heard the last of him," warned Zeke.

"I know, but perhaps he'll think twice about bothering us for a while. I don't mind the cleaning of the boots. We all do that. It's the way in which he says things. He's a pompous ass!" laughed Josh.

"Come on. Let's eat, you fool," chuckled Zeke as he put an arm over Josh's shoulder and turned him toward the dining hall.

In the weeks that followed, Daniel and Josh rarely spoke. Josh still cleaned the boy's boots, but little else. Besides, Josh was having a hard time keeping up with Abercrombie and his history class.

As they practiced their swordsmanship on each other, Zeke would shout out questions to Josh who would struggle, but would eventually find the answers somewhere in his head. There were many facts he stored away, and he just was not sure of their meanings or importance.

Zeke got a B on his mid terms while Josh got a D. They both vowed to try harder to beat old man Abercrombie. They were studying in the small library in the building next to the dining hall.

"What are you reading?" asked Josh as he looked up from his notes.

"Oh, it is a letter from home. Mom wrote to tell me they're planning a big homecoming Christmas celebration for me," beamed Zeke.

"That's great," replied Josh with little enthusiasm.

Zeke quickly finished the letter, his face bubbling with pride. "What are you doing for Christmas?" he asked as he folded up the letter.

"I don't know," replied Josh without looking up.

"Have you heard from them yet? You are going home, aren't you?" asked Zeke, well aware that Josh had not received any mail since arriving at school.

Josh looked up from the book. Already his eyes were watery. Zeke looked into his eyes, already wishing he had not asked the question. He could sense that his friend was hurting. He did not know why Josh's family refused to write. Josh and Zeke had so little privacy; he just didn't have the chance to ask.

"I've heard nothing. I'll make plans to stay here. Maybe I could help Ike in his shop."

Zeke's face suddenly sparkled as a huge idea just over-whelmed him. "Why don't you come home with me? You could see Maine, meet my family, and we could have a blast."

The idea shocked Josh. He didn't know what to say. He was afraid to say yes. "I don't think your parents would want a stranger in their house at Christmas time."

"Stranger?" Zeke looked left and right as if searching for one. "I don't see a stranger around here." He paused and looked Josh straight in his eyes, "I do see my only best friend in the whole wide world sitting across from me. My family would take great delight in meeting this crazy person, my best friend."

He had said it twice, as if making sure Josh heard him. "Well, maybe..."

"Good. It's settled then," said Zeke quickly. "I'll write them today and obtain their permission." He quickly started arranging the paper for his letter. "Now what was Napoleon's last battle?" he quizzed Josh once more.

Josh gave him a frown, still savoring the thought of spending Christmas with Zeke. "Do we have to study some more?"

"Are you going to let Frederick the Fart beat you? Are you?" taunted Zeke.

"Hell no. Let's see..."

FOUR

Zeke encouraged Josh to send a note to his folks to let them know he was not coming home to South Carolina for Christmas, but Josh was angry they had not written him, and so he refused to write a letter. Still, as the train rolled along the tracks, Josh could not believe he was heading north to Maine with his best friend Zeke, and even farther away from his family. He wondered if they still hated him.

They had been traveling for a few hours on the second day of their journey, and already Josh noted that the accents of the voices he overheard on the train had changed greatly. He quickly became a member of the Southern minority on the train.

He enjoyed overhearing conversations of the people around them. He heard all kinds of interesting things like the men who were discussing expanding the railroad to the west, and two men who talked about a new ironclad boat they had seen. Josh yawned and turned to his left to find Zeke sound asleep, his head propped up against a window. Josh picked up a newspaper someone left behind after getting off in Philadelphia. The train had been packed ever since leaving Washington. Since he had plenty of time on his hands, he read every word in the newspaper, even the advertisements. He saw an ad selling a new plow for three dollars. He shook his head in amazement, knowing his daddy would never have paid that much.

He was particularly engrossed in a story about Harper's Ferry and the arguments made for abolishing slavery. References that grossly assumed that all slaves were treated like those in Harriett Beecher Stowe's novel Uncle Tom's Cabin just made him sick. He knew his family treated their slaves very well, providing everything for them. He then read about a man from the Midwest, named Abraham Lincoln, who was a part of the newly formed Republican Party, and this reporter was suggesting that more than likely Lincoln would run for his party's nomination for President of the United States. What disturbed Josh the most was that Lincoln, if elected, was promising to abolish slavery, and magically preserve the Union at the same time, or at least that was what the reporter implied. Josh had already heard talk back home that if slavery was considered illegal and abolished, the South would leave the Union. He couldn't imagine such a thing.

As he was reading, a loud fat man with a huge cigar on his right hand, and a shiny gold ring on his ring finger, said boldly, "Lincoln looks like a monkey and talks like one, too." Josh thought the man's wrinkled plaid suit looked vaguely similar to the one he saw on a monkey dancing for an organ grinder in the station in Washington. He chuckled at the thought.

The man across from him wore a gray suit and was frequently drinking from a flask he kept inside his coat pocket. "Gentlemen, there is no longer a need for slavery. It's holding us back. If the Southerners paid fair wages, then the darkies would turn around and spend their money on goods shipped from our factories up north. As it stands now, the South buys little from us, but wants us to buy all their cotton."

A few others agreed with him but the fat man responded, "You forget such practicalities from our friends in the South. Southerners have no manners and are just ignorant farmers. I hear they inbreed down there. They don't know what they're doing. They're no more than barbarians."

Josh chewed his lip as he slowly slid the newspaper down a bit, so he could see the fat man that was doing all the talking.

The fat man continued, "If Lincoln runs, I'll vote for him, but I just hope I don't have to look at him! Maybe they won't put his picture in the paper. It could cause one to lose an appetite."

Josh spoke before he could stop himself. "It doesn't appear that anything has ever made you lose your appetite!" Josh's heart began pounding in his head.

The four men were shocked that an outsider joined their conversation without invitation. The fat man appeared angry at first, and then realizing his foe was but a young cadet who spoke with a Southern accent, he laughed, "I see we have a gentleman from the South with us today. Aren't we so lucky?" he chuckled with his friends sarcastically. "Tell me, young man, does your family own slaves?"

Josh should not have argued with him, but he did, "Yes, sir, over three hundred."

"My word, my word, don't you feel guilty for mistreating those poor Africans?"

"We don't mistreat our people. We take good care of them. We feed them well and give them medicine and..."

"And they are forced to work in the fields in the hot southern sun without even a penny's wage. The Southerners are just too lazy to do the work themselves, isn't that true, lad?"

"Well, I can see you've never worked a day in the hot sun!" cut in Josh. "If we paid labor to bring our crops and especially our cotton, that suit you're wearing would cost ten times more."

Zeke awoke and frowned. He wasn't in the mood for a fight today. They were almost in New York, and he hoped they would be home by dark. Anxious to see his family as soon as possible, he would rather see Josh's smile and radiant blue eyes than to see the hair stand up on the back of his friend's neck as it did now.

He whispered to Josh, "Josh, please. Let it go. You can't win an argument on the slavery issue. No one can."

The man in the gray suit smiled at Zeke, "Right you are lad. There will come a time when our 'beloved' elected officials will decide the issue for us, but I fear that if a new law makes the South stopping using slaves as laborers, then the result could be far worse than slavery itself."

The man's comments brought silence to the group. Zeke stood up, "Come on, Josh. Let's get something to eat."

Josh reluctantly followed his friend into the next car where a Negro man served sandwiches and drinks from a small bar. They bought two of each, and sat down at a table to eat.

"Why did you get into that discussion? You're in the North now. You're outnumbered," chided Zeke.

"Outnumbered? Have you ever seen me run from a fight? Have you?" asked Josh between bites.

"No, but..."

"Just because I'm in the North doesn't mean that I can hide the fact that I'm a Southern boy, born and bred, and proud of it."

There was cold silence between the two friends.

Then Zeke laughed, "Born and bred? Are you kidding me? I can't believe you said that. You're so funny. It sounded more like a meal at the eatery!" laughed Zeke. He changed his voice to a proper New York accent and that of a waiter, "Sir, would you have the chicken, the stuffed turkey, or the born and bred boy from the South!"

Josh giggled so hard that the coffee he was drinking spilled on his hand. "Ouch! Now look what you made me do," he laughed.

Zeke stunned him with a comment that he just blurted out so quickly he couldn't stop himself. "Josh, you have the most fantastic blue eyes."

A deathly silence fell between them as Josh suddenly realized that Zeke had been thinking the same thing he had. Josh's pale face turned a light pink. He lowered his voice to a whisper, "So do you, my friend. I love it when they change to hint of gray, and then back to ocean blue. I can always tell when you're in a good mood because they become very blue."

"Yeah, and I can always tell when you're ready to clench your fist and poke somebody in the nose like you did Daniel. The hair stands up on the back of your neck, and your eyes turn into swords ready to run your opponent through," laughed Zeke.

Josh chuckled, "They do not."

"Yes, they do. I'm just lucky I'm on your side."

They paused again. Words seemed to have escaped them.

"Even on the slavery issue?" asked Josh, breaking the silence.

Zeke dropped his head; a bit angry with Josh. "You just won't let it go, will you? Do me a favor. Promise me that from this minute on, you and I will never again discuss slavery. Promise me. Promise now!" demanded Zeke, his lower lip pouting if he was really angry and determined.

"And if I don't?" teased Josh.

Then I'll tell everyone on this train that you have the smallest penis in the world!" quipped Zeke.

There was another long pause as the revelation of what Zeke just said sank in.

Josh asked, "How do you know what size penis I have?"

"I saw it when we were trying to get your long johns on you, and besides, you fool, I see it poking through the long johns every morning when you get out of the sack. I don't know what you dream about, but it must be someone really special."

Josh face flushed beet red this time, "You're terrible. You get hard yourself, you know."

Zeke leaned forward in a grinning low whisper, "Not like you. Heck, we could hang the academy flag off you!"

The boys broke into howls causing surrounding passengers to tell them to pipe down. They tried, but the more they tried, the bigger the giggles became. They couldn't stop themselves. They quickly swallowed the rest of their sandwiches, walked to the end of the train, and stood on the back railing.

"It's cold out here," protested Zeke.

"I know, but I've got to pee."

"What? Here?" protested Zeke.

"Put your back to the door so no one can see, and I'll let it fly," urged Josh.

Zeke turned around, laughed, and walked over to the glass door and put his back to it. "Go for it!"

Josh quickly undid his fly and began pissing off the back of the train while Zeke laughed.

"My turn, my turn!" said Zeke.

Josh and Zeke swapped places.

"I can't believe I let you talk me into the wildest things. Here I am about to pee in front of the whole world."

"We're in the woods. There's no one to see. Hurry up. I'm freezing. It's December, you know," argued Josh.

"Okay, here goes."

The train suddenly went through a tunnel and the sky went black. Neither boy could see.

"Zeke?"

"Josh?"

"I can't see a thing," replied Zeke.

"Just don't piss on me!" laughed Josh.

Then suddenly, they broke into daylight once more and the train braked. They exited the tunnel, rounded a bend, and entered the town of Newark, New Jersey and instantly went under a walkway bridge filled with ladies out for a stroll. Zeke had started peeing and couldn't stop. The ladies saw him and pointed. Two ladies fainted. Josh started screaming with laughter. Finally Zeke finished and dove for Josh who bear hugged him as the two spun round and round laughing their heads off.

It was a momentous occasion, not for the chuckle they would always remember, but it was the very first time the two friends really hugged each other. They didn't let go of the embrace quickly, but rather held on as they spun around and around laughing. Like Colonel Lee said, it was a day of history for them—a day that was very special and not soon forgotten.

A few hours later, the two friends arrived in Grand Central Station in New York City, and quickly debarked from their train. The conductor told them they had an hour before the train to Boston, where they would transfer to Portland. They moved their bags to the baggage car of the next train and then bounded excitedly up the long steps and onto the streets of New York. Zeke had come through New York on his way south, but had been afraid to explore. Josh had never been there, and couldn't wait to see everything possible.

Hungry once again, they stopped into a pastry shop and bought several small cakes, crossed the street, and sat down on a bench to eat them. The boys were busy taking in the sights of the large city of New York and marveled at all they saw. Even the gas street lamps amazed them. They hadn't noticed the boy eyeing them very carefully as he casually walked toward their bench. When he got close enough, the boy shot quick glances in all directions, snatched the remaining cakes in the bag left on the bench beside Zeke, and took off running.

Josh and Zeke leaped to their feet and took off after the daring boy. They darted through the crowds of shoppers and business people, dangerously crossed the busy streets filled with wagons and vegetable carts, and darted down an alley, crossed another side street, and then down another alley.

"We've lost him," exclaimed a puffing Zeke.

"Geez, I hate to be stolen from," protested Josh.

"Well, I guess we've seen the best and worst of New York. Let's get back to the train station."

"Maybe the boy needed those cakes more than we did," added Josh. "Let's go."

As they began their walk, they crossed the street, and as they entered the next alley, the boy they had been chasing suddenly stepped out of a doorway, and nearly ran into them. Seeing Josh and Zeke, he hastily darted back in the doorway, but this time Josh was right on his tail like his old dog Junior on the trail of a possum.

They climbed a set of stairs, and then Josh tackled the poor boy in the hallway. Josh quickly scrambled to get on top of the boy, and reared back to pound him when the door beside them suddenly opened.

A dirty, unkempt lady appeared in the door holding a screaming baby in her arms. A three-year-old girl clung to her mother's dirty dress.

"Please don't!" she begged. "Please don't hurt my son!"

Josh stopped as Zeke came up beside them.

"Is this your boy?" asked Josh. She nodded yes. "Your son stole from us," he accused.

"Please wait," she pleaded as she turned from the door and returned carrying their bag of cakes. "Is this yours?"

"Yes, Ma'am. That's ours."

"Jeremy, you told me you bought this with money you earned. You're going to get quite a blistering for telling me that tale, young man. Get in here right now!" she demanded.

The boy was apparently more afraid of her than Josh. He quickly scrambled from beneath Josh and darted into the room, pushing the door back. Zeke and Josh saw what kind of a place they lived in. It was unkempt, smelly, and dirty. There was no heat, and everyone was shivering. Zeke didn't know what to say.

Josh shook his head, "Ma'am, I've already eaten enough. Why don't you and your family enjoy the cakes as our treat?"

"No, we couldn't. We can't take a hand out. We're not beggars," she added proudly.

Josh searched his mind for a solution, "How about this? To tell you the truth, after chasing your boy, we're lost. If you'll let him show us the way back to the train station, then he will have earned the cakes for you. Is that a deal?" he said smiling with all the charm he could muster.

She smiled back. "You're a kind boy and from the South, too. Jeremy, apologize to these gentlemen, and lead them back to the station, and then get your butt back here on the double."

Jeremy did as he was told. Josh and Zeke tipped their hats to the lady while Josh winked at the little girl. They turned and walked back down the stairs to the street.

"How old are you?" asked Josh of Jeremy.

The boy with the blond, but dirty hair, replied, "Thirteen."

"That's a good age. Is your dad out of work?" asked Zeke.

"What dad?" replied Jeremy with bitterness in his voice? "He left when I was six."

"Does your mom work?" asked Josh.

"She cleans offices when she can get the work. Times are hard." He stopped and pointed down the street, "There's the station at the end of this corner. Do you see it?"

"Yes, thank you," replied Josh. The boy started to turn and leave, but Josh caught his arm. "Listen, Jeremy, had it not been for your mother's interference, I would have thrashed you within an inch of your life for stealing from me. Please don't make that mistake again. The next person might not be willing to stop. They might have a dagger and run you through! Do you understand?" A lump swelled up in the boy's throat so he just nodded. "Good. You're the man of the house now. You're going to have to find work doing something. That's what you should spend your time doing—not stealing. Your family needs you. If you go off to jail for stealing, what good are you to them? Do you agree?" Josh almost chuckled at how much he sounded like his father. The boy, a bit more frightened, nodded a slow 'yes'.

"Good, now how far from here to the Henderson Freight Company? Do you know it?" asked Josh as Zeke looked on in puzzlement.

"Yes, it's on Thirty Seventh Avenue."

"Good. Remember this name—Arthur Wilcox. He's the owner. He and my dad are old friends. Dad ships a lot of stuff to him. My name is Josh Johnson." Josh stopped and turned to Zeke. "Give me dollar."

"A dollar?" protested Zeke.

"I'll pay you back," replied Josh as Zeke handed him a silver dollar. "Now, Jeremy, I'm going to loan you a dollar, and you're going to pay me back one day, agreed?"

The boy took the shiny coin and smiled broadly, "Yes, sir. I agree."

"Good, now you spend some of that on some food for your family and a new shirt for yourself. Clean yourself up a bit, and go see Mister Wilcox. Tell him I sent you. What's my name?"

"Josh Johnson."

"Good boy. You tell him I said you were the fastest runner I have ever seen. I almost never caught you, now did I?" They both chuckled. "Tell him you would make a good worker, and would be willing to do anything.

And Jeremy, the next time I come through New York, I'm going to stop in and see if you're working instead of stealing. If you're working, I'll buy you dinner. If you're stealing, well, I'm going to beat you to a pulp. Do you believe me?" Josh squared the boy's shoulders and looked him straight in the eyes.

Jeremy gulped and smiled slightly. "Yes, sir, I believe you, and thank you."

"Good. Point the direction to us." Jeremy pointed to their left. Josh nodded, "Thank you. Run along now. Take care of your family. Good luck."

"Bye, sirs. Thanks!" called Jeremy as he began running back toward home, clutching the silver dollar tightly in his hand.

Josh and Zeke began walking toward the train station.

Zeke gestured with his hands at Josh. "That was unbelievable. You are very clever, and very kind, my friend," stated Zeke. "You helped them without them feeling like they were charity cases. Remarkable."

"We all make mistakes in this world. Changing our ways is the best way to apologize. Did you see where his family lived? I tell you, we treat our slaves far better than you treat your poor," stated Josh.

Zeke quickly lifted a finger at Josh, lifted his eyebrows, and warned him, "You promised, no more talk of slavery."

"Okay, okay," chuckled Josh.

"But you're right. This world isn't perfect, is it?"

"Nope, but I am!" laughed Josh as he knocked Zeke's hat to the street, and took off running for the station.

Zeke snatched up his cap, and took off after him, "Yeah, right!"

The train was running behind schedule. Zeke's mom had planned a fancy dinner for the two cadets, but it was half past ten when their train finally rolled into Portland. His father had gone to the station to wait on them, while his mother put the rest of the family to bed. Richard and James slept in a room at the end of a short hallway, and their parents slept downstairs.

Zeke pictured the entire clan waiting on the platform standing in the same spot where he had left them a few months ago, with their arms high in the air waving at him. However, with the lateness of the hour, there were but a few people on the platform, and there was snow everywhere. He was disappointed but said nothing.

Upon seeing his dad, his face broke into a huge grin, "Father!" called Zeke as he stepped from the train.

Josh watched as Allen Robertson ran across the last seventy-five feet that separated him from his son. Zeke was fifteen years old and to many, a grown man already, but it made no difference to Allen. He bear hugged Zeke and swung him around like he was six years old, and to Josh's complete surprise, the man kissed Zeke on the top of his forehead and said, "Welcome home, son. I've missed you. I love you."

"I love you, too."

Josh's heart nearly broke. He quickly turned away. The sight of their embrace touched him deeply. His emotions were in turmoil. He was exuberant that his friend had the love of his father, and he was saddened because he had lost his own father's love. Zeke grabbed him by the arm and spun him back around. "Dad, this is my very, very best friend in the whole wide world, Josh Johnson. Josh, this is my dad."

Josh removed his right hand from his glove, stuck it out, and smiled, "I'm very pleased to make your acquaintance. I've heard so many things about you."

Allen took Josh's hand and shook it firmly, quickly putting Josh on a man-to-man basis, "And I yours."

His Father added, "Come on, let's get out of this cold weather. Your mother has your supper warming on the stove."

"Sounds good to me, let's go," grinned Zeke.

The Robertson's house was an easy buggy ride from the seaside village of Portland. The house was set back about a hundred feet from the ocean on a huge rocky cliff overlooking the sea, but it was hard to tell where it was as snow had started falling, and it was soon almost blizzard conditions. Josh was grateful it was only a ten-minute ride. He was already freezing and wondered why people liked living this far north in the first place. Josh spotted the house in the distance because there was a candle lit in every window of the house.

"Why all the candles?" asked Josh.

"We do it every Christmas," replied Zeke.

"But this year is special. We wanted everyone in the town to know our son is coming home," added Allen with great pride.

"Oh," replied Josh quietly, recalling that only the kitchen candles were lit when he left home for school. Allen stopped the buggy in front of the house.

"You two get out here, grab your stuff, and head into the house. I'll unhitch the team. Go on now, get!" he ordered in a friendly way.

Zeke grabbed his satchel and followed by Josh he made their way up the snow covered steps and into the two story New England gray house. It was trimmed in white with a big deck that went all the way around the house.

Zeke pushed in the door, and together, he and Josh crowded inside. "Mom, I'm home."

Josh spotted an Irish lady with bright blue eyes quickly making her way from the kitchen. "Oh Zeke, darling, you're home. You're finally home. We've missed you so." She hugged him tightly then kissed him quickly on the mouth.

Zeke blushed at being kissed by his mom in front of Josh. "Mom, this is my best..." Josh cleared his throat loudly and gently shook his head no. Zeke chuckled, "He's modest, Mom. This is my best friend, Josh Johnson."

"I'm so pleased to meet you, Josh."

Josh stuck out his hand. "I'm pleased to meet you, ma'am."

"I'll accept no handshake from a friend of my son. Come here. Give me a hug! I bet you could use one, too. Am I right, dear?" Before Josh had a chance to answer, Elizabeth Robertson grabbed and bear hugged him tightly, and to everyone's surprise, she kissed him quickly on the lips as well. "Now don't you feel like you're home now?" she laughed.

"Yes, ma'am," Josh blushed. Zeke chuckled as he elbowed Josh. None but Josh knew how special and needed that hug was.

"Mom, we're starving. Something smells good."

"It's me that smells good, but come on. Off with your coats and come into the kitchen where it's nice and warm, and I'll serve you some dinner."

The boys followed her into the kitchen. Allen joined them presently, lit a pipe, and fixed himself another cup of hot steaming coffee. The family, minus the younger brothers who were already asleep, settled down to eat and chat. By midnight, the two boys had eaten two helpings of everything, and enjoyed dessert as well. Now they were both yawning.

Elizabeth stood, walked around the back of her son, and gave him another hug, kissed him on the top of his head, then nodded to her husband, "Allen, we're keeping them up. They must be exhausted. I changed the sheets on your bed. Your dad made you a fire and heated the water for a bath. You boys are sweet, but traveling two days with no bath, my lord, you smell like skunks!" teased Elizabeth.

"Gee, thanks, Mom," laughed Zeke.

"Off you go. I love you dears. Sleep well. Sleep as long as you like. I've marketing to do in the morning, and the boys will be heading out with your dad, so sleep in and catch up. We'll have a nice chat tomorrow. I can't wait to hear all about your school. Off you go now," she ordered as she hugged them once more and sent them upstairs.

At the top of the stairs, Zeke whispered and pointed down the hall. "My brothers sleep down there. This is the water closet."

"The what?" whispered Josh?

"It's like an indoor outhouse. My dad read about it a newspaper and ordered it. As you can tell, it gets pretty cold up in Maine. Taking a potty in the outhouse could cause one to freeze to death. We can pee in there. Come on."

Zeke led him into his room at the other end of the hall. His mom had lit a lamp for him, and his dad had built a good fire so that Zeke's bedroom was warm and cozy. The walls of the house were a foot thick to help keep them warm, and a low ceiling that was just inches above their heads. There were pictures of ships on every wall. In one corner was a large wooden tub.

"What is that?" asked Josh.

Zeke shut the door behind them and set his bag down. "That's a Japanese tub."

"A what?" replied Josh as he set his satchel down and walked over for a closer inspection.

"A rich Japanese man sadly contracted smallpox when he came to America. He had no family so they auctioned off his things to pay his debts. I bought it with some money I saved, and I purchased it for two dollars because no one knew what it was. I had read a book about Marco Polo and he described just such a tub. Come on, I'll show you how it works.

"There's a pipe that goes in at the bottom and comes out at the top. Do you see it? Well, the pipe is really a loop that goes through the fireplace. The water goes from the pipe to a narrow copper coil that thins the water out, so the fire can heat it quickly, and then the hot water returns to the tub."

"What pushes the water?" asked a still bewildered Josh.

“Yet another adaptation of an invention. Do you remember how much the wind was blowing outside?"

"Yeah, I nearly froze my balls off!" grinned Josh.

"Well, we're on the ocean. There's always a breeze. Therefore, I copied a windmill out of a catalog, and made a miniature one that I have mounted over the kitchen roof. It turns a shaft that comes through the wall right here, and hooks to the top of the pipe. The shaft turns a small pump that pushes the water through the copper pipe, then back into here, and presto, we have a hot water tub."

"You're crazy," laughed Josh.

"Last one in is a rotten egg!" grinned Zeke as he began jerking his clothes off.

"We can both get in?"

"Yeah, come on!"

Josh was too tired, cold, and weary to argue. He began stripping out of his clothes, and after just a few seconds, they were both down to their long johns. Zeke hesitated a second and looked at Josh, who was also hesitating. They both chuckled and down went the underwear. Zeke climbed in first, and Josh quickly followed sitting opposite him. The problem was what to do with their legs, which ended up being sort of intertwined with the others.

"This is wonderful," grinned Josh.

"Heavenly," sighed Zeke as he slowly slipped his head beneath the water and then came up spitting water at Josh like a seal. Josh quickly copied him.

However, for the next thirty minutes they said little. The soaking hot water soothed them far beyond their expectations. They could see each other's erections in the clear water as they sat but thirty inches apart, but neither boy said anything. They gleefully gazed into the other's eyes, but knew not what to say, or even how to express what they felt deep in their hearts. Of all the books they had read, not one word had prepared them for the love that had already bonded them together, and continued to grow inside of them, anxiously waiting to burst out.

Zeke climbed out of the tub first, grabbing a towel and drying off. He then handed one to Josh as he climbed out. Zeke bent down to pick up his long johns.

"Gee, these stink. They need a washing," he said.

"What do we do?" asked Josh as he dried off and looked over at naked Zeke.

"I'll rinse them in the tub and hang them over a chair near the fire to dry over night."

"What'll we sleep in?" asked Josh as he helped wash his own long johns.

"The bed silly," grinned Zeke.

"I mean what do we wear."

"What do you wear when you go skinny dipping in the swamp?" asked Zeke.

"Oh," sighed Josh almost wickedly while rolling his eyes.

They quickly spread out the long johns over a chair. Zeke turned down the lamp, went over and pulled back one quilt, then another, and then another, and then a sheet.

"Three quilts?" asked Josh.

"It gets below zero up here, you know. It's a feather bed. You'll feel like a king compared to that army bunk at school. Climb in," ordered Zeke as he held back the covers.

Josh climbed in, Zeke quickly slid in behind him, and though the bed was small, they managed to keep a few inches between them. After a moment of silence, Josh finally broke the quiet.

"You have a fantastic family."

"Yeah, I know, but thanks."

"My feet are cold."

"I guess we should have put socks on, but they probably stink, too," Zeke chuckled.

"But they're cold," protested Josh again. "Here. Feel this!" Josh slid his feet over and put them against Zeke's bare leg.

"Geez! You're right. What is it they say, cold feet warm heart," Zeke grinned, but he didn't pull his legs away from Josh's feet.

Josh didn't pull his feet back either. "Sleep well, friend."

"You, too, thanks for coming with me. I would have missed you something awful."

"The same here, and thanks for having me. Night."

"Night," replied Zeke.

Josh closed his eyes, but all he could see was Zeke's blue eyes, and now his naked body as he recalled him getting out of the tub. Zeke had the same problem, but neither boy said anything more. The minutes ticked by, but the boys couldn't sleep just yet. They were exhausted from the long tiring trip, but somehow they felt different lying next to each other in the same bed. Their minds searched for answers to the questions that had overwhelmed their minds on many nights at school, but finally, with no answers discovered, Zeke stretched, turned on his side away from Josh, yawned as if asleep, and backed up just slightly against Josh. Josh turned toward Zeke, yawned, and then gently moved his arm across the pillow. Zeke sighed, lifted his head just slightly, allowing Josh's arm to slide down and under Zeke's neck. Zeke slid back a little more, enjoying the warmth that seemed to just glow from Josh's body like a log pulled from a hot fire.

Josh responded to the warmth he felt from Zeke by sliding forward just a bit. The top of Josh's thighs moved cozily against the back of Zeke's legs.

Zeke felt the tip of Josh's erection against his backside and shivered slightly. Zeke slid back another inch or two until his back was firmly against Josh's chest. Josh moved his chest until it touched the back of Zeke's shoulders. The sunburst glow of the fire made their hair and faces glisten. Though his eyes were heavy, Josh could not take his eyes off Zeke. They still said nothing to each other. Josh tightened his arm under Zeke's neck and pulled him even closer. Zeke reached over Josh, found Josh's left arm and pulled it back over his stomach, allowing his fingers to rest on the back of

Josh's hand. Josh's opened palm was now resting just above Zeke's abdomen, the very one he had dreamed about on so many cold nights at the Academy.

As if even an eighth of an inch mattered, they managed to cuddle up even closer, and now confused, but deliriously comfortable and warm, their hearts now beating as one, and their breathing harmonious, they finally drifted off to sleep.

FIVE

It was late morning by the time Josh opened his eyes, and then gently, he let out a slow and almost silent breath and yawned. At first, he was quite confused as to what his eyes saw above him, and even where he was. As his mind slowly awakened, he remembered the room was in Maine, and the bed he lay in belonged to his best friend Zeke. The snow had continued falling all night long, and the sun was almost blocked from the piles of snow on the windowsills.

He was lying on his back beneath the three quilts. Somewhere in the night, Zeke had turned into him, and now rested his head on Josh's almost hairless chest. Zeke's tender pink lips were barely touching Josh's left nipple, his right leg pulled up between Josh's legs, the knee of which was resting firmly over Josh's genitals. His right arm was under Josh's left armpit, and his left hand somehow under Josh's back. Had it not been for the soft feather bed, the position would probably have hurt Josh's back, but as it was, it was the happiest, most comfortable moment of his life.

He could feel his erection beneath Zeke's knee, and he was surprised to find his right hand lying casually over Zeke's soft, warm butt. He felt it gently, and then felt his own erection swell even more without even touching it. Zeke's hair was tickling his nose, but he dared not sneeze. He wished he could remain in this position the rest of his life.

He softly kissed Zeke's hair. He couldn't believe he had been allowed to do so. He had never kissed another human being's hair in all his life. He had never held Knobby like he was holding Zeke. He had entered Knobby, but he never loved the poor boy. He realized at that very moment that he did love Zeke. In fact, he thought, he was in love with Zeke. He had never been in love before. It was a confusing love between a man and a man, but he loved him nonetheless, and pushed all negative thoughts away, at least for this very special moment.

He kissed his hair once more and then again, savoring the smell, the touch, and the softness of Zeke's body. As Zeke's essence drifted into Josh's brain, he felt his heart was about to burst. Josh felt that surely there could be nothing more that would make him feel more euphoric or more jubilant than he did right now. He noted something stabbing him in his side. He felt it throb. It was then he realized that it was Zeke's erection. His heart skipped a beat. He wondered if Zeke felt for him the way he felt for Zeke.

Then the magic of the moment frightened him. What if Zeke awoke and he was embarrassed by it all? What if Zeke rejected him? What if Zeke called him an abomination? What if they sent him back to school all alone? What if...

Zeke stirred slightly. Josh held his breath. Zeke sighed. Josh froze. He was afraid to move and afraid to breathe. Zeke quietly cleared his throat. Josh's pulse could be seen in his temples.

Zeke tenderly kissed Josh's chest, his nipple, and then slid his right hand down to Josh's tummy and softly rubbed it back and forth. Josh allowed his heart to beat once more.

Zeke began to allow his fingers to caress him. Zeke shocked him by allowing his right hand to gently rub Josh's stomach in tiny slow circles that kept slowly meandering their way down Josh's body until they were just below his navel. Zeke pulled his right leg back a bit and then pushed his knee gently into the bottom of Josh's testicles. A shiver went up Josh's spine. His heart pounded loudly.

Zeke's hand drifted down across the top of Josh's. Zeke allowed his hand to move to the side of Josh's penis, and then gently planted it deep into Josh's blond pubic hair. He began running his fingers in circles feeling the softness of the usually hidden hair. Josh shivered once more. He pulled in on Zeke's buns while allowing the fingers of his left hand to slide to the back of Zeke's head, enjoying the softness of his brown hair. He kissed Zeke's head once again. Zeke, having toyed with him long enough, allowed his hand to slowly encircle Josh's erection and began to slowly pull and tighten on it. Josh sighed as he moved his left hand from Zeke's hair and slowly moved it across the back of Zeke's bare back and down across his own chest and down to where he could feel the muscle throbbing at his side.

Josh could hear his heart beating. Josh felt the tip of Zeke's erection. His heart pounded harder in his chest. He kissed Zeke's hair once more. Zeke kissed his chest. Josh's hand closed around Zeke's tool and squeezed. As the seconds passed, their lungs heaving, their hearts hammering, Zeke slowly turned his head from Josh's chest until he could gaze directly into Josh's eyes. In the beams of the clear morning sun as it fought its way through the frosted windowpanes, he found Josh smiling and staring right back into his eyes. They stopped their pulling and squeezing almost simultaneously, and still without a word being said, they gazed and smiled. Zeke moved closer to Josh's face. Josh let go of Zeke's erection, and then reached over, placing both hands on Zeke's buns, and pulled him closer to him. Zeke let go of Josh, moved his hand up and under Josh's left arm, moved even closer, and then sliding on top of Josh, Zeke lightly kissed Josh. It was a tender, gentle peck. Josh then kissed Zeke just as tenderly. They kissed again, just a slight peck at first, as if testing to be sure that God wouldn't strike them dead. They tested the waters once more, then still staring into each other's radiant blue eyes, they finally closed their eyes, and for the first time in both their lives, they passionately kissed. While still kissing, they pulled tightly into each other until their tongues began to explore each other's mouths. Minutes became hours and might have become days had they both not simultaneously exploded like rockets on the Fourth of July.

The hot, wet juice mixed on their skin. As it cooled and became sticky, their passion cooled. Zeke abruptly pulled back from the kiss, stared at Josh, and then suddenly sat up.

"What have we done?" he whispered.

The frightened and ashen look on Zeke's face scared Josh. Male sex was not new to him. He had experienced playing with another boy. He felt no guilt. No remorse. He felt only passion, love, and joy. "It's okay," he whispered reassuringly.

"No, it's not okay. We've made love like a man and wife," responded Zeke coldly.

Josh chewed his lip. He became very nervous. "I know. I don't quite understand it myself, but I know I love you and..."

"I love you, too, but not like a wife. You're my best friend and..." said Zeke quickly in a panic. Josh noted how wrinkled with worry Zeke's brow became.

"I'm much more than a best friend, and you know it," shot back Josh, a bit hurt that Zeke had not acknowledged that there was something special between them.

"How can you be more?" Zeke stepped from the bed, his erection quickly subsiding. A last drop of sperm hit the floor beneath him.

"I don't know, but I know you felt it. Didn't you?" urged Josh.

"We must clean ourselves up. Someone might see us. This can never happen again," began Zeke as he found a cloth in a box in the corner and began wiping the juice from his stomach. "I can't believe we did this. This sticky stuff will probably eat our skin up. It's meant to make babies."

Josh couldn't help but chuckle, "Zeke, calm down. You're being ridiculous. I've had Knobby's juice on me, I've put mine in him, and it doesn't hurt..."

"You've done this before?" accused Zeke with a frown, and then a realization that he was really the naive one.

Josh dropped his head, quickly wishing he had not made such a crucial mistake, wishing he could erase the previous sentence, but he loved Zeke too much to begin lying to him. He immediately told the truth, "I used to play around with a friend back home. Nothing serious, we were horny for Pete's sake." However, he purposely left out that Knobby was Negro and a slave.

"Get up. Get dressed. Someone might come in and see you lying there and..."

"And assume we had sex together. I don't think so. It's beyond most folks' wildest dreams," said Josh as he climbed out of the bed, cleaned his chest, and began pulling on his dried long johns.

"We'll never speak of this again. It didn't happen, and it won't happen again," stated Zeke.

"Okay, okay, just calm down. You're just scared. I'd never do anything to hurt you, and I'm sorry if what we did hurt you. I was expressing the profound love I have for you. I thought you were doing the same."

"I don't know what in the hell I was doing. Come on, let's get some breakfast," replied Zeke as he slipped on his pants, grabbed his boots and shirt, and headed down the stairs.

Josh did not move at first. He looked back at the bed and quickly replayed the evening and his moment with Zeke. If they never did it again, he would still die a happy man. Even if Zeke demanded that he wear three pairs of pants while sleeping in the same bed with him, he would still love Zeke. He knew that he would love Zeke for the rest of his life, and far more than anyone else on the planet would.

They ate a late breakfast of honey muffins Zeke's mom left them on the stove, but they barely talked. Every time Josh asked a question about Maine or Zeke's family, Zeke answered in simple one-syllable answers. Josh wisely decided to quit trying, giving Zeke more time to absorb what had happened.

They wrapped up in their big coats, braved the winter elements by rushing out the door, slipping in the snow down the steps, and soon were throwing snowballs at each other as they made their way to town. By the time they arrived at the first storefront, a boat supply shop, Zeke had begun talking and laughing again, causing Josh to say a quick prayer of thanks.

Once inside the shop, an old sea dog quickly met them, or at least that's what Zeke bravely called the eighty-year-old man sitting in a rocking chair by the potbelly stove while puffing on a huge pipe. It made him look much like a big steam locomotive. Josh tipped his hat at the man while they slipped out of their big coats. Zeke quickly explained to Josh that he had spent many summers working in this shop, stocking supplies, and just about anything that needed done. A tall bald man carrying a box came up to the counter and set it down.

"Mister Kendall, how are you?" asked Zeke as he brushed the snow from his hair.

"I'm very well, dear boy. You're looking rather smashing. Home from school I see. Who is this handsome-looking soldier?" he said with a grin. Josh quickly surmised that Mister Kendall was a man that loved to tease and show off his wit. He liked him immediately.

"Ah, Mister Kendall, I'm pleased to introduce you to my roommate and friend. This is Josh Johnson," stated Zeke while removing his glove and gesturing to Josh.

Josh shook Mister Kendall's hand firmly. A firm handshake was something he was always determined to offer. He didn't want anyone thinking he wasn't manly. Wait, Josh thought. Zeke didn't introduce me as his best friend as he had done with everyone else. Was it an oversight or an intention? He wondered if things had really changed that much since this morning. He tried to smile at Mister Kendall, but worry lines wrinkled his brow. He chewed his lip.

"Ah, yes. It is a great pleasure to meet you, Josh Johnson," he pronounced his name clearly, while shaking his hand repeatedly and looking directly into his eyes. "I see they've been feeding you kind of poorly at that school. I have some new peppermint sticks on the counter. Shall we try one?"

"Yes, thank you. It's very nice to meet you," added Josh, feeling a bit awkward.

Mister Kendall stopped dead in his tracks and turned back to Josh. "You're from the South, aren't you lad?" he said with a confused look on his face.

Josh suddenly felt like he been accused of a crime, but his pride made him pull his shoulders back and take a deep breath, "Why yes, sir. I am from Charleston, South Carolina."

Zeke knew Mister Kendall liked to talk about politics, so he tried to steer everyone toward the counter. "Where are the peppermints?" he asked hopefully.

Mister Kendall replied quickly without letting his eyes leave Josh's face, "In the big green paperboard bucket." Pointing without looking, "Help yourself." He sized up Josh a little closer. "Josh, where do you stand on this slavery issue?" he asked while pushing his lower lip out a bit with the tip of his tongue, the smile quickly fading from his face. He relit his pipe taking a puff.

Josh smelled the cherry tobacco aroma. It reminded him of his grandfather. He suddenly longed to see him. "Sir, I'm on holiday with my very best friend in the whole world. I often feel like I'm a foreigner when I'm north of the Mason Dixon line so with all due respect, sir, I shall refrain from answering your question. To do so would cause me to get my ears boxed by my best friend." He emphasized the words "best friend" carefully, hoping to rekindle that status once more with Zeke. And then with a bit of a sly grin, and a wink to Zeke, "However, Mister Kendall, should you have the great pleasure and fortune to visit my beloved South, and especially my home in Charleston, I would be happy to serve you some of our fantastic home grown tea. And then with great enthusiasm, I shall explain to you my exact position on slavery."

Josh's bold but witty and clever response drew a snicker from a thankful Zeke, and a grin from Mister Kendall himself. The boy had been fair, very polite, and respectful. He surmised that Zeke had chosen his friend with great care, and he liked the choice. "Very well, son, very well indeed."

Josh attempted to change the subject, "My, my, sir. I've never been in a finer shop than this. I believe you have enough supplies to outfit the King's navy," he said politely and deliberately.

Mister Kendall was not fooled, but neither was he one to turn down a compliment. "You're right, and thank you for your kind words. Now come on over here before Zeke eats all the candy. He is such a pig," he teased.

Mister Kendall, Zeke, and Josh toured the shop, playing with harpoons and cannon balls, and they listened to several of Mister Kendall's famous whale stories. After about an hour, Zeke and Josh waved goodbye, and crossed the street to the general merchandise store.

Josh was busy taking in the aroma coming from the coffee grinder counter when Zeke suddenly returned from across the store with a pretty girl of about sixteen. Josh immediately noted that Zeke was holding her hand. She was smiling and trying to slow Zeke down as he pulled her toward Josh. Josh forced a smile. She blushed.

"Josh, this is Rebecca. Rebecca, this is Josh, from my school. She and I have been sweethearts for years," he added.

Josh's face was smiling at her, but his brain was analyzing what he just heard. Once again, he had been demoted from best friend status, and now Zeke was suddenly announcing he had an old girlfriend of many years, a girl he had failed to mention even once during their last hundred and twenty days together. It puzzled Josh, but he was determined to make a good impression on all of Zeke's friends and family. He smiled a bit more, "I can see why. Rebecca, I do believe you're the prettiest girl in Maine."

She blushed again. Even Zeke blushed a tad. "Why thank you, Josh. You have the funniest accent," she added.

"Yes, yes I do," he began sarcastically, a bit annoyed at having been told he has an accent when everyone knows it is these stupid Yankees that have the accents. "Down South, you see, as children, we are forced to eat ground cornmeal for breakfast. Some call it grits. It sticks to your teeth and your gums, and the next thing you know, you've developed an accent. What's your excuse?" he coldly asked.

"Pardon?" she didn't understand.

Zeke broke in quickly while giving Josh the evil eye look, "Come, Rebecca, help me find something for my mother's Christmas present." He turned her away from Josh.

"It was nice to meet you," she said to Josh, looking back over her shoulder.

"My, dear," he began in as thick a Southern accent as he could manage, "the pleasure was all mine."

Zeke rolled his eyes at Josh while escorting Rebecca to the other side of the store. Josh slowly turned around and then once he had his back to them, he snarled quietly, "You half-brain twit!" Then he let his anger subside and almost laughed at his daring and reckless wit. He couldn't believe he had responded to Rebecca so quickly and fiercely, and he was sure Zeke would make him pay a price for it at a later time.

Josh and Zeke spent the rest of the day in town then stopped by the docks on the way home to see the family's fishing fleet and his dad's office. Josh was thrilled to see the boats, and wished the weather were warmer so they could go out for a sail. Zeke's dad suggested he come back in the summer to enjoy the ocean. Josh replied he would love to, but was miffed when Zeke did not immediately concur.

The Christmas dinner was as good as back home. The table was filled with lots of home cooked dishes, and Josh was surprised to find that a Maine turkey tasted as good as a Carolina bird. For the past two days and nights Josh dealt with Zeke's mood swings. Josh had just about figured out when Zeke was going to be friendly, and when he wasn't.

It seemed to him that when they were alone and out of the house, Zeke was nice as usual, but when they were in the house or amongst any of the townspeople, then Zeke seemed to put some distance between them. Unfortunately, his theory was not one hundred percent accurate, as more than once he had been proven wrong when he found himself walking with Zeke, but talking only to the face he saw every day in the mirror.

Tired of waiting on Zeke to come around, Josh began to spend more time with Zeke's brothers, Richard, James, and baby Timothy. He soon discovered James was an avid chess player, and it took a lot out of Josh to recall his grandfather's moves so he could beat young James. He found himself daydreaming about the winters he used to spend learning to play the game from his grandfather, but he soon had to force such memories from his mind, as it saddened and hurt him. No one from his family had written him since he left the plantation. Spending money had been sent to the school's office, and he drew from the account when he needed a little cash. It worried him that perhaps Zeke would soon be like the rest of his family, cutting him off forever.

Two nights after Christmas, with the wind howling outside, and the snow continuing to come down, Josh and Zeke left the kitchen after a late night snack of cold turkey and biscuits, and headed up the stairs to bed. Zeke stopped by the water closet to pee, while Josh went on to Zeke's bedroom. He put a few more logs on the fire, walked over to the hot tub, and noted that the water was coming in so fast that it made little bubbles that quickly floated to the surface.

The cold Maine winds chilled him to the bone so he quickly stripped out of his clothes, and climbed into the big tub. The warm water quickly took the chill from his bones, and allowed him to slowly relax and unwind. He slipped off the wooden seat and dipped beneath the water just as Zeke came into the room. Zeke scanned the room, but did not see Josh in bed. He had been deliberately coming to the bedroom last, hoping Josh was already in bed, and if lucky, already asleep before he turned down the lamp and crawled in himself.

Not seeing Josh, he soon noted the pile of clothes on the floor, but again saw no one in bed and there appeared to be no one in the hot tub. He shut the door, and called Josh's name, "Josh?" he whispered. No one replied. "Josh?" He walked over to the tub.

Josh suddenly came up from beneath the water, and spit water like a seal right into Zeke's face. Zeke was so shocked, he just stood there stunned, the water running in tiny streams down his face and dripping off the tip of his nose onto his shirt.

"Gotcha!" laughed Josh.

"Thanks," said Zeke sarcastically, as he turned to go sit on the stool and take his boots off.

"Come on in. There are bubbles in the tub tonight," urged Josh.

"Bubbles?" quizzed Zeke as he walked back across the room in his stocking feet to look.

"Yeah, they're coming out of the water pipe."

Zeke leaned over the edge of the tub. The inlet pipe was beneath Josh's wooden seat and he had to look right at Josh's genitals to see where they were coming from. He heard the wind howl. He turned away and began pulling off his sweater and then his shirt. "I guess the wind mill is turning so fast that it is creating turbulent bubbles in the water."

"Whatever. They sure feel soothing as they float up against my skin."

"That's good," replied Zeke as he stepped out of his pants, pulled back the covers, and still wearing his long johns, he crawled into the bed, and pulled the covers over him.

"You're not coming in?" asked a disappointed Josh.

"No, I'm tired. I'm going to sleep."

"Suit yourself. May I ask you one more thing before you fall asleep?" Josh had softened his voice.

"If you must," replied Zeke as he turned to face the opposite wall from Josh.

Josh hesitated, but he had already grown accustomed to Zeke's indifference toward him. "Would you prefer I catch a train back to school tomorrow, cutting my visit with you and your family short?"

Zeke did not answer right off. "Why would you want to do that?"

"I think it is rather obvious that you are uncomfortable around me, that you no longer consider me your best friend, and that you don't want to spend time with me. I think I..."

Zeke cut him off, "What do mean I no longer consider you my best friend? I never said that!"

"When was the last time you introduced me as your best friend? I'll tell you. It was the first night I arrived here. Since then I'm just a friend."

"Oh, you're being silly. It is just semantics. Just because I don't tell total strangers you're my best friend doesn't mean you're not. I just didn't want to imply..."

Josh broke in, "That we're more than best friends?"

Zeke chewed his lip, and set his jaw firmly, and then whispered through clenched teeth. "We're not more...we're just best friends."

Josh felt like one of Shakespeare's daggers just stabbed him deeply into his heart. "Oh," he replied quietly. He could think of nothing else to say short of starting an argument, and he didn't want that. He wanted to get things back to normal, but it just seemed they found something to fuss about at every opportunity. He would decide before morning if he would leave early.

Zeke said nothing more either. He pulled the cover up tighter beneath his chin, and listened to the wind whistling through the cracks in the windowsill. He heard Josh step out of the tub, and could even hear him drying off. He continued to face the wall, but closed his eyes and in his mind, he could see Josh standing there, dripping, drying off and naked. The fire seemed to make Josh's skin shine a soft pale orange. In his brain, Zeke could see Josh's erection, so he instantly forced his eyes to open to stop the dream. He felt himself. His tool was hard. Now angry with himself, he began grinding his teeth.

Josh decided to rinse his long johns out, and then he spread them across the chair to dry overnight before gently slipping beneath the covers, trying not to awaken Zeke, and being ever so careful not to bump up against Zeke. His skin was warm and toasty. Zeke could feel the warmth from Josh's naked body on his back. His nostrils flared at the scent of the soap that Josh used in the bath. Josh smelled amazingly clean and fresh. It was a smell he liked.

Zeke closed his eyes but once again, in his mind, he instantly saw Josh lying there beside him in the nude. His brain replayed their first night. His erection became harder. He popped his eyes open. After a moment, he closed them again. He saw himself kissing Josh. He opened them again. He sighed. His thoughts were churning. He could not stop his thoughts.

Josh had not been able to fall asleep just yet either. He was considering that his stay was making his best friend miserable, and perhaps he would be doing Zeke a favor if he left. Nevertheless, he was also concerned about what would happen to him if he returned to school, as there was no place for him to stay. He could not go home. He forced his eyes to close. Sleep still did not come. The answers to his dilemma did not come easily for him. To his amazement, Zeke turned toward him. Josh kept his eyes closed, pretending to be asleep. The fire cast deep shadows across the room, but just a bit of light shone across Josh's hair, and across the top of his face. The light created a tiny shadow over his nose, and just a small beam of light over his lips. Zeke studied Josh's hair and longed to touch it. He imagined the intense blue eyes, where he now saw nothing but shadows, and wished he could again. He noted Josh's tender lips, and recalled the warm, wet, penetrating, invigorating tongue that was resting silently behind those wonderful lips.

Josh felt he could feel Zeke's eyes, but still he lay still. He was completely bewildered when Zeke's hand gently slipped over to his stomach, and began to softly caress his skin. His penis leaped to full mast, but he still did not move, pretending to be asleep, wondering if perhaps it was easier for Zeke to touch him when he thought he was asleep. It did not matter, as he desperately wanted to be touched.

Zeke's hand moved down, feeling the softness of Josh's pubic hair. Slowly, Zeke's fingers began to play with Josh's erection.

Josh's mind was racing for answers as to what he should do. Zeke moved not just a little closer, but right into Josh's side, pulled his upper leg and knee into Josh's groin, and gently laid his head down on Josh's warm chest, listening to his heart.

Then unexpectedly, Zeke looked up at the still frozen posture that Josh fought to maintain, "You're still my best friend, and I'm yours. I don't want you to leave. I would miss you terribly. I love you."

Josh's eyes popped open, half afraid of what he had just felt and more importantly, what he had just heard. He was afraid it might just have been a dream. The firelight caught Zeke's moistening blue eyes. He saw the earnest there, and knew instantly this was no dream. A tear slid from the corner of Josh's eyes.

"Then why do you treat me like a cold fish?" asked Josh.

Zeke chuckled, "A what?"

"You're a sailor? You treat me like I was cold and slimy, and you can't wait to get away from me."

Zeke squeezed Josh's erection. "You're crazy. I do not."

"Zeke, whenever anyone else is around us, you treat me like a bastard child." He had said it boldly, but sincerely.

Zeke thought about the comment for a moment. "I'm sorry. You're right. I don't know why. I don't want to hurt you. I just feel..."

"Guilty?" asked Josh.

"Perhaps, I mean, is this something we're going to grow out of. We'll get married to some nice girl one day, and have a bunch of kids."

"I don't really know. I don't know if there is anyone else that has feelings like we do," replied Josh.

"But, it's not normal. What life do we have like this?"

"Who is to say what is normal? I've never been normal. I don't want to be like everybody else. I've learned I don't need anyone else's approval, but I want yours. If our love continues for each other, then maybe we'll have to live in a place where we can be ourselves."

"You mean on a deserted tropical island?" asked Zeke.

"Sounds good to me, or perhaps in the Rockies? I just know that right now, being with you makes me feel alive, makes me so happy that I just know I'm going to bust. If I die before I wake, I will have died happier than I've ever been. I love you, Zeke Robertson. I really do."

Zeke sighed, as a slow tear fell down his cheek and bounced onto Josh's bare chest. "And I love you."

"Don't feel guilty. You're ruining the love, the joy, and our happiness. What we do is our business, and no one else's. I'll fight the first man that tries to interfere. Together, we can conquer the world."

Zeke leaned up and kissed Josh strongly and passionately on the mouth, their tongues instantly exploring. Josh pulled him closely and reached down to feel Zeke's buns, but the long johns prevented him from feeling the beauty of Zeke's flesh. He snapped opened the flap and allowed his hands to slip inside.

Over the course of the lovemaking, Zeke managed to crawl out of the long johns while still kissing Josh at the same time. They made love long and intimately, and then spent the rest of the night cuddled tightly in each other's arms.

SIX

The good news about being back at school for the second semester was the freshman hazing was now over with, and Daniel now had to do his own boots and chores. However, it didn't stop his hate for Josh and even Zeke, simply because Josh and Zeke were friends. Daniel constantly kept thinking of ways to get even with Josh.

Zeke was still tutoring Josh in his history lessons, and they had a big test coming up on Monday that they were busy working on. The mid-February weather turned very cold. Petersburg became very chilly, fogged in, damp, and dreary. Josh longed for spring, the southern summer sun, and especially swimming in the swamps. He wondered if he would ever be allowed to return there, or allowed to go home for the summer.

"Are you daydreaming again?" complained Zeke as he thumped Josh in the back of the head with his index finger as he returned to their table in the library with yet another book.

"Ow!" said Josh aloud.

The room of students all turned and said in unison, "Shh,"

Josh gestured an apology by dipping his head and smiling, and then whispering to Zeke, "Of course not. I was just allowing the events of history to settle in my mind."

"If you don't get to work on reading that book, I'm going to settle my foot up your butt," threatened Zeke with a slight grin.

Josh gestured for Zeke to come close enough for him to whisper even softer, "You mean my cute butt, don't you?"

Zeke almost burst out laughing, but managed to cover his mouth, and regain his composure, and whisper back into Josh's ear, "If you don't finish that book, I'm going to kick your cute butt."

"That's better. Now don't bother me, I'm reading," chuckled Josh, as he pretended to shoo Zeke away.

Zeke sat down across from him and just gazed lovingly into Josh's ocean blue eyes as Josh returned to his book. After a minute, Josh glanced over his book, and smiled back at Zeke. They both grinned slightly, and then Josh returned to his reading. Their love had managed to survive the trip to Maine, but at school, it was now less of a physical thing, and more of an inner thing, as they had almost no privacy at school, and didn't dare take any risks. They had been plotting for Easter spring break in March when they had a whole week off from school. They were saving their money, and planned to rent a room in Washington for their vacation and lots of catching up on making love. Josh and Zeke stayed late in the library, and were the last cadets to leave. They pushed themselves to study hard, and Josh now had a reason to excel. He wanted to please Zeke. He wanted to stay in school with Zeke. He had never worked harder at schoolwork.

When reveille sounded, they woke with a start, leaped out of bed, made their quick trip to the latrine, and quickly reviewed their notes until time for roll call and breakfast, then more note reading until the first class bell.

Frederick Abercrombie looked meaner than ever when Josh walked in the room. Josh sensed that somehow the man had already managed to make the already-hard exam even harder just because he was in the class. Each cadet was told to clear his desk of all his books and papers. Then the professor handed out the exams, checked his gold watch, and told them to begin.

Zeke went through the first page faster than Josh, but Josh was doing well; far better than usual, and was hoping page two wasn't much harder. By the time the hour-long exam was completed, Josh found himself exhausted from the stress, and his hand hurt from the quick and furious writing he had done. They were ordered to leave their exams face down on the desk, and to leave the room. Josh and Zeke quickly left the room greatly relieved the exam was over.

Daniel moved close to Josh's table, looked across the room to see if anyone was watching him, and then nodded to Eli. The boy took his cue and walked quickly up to Professor Abercrombie.

"Sir, do you believe that history will be repeating itself on the slavery issue in the United States? I mean are we going to fall just like the Roman Empire." Eli tried to sound sincere, but more importantly he moved around the professor so that when Abercrombie looked up at him, he would not be able to see the rest of the room.

Daniel waited patiently for the last cadet to leave the room, then slipped a sheet of paper from inside his coat, lifted Josh's test paper and put the paper underneath it. He then checked to see if anyone had seen him.

"Well, Mister Brown. You could be on to something there. The Romans did indeed expand too fast, leaving little support for the vast empire, but they also became politically and morally corrupt. I don't think we've gone quite that far here in the United States, but as to the slaves...."

Daniel cleared his throat as he turned to leave the room. Eli took his cue, and gladly cut Abercrombie off, "That's great, sir. Thank you very much. I have to run and study my math. Thank you, sir. Brilliant."

Eli quickly left the room, leaving Abercrombie confused, and somewhat suspicious of Eli's motives. He walked from desk to desk picking up the exams. When he lifted Josh's exam, the sheet of paper that Daniel placed there fell to the floor. Abercrombie bent down and lifted it up with his right hand, immediately realizing that it was a cheat sheet. He held up the last test he had picked up in his left hand, and discovered the paper and the cheat sheet belonged to Johnson.

He stacked the two papers together, put them on the top of his pile, and then looked out the window and spotted Josh and Zeke heading across the campus. He had always despised Josh from the first day they had met. The boy had knocked him down, and he was a poor student as well. He saw a chance to get even. He saw a way to get Josh kicked out of school. He grinned broadly as he began preparing his case for the Academy Commander. He looked up to see a student coming down the aisle toward him with perhaps another question.

By three in the afternoon, Josh and Zeke finished their last exam, and had just returned to their cottage to fall down on their bunks and rest a bit before riding practice. Two senior cadets suddenly entered the room. Zeke spotted them first, and the color left his face. They were carrying muskets. He had never seen two cadets carrying muskets into their cottages. All rifles were locked in the armory.

The two cadets came to an attention, and the senior ranking cadet spoke loudly and plainly, "Johnson, Josh. You are to consider yourself under arrest. You'll accompany us to the commander's office immediately."

Josh turned around, shocked at what they had just said. "Under arrest? For what?" he asked.

"For cheating. You have disgraced the school and the corps," shot back the cadet, "Now come with me."

"Josh would never cheat," broke in Zeke.

Josh stood. "I'll go with you, but I didn't cheat. Who is accusing me?"

"Professor Abercrombie."

Josh led them from the room. Zeke stood by in shock. "Abercrombie?" he asked himself.

Daniel and Eli quickly turned their faces from Zeke. They were desperately fighting an urge to laugh. Daniel finally spoke, "I always knew Josh was no good. He'll be kicked out of school. That's the end of him. Hurrah, I say,"

Zeke took four quick steps, spun Daniel around as he was taking off his shirt, and hit him with a solid right hand upper cut to the jaw. Daniel fell to the floor in a heap and out cold. Eli started to jump across the bunk at Zeke, but Zeke turned quickly at him, his fists up and ready. Eli backed off. Zeke returned to his bunk, grabbed his coat, and headed out the door for the administration office.

When he reached the office door, he found the two musket armed cadets standing at attention on either side of the door. When Zeke got closer, the ranking one spoke again. "You can't go in. No visitors."

"I need to speak to Josh," pleaded Zeke.

Josh could hear Zeke from inside as he sat alone on the wooden bench waiting to see the colonel. He longed to talk to Zeke, but Zeke was told to return to his cottage, or he would be given five demerits for disobeying. Zeke paced back and forth for a few seconds, frantically ringing his hands, feeling the bruised knuckles he had just received from Daniel's chin, and then walked around the corner of the building and out of sight of the guards.

Josh sat there motionless for the first half hour, and he could just slightly overhear Colonel Lee discussing a purchasing problem with the sergeant. He noted a leftover newspaper on the bench beside him, picked it up, and began reading.

He was soon surprised to find that the man he had read about on the train heading to Maine had been elected as the first Republican President of the United States. His name was Abraham Lincoln. Josh read on to discover that Lincoln would become the 16th President of the United States by winning 1,865,593 votes, defeating both Douglas and Breckinridge. He was amazed to think there were over a million people living in the United States. He guessed he had only seen a few thousand Americans in his lifetime. He found an article about the South that said they would be forced to secede from the Union, but that Lincoln promised to preserve the Union, while still trying to find a solution on the slavery matter.

The colonel's door suddenly opened and the sergeant appeared. Josh immediately dropped the newspaper and got to his feet. The sergeant nodded while giving Josh the once over with his eyes. He already heard the rumor, and already convicted Josh as he left the building.

"The Colonel will see you now," said Cadet Jones.

Josh promptly walked through the banister railing and into the colonel's office. Cadet Jones shut the door behind him. Zeke leaned up against the wall outside the colonel's window. Josh saluted, and held his shoulders back as straight as he possibly could.

The colonel looked up and saluted. "Professor Abercrombie has accused you of cheating on today's history exam. What do you have to say for yourself?"

"May I speak freely, sir?" asked Josh.

"By all means, speak your mind, boy."

"Sir, there is no way in hell I cheated on that exam. I've been working my butt off for six weeks to prepare for that test. If I had planned to cheat, I sure wouldn't have worked that hard to study. Someone has set me up, sir."

Zeke flinched when he heard Josh cuss in front of the colonel. The colonel took in Josh's statement while studying the boy very carefully.

"Why did you come here, son?"

The question caught Josh off guard. It took a second to answer. "Truth is, I didn't want to come here. I was sent here because I had nowhere else to go. Nevertheless, sir, after just six months here, the Academy is my home, my family, and my friend. I don't want to leave, and would fight the first man that tries to run me out!"

"I can see you have a temper. Sometimes in battle, a temper is a good thing, giving you that extra adrenaline rush you need to get the job done. But sometimes it can cause a man to do foolish things."

"Sir, I did not cheat. Never have. Never will."

"How do you propose to prove your innocence? The professor found this cheat sheet underneath your exam."

"Under it? Sir, when I left the room there was only the exam on my desk. Do I look so stupid that I would leave a cheat sheet on the desk for the professor to find?"

Zeke flinched again at Josh's boldness.

"No, I guess not, but an accusation of cheating is a serious matter. There must be a thorough investigation. I'll set a hearing for next Tuesday at three. You may seek counsel if you so desire."

"Yes, sir. Thank you, sir."

"Very well. That is all."

Josh saluted once more, and the colonel stood and held his salute while carefully studying Josh's eyes. It seemed like an eternity to Josh, but he did not back down from looking directly into the colonel's eyes. Satisfied, the colonel finally let go his salute, and Josh left the room.

As he rounded the corner, Josh ran head on into Zeke.

"I can't believe this. You should have heard..."

Zeke grinned, "I did hear. I was just outside the colonel's window. Come on. We've got to talk."

Zeke led Josh across the grounds and into the stable. The place was empty as everyone was already out on the riding field. They went up to the loft, checked carefully to make sure they were alone, and then Zeke gave Josh a huge hug, and kissed him passionately. They had never kissed on campus before. Josh was surprised at Zeke's audacity.

"What was that for?" asked Josh.

"Just thought you might need one. Want me to take it back?" teased Zeke.

"No, but what are we going to do?" Josh sat down despondently on a bale of hay.

Zeke joined him. "Well, it's obvious that you've been set up, and it's an easy bet that the culprits were Daniel and Eli."

"It could have been Frederick the fart. He's pretty clever. I don't think they are going to take my word over his," stated Josh.

"By the way, when you see Daniel, you should note his jaw has swollen a bit," said Zeke with a sly grin.

"His jaw? What did you do?"

"I gave him a good punch. He fell to the floor, out cold."

Josh chuckled. "I thought I was the fighter around here."

"You're the loud mouth. Do you realize you just cussed in front of the colonel?"

"I did?"

"Yes, you fool. Now let's think this through a minute."

"Will you go with me to the hearing and be my counsel?" asked Josh tenderly.

"Of course, I will. You're going to have to be on your best behavior until this hearing. Don't let Daniel trick you into a fight, or do anything that might weaken your case. Promise?"

"Yeah, sure. Anything. I just can't be kicked out. Where would I go?"

"I heard what you said in there. I'm your family now. I'm your friend. I'm all you'll ever need." Zeke kissed him again.

"I'd sure like to curl up with you right now," grinned Josh.

"That's all we need before the hearing. Nope, first we win this hearing and then we celebrate in Washington on our holiday. Deal?"

"Deal!"

Tuesday came all too quickly. Zeke interviewed most of the corps looking for clues. He hoped they were ready. The cadets arranged the dining hall tables into a court-like setting with the colonel presiding over the hearing. Abercrombie sat at one table, Josh and Zeke at the other. The professors sat behind them followed by the entire corps. The tension was tight in the room. When the colonel entered the room, all stood and saluted.

"Be seated, gentlemen. Let's get started. Professor Abercrombie, would you please come forth and examine these two documents?"

Abercrombie stood and walked over to the colonel, and took the documents from him and studied them for a long minute. "This is Johnson's exam, and this is the cheat sheet I found beneath his exam."

"Did anyone else cheat?"

"No, sir."

"Any chance another cadet may have slipped this beneath Johnson's paper?" asked the colonel. Zeke and Josh knew that was exactly what happened. It felt good knowing the colonel had asked the question.

"No, sir. I kept my eye on the cadets during the entire exam and even until the last man left the room. No one could have slipped it there."

"Do you have anything to add?"

"Yes, sir. Johnson has been a poor student all year. I graded his exam. He made a ninety-two on that one. That is ten points higher than he has ever made. I don't think he could have done that without cheating. He's just not capable."

"Thank you, Professor." The colonel did not like the Professor's harsh analysis, but he kept a stiff lip. "Counsel, any questions of this witness?" asked the colonel as he looked over to Zeke.

"Professor Abercrombie," began Zeke nervously, never dreaming that he would ever play the role of a lawyer. He also did not relish the idea of quizzing Abercrombie. The payback could be a long semester in his history class. "Did you see anyone place the cheat sheet on the desk?"

"No, I did not," replied the Professor, not at all happy to be questioned by one of his students.

"Was anyone standing near Josh, I mean, Johnson's desk after the exam?"

"Most certainly not. I was watching all the students carefully."

"So in your opinion, no one but Josh could have put that cheat sheet there. Is that right?"

"Precisely."

"Does it make sense to you that a person would cheat on a test and then leave the evidence behind?"

"My experience with Johnson is that he doesn't have the mental capacity to make logical decisions like that."

The corps chuckled. Josh almost wanted to leap from his chair and push his fists deep into Frederick's face, but Zeke had anticipated the answer and stood between them.

"That's all I have for now, sir."

"Very well," said the colonel. "My office has no more witnesses. Do you have any that you want to call?"

"Yes, sir. I would like to first call Professor Wilkins," stated Zeke boldly.

"What has Wilkins got to do with this?" protested Abercrombie.

"Professor, if you'd be so kind as to keep your questions and opinions to yourself. You're not on trial here. You're simply a witness," rebuked the colonel, delighting in the opportunity to finally chastise Abercrombie a bit.

Professor Wilkins came from his seat amongst the cadets and sat in the chair to the right of the colonel. Zeke walked up to the colonel. "Sir, may I borrow these two documents for just a moment?" The colonel did not reply, but simply handed them to Zeke. Zeke walked over to the Professor, and handed him the two documents. "Professor Wilkins, would you carefully examine the handwriting of the two documents?"

Professor Wilkins lifted the gold-rimmed spectacles he kept on a black cord around his neck, and carefully squinted through them as he examined Josh's test paper and then the cheat sheet.

Zeke waited on him to finish and then asked his next question. "Now, sir, did you bring the samples of writings I requested?"

"Yes, I've brought several of Johnson's papers from my class."

"Very well, would you compare the writing of Johnson's English papers with that of his test paper?"

Zeke waited patiently for the professor to study each one carefully.

"They're the same," he announced. There was a murmur from the cadets.

"And how can you tell that Josh's English paper and his history test paper are done by him?"

"I've been teaching English to cadets for over thirty years. I know handwriting. Johnson's is one of the worst I've ever seen. I'd recognize it anywhere. I almost go blind just trying to grade his papers!" The cadets chuckled once again at this remark. Josh blushed a bit.

"But how can you be so absolutely sure?" asked Zeke.

"Here, I'll show you. Do you see that letter *J*? Well, most of the boys start low with the first loop of the *J* then come down and continue the second loop and end up right where the first began. Not lazy Johnson. He always slops right on past it and into the next letter. In addition, look at his *S*'s. They look like bad figure eight's," added the professor.

Josh was beginning to wonder if Zeke had turned on him, as he was making him to appear to have the worst handwriting of any student in the school.

"Very good, Professor. Now would you look once again at the cheat sheet? Do you see any J's or S's that appear to be Johnson's?"

The room fell silent as they now all caught on to what Zeke was after. So did Josh, as he began to nervously chew his lower lip. Slowly, the professor compared the cheat sheet with his samples of Josh's handwriting.

Finally, he dropped his hands as he set the papers down, removed the glasses from his nose, and looked up at Zeke.

"Cadet Robertson, this cheat sheet was not written by Johnson. There is not one single J or S or any other letter on this cheat sheet that is like Johnson's terrible handwriting style."

The cadets cheered. Josh broke into a smile. The colonel was pleased, but kept his composure in check. His steady gaze into Josh's eyes a few days ago had told him Josh had been telling the truth. He now fully believed what he saw, but still, he was determined to remain impartial and called for silence.

Zeke turned back to the professor, "Sir, thank you very much for your help in this matter."

"You're very welcome," replied the professor as he handed the two documents back to Zeke, and returned to his seat amongst the cadets.

Abercrombie leaped to his feet. "That still doesn't mean that Johnson didn't cheat. It only proves that he was smart enough to get someone else to print out the cheat sheet. Perhaps even his best friend, Mister Robertson," accused Abercrombie as he sneered in Zeke's direction.

Zeke began a rebuttal, but the colonel beat him to it, "Professor, I've already reminded you once that you are a witness and not a prosecutor. Now sit down and be quiet." Then the colonel looked over at Professor Wilkins. "Wilkins, would you recognize Robertson's handwriting?"

"Yes, I would, and I had guessed you might bring that up. I have samples of his handwriting, and I must say his is quite good with the exception of the letter L. He really leans it over. All the L's on the cheat sheet are straight up. That's not his work either."

"Thank you, Professor. You've been most helpful," and then to Zeke, "Cadet Robertson, this handwriting report is very interesting, but not completely convincing. There is still the matter of who put the cheat there, and did Johnson use it or not?"

"I have another witness, sir," replied Zeke.

"Very well."

"I call Lieutenant Jamerson."

The cadets murmured at the surprise calling of Jamerson. Josh looked back as Jamerson stood and began walking forward. As Jamerson paced by, Josh's eyes focused on the intense stare that Daniel was giving him from the front row.

"Mister Jamerson, were you in the vicinity of the history classroom after the exam in question?" asked Zeke.

"I was."

"And why were you there? Haven't you already taken freshman history?"

"Of course I have, I'm a senior. I was there because I wanted to ask the professor about the talk in the newspapers about the Crittenden Compromise. I am writing my senior research paper on the slave verses free state issue, and quite frankly, the compromise's plausibility puzzled me."

"So you were waiting for the exam to finish to ask the professor a question?"

"That's right."

"When you approached the door, had all the cadets left the room?"

"All but two. One was talking to the professor, and the other was coming up the aisle."

"Was it possible for the professor to see the entire classroom from the position you found him in when you approached?"

"No, he had his back on the classroom while talking with the student." The cadets shifted restlessly at this new revelation. Abercrombie clenched his fists nervously as he listened to the student's response.

"I see, so someone else could have put the cheat sheet under Johnson's exam as he had already left the room. Now, Mister Jamerson, Mister Johnson's desk is to the left of the center aisle of the room and the third one down. Where did you see the cadet leaving the room when you came to the door?"

"He was coming up the center aisle." The cadets grumbled this time. Josh felt like his stomach was churning.

Zeke paused to allow this interesting fact to take hold. "Now, Mister Jamerson, please think carefully, what was the name of the student who was talking with the professor while he had his back turned on the classroom?" added Zeke.

"Brown, Eli," stated Jamerson clearly.

"I see, so Mister Brown had obtained the professor's attention. If you'll pardon me a moment Mister Jamerson," begged Zeke as he turned to the audience, "Professor Wilkins, did you bring the sample of Mister Brown's handwriting from your class?"

"Yes, I did," he replied as he stood holding it up.

"Does it match the cheat sheet?" asked Zeke.

"No, it does not." The cadets anticipated a match, and were disappointed. Eli felt like a Christian being thrown to the lions. He wanted to bolt from the room. He wanted to speak out, and say it was Daniel, but his eyes caught sight of Daniel's menacing and threatening gaze, so he quickly clamped his teeth shut and said nothing.

"Very well," thanked Zeke as Wilkins sat back down. "Now, Mister Jamerson, who was the only other student coming up the aisle?"

A hush fell over the room. Jamerson spoke clearly, "It was Carpon, Daniel." The corps began murmuring rapidly. The cadets seated to either side of Daniel slid away, leaving him sitting all alone and out on a limb so to speak.

"Your attention, please!" urged the colonel as silence once again fell on the room.

Zeke turned and deliberately winked at Josh. Josh thought his heart was going to leap right out of his chest. He could not even swallow he was so nervous.

"Professor Wilkins, did you bring a sample of Mister Carpon's handwriting?"

"Yes, I did," he replied as he once more stood and held it up.

"Does it match the cheat sheet?"

"Mister Carpon had to take my Freshman English class twice before he passed. I have many samples of his handwriting. I pulled them all out. He always wrote quickly which means his natural style would come out in spite of himself. A person that writes slowly and deliberately can sometimes change parts of his style, but never all of it. In other words, there was nothing deliberate in the writing of his test papers in my class. However, the cheat sheet was written in a very deliberate style, as if trying to hide the true identity of its author, but Mister Carpon makes two distinct kinds of letters. The letter *C* from his surname is always made with a very tiny curl at the top and then a bold semicircle curve to the letter whether it is a small c or a capital C. He also makes an unusual letter *P*, again with a small starting circle identical with the circle, which begins his letter C. I found twenty two examples of these individual letters on the cheat sheet."

The cadets stood up and cheered. Daniel tried to make a break from the room, but the cadets swarmed him, and brought him back to the front of the room, sat him down in his chair, and held him there. Attention was called, and every one ordered to be seated. Daniel looked defiantly at Josh, and he proudly returned his gaze.

"Johnson, it appears the truth has indeed come forth, and I apologize for any stress this accusation may have put on you. Your record remains clear and intact, and you are returned to full cadet status. You are to be commended on your score on this exam, and I'm told by our librarian that you and Robertson spent more time in that library preparing for this exam than any other student in the corps."

Zeke and Josh were pleased the colonel had apparently done a bit of investigating on his own.

"Furthermore, you are one smart cadet in seeking your representation in cadet Robertson. Robertson, you'd make a fine lawyer. Well done."

"Thank you, sir."

Zeke returned to Josh's side, and together, they sat there proudly.

"As for you, Carpon. You are hereby removed from the corps, and banned from this academy. You shall not return. Cadets, you are never to speak this student's name again. He has shamed the academy. We will never speak of him again. Lieutenant, please remove Carpon from the premises immediately, and put him on the first train out of here. As for Mister Brown, I don't doubt that you had something to do with this incident. You are hereby placed on probation. One mistake, sir, and you'll be kicked out of school, too. This hearing is hereby adjourned!"

The cadets swarmed the table. Zeke gave Josh a big hug. Everyone began patting them on the back and cheering. Professor Wilkins came over to shake their hands, as did the colonel. Humiliated, Professor Abercrombie quickly left the room. Daniel could be heard screaming obscenities and threats at Josh and Zeke as he was marched off the campus.

Later that night, Eli was severely beaten by a group of masked cadets in the latrine. Zeke and Josh had nothing to do with it but by dawn, Eli and his belongings disappeared.

SEVEN

They arrived at the Hotel Baltimore at dusk, having left the Academy after their last class, caught the train to Richmond, and then on to Washington. It had been almost three months since they had been off campus together, and they felt like a big burden had been lifted from their shoulders. They had become good at acting like they weren't in love, but upon arriving in the capital city they now felt a very special freedom. There was no one in Washington that knew them, so they could be themselves, at least behind closed doors.

They couldn't wait for the clerk to give them the key to their room. They rapidly ran up the stairs, found their room on the second floor, unlocked the door, dashed in, and locked the door behind them. The room was but fourteen feet square with a bed in the center and a tall window on each side of the bed. They smiled and nodded as they each picked a different window to run to, whereupon they simultaneously jerked the shades down, blocking the world from their view. Instantly, the last bit of social pressure instantly fell from their shoulders. They were finally alone.

"Now?" asked Zeke.

"Now!" yelled Josh.

The two cadets started rapidly unbuttoning their uniforms, dropping them to the floor in a heap until they were down to their long johns. Josh toyed with the button on the front of his long johns, slowly unbuttoning one button at a time. Suddenly, he laughed and jerked the long johns off as well. Zeke quickly downed his own. The room fell quiet as they proudly stood before each other in the nude. Zeke made a move for the bed. Josh leaped through the air and tackled him. Together, they fell onto the bed, and quickly began kissing and probing as if literally starving for affection.

The minutes and hours ticked by, and they missed the dinner hour. They had long ago forgotten about eating. They left the bed only to use the small private bathroom, a luxury they had insisted upon, and to take a crowded bath together. They slept in. Their lips were chapped from the constant kissing and sucking. Their tools were sore from the long, excited erections, but they didn't care.

Starving, they finally dressed, and walked down to the hotel's dining room for lunch. They ate everything they could get their hands on, and then took a stroll to tour the city.

Washington wasn't as big as New York, but still the streets were busy. They bought a newspaper that was filled with stories about slavery, secession, and possible war. They found many editorials and debates about states' rights, and they couldn't help but snicker at the terrible cartoons depicting Abraham Lincoln, most often as a tall skinny monkey.

Zeke noted an article about an ironclad boat being built on the Potomac so on the second day in Washington, they hiked over to the river to see the shipyard. While still cool, they enjoyed the hint of spring as the trees were beginning to bud, and the sun felt warm on their pale faces. They walked along the edge of the river until they came to the shipyard. Zeke was thrilled to see so many of the tall-mast ships that were moored there, and wished he could take Josh sailing, but knew they shouldn't waste their tightly budgeted money on such a thrill.

They walked from dock to dock, talking about the boats, and not really paying any attention to what lay ahead when suddenly they came upon a construction crew working on an oddly shaped small boat made of iron plates. Zeke noted a drafting table under a shed and spotting no one around, he began looking at the plans. He always wanted to be an engineer, and marveled at the design of this future boat.

"What is it?" asked Josh.

"It appears to be an underwater boat?" replied Zeke as he scanned another page.

"A what? Are you serious? How can a boat go underwater?"

"I don't know."

A man walked up with a pencil in his ear. He had blond hair, and was in his fifties. "What are you doing, lads?" he asked.

"I'm sorry, sir," apologized Zeke. "We're cadets and well, my family owns a shipping fleet out of Portland Maine, and I'm interested in engineering, and your new boat just caught my curiosity."

"I see," said the man as he lit his pipe. "Well, my name is John Ericsson. I'm from Sweden. I came to this country to be an engineer. You're looking at the plans of the very first combat iron boat. It has a single turret in the center than can swing around in a three hundred sixty degree circle allowing it to fully blast the stuffing out of any enemy ship. She is virtually indestructible."

"Amazing," replied Zeke.

"Yeah, I think so, too. How's school coming?" he asked.

"Very well, but we're only freshmen. We have a ways to go just yet. I'm going to pursue engineering."

"I see, well, there are no schools around here for engineering. Perhaps you two boys might like a summer job here on the docks. It's hard work, but you might learn a thing or two."

"That would be fantastic," grinned Zeke. "My name is Zeke Robertson, and this is my best friend, Josh Johnson."

Josh beamed at the sound of being publicly called Zeke's best friend once again.

"I'm pleased to make your acquaintance, boys. Just remember my name, and give look me up when you get out of school for the summer, okay?"

"Great. Thank you," said Zeke. "Well, we'll get out of your way. Thanks again for taking a few minutes with us."

"Bye, boys," said Erickson as he began making calculations on the edge of his plans.

They wandered about for most of the day, finding both adventure and fun in almost everything they came across. They stopped in the park to hear an abolitionist preach from a wooden box about the sins of slavery. Zeke could tell that Josh was about to begin an argument with the man, so he quickly pushed Josh down the street. They turned a corner and saw a sign that had Ford's Theater painted on it.

"Is there a play tonight?" asked Zeke

"There's a handbill pasted on the wall. It says, "The Merchant of Venice,”" read Josh.

"Great. Let's go back to the hotel, take a nap, eat dinner, and then come back here for the performance tonight. I've never seen a live play," said Zeke excitedly.

"It's by William Shakespeare. It'll be boring. I've read Shakespeare. I promise you, he is very boring," replied Josh as they began walking back to their hotel.

"You read Shakespeare? Ah, that's a laugh. I didn't even know you could read!" teased Zeke, as he knocked Josh's cap to the street and took off running.

Josh grabbed his hat and took off after Zeke. "I'll catch you. You know I'm faster."

Zeke glanced back, "Not this time. You're getting fat and old from all that sex..." Zeke reached the corner and crashed into a parked buggy.

Josh laughed at him as Zeke fell to the street, but before Josh could get there. Two men stepped from the curb. The bigger one placed his foot on Zeke's back, preventing him from getting up. The other reached down and plucked Zeke's wallet from his pocket.

"Hey, give me that back! Let me up!" protested Zeke.

"Cut him," ordered the smaller man.

The big man pulled a knife from his waist, reached down, grabbed Zeke’s head by a fistful of hair, and jerked it back. Zeke screamed out at the pain. The big man intended to cut Zeke's throat, but neither man saw Josh rushing up the street after Zeke.

Seeing the knife glitter in the afternoon sun, Josh leaped through the air and knocked the big man off Zeke by driving his head hard into the man's back. The big man tumbled over, but came up quickly with the knife swinging dangerously in front of him. Suddenly, he took a swipe at Josh, cutting him on his left arm. Josh flinched at the pain, but managed to catch the man with a rapid uppercut to his chin.

Zeke scrambled to his feet when he saw the little man about to run. Zeke tackled the man and hit him twice in the face. The man quickly handed him back his wallet. Zeke snatched the wallet, stood, kicked the man in the ribs, and turned back to help Josh.

The big guy took another swipe at Josh. A crowd gathered to watch the fight. Someone called for help. The man swung again. Josh jumped back. Zeke searched the ground for a board or stick, or something he could use to knock the knife from the man's hand. He spotted a passerby's wooden cane, and ran to 'borrow' it by snatching it from the man's hand.

He turned back to the fight just as the smaller man had gotten to his feet, and pulled a small derringer from his inside coat pocket, taking aim at Josh.

Zeke didn't hesitate or even consider the possibility of being shot himself. He swung the cane down hard across the man's right arm as he was trying to take aim at Josh. He had swung so hard that the bone in the man's arm snapped. It was a loud splintering crack that made everyone grimace at the awful sound. Even the big guy froze for a split second.

Nevertheless, not Zeke—he swung back around with the cane and hit the man hard across his wrist, knocking the knife to the ground. The stunned man grabbed his throbbing hand. Josh rushed in, hit the man twice in the face and once in the gut, and then kicked him hard in the groin. The man tumbled to the ground in a heap, clutching his groin. Goliath had been defeated, thought Josh.

Zeke turned once again to hit the smaller man and found the gun still on the ground, but the man was nowhere to be found. Zeke bent down, picked up the gun, and stuffed it in his pocket.

A constable appeared, heard Josh and Zeke's account, and hauled the big guy away to jail. The crowd cheered. Josh and Zeke took a playful bow, and then dusted themselves off. Zeke returned the cane to its owner, and apologized for having borrowed it. The man was quite nice and said it was no trouble. Then the man did an odd thing, or so thought Zeke. The man winked at him. Zeke just innocently smiled back, and then turned to find Josh, so they could head back to the hotel.

"Excuse me. Excuse me, please," said a man in a black bowler hat, spectacles, black stringy hair, and a weathered rumpled black suit and white shirt. He carried a writing pad in his left hand and pencil in his right. "I'm Ronald Livingston. I'm a reporter for the Post. May I have your names? I'm going to do a story about street crime. You guys sure did handle that big fellow."

"It was nothing," replied Josh. "I'm Josh Johnson. This is Zeke Robertson."

"That's funny," replied the reporter.

"What's funny?" asked Josh as he gave the man a puzzled look.

"Your name, Josh Johnson," replied the man.

"My name?" asked Josh, the smile falling from his face.

"No, I don't mean it's funny as in making fun of you, just that they are filled with alliteration."

"A-lit-a-what?" asked Josh.

"Alliteration. That's when you make a sentence using the same letter for the start of each word. Both your names begin with the same letter. You know, as in Josh Johnson, or JJ.

"Oh," replied Josh.

"Oh," echoed Zeke. They were both thinking the man was surely off his rocker.

"Pardon me for saying this," he stopped to move them away from the crowd, "but are you two good friends," he said emphasizing the word "good." They both nodded affirmatively. "Really good friends?" They again nodded. "I see, well, there is a small group of friends like us that meets at private pub. Let me write the address down for you." He quickly scribbled the address down. "I've got to get to work. Your names will be in the newspaper tomorrow. Good job. In addition, if you two love each other as I suspect, then come to that address after ten tonight. You'll meet some other very interesting people who have something in common with you."

Before they could reply to his last comment, he pushed through the crowd and was gone. "How'd he know that we..." Zeke caught himself as a passerby pushed around them.

They began walking down the street. Josh scratched his head. "I don't know. Maybe he was just guessing. I mean, just because I saved your life and you owe me..."

"You saved my life? I saved your life. He was about to shoot you," broke in Zeke.

"I recall you were about to get your throat cut when I knocked that guy off of you."

"Yeah, right," grinned Zeke sarcastically. "I could have handled him. How's your arm?"

"Hurts, but it's not bad. No stitches. We just need to wash, and tie a bandage around it."

Zeke leaned in to Josh and whispered, "Does this mean you can't have sex tonight?"

Josh smirked back, "Tonight nothing. I'm ready right now. I'll race you to the hotel." Josh took off running with Zeke quickly jogging behind him.

"Is it time for the curtain to go up?" quizzed Josh already impatient and bit worried about having to sit through a production of Shakespeare.

Zeke checked his pocket watch, a gift from his parents on his birthday. "Yep, any minute now. Do you see those box seats with the American flag hanging in front?"

"Yeah, so what?"

"I overheard the lady on the other side of me say that is the President's box."

Josh gave him a look through the top of his eyes as if he were looking over glasses. "Do you mean to say that is where Abraham Lincoln sits when he comes here?"

"Yep, guess so."

"Geez, do you think we'll get to see him?"

"No one in the box as of yet. He might not come tonight. The play has been here for a week already," replied Zeke just as the lights dimmed and the curtain went up. "Shh, here we go."

After the show ended, Zeke and Josh followed the crowd into the street where buggy after buggy picked up Washington's theater crowd. The two cadets stood around and watched to see if Lincoln came out, and soon disappointed he didn't.

"Are you hungry?" asked Zeke.

"No, I'm fine. Shall we find that pub the reporter told us about?" asked Josh.

"I dunno. Do you think it's a setup? We could get robbed."

Josh laughed, "We don't have much money on us. The rest is hidden in the hotel. Let's go. Where's your sense of adventure?"

"Okay, but how do we find it?"

"Here, give me the slip of paper, and I'll ask one of these buggy drivers. They probably know every street in town."

Josh took the address and tried the first driver he came to. Zeke watched as the man shook his head. On Josh's second attempt, the man gave him a hard cold look, and then pointed down the street while Josh kept nodding.

"Did you get it?"

"Yes, but oddly I don't think the man wanted to tell me. Let's go. It's about six blocks from here."

Josh and Zeke walked and talked about the play, and how Josh hated to admit that he liked the play, in spite of the fact that it was written by Shakespeare. They turned down the street the driver indicated, and then watched for street numbers painted on the dark buildings. There weren't many gas street lamps, and they were having trouble finding the right street. They crossed an alley. Zeke thought he saw someone move down the alley. He wasn't anxious to get in another knife fight, and so he began to question whether they should try to find this pub or not.

"Josh, this doesn't appear to be a good side of town. Why don't we just go back to the hotel?"

Josh saw the worry line across Zeke's brow and patted his shoulder. "I'll find it. Don't worry."

Two men came around the corner holding hands. Zeke nearly jumped out of shoes. Josh became alarmed as well. The two men spotted Josh and Zeke, unclasped their hands, and crossed the street in front of Josh and Zeke. Then the men turned down an alley. Josh and Zeke sighed; greatly relieved the two men weren't robbers.

"Let's go," protested Zeke.

"Wait a minute! Now I understand. Did you note something a bit unusual about those two men?" asked Josh as he spun Zeke around to face him.

"No, I was just glad they didn't harm us."

"They were holding hands, at least until they spotted us."

"They were what?"

"Holding hands," grinned Josh.

"Oh, my lord!"

"Let's follow them. Come on," added Josh before Zeke could protest. Josh grabbed Zeke's hand and pulled him down the alley. The two men were a hundred feet ahead of them. Reluctantly, Zeke followed. "Hurry, we'll lose them," urged Josh as they began trotting along.

"I see them," said Zeke.

They walked quickly and soon they were but fifty feet behind the two men who hadn't noticed they were being followed. Josh and Zeke noted they were holding hands again. When the two men crossed an alley, they walked but twenty more feet, and suddenly disappeared. Josh and Zeke crossed the alley, walked the twenty feet, and then began circling.

"Which way did they go?" asked Josh.

"I don't know. They were standing right here and then poof—they were gone. It was like a magician's show," added Zeke. "I think we'd better go."

"Shh," whispered Josh. "Listen."

Zeke strained his ears and sure enough, the two boys could faintly hear a piano playing.

"Down this way," said Josh as he followed the sound of the music into the entrance of a building, but instead of going up the steps, they took a right turn, and went down a spiral staircase to the basement. The music became a little louder. At the bottom of the stairs, they saw a door with a gas lamp on the wall beside it.

Cautiously, Josh and Zeke walked toward the door. The music became a little louder.

"Shall I knock?" asked Josh.

"I think we should go..." began Zeke.

"Where's your sense of adventure?" broke in Josh as he grinned mischievously.

Just as Josh reached up to knock on the door, the door suddenly opened. Instantly, the music echoed off the walls surrounding them. A big man in a white suit, white hat, and black cane bumped into Josh and Zeke as he came out of the doorway. They both smelled the whiskey on his breath.

"Oh, excuse me, dears," said the drunken man as he stepped back, took a good hard look at Josh and Zeke, and then politely bowed. "I'm so sorry." Then the man giggled, "I'm so sorry I'm leaving when you two handsome boys are just arriving. Well, don't mind me, get your butts on in there, and have some fun." He held the door back for Josh and Zeke to enter.

The two boys were stunned at being called 'dears', but their curiosity gave them enough energy to take a few steps forward. Inside they found a very low ceiling and a crowded bar. The bartender was busy serving several men at the counter. Zeke and Josh scanned the room. There was not a woman in the place. They were only men and to their surprise, several of the men had their arms over the shoulders of their companions. They both spotted two men kissing in a darkened corner.

"What can I get you?" asked a burly fellow with bright red hair from behind the bar.

"Two beers," replied Josh quickly. Zeke had been unable to get any words to come out.

"Two beers it is," he replied as he quickly filled two mugs of beer and brought it to them. Josh gave him some coins. "This is Al's Place. I'm Al. And you are?" he had stuck out his big hand.

Josh took it and shook it firmly. "I'm Josh Johnson and this is Zeke Robertson."

"I'm pleased to make your acquaintance," he said with a warm smile. "Am I to presume you two are lovers?"

The astounding question nearly scared them both to death. Josh could only nod affirmatively. The man grinned. "That's wonderful. Well, this is your first time here so let me give you a few tips. First of all, you're not alone here. All of us here prefer the company of men. You can hold hands, kiss, do whatever you like, as long as you buy a beer or two from me," he added with a grin. "If anyone tries to make a move on you, then you just holler my name, and I'll knock the stuffing out of them. Why don't you take your beers and sit over at the table near the stage. It'll be show time in just a while. You'll like the show. Now go on. Have a good time. Relax. You're among friends here. You'll be fine."

Josh and Zeke followed his friendly advice, picked up their beers, and began walking slowly to the table Al pointed out to them. The men around the room gave them a good hard up and down look, as they were the new boys in town. Josh instantly knew what the slaves must have felt like when they were put on the auction block in the slave market in Charleston. It felt weird knowing they were looking at his butt and his crotch while sizing him up. It was also kind of flattering to have them looking. Josh pulled his shoulders back and kept his tummy firm. He even tried to smile. Zeke was far more nervous, but did his best to force a smile as they sat down.

Josh and Zeke didn't say anything to each other for almost twenty minutes as they stared back at the men around the pub. They were completely dumbfounded to find other men who felt as they did. Their breath was labored, and their hearts were pounding. Slowly, Josh slipped his hand over into Zeke's lap, took his hand, allowed his fingers to intertwine with Zeke's, and then squeezed.

Zeke smiled at Josh and squeezed him back. "I don't know what to say. I guess I figured that we would one day grow out of our love for each other. But these men are older and they're still..."

"In love?" Maybe we aren't going to outgrow our feelings. I, for one, would be happy to spend the rest of my life loving you."

Zeke turned to look intensely into Josh's blue eyes. They both smiled. "Shall we?"

"Shall we what?"

"Kiss," whispered Zeke.

"Why the hell not?" laughed Josh as he leaned forward and kissed Zeke in front of the entire pub.

To their surprise, not one single person in the bar gave them a sneer. They didn't even seem to notice. More confident, Zeke and Josh kissed again.

Suddenly, the piano player, a tiny little man with a baldhead and big glasses, began playing a fanfare, and the men around the bar started applauding. A simple thin, tattered curtain parted and a performer stepped out and began singing. It took Josh and Zeke a full minute before they realized the woman singing was really a man dressed as a woman, including a full wig. They sat before her, completely mesmerized. The woman sang short little ditties that were all bawdy and funny. Josh and Zeke had never heard them before, but they laughed harder than anyone else in the room. They gave the performer lots of applause and were only saddened when it was over.

Josh and Zeke stayed way past midnight before finally deciding to head home to the hotel. Al stopped them at the door. "Are you boys okay?" he asked.

"Fine. Thank you, Al. We had a great time," stated Zeke.

"Is it like this every night?" asked Josh.

"Every night. People like us have to be very secretive, or we could get our heads bashed in," warned Al.

"Don't worry. We wouldn't tell. Can we come back?" asked Josh.

"I hope you will, and listen, if you ever need a friend, just call on me. I run a boarding house upstairs and I've always got a spare room for rent if you're in town on holiday."

Zeke surprised Josh by quickly responding to Al's invitation, "We'll be working at the shipyard this summer while on holiday from school. Perhaps we could rent a room for the summer."

"I'll hold one for you. Just five dollars a week," added Al.

"Thank you. It'll be about the middle of May."

"Splendid. Good luck to you. Come again." Al shook their hands firmly and held the door for them. Josh and Zeke stepped out into the cold air, took each other's hands, and began making their way back to the hotel, deliriously happy and excited.

EIGHT

Most of the boys gathered in front of the administration building just before lunch to see if they had received any mail, but long ago Josh gave up hope of receiving a letter from any of his relatives. So to avoid disappointment, he never joined in the mail frenzy. He just stayed in his bunk until the bugle sounded for lunch.

Zeke, on the other hand, went daily to mail call, and generally received at least a letter a week from home, sometimes a note from his grandfather, and even his older brother had written a couple of time. Zeke stood in the back of the circle of cadets as he waited to hear his name called.

Cadet Jones was in charge of calling out the names on the envelopes and parcels. He stood on a crate so all could hear, and so he could spot the recipient. "Simpson!" he called, then tossed a letter to a blond headed guy from Pittsburgh. "Smith!" Two boys started forward. "Smith, Paul!" he added. "Sorry, Jim," he apologized as there were two boys named Smith. The latter stepped back with a disappointed frown on his face. "Maybe next time," encouraged Jones.

"Johnson, Joshua!" called Jones abruptly.

No one moved forward.

"Johnson, Joshua!" repeated Jones. Again no one moved.

Jones was about to move on to the next name, when the realization of the name finally sunk deep enough into Zeke's brain. "I'll take it to him!" he yelled as he pushed his way through the cadets.

"Thanks," replied Jones as he passed the letter to him before going on. "Henderson!" he called.

Zeke took the envelope, read the return address, and made his way through the crowd and began running for the cottage completely forgetting he might have received a letter, too. He found Josh half asleep on his bunk. Zeke slammed the door, rattling the coats and hats hung by the door. Josh flinched at the bang of the door.

"Geez! You scared the piss out of me," complained Josh. "'Are you trying to wake the dead three counties away?"

Zeke ran to him. "Guess what?"

"What?" replied Josh as he settled back down to continue his nap.

"You got a letter today."

Josh opened one eye. "Me?"

"Yes, you! It's from South Carolina," grinned Zeke.

Josh immediately sat up and slowly took the letter from Zeke and turned it around so he could study the handwriting. "It's my mom's handwriting," he whispered, his heart now racing.

"Well, go ahead. Open it!" urged an equally excited Zeke.

"I'm afraid to. What if she is writing to tell me not to come home? Perhaps writing to tell me to never write them again? Or to..."

"They wouldn't do that. You're their son. Open it," urged Zeke once again, as he sat down beside Josh.

Slowly, as if expecting the letter to explode, Josh opened the envelope, and began reading the letter. Zeke read right along with him, but Josh read it aloud anyhow.

"Dearest Joshua. I hope this letter finds you well and happy. We received a report from your school. I'm pleased with your grades, and I hope you're studying hard for your upcoming end-of-year exams. I received your letter today requesting permission to spend the summer working in Washington at the shipyard with your friend Zeke. I think that would be most wise, and I felt it would be a continuing part of your education at the Academy. I've sent the school a letter enrolling you for next year. I've also sent them money for your bill, and there should be some leftover funds you can pick up when this term is over to help you with your room and board this summer. Your grandfather died just after Christmas and his dear wife, Elizabeth, just couldn't bear this world without him. We buried her just six weeks later. Keep up your grades and have a good summer."

Zeke knew the letter was too short, and yet heavily packed with news. He glanced around the room, and was pleased all the cadets were still at mail call. He put his arm around Josh as tears slowly slid down Josh's cheeks and dripped onto the parchment.

"I'm very sorry about your grandparents. I can't imagine how badly you feel," attempted Zeke.

"Thanks. I wish I could have said goodbye to them. No one was allowed to see me off. Now I'll never be able to say goodbye to them." He suddenly sobbed heavily. Zeke patted his shoulder, desperately wanting to take him into his arms, but feared being caught, and expulsion from school.

After a while, Josh dried his eyes, folded the letter, and put it with his other papers on the shelves by his bunk. "I guess the good news is that I can now go to Washington with you for the summer." He tried to smile, but he just couldn't.

Zeke looked into his watery eyes and nodded, "Let's just hope my parents concur as well."

"You don't think they would say no, do you. I'd be alone all summer," added Josh apprehensively.

"I don't know what they'll say. Let's get to lunch. You need something to eat and to put this behind you. We've got the fencing tournament this afternoon," began Zeke enthusiastically, as he pulled Josh onto his feet.

"I'm not very hungry..."

"Yeah, but you hate to see me eat alone. So let's go," refusing to take no for an answer.

As they made their way across campus, Josh suddenly spoke up, "She didn't say I couldn't come home, just that it would be okay for me to stay in Washington. However, you know, I think I can read between the lines of her note. If they didn't tell me about my grandparents' deaths, nor invite me to the funerals, I guess it's rather obvious that they don't want me back, huh?"

Zeke wrestled for a comment to encourage his friend, though he knew Josh spoke the obvious truth. "No matter, we'll have far more fun in Washington than you ever had in that god forsaken mosquito infested swamp of yours!" Zeke knocked Josh's cap to the grass and took off running.

"Hey! What do you think you're doing? I'll get you!" Josh snatched up his cap and took off running after Zeke. "You'd better run fast 'cause when I catch you, I'm going to beat the living daylights out of you!"

The school's annual fencing tournament was held on the parade grounds. Names were drawn from a hat where all the cadets entering the contest placed their entry slip. No freshman ever won the hard fought tournament, but the fencing instructor urged Zeke and Josh to enter, as they were the best in their class. Josh's first opponent was a sophomore from Texas. His name was Ernie Polk. He was very good and a bit taller than Josh, giving him a slight advantage. Zeke watched nervously on the sidelines as Josh took on Ernie.

At first, Ernie had Josh on the defensive, and Zeke knew that Josh was losing points quickly, but determination was a rallying motto for Josh, and he quickly began working until he had won the match just as time was called.

Zeke congratulated Josh, and then took on his first match, a junior from Ohio, Bill Smitherson. Bill was Zeke's height, but a bit chunky in build, and a loudmouth as well. He picked at Zeke verbally before the match began. Zeke didn't respond to Bill's attempt to rattle him, but rather kept his concentration on his plan of attack. Zeke was only slightly better than Josh, and as it turned out, Smitherson was all bark and no bite. Zeke put him away quickly.

Two hours later, Zeke and Josh barely survived six exhausting preliminaries. Their instructor was quite proud of his young students. It was now down to the final four, two seniors and the two freshmen, Josh and Zeke.

Zeke was up first, taking on Roger Fierson from Virginia. Roger's dad was one of Virginia's senators, and his family was from a long line of military servicemen. Roger was a tough competitor, and matched Zeke point for point. Josh was yelling for Zeke. Roger's experience was a plus for him, but Zeke kept his cool as Roger took the offensive, backing Zeke up systematically. Josh nervously chewed his lip as he took pauses between yelling for Zeke and chewing.

Zeke never lost his concentration. He allowed Roger to stay on the offensive long enough to learn his moves, size him up, plan a strategy, and to allow him time enough to get a bit cocky and overconfident—or so Zeke hoped. Then suddenly, Zeke made a quick side step and stabbed. He scored a touché. He stepped back again, fended off an attempt to score by Roger, and then touché once again. Zeke's sudden remarkable comeback made the score three to two and to Roger's favor.

Josh was screaming at the top of his lungs, encouraging Zeke to attack. Zeke didn't hear him. He was concentrating intently as he lifted and stabbed, barely missing a score, and oblivious to everything around him. Quickly he blocked a counter, and then in a lighting stroke, he scored again. The match was now tied. Josh leaped into the air over and over again cheering wildly. The rest of the freshman class was also yelling and screaming for Zeke.

The taunts of the rookie freshmen upset Roger, and he made the mistake of letting his temper get the best of him, as he momentarily dropped his guard. Zeke seized the opportunity and scored a jarring blow to Roger's shoulder just below the neck. Josh leaped into the air as the judge gave Zeke a point, making the score four to three to Zeke's advantage.

That last point stung Roger through the padding. It also hurt his pride as no senior ever lost to a freshman. His classmates began chanting for him. He felt the bruise that was already swelling beneath his vest. He let out a long sigh, and then attacked venomously. Zeke fended off blow after blow, stab after stab. Sweat rolled down his cheeks as he defended himself over and over again. Zeke hoped that Roger would soon wear himself out. Josh nervously chewed his lip as Zeke was again being forced backward step after step as Roger continually swung at him. Zeke was losing ground, and if he wasn't careful, he could step too far backwards, and right off the marked playing field.

However, Roger's strength was failing him. His arms ached much like a boxer who punched too fast and excessively. Just as it appeared that Zeke couldn't back up another step, Zeke began to swing from defense to offense.

Roger thought sure he had worn Zeke down, and when Zeke suddenly came back at him, he was already mentally defeated. He had no strength left to attack.

Zeke ducked at a wildly aimed high blow, and then lunged quickly and touché Roger just over his heart. If it had been a real sword match, Roger's heart would have been pierced. Suddenly, the timekeeper blew his whistle. Time ran out. The stunned senior just looked down at his chest. The match was abruptly over. The astonished crowd fell silent as the realization took hold. Roger had been defeated in front of his classmates by a freshman. Josh half expected a fight to break out, but it had been a thrilling, quality match. Everyone admired the two combatants as the entire academy began slowly applauding Roger and Zeke.

Displaying the mark of a true gentleman, Roger brought his epée straight up and saluted Zeke, who quickly returned the salute. A huge smile spread across his face. The fencing instructor joined in the applause, as the entire freshman class began to cheer and chant Zeke's name.

"Way to go, big guy," beamed Josh as he slapped Zeke on the back.

"Thanks. Now it's your turn," grinned Zeke.

"Yeah, right," replied a nervous Josh.

As the match began, Josh quickly scored the first point, but his opponent, the other senior, was a tough and smart competitor. He soon had Josh four to one. Josh desperately scored another point, but soon time ran out, and Josh was defeated. Now there were only two, a senior, and a freshman, preparing to duel for the championship.

"I tried to wear him down for you," grinned Josh, not too bothered at losing, as he had never fenced before coming to the Academy, preferring to ride horses instead. He was just as happy with Zeke winning instead. It was a feeling he never experienced before. It was pure pride he felt in watching someone he loved succeed. He didn't quite understand the feeling, but he knew it made him extremely happy.

"Yeah, I can see that. He was very confidant and grinning the whole match," replied Zeke, as he prepared for the final match.

"But you can take him. I know you can," said Josh as he patted Zeke on the back.

"You think so?"

Josh leaned into Zeke and whispered, "Yes, he drops his right shoulder, and then lifts it quickly right before he lunges. Remember that, and put it to our advantage," urged Josh.

Zeke gave him a bewildered look. "Our advantage? I thought it was me that was about to face this guy."

Josh whispered even lower, "I'll be right inside your heart so don't let him stab you there. Now get your butt in gear, and let's win this thing!"

The instructor walked to the center of the audience and raised his hands to urge the cadets to be quiet. "Gentlemen, we have come to the last match of our school tournament. Each man has won eight other preliminary matches to get to the championship round. As I introduce the competitors, please give them a grand hand for the magnificent efforts. In getting to this level, they have distinguished themselves above all others. The first man is Brice Caldwell, a senior from Georgia." The crowd cheered, especially the upperclassmen.

Then the instructor introduced Zeke. "I'm pleased to present his opponent, a very talented freshman from the great state of Maine, Cadet Zeke Robertson."

The freshman yelled and screamed while the upperclassmen booed and hissed. Zeke heard nothing. He kept his eyes on Brice Caldwell. He watched how he walked. How he flexed his sword. He studied everything the cadet did. Several seniors patted Brice's back, urging him to win.

The instructor began the match. Josh expected Zeke to once again be on the defensive for the first few minutes of the match, but Zeke abruptly strayed from his previous game plan, faked a lunge to his left, sidestepped and touché Brice in the left arm, effectively scoring the first point.

Josh leaped into the air once more. The freshmen cheered. Brice lifted his weapon, using more caution in his approach. The next few minutes were fierce attack and counterattack sequences as each man tried to score. In the end, Brice scored with a touché on Zeke's upper right arm.

Then just as quickly as the match had begun, Brice touché again, this time right in Zeke's stomach. Zeke vehemently defended himself for the next few minutes. In his mind, he saw Brice's shoulder dip then quickly lift, but Zeke had been too slow to respond, and Brice scored another point. It was now three to one.

Zeke knew he should have won the last point. Josh had spoken the truth, but up until now, he had found such a simple thing just too hard to believe.

After several minutes of counters, Brice dipped, but this time Zeke flung his sword down harshly on Brice's epée just as the senior lunged. Zeke stabbed him in the side as the stunned Brice fell to the ground on his knees.

Embarrassed, Brice got to his feet a little too quickly and lunged once more at Zeke. Zeke anticipated the bold move, blocking the shot, and then once again touché Brice in the hip. The score was now tied. Josh and the freshmen were cheering madly. The upper classmen began chanting Brice's name.

Brice took a deep breath, nodded slightly to Zeke, and then began swinging hard and fast at Zeke, as the younger boy bravely defended the barrage. He soon found himself being forced backwards in the process. After nearly being run through, Zeke tripped over his own feet, and Brice lunged. Zeke found himself off balance and therefore couldn't counter, and was stabbed hard in the right shoulder.

He flinched at the pain while wondering what he was going to do to win, but Brice gave him little time to recover as he quickly launched another impressive attack, hoping to win his final point.

Josh screamed at Zeke, but Zeke's concentration remained steadily on the man swinging the blade at him. He defended blow after blow hoping to wear Brice down, but Brice never slowed down, and Zeke began to wonder just how many swings the senior could deliver.

Then abruptly, in the middle of all the hard swings, Brice's shoulder went down. Zeke sidestepped, swung down hard, then countered quickly, and stabbed Brice in the heart—a solid convincing point.

Shocked by the point, Brice's temper got the best of him. He swung his free hand into Zeke, knocking him to the ground. The instructor's hand went up in protest. A verbal warning was given. Two warnings and the match would be forfeited, but Brice continued roaring his way toward Zeke. He slashed the air rapidly with his epée. The swish-swish sound of his blade through the air could be heard even over the loud cheering. Zeke quickly scrambled to his feet while protecting himself from Brice's menacing and powerful swings.

On and on they swung and stabbed, each boy desperately trying to win the final victory point. Zeke's arms and shoulders throbbed and ached. His heart was racing. He felt sure that at any moment his epée would break, as he had used it over and over again to defend himself from Brice's determined and tenacious attack. The unrelenting attack continued for several more minutes. Then just for a brief moment, Brice let up allowing the blood to flow through his arms and fingers. In that instant, Zeke seized his opportunity. He surprised everyone by rushing Brice, causing the boy to leap backwards losing his balance. Recovering, Brice felt briefly he had a moment to win the match. He dipped his shoulder to lunge.

Just as he lifted, Zeke lunged forward, and scored a direct touché in the boy's chest. A solid point scored just as the timekeeper blew his whistle. The match was instantly over. The surprised and angry senior dropped his sword, and threw a punch to Zeke's face, bloodying his nose. Josh leaped on Brice's back, and began beating him wildly about the head. Other seniors took on the freshmen until they abruptly heard the sound of the instructor's pistol as he fired into the air.

"Attention!" he called.

The cadets stopped fighting instantly, and scrambled to attention.

"That's better. Gentlemen, we have just witnessed an impressive battle. Both men deserve our respect. It is a great shame that only one could win. It is also a shame that the loser displayed such shameful conduct. For that deed, Mister Caldwell, you have just earned yourself five demerits, and you shall go to bed with no supper tonight. As for our winner Mister Robertson, you have my respect and admiration. Congratulations!"

The crowd cheered. Josh ran to Zeke, gave him a bear hug, and then began swinging him around in circles. The seniors left the parade ground in silence. The freshmen celebrated by lifting Zeke to their shoulders as they ran around the parade grounds. They now felt invincible.

The next afternoon, the horse-riding tournament began. Points were awarded based on the various skills required. Zeke was in fifth place after three events, but Josh was in first. He was far more confident of his riding ability than in any other area of the Academy's education program. Colonel Lee, a horse lover himself, had ridden to the outer field on his favorite mount to watch the afternoon's events.

Josh was the first to ride through a slalom type course while keeping his hands in the air. This event required expert legwork, and Josh was the only cadet to receive a perfect score. Zeke touched two poles, and Roger was once again in the running, scoring on all but one, moving him up to second place behind Josh. That put Zeke in a tie with Brice Caldwell for third place. Brice kept revenge on his mind, and determined to beat the two freshmen at all cost.

The final event of the day was a combination horse race and obstacle course. The top ten point finishers were at the starting line. They were to race along a course outlined by red flags. From time to time, they had to jump over stacked bales of hay, leap over fences, and finally they had to draw their swords and stab a bale of hay swinging by a rope from a tree limb.

The instructor fired his pistol to start the race. Zeke's horse became alarmed at the gunshot and headed off in the wrong direction, which was right through the spectators. The crowd laughed at him, but the deeply embarrassed Zeke still managed to get his horse turned in the right direction, and took off after the running pack ahead of him at a full gallop.

Josh quickly took the lead, sailing over the first stack of hay with plenty of room to spare. Roger was right on his tail followed by Brice. At the next fence, Josh once again sailed over, but Roger's horse caught his rear hoof, and stumbled a bit before regaining his rhythm. This allowed Brice the opportunity to pass him. Very determined to catch up, Zeke sailed over the next obstacle at blinding speed. He passed a couple of riders and moved up to sixth place.

Josh glanced back and saw Brice just two horse-lengths behind him. He had enough racing experience as a boy under his grandfather's tutelage to know that Brice's horse could over take him, so he dug in his heels and tried to gain a bigger lead. Brice was determined to win this match after losing to Zeke in the fencing contest. He had already scored just enough points that if he won the race, he would end up beating Josh by a single point.

The next obstacle was the swinging hay bale. Josh drew his saber and lunged successfully. Brice drew his saber and stabbed the bale without slowing down his horse. Josh placed his sword back in his scabbard while kicking his horse. He then hunkered down low in preparation for crossing the upcoming creek.

Brice didn't replace his sword. The two riders cleared a hill and were momentarily out of view from the rest of the cadets. Josh and his horse flew down the other side of the hill and hit the water hard, splashing water all the way to the far bank. His horse began to walk as fast as it could through the four feet deep water. Brice's horse hit the water hard as well, soaking Josh, but Josh wisely kept his face forward, keeping his eyes from being covered with mud.

Suddenly, and to his complete surprise, Josh felt the sting of Brice's sword as the senior hit Josh across the upper back and shoulder with the flat of the blade. It felt as if his dad's whip had flayed him. Josh wanted to leap from his horse and beat the stuffing out of Brice, but instead, he held his anger in check, and kicked his horse onward.

Just as Josh made it to the bank, Brice hit him once again, nearly knocking Josh from the saddle. The blade turned a bit this time, and bit into the soft flesh of Josh's back. Josh flinched at the pain. His horse took off so abruptly that the blade scathed the horse's rump as well. The poor horse leaped forward, nearly flinging Josh into a nearby tree. He fell to the right side of the horse and barely hung on. How he hung on was even a surprise to him, but his strong legs clung on tightly as he temporarily let go of the reins, grabbed two big fistfuls of the horse's mane, and swung himself back on top of his horse. His horse lost some speed while Josh righted himself in the saddle. In the meantime, Brice used the flat of his blade to beat his horse and quickly took the lead.

Angry, and more determined than ever, Josh squeezed his legs tightly, and took off after Brice. They topped the hill and the crowd immediately realized that Brice had taken the lead. The upperclassmen began to cheer. Zeke raced through the water, passed two riders making their way across the creek, and moved himself up to fourth place, topped the hill, and instantly yelled for Josh to go.

Three hundred yards was all that was left. The riding instructor was not at all pleased to see Brice swinging his sword wildly at his mount, but at the moment, there was nothing he could do about it. He would have plenty to say later.

Brice had but a full horse length on Josh, and Josh didn't seem to be moving up. They topped another hill. Josh gave his horse another squeeze, and the horse responded by moving up beside Brice. Realizing his lead had diminished, Brice angrily swung his sword at Josh, but Josh had not let his eyes leave Brice this time. Brice tried to kick at Josh, but Josh kept his head down, squeezing harder.

Brice swung once more with his sword. Colonel Lee lifted his binoculars to his face just as the boys came over the final hill leading across the pasture to the finish line. He saw the senior swing the sword. He was sorely disappointed at the bad sportsmanship being displayed. However, his disappointment soon became a grin.

Josh saw the swing of the sword coming toward him. He ducked down just as the blade missed him, lunged out with his fist, and caught Brice harshly in the forearm. The sword fell to the ground bouncing on the rocks beneath them.

Zeke's horse leaped past the third place rider and stepped on the blade, snapping it in half.

"Go, go, go!" yelled Zeke.

Relieved the sword was no longer a problem, Josh hunkered down behind his mount's big neck, and squeezed as hard as he could.

Brice cursed. The two horses were neck and neck with only fifty feet to go. The crowd cheered. Colonel Lee suddenly let out a yell of support. All hands were in the air. The finish line was marked with a simple white string. Josh could see it. He could feel the earth shaking beneath him. He stayed low. He didn't dare look at Brice. He kept his eyes on the string—twenty feet to go.

Josh's horse crossed the string by half a length, clearly winning the race. The crowd cheered. Zeke raced in right behind Brice winning third place. Embarrassed, Brice kept riding through the crowd toward the barn.

Colonel Lee pulled his horse up alongside Josh, climbed down, then took off his leather glove, and reached out and shook Josh's hand.

"Well done, Johnson. Well done indeed!" said the colonel.

"Thank you, sir. Thank you very much."

"You'll make a fine cavalry officer some day. Keep up the good work," added the colonel as he climbed back on his mount.

"I will, sir. I will."

Josh grinned as big as he could. He searched the swarming crowd of cadets until his eyes caught sight of Zeke. Zeke gave him a cocky salute, and then laughed heartily. Josh threw his hands into the air, and yelled as loudly as he could. They had both done what no other had done before them. They had beaten the seniors in two key events. They were jubilant.

NINE

Over the course of the following summer, Zeke and Josh often felt like they somehow magically moved themselves to another planet. The boarding house room that Al rented to them became their private castle, where they could hug, kiss, and talk about their love without fear of persecution. They loved their weekend late night visits to the bar below the rooming house, which allowed the opportunity to meet other male couples, and enjoy many fine dinners at their homes throughout the Washington area. They made many new friends and learned much from their experiences. Josh and Zeke were astounded to find out what each of their new friends did in their public lives. There were senators and representatives, newspaper editors, presidential aides, military leaders, a judge, and they even met a member of the clergy. Their confidence was bolstered, and their spirits lifted. They accepted the fact that their love for each other was not just a phase they were going through. Their love for each other was indeed real.

However, outside their castle walls, the world around them was rapidly falling apart. Every restaurant and bar was filled with conversations and arguments about slavery, and the possibility of the South seceding from the Union. Zeke made Josh promise not to enter into any of these discourses, but quite often Josh found himself chewing his lip as Zeke hustled him away from a potential political fight. Zeke begged Josh to learn to hide his Southern accent, and Josh would oblige, but only in a comical, kind of hokey sounding Northern accent until finally Zeke gave up.

The work had been hard at the shipyard with Zeke learning as much as possible about engineering from John Ericsson. The ironclad boat was almost complete just as the month of August was coming to a close. Josh found the engineering opportunity a bit boring, and the necessary math way over his head, so he preferred to work right alongside the big steel workers. He spent the summer carrying hundreds of pieces of iron, and thousands of hot bolts to the fitters. His muscles became very well developed, and Zeke somewhat envious, but not willing to give away his opportunity to learn boat design from Ericsson himself.

Zeke learned that Ericsson experienced quite an adventuresome life in his fifty-seven years. He had only been twelve years old when he began to learn drafting. During his seven-year stay in the Swedish army, he won many awards, and even a promotion to captaincy for his outstanding maps and drawings. He lost a prize competition for his early steam locomotive, but it was the loss of the contest that made him more determined than ever to succeed with his drawings, beginning with a variety of marine designs.

The first noted invention was that of a new naval engine design to be used below the waterline, which won an award of $2,000 from the British admiralty. It featured a screw propeller which shipmates scoffed at until they saw how easily the boat made its way through the water. He used his knowledge to make the first steamboats to cross the Atlantic in 1838.

As a result of his success, the United States government hired him to build an iron vessel fitted with his engine and propeller at a British shipyard. Upon completion, he journeyed with the boat to America in 1839 and began his operation in New York. The government once again hired him to build the latest design, the Monitor. The locals called it a cheese box on a raft, but he paid them no mind because soon he displayed all the power his little vessel possessed.

Josh and Zeke knew the boat wouldn't be launched by the end of summer, and they were saddened they wouldn't be there with the others come bon voyage day. The academy started September first, and so they spent their last days in Washington saying their goodbyes to their friends.

The very last morning in town, they stayed in bed as late as they could. They would miss sleeping together, especially the cuddling and kissing. They also put all they had learned about sex to good use—very good use. By the time they boarded the train for Petersburg, their lips were chapped and their tools too tender to touch.

Josh and Zeke were surprised at how happy they were to be back at the academy. The old seniors were gone, and they were no longer freshmen. They spent their first days at school riding through the countryside, practicing their fencing skills, or helping to prepare the new gun range that had been built over the summer. Beginning with this semester, all cadets were required to learn how to properly load and fire pistols, rifles, and cannons. Josh and Zeke took to this class quickly, with Josh impressing the entire school up with his dead reckoning eye. Using his pistol, he hit the silver-dollar size bull's eye more often than any other cadet.

Another favorite class of theirs was war strategy as taught by William C. Gethridge, an older gentleman who served in the Queen's army before retiring to the States. The course was really another history class, but Gethridge showed the students the mistakes that were made that often caused the loss of an entire battle, and sometimes even a war. Josh and Zeke were amazed at the simple mistakes the world's greatest generals often made.

Gethridge tricked the class by asking what was the greatest weapon today's modern armies had in their possession. Josh guessed the cannon. Zeke proposed the new ironclad boats. Gethridge explained that the greatest tool a modern general had was information. The lack of information was the very reason so many major catastrophic mistakes were made in the wars of the past. Today, there were newspapers, trains, steam locomotives, and even the telegraph that could easily give the generals better eyes and ears, and a greater chance of knowing their enemy's movements. Still yet, good military information came from those trained to observe, estimate accurately, and predict the plans of the foes.

Gethridge predicted that the real heroes of the next war would be the scouts who provide the information. As Josh listened, he knew that the job of a scout was exactly the kind of thing he was looking for. It required a man to be a jack-of-all-trades. First, he had to be an excellent horseman, as well as a good shot, and an able swordsman and fighter as sometimes a scout would be discovered behind enemy lines. If the information that was stored in his brain was to get to his general, he might often have to fight and elude his way to safety.

Zeke stuck to his original plan to be an engineer, but agreed that scouting certainly suited Josh. After a month of school, Gethridge set the class up on a field trip. Part of the class was the attacking enemy and the other half was designated as the defenders. He appointed leaders and sent the "armies" into the woods. The leaders appointed scouts. Josh volunteered to be a scout for his team.

Within the hour, Josh discovered the enemy approaching the school by the riverbed. He rushed back to his lines by twice jumping a high pasture fence on his mount and then screeching to a halt while leaping from the saddle to give his information to the team captain. They quickly planned a flanking attack, catching the enemy with their backs to the river and nowhere to run. Josh's team won and scouting became something he talked about far more than his roommates wanted to hear. He was always dreaming of evasion tactics and tricks.

Hearing nothing from home, Josh wrote that he was once again heading north to Maine to spend Christmas with Zeke and his family. Zeke wrote to his parents that they would be arriving on the afternoon of December 20, 1860. School let out on the seventeenth. Josh and Zeke packed their stuff quickly after their last class, and dashed to town to catch the next train to Washington, where they planned to spend a few days with Al and the gang before heading north. Al reserved their favorite room for them.

They had been so busy over the past few weeks preparing for the mid-semester exams they hadn't had the time to keep up with local events. Josh and Zeke settled in an empty booth at the end of the rail car, and soon snoozing as the train headed north. Josh later awoke with a start after hearing a man angrily curse the state of South Carolina.

The man had a black mustache, pale white skin, and appeared to be a reporter with his notepad in hand. "If South Carolina stupidly secedes from the Union, Lincoln will be forced to fight them."

Another man broke in, "But Lincoln hasn't even been inaugurated yet. Nothing will happen. It'll just force Lincoln to settle with the South over the slavery issue once and for all."

"I'm telling you, the South will not concede. They need the slaves to harvest their crops. They put themselves into a corner by not diversifying their sources of income. They'd starve without the slaves. They have to fight."

Josh slowly sat up. He was chewing his lip, desperately wanting to join into the discussion, when Zeke quietly slipped his hand over and squeezed Josh's forearm. Josh thought he was still asleep. Josh looked over at Zeke's eyes and smiled.

Zeke grinned, "You promised you wouldn't discuss politics," he began in a low whisper, "and if you don't keep that promise I'll get two rooms at Al's."

"You wouldn't!" frowned Josh playfully.

"Don't be so sure!" shot back Zeke.

Josh poked him with his elbow in the ribs. "Okay, you win. How much longer until we're in our room," he stated carefully.

"Three hours and fifteen minutes exactly," replied Zeke after glancing at his pocket watch. "Rest your eyes. It'll go by faster."

Josh leaned into him and whispered, "Can't. Every time I close my eyes, I find myself dreaming of you, and that's making my britches tight!"

Zeke fought back a chuckle. "You're incorrigible."

"Yeah, I know," grinned Josh. "I'm terribly in love with you."

Zeke dozed off once more while Josh snatched up a forgotten newspaper dated yesterday. Josh hadn't read one since long before exams, and as was his custom, he read everything, even the classifieds. He read an article about an Italian patriot Garibaldi, a military leader who invaded Sicily and Naples. He closed his eyes until he could see his geography map in his head to recall exactly where Sicily was. He didn't understand why they were fighting. He then read about Sardinia-Piedmont who had seized the Papal

States in Italy, but he became bored with European news bits, and turned the page.

He came upon a sketch of a contraption by a man called Jean Joseph Etienne Lenoir. The picture was of something he called an internal-combustion engine. Lenoir just received a patent on the thing, and it was supposed to help further along the industrial machines of the future. The man envisioned wagons pulled by his engine as opposed to horses. Josh got a chuckle out of that nonsense while making a note to show Zeke the article when he woke up.

He read with delight any news from the South. He read about the expansion of Charleston harbor, and longed to sit high on top of the stacked bales of cotton as he had done as a boy and watch the ocean voyaging ships enter the harbor and moor in front of him. He read about the growth in Atlanta, and how that little city had grown to become a large shipping and rail junction for the South. He read about traveling plays and musicals, and wondered if he and Zeke would have enough spare time to attend a Ford's Theater production in their brief stay in Washington. He also noted an article about some general's inspection of the cadets at the Citadel in Charleston. He had thought about going to school there, and even talked it over with his grandfather before the incident with Knobby. Goodness, he wondered to himself, had he been able to go there instead of Petersburg, he would have only been a few hours ride from home. He chewed his lip. That was never to be. He had made the mistake of being caught. He promised himself he would never put Zeke in the same jeopardy as he had put poor Knobby. Then he realized, had he gone to the Citadel, he would never have met his beloved Zeke at all.

With his reading of the newspaper finished and folded beside him, he soon fell asleep as the railcar continued jostling its way north.

The sounds of Washington soon brought them awake as passengers began scurrying about collecting their belongings and preparing to depart. None was more anxious to get off the train than Zeke and Josh. They quickly grabbed their bags and leaped from the train as it slowed down at the station. After a summer in Washington, they knew precisely the shortcuts and alleyways to take to get them to Al's rooming house.

They stopped briefly at a small deli to grab a sandwich and to sip some apple cider. This was an early supper they gobbled down quickly, and headed back out the door. They were breathless by the time they got to Al's door, and just as Zeke was about to knock, the door opened, and there stood Al with a broom in his hand.

"I was just about to sweep the steps and glory be, it's Zeke and Josh. Come here, boys! Give me a hug!" urged Al by opening his arms wide.

Josh and Zeke quickly obeyed, as Al squeezed them together tightly. "Is our room ready?" asked an anxious Josh.

"Hold on now," teased Al. "Aren't you going to even ask how I am doing?"

"How are you?" they both recited simultaneously.

"I'm good. I'll save a late supper for you. We settle the account then. Show time is ten. We have a special artist for you tonight. Here's the key. It's good to see you. Have fun!" he laughed as he pretended to sweep the eager boys inside.

"Bye, Al," they called together without looking back.

They raced up the steps, opened the door, stepped in, dropped their bags and without even slowing down to pull the shades, they stripped out of their clothes, ran to the windows, yanked down the shades, and dove onto the bed. They made love for just over two hours, then took a hot tub bath together, and went back to bed. Eventually and almost reluctantly, they were dressed and headed down to the bar.

They were greeted by many of their summer friends, and met a few new ones as they entered the bar.

Al waved them over to the bar while lifting two plates covered with red-checkered napkins. "Here you go, boys. Suppertime! You can only live on love for so long before your body needs some victuals!" he teased. "There's a table near the stage. How about a beer?"

"Absolutely," grinned Josh as he handed Al two bits for the dinner and the beer, and the money for their room. "I've longed for the taste of a good beer."

"Me, too. What's for dinner?" asked Zeke as he sniffed the plate through the napkins.

"Young hens, potatoes, and beans, and I threw in some cornbread, too. Now, go on. Your dinner's getting cold," he waved them on with a grin, and a playful swish of his bar towel.

"Thanks, Al," they called back as they made their way through the crowd, found a table and sat down.

"Does it seem like more people than usual tonight?" asked Josh.

Zeke didn't reply, but lifted the napkin and grinned, "Yum, yum! This looks marvelous."

"Yeah, you're right," replied Josh as he tore off a leg and devoured it.

Zeke took a bite, and then turned around to check out the crowd. "You're right. Almost every table is full and there's a few standing by the wall. Do you think being a homosexual is becoming popular?"

Josh turned his head toward Zeke abruptly and chuckled, "Yeah," he began sarcastically, "I understand old Abe Lincoln has become one as well."

"Ooo," laughed Zeke. "What man alive would go to bed with him? He looks like a monkey!"

They both laughed at themselves as they continued digging into their meal. Suddenly, the piano player stopped his tune, and began a fanfare as Al rushed to the stage.

"Gentlemen! Gentlemen! May I please have your attention? We have a special guest tonight. Well, actually we have several special guests. Let me quickly point out, as if you horny rascals hadn't already noticed, but down front, Josh and Zeke have stopped off to see us on a break from school."

The crowd of friends cheered and clapped. Jeremy Livingston, the reporter from the Post, who had given them Al's address, stood up. "I guess that explains why I keep hearing bed springs squeaking on the floor above me!" The crowd roared with laughter. Josh and Zeke blushed and laughed.

"Give them a break. They can't do the 'you know what' at the academy, and so they had a little catching up to do. Welcome, boys. We're glad to see you doing well. Now where was I? Oh yeah, our special entertainer tonight is visiting Washington with the road company from Offenbach's 'Orpheus of the Underworld' at the Ford Theater. His name is Jean Claude. He's French and very handsome. He's here to sing a few special songs he wrote for our ears only. Let's show him how grateful we are! Please welcome Jean Claude!"

The curtains parted as the applause began. A man in a military dress uniform costume stepped through, drew his sword, and saluted the crowd. Al had been right as Josh and Zeke found themselves completely mesmerized by his handsome features. He was tall, slender, with a tender smooth face, and a pencil thin mustache just under his nose. His eyes were wide and bright. The dark brown pupils just seemed to glisten in the candlelight. He nodded to the pianist.

The first song was about a soldier who had fallen in love with his sergeant, the jest of which was that the sergeant kept fending off the poor soldier's pathetic attempts to kiss him, until one day the sergeant came down with a huge case of constipation after eating way too much cheese. Alone in their tent, the sergeant rolled left and right in agony as the abundance of cheese caused him great digestive discomfort. The young soldier told him how he could solve the problem, but the sergeant wouldn't listen. Finally, many hours later and way late into the night, the poor sergeant's knees drew up to his chest in anguish. He awoke the soldier and begged him to do whatever he could. He just couldn't take the cramps and the pain any longer. He also said he felt like he was giving birth to a cow. From time to time, the crowd would laugh, chuckle, and even applaud at the humorous and captivating song. Josh and Zeke had never heard such a song in their entire life, and were both anxious to hear the ending of this tale.

Jean Claude stopped his story abruptly and said in broken English, "And do you know how this young lover helped his poor old sergeant? Well, I'll tell you," he added as he nodded to his pianist once more.

The story went on that the young lover pulled down the pants of the sergeant and turned him over on to his stomach. Then he dropped his own pants, smeared a little cooking fat on his rod and on the count of one, two, three, he drilled the sergeant deep and hard. The sergeant moaned and groaned, but the lover was finally getting his reward. After an hour of in and out, his bare buttocks quivered and shook, and then he let go his entire bladder into his sergeant's bum.

"And do you know what happened?" taunted Jean Claude.

"A few minutes ticked by, then suddenly, the sergeant leaped from his bunk and ran out of the tent toward the woods where soon he was emptied of all his poor cheese!" sang Jean. The crowd roared with laughter and assumed the story was over as they clapped wildly. But as the applause began to die, Jean Claude turned back to face his admirers and said, "But later, the next night, the soldier came into the tent after a late watch of guard duty, only to find the sergeant laying naked on his bunk face down. The soldier asked if the poor sergeant was constipated once again. The sergeant laughed and said, "Hell, no, boy! Just drill me again. I'm in love, I'm in love, and I'm in love!"

The men stood, cheered, and laughed. Josh and Zeke were right down front. Josh felt Jean's eyes as he scanned down Josh's front side and then looked over at Zeke and gave him a long stare as well. Josh and Zeke had really never experienced such probing eyes before, but took them as a compliment, and cheered right along with their friends.

The actor performed a few more songs and then left the stage with the crowd still cheering. Minutes later, his costume put away, Jean Claude came through the curtain and came right up to Josh and Zeke.

"Good evening, gentlemen," he said politely with his thick French accent. "May I join you?" He motioned to a free chair.

"Sure, help yourself," said Josh, a bit light headed from his second beer and sounding very Southern.

"Thank you," replied Jean Claude with a polite nod as he sat down.

"We enjoyed your performance immensely. Are you performing 'Orpheus' tomorrow night?" asked Zeke.

Al brought Jean a beer. "Thank you my good man. You're such a dear," grinned Jean. Al blushed. Josh and Zeke giggled. Then back to the boys, "Yes, would you like to come?"

"Yes. We try to go to Ford's Theater every time we're in town," stated Zeke.

"What are your names? I'll leave a pass for you at the door. Perhaps you can join me for dinner afterwards, and then back here to Al's for a drink."

"I'm Zeke Robertson, and he's Josh Johnson."

"Zeke and Josh," echoed Jean as he shook both their hands. "Very well. Just ask for the doorman and use my name for the pass." He leaned a bit closer to the table, took a long draw on his beer, and said in a lower whispery voice, "I guess you two know that you're the handsomest men in this pub."

Josh exclaimed, "You're kidding!"

"You're the best looking men in the bar," stated Jean more proudly.

"Well, thanks for the compliment. You're pretty handsome yourself," sniggered Josh.

Jean was a bit put off with Josh's drunken drawl and turned his attention more toward Zeke. "Are you going with this Southern boy?"

"Going where?" asked a naive Zeke.

"Are you two lovers, for God's sake?" said Jean quickly.

"Yes, we are," said Zeke apprehensively.

"Good for you. You're made for each other. You both have such radiant blue eyes. I could see them from the stage. In addition, you're both so damned cute. I don't suppose you'd be interested in a little threesy tonight?"

"What?" asked Josh?

Jean smiled wickedly, "A little two on one, if you know what I mean?"

"Oh..." sighed Zeke.

"I could teach you a few things about how the French boys make love," urged Jean.

"I don't think so. I've never done it with anyone but Josh. I love him. I love no other."

Josh was pleased at Zeke's reply, but still couldn't help putting his two cents in, "I doubt if there is anything we can learn from anyone. When we make love, the sun stops and the moon quivers!" Josh laughed loudly.

"Very well. If you change your mind, please let me know. I'm very good. Let me shake a few hands, and we'll see you at the theater tomorrow night." Jean pretended to tip a hat as he stood from his chair, and began making his way from table to table like a politician.

"Can you believe that guy?" asked Josh.

"Some ego. I was shocked by what he wanted to do with us," added Zeke.

"Well, hells bells. Might be fun. I bet we could drill him deeper than that old sergeant got!" laughed Josh.

"Yep," added Zeke in a badly faked Southern accent, "by the time we finished drilling him as deep as our dicks go, there'd be a geyser shooting up into the air out of his butt!"

Josh spilled his beer he laughed so hard. Zeke's eyes watered a bit from chuckling so much that they both decided it was time to go. They made their way up the stairs, stripped out of their clothes, took a long piss in the pot, and snuggled under the covers together.

They didn't get up until lunchtime, and so they decided to bundle up and take a stroll through the city. They made it to the harbor and were pleased to see Ericsson's ironclad floating in the water. They longed to take a good close look, but the winter winds coming off the water soon sent them scurrying into a nearby bakery. They bought a few pastries and some coffee, and stood at a counter to eat their lunch. Josh and Zeke soon heard the nearby men discussing secession.

"I heard they plan to vote on it tomorrow," said the first man.

"I just don't see how splitting up the Union is going to help anything. Is America to become like Europe, all kinds of tiny little countries fighting each other?"

"I don't know. I got rid of my slaves years ago, and I'm doing just fine," replied the first.

"Yeah, but you don't have acres of crops. You're a shipping company. You don't need a lot of personnel to get the job done."

"I know, but slavery is just barbaric. I don't even let my ships carry slaves anymore."

"I guess that cost you a bit."

"Yeah, but I've already made up for it. Now there's plenty of Northerners who want a cargo company that doesn't ship slaves. I've ended up with even more business than I had before."

"You're a lucky man. How's your dear Martha doing? Is her breathing better?"

Zeke pushed Josh out of the store. "You did good. I was afraid you were going to say something."

"I keep my word when I give it," replied Josh.

"I know you do, but sometimes your mouth starts up before your word catches it," grinned Zeke.

"You're weird. Absolutely weird," laughed Josh.

They turned down an alley. They were alone. Zeke added, "I must be, too, because I love you with all my heart."

"Would you kiss my butt?" asked Josh.

The request stunned Zeke. He thought a second while a slow grin crept across his face. "I just kissed it this morning. I kissed it right there!" he touched Josh's lips with his finger, and then took off running.

"I'll get you!" yelled Josh as he chased after him.

Josh and Zeke had never seen anything like Offenbach's 'Orpheus.' They also had never had such good seats. Jean Claude kept his word, and the passes were waiting at the door for them. They were thrilled to get in free, but overwhelmed at the fine seats they had.

They made their way backstage afterwards, and were shown to Jean's dressing room by a grumpy old man who was a stage manager. He gave them the once over, and then as he walked past them he said, "I hope you two boys don't give him any sickness." He didn't wait or even look back for a reply.

"What'd he mean by that?" asked Zeke.

Another man came by. He also gave them a contemptuous look.

"I don't much like it back here. Maybe we should go," urged Josh.

"I agree, but Jean's been ever so nice to us. Let's tell him how much we enjoyed the show, and we'll see him at Al's."

"Okay," replied Josh reluctantly.

Zeke knocked at the door. They both recognized Jean's voice from inside. "Who is it?"

"Zeke and Josh," replied Zeke.

"Very well. Come in and close the door," he replied quickly.

They stepped inside, closed the door, and turned around to find Jean struggling to get out of his last costume, a long regal-looking robe. As he pulled it over his head, they were stunned to discover Jean had absolutely nothing on underneath. Their young eyes couldn't help but stare at Jean's penis. Jean peeked out the top of the robe as he pulled it over his head, and slowed down his struggle a bit to give the boys plenty of time to take him in. He studied Josh and Zeke's pants, and immediately noted the growing bulges.

"Oh there, I finally got the darn thing off," he said as he pulled the rest of the robe over his head and laid it on a chair. How are you?" he asked as he reached to shake their hands while still nude.

"Fine," replied Zeke, now trying not to be caught looking at Jean's privates.

"Well," replied Josh while staring at the ceiling.

"Am I embarrassing the two young lovers? I'm sorry. Let me get dressed, and we'll get some dinner. Did you enjoy the show?" he began pulling on his clothes while turning as he bent over so they could see his soft, but tight buns.

"Yes. It was splendid," replied Zeke.

"I'm so glad you came," said Jean.

"The seats were the best ever. We can't thank you enough," added Josh.

You could suck me," stated Jean quickly, and then laughed as Josh's and Zeke's mouths fell open. "That's almost wide enough!" Then he chuckled, "Just kidding, boys. Relax. You're so uptight." He pulled his coat on. "Let's go."

He then stepped out the back door and onto the street. Jean stepped between Josh and Zeke, put an arm in theirs, and led them off down the street, singing a little tune in French. They didn't know what he was singing about, but they laughed anyhow. After dinner, they all had a few beers. Josh was getting a bit drunk and Zeke wasn't far behind him. Jean bought them another round. Zeke soon had to pee and stood to leave. Josh muttered something about Zeke doing a good piss for him, too, as he was too drunk to go. Zeke left the bar by the back door, and went down the alley to pee in a ditch.

Jean soon excused himself saying he had to talk to Al. Josh waved bye to him, and took another long gulp of his beer. His head was swaying and he felt like his eyes were circling about his head. He had quite a buzz.

Jean looked back to see if Josh was looking then darted out the back door. Jean crept up behind Zeke just as Zeke was finishing his piss. Jean waited until the last drops of urine hit the mud, and then he knelt down and spun Zeke around like a child's top. Zeke was too light headed to figure out what had happened. Jean immediately went down on Zeke's tool and began working it.

Zeke glanced down and into the shadows. He could just make out a figure about Josh's size and a head of hair. He began to stroke the hair, assuming it was Josh that was on him. Zeke's penis began to swell. Jean worked harder. Just as Zeke's hot juice exploded, Josh stepped from the bar.

Zeke glanced up and clearly saw Josh's face in the lantern light by the doorway. He gave Josh a puzzled look, glanced down once more at the head of hair, and then back at Josh. Josh began walking toward him, swaying as he walked.

Having swallowed all, Jean suddenly stood, kissed Zeke, "Fantastic, my friend. You are fantastic!"

Josh heard the Frenchman. He had seen him kneeling before Zeke, but it was Zeke that reacted first. "You sorry son of a bitch. I thought you were Josh. I didn't give you permission to..."

"But you enjoyed it nonetheless, no?" laughed Jean Claude.

Zeke belted him in the mouth in a flash. The Frenchman fell back. He touched his bloody lip as his anger overwhelmed him. In a flash, he pulled a hidden derringer from his coat pocket, and began to take aim. Zeke froze. He had nowhere to run and nowhere to hide. Jean sneered as he pulled back the hammer with his other hand, and prepared to fire.

Josh kicked hard from behind and his boot went up deep into Jean's crotch. The toe of the boot smashed hard into Jean's testicles. The gun sailed into the air. Jean grabbed his crotch, screamed, and bent over trying to get his breath. The gun hit the street and fired wildly into the air. Josh kicked Jean again in the butt, sending him sprawling into the open, muddy latrine where Zeke had just pissed. Jean was instantly covered in the slime as he pulled his knees into a fetal position, desperately trying to get some air back into his lungs, and stop the pain all at the same time.

"Are you all right?" asked Josh as he came over to Zeke.

Zeke started to cry, "I'm sorry, Josh. I thought it was..."

Josh turned him back to the rooming house. "Hush. I didn't trust that fast-tongue bastard from the moment we met him. I was pretending to be drunker than I was. I caught him studying you. I knew he was on the prowl. I knew he would make his move, and I would nail him and anybody else in the world that lays a hand on you. Come on. Let's go to bed. My turn," he said wickedly.

"You're unbelievable. You used me as bait?" asked Zeke.

Josh chuckled. Zeke seemed to get madder. His face blushed red. Josh poked him playfully in the arm. "It takes a worm to catch a big fish. We caught him, didn't we?"

"Are you saying I'm a worm?" asked Zeke, still pretending to get madder.

"Not you," laughed Josh. "Just your dick!"

TEN

At just past five on the morning of December 20, 1860, Josh and Zeke boarded a train for New York that would take them on to Portland, Maine. They had enjoyed their stay and their freedom in Washington so much, that they found it very hard to leave, but both boys were also looking forward to visiting Zeke's family, soaking in the hot tub, and snuggling together beneath the heavy quilts.

The train rambled along the route to the north and with each passing mile, it felt like it was getting colder. Not long after leaving Philadelphia, snow began falling along the tracks. The conductor told them there was six inches of snow in New York that fell just yesterday while he was heading south. Josh found snow fascinating, but still missed his warm afternoons lying nude on the hill overlooking his swimming hole in the swamp. When he got this far north, he only seemed warm when he was lying naked at Zeke's side.

The day had been long and hard with only a brief stop over in New York before continuing on. Zeke checked his watch and knew the train was already running behind schedule. He frowned a bit and reluctantly went back to sleep. Josh searched the rail car for more newspapers to read. The train rolled to a stop at five fifteen that afternoon. The conductor went about waking everyone as the cars began slowing down. Both boys yawned, then tried to shake the sleep and weariness from their bodies, quickly straightened their clothes, and then gladly leaped from the train as it finally pulled into the Portland station.

This Christmas, the entire family managed to make it to the train station, and they all ran up and hugged Zeke first, and then quickly hugged Josh, not at all wanting to leave him out. The Robertson family had adopted him, not knowing about his secret relationship with their son. While they were standing on the deck of the rail station, a man wearing a small black hat and white shirt with a black bow tie, and a pencil stuck over his ear came running frantically from the telegraph office. He stood on a nearby bench and yelled, "Hear, ye! Hear, ye! South Carolina just seceded from the Union! I repeat South Carolina seceded from the Union!"

"Oh my goodness," replied an alarmed Elizabeth.

"Let's get the children home," urged Allen Robertson as he began pushing his family away from the gathering crowd. "Everyone get in the buggy. Let's go."

Everyone obeyed but Josh. He stood not twenty feet from the telegraph operator trying to make his mind up as to how he should react to the news. Meanwhile, other passengers and locals alike encircled the telegraph operator and began making their own comments.

A burly bearded man with a pipe blew a puff of smoke and then spoke up, "I knew when Lincoln was elected this would happen. The South would rather fight than give up slavery."

A tall man who looked much more like a lumberjack than the sailor he was, spit out the tobacco juice from his mouth and replied, "There will be others following South Carolina's lead. We're headed for war, unless Lincoln just lets them go."

The telegraph operator spoke up, "He's already said that while he doesn't want war, he will fight to protect America's property and forts in the South."

The burly man spoke again, "I can't believe those Southern politicians are so ignorant. This action will destroy their economy."

The town's lawyer spoke, "It's not a matter of economics, and maybe not even an issue of slavery. It's more a matter of states' rights to govern themselves. Slavery is just the tool. It's a matter of pride."

"Yeah, right. Redneck, stupid pride," replied a man from the back of the crowd. Others agreed with him.

Josh took a step forward, anxious to speak up, when suddenly he felt a hand grab him by the back of his collar and start pulling him backwards. He struggled to break free, tripped slightly, then spun around with his fists clenched, and ready to swing at whoever was pulling him.

However, his fists fell to his side the split second his eyes focused on Zeke who said but two words, "You promised!"

"But, South Carolina has seceded!" protested Josh as if his father had told him to go read his Shakespeare, and he had just thought of a fantastic excuse.

"You're in the north now. You're outnumbered and out gunned," grinned Zeke briefly. "Our strategy classes would say it's time for you to regroup, rethink, and re-plan, and not to take on an impossible offensive. Wouldn't you agree?" asked Zeke strongly.

Josh thought for a second, and then slowly smiled, "Damn! How'd you get to be so smart?" He paused for a second then added, "Okay, okay. Let's get out of here. I'm starved."

Zeke silently said a prayer of thanks as they crossed the rail station, leaped off the deck, and ran across the street to the family waiting in the buggy.

Zeke whispered to Josh just before reaching the buggy, "I learned it from someone I love very much."

They were climbing on the back of the buggy as Allen hit the reins. With the family sitting so close, Josh couldn't say a single word of reply to Zeke's whisper. He just stuck his thumb into his chest as if to say, "me?"

Zeke nodded. Josh smiled and winked at him.

Their second Christmas together was even better than the first. They spent their days helping the family with the shipping business, shopping, and playing. Josh preferred the latter, but he put his newly acquired summer skills to work around the dock, generally helping everywhere possible. He didn't want to seem like a freeloader, and it took a bit of pleading on Zeke's part to get Josh to take a few hours off and go riding with him.

Though the weather had turned bitter cold with many days of snow, quite often the sun shone brightly when Josh and Zeke would ride to the top of the cliffs overlooking the Atlantic Ocean. The view was magnificent, and for a while, neither boy spoke. Josh noted the chunks of ice floating in the ocean, and grinned when he saw a sea gull land on the ice and ride it for a while. They felt lucky to be alive, to be able to experience such splendors and, above all, to have the love of the other.

"What happens if war breaks out between the South and the North?" asked Josh bluntly, disturbing the silence.

Zeke frowned. This discussion had come up quite often since South Carolina seceded. "I wish I knew. We're in school. We should stay in school. Let the politicians fight the war."

"That's pretty naive, Zeke. You know better. Politicians never fight. They don't commit their sons, but the sons of other mothers to do the fighting. Other children bleed, not theirs."

"Let's finish school then move out west, far from slavery, far from the North and South, and..."

Josh interrupted him, "And far away from anyone that knows we love each other."

Zeke didn't reply, but nodded slowly. "I guess we can't live here in Maine. There'd be too many questions as time went by, especially if I didn't marry like everyone else."

"And we can't go to the Johnson Plantation. At least I can't. The cat's already out of the bag there!" Josh smirked as he shook his head and hurled a twig he had broken off a tree limb into the ocean.

"Maybe we should sail to some exotic island," teased Zeke.

"Hey, I like boats, but I like riding horses better. I like your idea of going west the best, but if war breaks out, the academy might close."

"Why do you say that?" asked Zeke.

"Over half of the students are from the North, and yet the school sits below the Mason Dixon line. There's no way a school with such diverse students can continue to operate in a normal environment while civil war is being fought around them. It is impossible. I'm afraid that you and I will be drawn into the conflict one way or the other."

"No, I'll not fight against you!" stated Zeke boldly.

"And I don't wish to fight against you, but what about our families and homes?"

"Why doesn't the South just give up slavery and then America can continue to grow without war?" asked Zeke.

"I know you're smarter than that. In the last five years cotton production has increased a thousand percent. The only way the South can keep up with the demand for cotton is through slavery. I read in an article on the train from Washington that the slave numbers have risen from just over a million slaves to now over four million. Would your dad suddenly give up his fleet of ships simply because the South asked him to? I suspect not. So why does everyone up here think the South should just cut loose their slaves, and let the economy that they've worked so hard to build just fall away. My family and many others would lose their livelihood, their homes, their plantations, and probably all that they own. That is land that my family has owned and worked hard to develop for many, many years. You don't throw away everything and make such sacrifices just because some stupid Yankee says you should!"

There was a long silence between the two friends. Zeke slipped off his horse and sat down on a log overlooking the ocean. "Wow, you've been preparing that little speech for quite a while, huh?"

Josh slid off his horse and sat down beside him, putting his arm over Zeke's shoulder, and then leaning in close. He lightly kissed him on the cheek. "You've had me muzzled for quite a while. I won't argue with a stranger. I won't even argue with your family, but I did need to voice my opinion. So let's think this thing through a bit. If the North invades the South, and starts killing my fellow South Carolinians, or my relatives, or even my family, do you think I could sit by and do nothing?"

Zeke eyes moistened. He knew Josh was right.

"Would you not fight to save your family or your family's business?" Josh waited for Zeke to slowly nod affirmatively. "Then that is the quandary of this secession. Which side are you and I on?"

"We can be on neither side or opposite sides. We could end up fighting each other," added Zeke.

"Precisely. That's what makes your idea of moving to the west perhaps our only solution. There we wouldn't know about the war. I wouldn't know if South Carolina had been invaded. I wouldn't even know if my family was attacked. Moreover, neither would you. I would assume that somehow things got worked out without anyone having to die, and what I don't know won't hurt me, right."

"But you'd wonder, wouldn't you? Even though they've turned their back on you, you'd still fight for them, wouldn't you?" asked Zeke rapidly, knowing the answer.

Josh chewed his lip, dropped his head, and replied in a quiet whisper, "Yes. Yes, I would," and then more boldly, "but I can live with the guilt of not helping them, I can't live with fighting against you or worst, living without you should you be killed in battle."

"Then the solution is really not much of a solution, is it?" asked Zeke.

"No, but it's the only way. We must go west. I don't know when, but I think we should make a plan and be ready. War could come at any moment, or a year from now. We should try to finish school, as we'll probably never return after we move west. Yesterday's newspaper says that Lincoln doesn't want war with the South. He's taking a wait and see attitude. Six other states have joined South Carolina in secession—Mississippi, Florida, Alabama, Georgia, Louisiana, and Texas. The Virginia legislature has called a conference of the states in Washington, D.C. for February 4th. Let's hope this attempt at a compromise is successful. If we're very lucky, maybe war won't happen, but we had better be prepared."

"So what shall we do?" asked Zeke, slipping his cold hand into Josh's hand, and squeezing it tight as they sat there alone overlooking the ocean."

"When we leave tomorrow, you should take all the cash you can get with you. Even take your savings out of the bank, and take anything else of value that would help us make the journey to the west should war break out. Let's ride to town and visit the telegraph station. I'll wire mother that I've been invited on an educational trip to the west, and that I need to buy a horse and provisions. I'll ask her to send my savings, and anything else I can get out of them."

"Where are we going to put all this money?" asked Zeke as he stood up from the log and looked down at Josh.

Josh stuck up his hand and Zeke slowly pulled him up. "I don't think we should trust the banks. If war breaks out in Petersburg, that's technically in the south, then the banks could be suddenly closed with our money on the inside."

Zeke suggested, "What about the administration office."

"No, I think we should bury it."

"Bury it?" chuckled Zeke.

"Yes, we may need get to it fast. If war breaks out, then we should immediately leave our classes, pack our gear, buy two horses, dig up our treasure, and head west as fast as we can, getting as far as possible from the war. If we don't, we could be required to serve in the army."

"Which army?" asked Zeke?

"That's the problem. I'd be recruited for the South, and you'd make a fine engineer for the North."

Zeke swung up into the saddle. "You have given this a lot of thought, haven't you?"

Josh swung onto his horse and pulled in reins, "Now that I've found you, I don't intend to let anything or anybody keep me from seeing you ever again. I love you."

"I love you, too. Race you!" Zeke kicked his horse hard, not waiting for a reply.

Josh accepted the challenge and kicked his horse hard as well. "Hee-yaw!" he screamed as the two friends galloped across the top of the cliffs, leaping over rocks and small fences. The cold wind made their eyes water as their noses and ears turned a bright red, but their hearts were hammering hard. They were in love, and in spite of the possibility of a terrible war, they were not easily going to let anything stop them from loving each other.

Upon returning to school, Zeke and Josh secretly removed a section of board from the floor in their cottage and hid almost five hundred dollars they brought back from Maine with them. To Josh's surprise, Cadet Jones informed him that his office had received a note for over a thousand dollars from his mother. Josh cashed in the note and put the money in the secret hiding place as well. He had trouble sleeping that night as he wondered if he would have preferred a letter from his mother or the thousand dollars. In the end, the choice would have been easy to make, but he wasn't given a choice, and thus accepted the outcome.

There were many debates around campus about South Carolina's secession, the possibility of war, and a there were a few fistfights between the southern and northern cadets. So far, Zeke and Josh managed to remain silently neutral. Colonel Lee called a meeting of the corps, and admonished them for falling prey to such irregularities in the ranks. While he was considered a Southerner himself, he said that in the academy, there were no borders, and they were to behave as first-rate soldiers. He expected them to always act as gentlemen.

Zeke remained proud of Josh, as he had yet to enter into any such arguments or discussions, preferring to talk about horses, hunting, or fencing. Virginia setup a meeting calling for a peaceful solution, and attended by seven slave and fourteen free states set up a meeting. They worked long and hard and in the end, they sent Congress several proposals, and some concessions by the Southern States. However, Congress ignored these resolutions, and accepted a bill by Senator Douglas that stated that Congress should not interfere with slavery in the states. The war could have been avoided right then, but this amendment was never ratified. No solution had been reached.

Josh and Zeke went to town for a haircut at Ike's and a good meal from Sarah's restaurant. Zeke was in the chair getting his haircut to the academy's standards while Josh sat near the potbelly stove reading yesterday's newspaper. He discovered no less than four articles about Lincoln. He was surprised to hear that numerous threats on Lincoln's life had been made public. Lincoln took the threats seriously, but never wavered in his determination to serve his country. He did, however, agree to take an unplanned route to Washington for his inauguration. Upon leaving his Springfield Illinois home, he told the audience of well-wishers, "I now leave, not knowing when, or even whether ever, I may return." It saddened Josh to think that such hostility might escalate into killing the President of the United States. However, as he read of a major plot against the President in Baltimore, and of how Lincoln was forced to abandon his special train and take a heavily guarded second train from Philadelphia to Washington to throw the hounds off his trail. Josh realized how confused and fearful the country was. War could very well happen, he thought, but he couldn't foresee any changes in people's opinions just because one side or the other won. It would all be for naught, he decided.

He then began reading an article on Lincoln's inaugural address where he assured the South that he respected its rights, urging them to forget about war. He said, "I have no purpose...to interfere with the institution of slavery in states where it exists. In your hands, my dissatisfied fellow countrymen, and not in mine, is the momentous issue of civil war. We must not be enemies."

But all accounts led Josh to believe that war was inevitable, and he was afraid that the result would be the end of his friendship and, more importantly, his relationship with Zeke. After their haircuts, they walked across the street to the restaurant. While waiting for Sarah to bring them a hot plate, Josh slipped his hand beneath the red-checkered tablecloth and quickly encircled Zeke's hand, smiled and nodded, which silently meant, "I love you."

Josh was way off in the far pasture riding his horse on the afternoon of April 12, 1861. He thought perhaps his horse had kicked a shoe loose or caught a small stone. He dismounted and lifted up the left front leg of the horse to inspect its hoof.

"Hold, boy. Let me see why you are limping. Be steady now. I won't hurt you," he said as he gently patted the horse's neck.

"Josh!"

Josh looked around for the sound of the distant voice and saw no one. He cleared a bit of mud from the horse's shoe, and spotted a piece of a sharp stick caught between the shoe and the hoof. He pulled it free, dropped the leg, and patted the horse. "You'll be fine now." The horse tested its hoof a time or two before actually neighing in agreement with his rider.

"Josh!"

He glanced up once more and this time he saw Zeke running toward him. Josh gave him a puzzled look, waved, remounted with a swing up into the saddle, and then kicked his horse and began galloping toward Zeke.

"Josh!" called Zeke once more.

Josh pulled his horse up to a stop as Zeke bent over. He was out of breath from the run. "What's up?" asked Josh.

"You...got...a... telegram," replied Zeke between gasps for breath. Zeke put a hand to his aching side.

"Yeah, who from?" asked Josh as he took the single sheet of paper from Zeke's hand. "Oh, my gosh! It's from my mother," he read aloud. "Josh. Hurry home at once. Your sister Mary has come down with smallpox, and is not expected to live much longer. She wishes to see you. Hurry with all haste. I've wired a train ticket for you to the station in Petersburg. Hurry. Mother."

"Oh my goodness!" exclaimed Josh. "I have to get there right away. My sister..."

Zeke reached up and stopped Josh from mounting his horse. "Wait, there's more news. I'm afraid it's bad. This morning, Brigadier General Pierre Gustave Toutant of the Confederate army ordered the firing on Fort Sumter in Charleston. War has begun."

Josh froze. While his ears heard Zeke's voice, his mind had yet to comprehend all the news that just entered his brain. "I must hurry to Charleston. When I return, we'll head west as we planned."

"Maybe I had better come with you. If we split up now, we might never get back together," pleaded Zeke.

"No, I can't take you to the plantation! How would that look? I don't know if I'm really welcomed there, much less you. They'll read between the lines. They would know I love you. I'll hurry there and rush right back.

Perhaps I can get some more money together and supplies to help us with our adventure to the West."

Zeke turned his head left and right and found no one. He reached down and pulled Josh's horse around a bit so that the view of the academy was now blocked. He hugged Josh tightly, and then kissed him quickly. "I love you. I'll always love you. I know you must go, but please hurry back as soon as you can. I'll stay here and wait for you. If they close the school, I'll stay with Ike and Sarah, okay? Just get back here? Do you hear me? Get back here!" Zeke was crying.

Josh fought back the tears. "I will. You know I will. I love you with all my heart. If you have to leave the campus, then take the money from the hiding place and wait at Ike's. I'll come back as soon as possible."

They hugged once more, and then Josh slid up on his horse and rode across the pasture with all haste. Zeke followed him on foot, never letting his eyes leave the back of Josh's head until finally he was out of his sight and gone. The tears slid from his cheeks to his shirt and finally to the ground. He knew that he must never cry over Josh in front of others, but here in the empty pasture, he let the tears flow. His heart ached, and the pounding of his chest grew until finally he dropped to his knees and sobbed. He feared he would never see nor hold Joshua Johnson ever again, and that thought alone broke him.

The train had been filled with conversations and suggestions as to the outcome of the war. Josh read for a while, but soon decided to sleep as much as possible because in his dreams he was still laying beside Zeke. He was awakening just outside of Raleigh when a fight broke out between two men arguing about slavery and secession. Josh did his best to ignore the yelling, and tried his best to go back to sleep.

By the time the train reached Charleston, he found the rail station abuzz with activity. Many Northerners had panicked and packed up all their possessions, and were awaiting the next available train to flee to the North. Josh immediately noted the new Confederate uniforms worn by the many soldiers that were everywhere unloading supplies, laughing, and cheering the attack on Fort Sumter the day before. Their uniforms were not that different from the one he was wearing from the academy. Josh learned that the small military garrison had surrendered the following day.

Josh exited the train and crossed the street just as a carriage came down the street with a man in his new Confederate uniform standing up in the back waving to the crowd that marched along side.

"Who is that?" asked Josh to a man selling fruit on the corner.

"That's Beauregard. That's the General that ordered the firing on Fort Sumter. He won the first battle of the war," replied the man.

Josh gave him a coin for an apple, "What happens next?"

"I guess all hell breaks loose. We fight the Yankees, and we keep the slaves. Although I don't have any myself, I hope to one day."

Josh didn't reply, but just tipped his hat and walked away. Josh was watching the cheering crowd as Beauregard smiled and waved. Then suddenly, Josh got a cold chill. He sensed someone was behind him, watching and following him. He clenched his fists, turned around abruptly, fully preparing to defend himself from an attacker.

"Master Josh! Is that you, suh? I's Samson. Is dat you?" asked a tall, muscular Negro man as he brought his hat down to his hand, and tried to keep his eyes on the ground as he had been taught, but desperately wanting to see Josh's face.

"Samson?" quizzed Josh.

The man's dark black face suddenly lit up. His mouth turned to a huge grin, "Yes, suh! Dis me," he replied as he reached for Josh's bag.

Josh let him have the bag, "You haven't changed a bit, Samson. How's Sally?"

"The buggy's over here, suh," replied Samson as he led Josh across the street. "Sally, my goodness. She is fine, very fine. She's been helping Mistress Johnson tend to poor Mary. She's got de pox."

"Let's go then. I want to see my sister while I can," said Josh as he climbed up beside Samson.

"Suh? Don't you want to ride in the back?" asked Samson as he picked up the reins.

"No, I want to break tradition. I want to see Charleston. I want people to see me. I want them to see that I left as a boy, and came back as a man and a cadet," stated Josh proudly.

Samson slapped the reins on the horses back gingerly. They began moving. Samson's face turned into a puzzle look, "Whatever you say, suh. Whatever you say," he muttered not understanding what Josh wanted nor why.

As they turned down King Street, Josh stood up and sniffed the air. He inhaled the salt air flowing in from the battery, and he wondered what the cannons had done to old Fort Sumter. "Turn around Samson. Ride by the battery. I want to see what happened."

"Yes, suh," replied the Negro man as he turned the horse around.

As they approached the harbor, Josh was surprised to find the beautiful Sunday Park had been made into an army camp. There were tents and soldiers everywhere. Cannons had been hauled in, and they all seemed to be aiming directly at Fort Sumter.

"Stop here," said Josh without looking back at Samson.

Josh stood up and shaded his eyes. He saw ships sailing all over the harbor, many filled with entire families sailing out toward Fort Sumter to see where the battle started and ended quickly. There was a festive air about the place. Everyone seemed to be rushing here and there. Josh saw Southern soldiers unloading supplies, and officers checking their field glasses. Slaves were boarding up the windows of the beautiful houses along the battery as if anticipating a hurricane. But as Josh sat back down, he knew they were expecting some kind of a response from Lincoln's army, and they intended to be ready to fight and ready to win.

"Move along, nigga," said a sergeant who approached them. My supply wagons can't get through with your bloody ass in the way!" he said roughly.

Samson picked up the reins, but looked to Josh for his orders. "Let's go home, Samson," said Josh as he stared at the sergeant somewhat defiantly.

Samson turned around and headed the buggy back down King Street toward the mainland and away from the peninsula of Charleston. Josh spotted a boy selling newspapers. He quickly found a coin in his pocket and bought one. He tucked it inside his coat, anticipating reading it later that night. For now, he wanted to take in all the sounds and smells of Charleston and the Low Country. It had been almost two years since he had been in the south—two long years. He had missed the hanging moss, the seagulls, and even the smell of the marsh.

The road was filled with the locals all heading to town to see what war looked like. Josh was still surprised to see everyone excited and happy as if a grand occasion had taken place and not the beginning of war. He knew from both his history classes, and his class on war strategies, that war left a terrible path of destruction. He knew the excitement would soon fall away and reality would move in like the black clouds of a winter storm. They left the sounds of the city and began the final journey home. He was excited and happy, yet terrified of what lay ahead. He tried not to think of how his parents might act toward him, and what they might feel, but rather to focus his thoughts on his only sister. Smallpox survival was not common. Once contracted, most folks died. He knew the odds were stacked against Mary. He prayed she would be okay. He hoped he would be okay, too. He fought to hold back his tears.

ELEVEN

The buggy turned from the county road, and soon began rolling along the Johnson property lines. Josh's eyes were scanning first to the left and then to the right, doing his best to take in the sights and smells of his beloved home. He wished a refresh to his memory of the adventures he had here as a boy, and recharge his brain cells, as he noted the various changes to the plantation while away at the academy. He saw a few hands in the field, but didn't recognize many of the slaves. He saw a newly developed cotton field. Workers were busy planting while others were pulling weeds. The trees along the edge of the fields had already begun to bud and turn green once more. It was springtime on the plantation, which was one of his favorite times of the year.

The buggy turned down the dirt road entrance to the main house his grandfather built many years ago. The trees on each side of the roadway seemed to have grown a foot or two in the past two years. At the end of the road he could see his home, the place where he was born, the very building he had grown up in, and he couldn't help but wonder if it was still his home.

He marveled at how big and wonderful his plantation home was. He saw his mother's roses and their beautiful buds. He noted her azaleas along the front of the house. He had forgotten about such simple beauties that only a mother could add to a home. The academy had no such luxuries and December visits to Zeke's mother were certainly not the time of year to expect flowers.

The buggy pulled to a stop. Samson waited for Josh to climb out, but Josh didn't move, so Samson climbed out and lifted up Josh's carpetbag and started for the house.

"Aren't you coming?" asked Samson as he stopped and spun around.

"I don't know," he replied, although he had hoped the family would be waiting on the steps for him. He had even dreamed they would run down the steps, grab him, and hug him to death like the father in the story of the prodigal son, or more recently like the Robertson family welcomed their son in Portland.

"You best come on, suh. Little Mary can't hold out much longer."

The declaration stung his face as hard as a wasp might have done. He immediately climbed down and followed Samson to the house. Samson opened the door and Josh stepped in. He immediately noted a few changes in the foyer, but over all, it was still massive and exciting. He saw his picture on the wall to the right, and was pleased it hadn't been taken down.

"Lord, child. Thank you, Jesus. My Joshua has come home," proclaimed Sally, Josh's long time maid. She had gray in her hair he noticed quickly before she swung her big arms around his neck and hugged him tightly. "How are you child?"

"I'm fine," he whispered, half afraid his voice might crack. "You're looking mighty fine, Sally. Can't wait to taste some of your cooking," he grinned.

She tapped his stomach, "From the looks of you, I believe I need to fatten you up a bit."

"How's Mary?" asked Josh.

"Not good, child. She's been asking for you every day for two weeks now. That's why Mistress Johnson sent Samson to town with the telegraph. Mary wanted to see you. She loves you, child. Let me have your hat and coat, and you go on up to see her. She's in her room."

Josh slipped off his hat and handed it to Sally. "I'll keep my coat, but thanks." He froze at the bottom of the big stairwell that hugged the curve of the wall as it went upwards to the second floor.

"Go on now. It'll be all right. Mary loves you. She asked for you, and she got her wish. Go see her," urged Sally. "Nothing changes her love for you. Nothing."

Josh didn't reply but nodded affirmatively. He knew there were twenty-six steps to the top as he had counted them over and over again while playing there as a child. When he reached the last step, he looked back down the stairs. Sally was still waiting there, motioning for him to go on, and smiling at him all the while.

He crossed the hallway and turned the doorknob on Mary's room. Immediately the smell of medicine hit his nostrils. He edged the door open a bit more and saw the face of Elijah, his little brother. Josh noted his sibling had grown quickly, and was taller and perhaps even taller than himself. Elijah caught sight of Josh, smiled, and waved silently.

Josh pushed the door open a bit more and sitting next to Elijah was his father, Richard Johnson. Elijah tapped his father's shoulder and pointed to the door. Richard slowly allowed his eyes to cross the floor until they caught sight of Josh. His father seemed to have aged ten or more years since he last saw him. He lost weight, his hair gray, and his skin wrinkled. He had never seen his father in such a poor state. Richard stared at him intently with such a cold, sullen look that Josh nearly stepped back and away. Another moment and he might have done just that, but his mother saw him. She left her daughter's bedside, came to the door, and pulled it from Josh's hand.

Josh saw his mother for the first time in two years, and felt surprised in finding her so pale and weary looking. Her hair was filled with gray strands that fell loose about her neck. He wanted to hug her, but she didn't offer, and so he held back. She took his hand and began pulling him toward the bed. She kept dabbing her eyes with a handkerchief that bore her embroidered initials in the corner. He had seen similar ones many times during his childhood.

"She's been asking for you, over and over again. She wanted to say goodbye to you, Josh. Please talk to her," encouraged his mother as she led Josh up to the edge of the bed.

Josh looked down at his sister. Her brow was a mass of sweat drops. Her lips were parched and cracked, her skin as pale as the snow in Maine, and her limbs feeble, weak, and meatless. She looked like a ghost, and had it not been her, he would have been frightened.

"Mary," he whispered. "Mary?"

She opened her eyes, the whites of which were streaked with red. She stared at him for the longest time. A wrinkle formed between her eyes.

"It's Josh," he said.

Slowly she smiled just slightly as if the struggle to smile was almost as great as the struggle to stay alive. "My, my, Josh. I've missed you so. How are you?"

"I'm fine. How are you doing?" he asked, knowing the answer.

"I shall die soon. I'm weak and my heart is about pumped out. I'm so glad you came." Without knowing the rest of the family was but a few steps away, she stated boldly, "Momma has missed you."

Josh turned around to find his mother sitting beside his father, the handkerchief blotting tears from her eyes. Josh couldn't think of anything to say. No words would come. She was the only sister he had.

"Josh, you look handsome in your uniform. I bet you'll be married before long. You should meet my friend Ellen. She's about your age and is staying at the Maxwell Plantation for a year. She's from England. You'd like her. She's really pretty and..." Mary suddenly coughed long and hard.

"Shh, Mary. Don't strain yourself," said her mother from across the room.

Mary stifled another cough. The veins in her neck were visible as she fought back the pain. She sighed deeply, "Josh, the family still loves you. They just have a hard time showing it. I love you and wanted you to know that before I..." The words trailed off.

"I love you, too. Thanks for telling me that. I've missed you so," he said as the tears he had tried to hold back began sliding down his cheeks.

She whispered, "I know." She was gone. The life left her body suddenly and quickly. He saw her facial muscles relax, and her head tilt to the side. He leaned down and closed her vacant eyes. Josh turned to his mother.

Rachel sobbed loudly, heaving, and desperately clutched her husband. Tears slid down Elijah's face. Josh turned back and chewed his lip while trying to place this picture of his beloved sister deep into his mind.

After a while, he turned and left the room. He crossed the corridor, entered his old bedroom, and was surprised to find it just as he had left it. He closed the door, fell down on the bed, and sobbed. Between the tears, he remembered the games he and Mary used to play. From time to time, a dream-like picture of Zeke would creep into his head, and he would smile, and then remembering Mary, he would cry some more.

The next two days were a blur to him. Relatives and friends came by the house. He politely shook their hands and thanked them for their condolences. Not one member of his immediate family asked him about school, but other relatives and friends did. He received many compliments on how sharp he looked in his uniform. By the time they laid Mary in the ground, Josh had begun to feel somewhat more relaxed around the plantation, but not in the house.

It felt weird passing his mother and father in the hall in silence. Elijah had come into his room to talk, but even he had little to say.

The day after the funeral, Josh saddled a horse, in spite of the blacksmith's objection that he should do it for him. Josh mounted his horse, galloped out of the barn, and crossed the road. He kicked his horse and they leaped over the fence, and raced across the pasture. He didn't know it, but his father had seen the display of skill that Josh developed with horses. He couldn't help but note that Josh indeed had a bit of his grandfather in him.

Josh rode across every field and marveled at how much the plantation had developed in the two years he had been away. He also saw the large number of slaves now working on the plantation. He thought he recognized a few of the slaves, but no one waved or spoke to him.

He came to the edge of the swamp and spotted a group of slaves chopping down the giant moss-covered trees. He saw a white man sitting on a horse nearby yelling instructions to the slaves. Josh pulled his horse up and walked slowly toward the man on the horse.

"Howdy, partner," said the man as he spat a wad of tobacco into the swamp water.

Josh noted the man's friendly smile, but still something told him this man was just too smooth to trust. Josh went along warily. "Hi. I don't think we've met. I'm Josh Johnson."

The man gave him a hard look, then smiled once more, and stuck out his hand. "Well, I'll be. I've heard stories about you..." Josh's mind began to race wondering what the man had been told about him, "but I prefer to reserve my judgment after I get to know a man. I'm Trevor, your dad's new foreman."

Josh had taken great care to shake the man's hand as firmly as possible. "I'm pleased to meet you. What are you doing here?" asked Josh as he gestured toward the swamp before them.

"We're going to plant some rice over here, but first we've got to get this section of the swamp cleaned up from the trees and the snakes."

It was a large swamp, but Josh still hated to see any of it go. There were twenty strong slaves sawing at the trees while others were chopping and sawing up the already felled trees to haul back to the plantation for firewood. Josh started to ask another question when suddenly a large pop was heard as a huge oak tree began to crack and snap. Enough of it had been sawed through, and then seemingly in slow motion it began to fall to the ground.

As Josh looked up at the tree, he suddenly realized the huge trunk was falling right toward him and Trevor, and not where the men had intended. Josh kicked his horse. "Look out!" he screamed to Trevor.

Trevor yanked the reins of his horse so hard that the horse leaped sideways, and then Trevor and his horse fell abruptly into the water. The lead man in charge of cutting the tree stood back and froze. As the big oak hit the ground and the water, a huge limb underneath buckled causing the trunk of the tree to kick back, whipping the legs from under the man who cut the tree, and then pinned him in the water. The man struggled to free himself, but the entire weight of the tree rested on his legs, pushing them deeper into the mud.

The man began to scream as he fought to keep his head above water. Trevor came up yelling and cursing as he tried to brush the mud and water from his clothes. Several of the slaves ran to help their fallen comrade, but as they got close, a large water moccasin fell from a nearby tree into the water and began swimming toward the pinned man. The slaves were terrified of the snake and ran for the shore.

"Snake! Snake!" yelled one of the men.

The fallen man saw the snake coming for him and began screaming over and over. Josh pulled his horse around and yelled at Trevor.

"Sir, there's a snake. Shoot it!" yelled Josh.

Trevor climbed back up on his horse. "The durn fool cut the tree wrong. He nearly killed us. Let the snake get him!" he scoffed.

Josh heard the poor slave's terrifying screams. The snake was but six feet away and preparing to strike. Josh snatched up a rifle from Trevor's saddle sleeve, took quick aim, and just as the snake leaped from the water to strike the man's face, Josh fired. The snake's head was instantly severed from its body. The Negro's face was sprayed with the snake's blood. The body of the snake flew against a tree, fell back to the water, and began floating away.

"Quick now, I'll watch for snakes. Let's get that man out of there. All of you get together and lift that tree," he ordered the slaves as he reloaded the gun.

"Hold on, sir. I'm the foreman here. I'll tell the darkies what to do," said Trevor.

"You work for the Johnson's, don't you?" asked Josh.

"Yes, I do."

"We pay you a good wage, do we not?" asked Josh.

"Yes, but..."

"No, buts. I'm a Johnson. You'll do as I say, or I'll run you off!" Then back to the slaves he said, "You heard me. Lift that log. Get that man out of there!"

The slaves, some of whom remembered Josh, quickly jumped into the water, and together, they lifted the old oak just enough to get the man's foot free. They brought the man to shore. Josh stored the rifle in Trevor's saddle, and then turned around to look at the slave.

"His leg is broken. You two men put him in the wagon and get him back to the plantation. That leg will have to be set so that you can walk properly, but you'll be all right. Hurry now. Get him some help."

Trevor trotted his horse over and looked down at the Negro with the broken leg. "You nearly killed me you son of a bitch. I'll get you yet."

Josh angrily replied, "I suggest you spend your time figuring out how you're going to get that log sawed up. I don't think my daddy pays you to just sit on a horse, or let one of his men die."

"I'm going to remember you, Master Johnson," replied Trevor sarcastically. Then to the rest of the slaves, "All right now. The fun is over. Let's get back to work."

Josh gave Trevor a hard stare. Without even trying to, Josh made another enemy at the plantation. He climbed aboard his horse, and followed the wagon back to the plantation and the slave quarters. Later that night in his room, Josh sat on the edge of his bed reading the newspaper he bought on the day of his arrival. He was fascinated by the events leading up to the firing on Fort Sumter.

He read about General P.G.T. Beauregard's demands that Major Anderson of the Union Army surrender Fort Sumter. The Major had refused. Beauregard's confederate recruits fired the first shots from Fort Moultrie at four a.m. on the morning of April 12th, 1862. Major Anderson didn't fire back until almost seven. After eight hours of bombardment, a flag of truce was drawn, and General Wigfall made arrangements for the Major and his men to withdraw from Fort Sumter.

So far, not one single person had been killed on either side, but ironically, as the Union troops were leaving the fort, the premature explosion of a cannon took the life of Private Daniel Hough of Battery E, First United States Artillery. He was the first man killed in the Civil War. The next day, Major Anderson and his men set sail for New York. Beauregard saw to it that Private Hough received a decent burial with full military honors.

President Lincoln called for the men who had seceded from the Union and fired on Fort Sumter to lay down their arms. The Southerners laughed at what they saw as Lincoln's weakness, as they were the very ones that had won the battle for Fort Sumter. Lincoln put out a call to recruit 75,000 troops. The Confederate government returned the call by asking for 32,000 men to take up arms against the Union. After years and years of arguing and debating, with the firing of a single cannon ball, the Civil War had begun.

Josh fell asleep after blowing out his candle. He began to dream about Zeke, and he began to feel his member swelling. He missed him so much and subconsciously, he decided that tomorrow he must head back north to Petersburg while he still could. Josh knew that he and Zeke must leave immediately for the West or they would never get out and the war would encircle them.

However, later in his dreams, he saw himself riding a white stallion and scouting for General Davis. He leaped over fences and crossed rivers. Suddenly, he and his men were attacked by a group of Yankees on their left. He turned his horse and charged the Yankees, leaping over a wall and pulling his saber, he stabbed one, two, three men, and then someone fired a pistol at him at close range. The bullet creased his forearm, and he dropped the reins to his horse, using only his legs as he had been taught to steer. He swung his horse around, lifted the saber high over his head, and just as he began to swing toward his assailant, he realized the Yankee that had fired on him was none other than Zeke. At the same moment, Zeke realized it was Josh he had fired on. The saber cut hard into Zeke's neck. Blood spewed over the chest of white stallion. Josh suddenly screamed out, and he awoke.

He laid awake the rest of the night, praying that Zeke was okay. His mind was settled in that he would leave with all haste the next morning.

The family was waiting for him when he entered the main dining room the next morning for breakfast. He smiled and sat down on a chair at the table his grandfather had made from a big cypress tree when he was a boy. He sat across from Elijah who winked at him. Josh returned the wink as Sally sat a plate of hot pancakes and eggs in front of him.

"Thank you, Sally. This smells wonderful," he said while smiling at her.

She didn't reply, but curtsied and retreated.

"Joshua," began his father, "I've been nominated by the Governor to serve in the Cabinet of the Confederate government. I leave this morning for Virginia."

Josh was awestruck that his father had spoken directly to him for the first time in two years, and then his words suddenly sank in. "But, sir, do you really think you can win this war with the North?"

Richard was a bit put off with Josh's sudden opinion. "I don't know, but we must try. If I had to give up my slaves, well, I'd lose the entire plantation. Surely, you don't want that to happen?"

"No, sir. I don't know what to think. I just wish there was another way. A lot of my friends at the academy are from the North."

"We have friends in the North, too, dear," broke in his mother. "It's all just a mess. Nevertheless, this is a great honor for your father. He must go and serve. They need him."

"I know, Mother, but..." began Josh.

"Listen, Joshua. I heard about how you saved that slave's life yesterday. I heard that Trevor was a bit cruel..."

"He's always cruel," his mother broke in once more.

"I don't like him, Dad," stated Elijah.

"He's got his faults, but it's hard to find a good white foreman these days. He's the best of the lot. But still, I don't trust him." Richard paused a second, wiped his lower lip with his white linen napkin, placed it beside his plate, and then looked straight at Josh. "Son, I need your help. I need to serve the South, but I can't leave my home in the hands of someone like Trevor. I need..."

Elijah broke in, "I can help, Dad."

Richard smiled at his younger son, "I'm sure you can, but you're only thirteen. Josh is almost eighteen. The Johnson Plantation needs to be led by a Johnson man."

"But I must get back to the academy. We have spring finals coming up soon..." protested Josh.

"I can tell that school has done a world of good for you. I saw you leap that fence yesterday with your horse, and the darkies tell me you blew the head off the snake in one clean shot. I imagine your school will be dismissed until this war stuff settles down anyhow. I don't suspect the war will last more than a few weeks, perhaps a few months. Once the North realizes that their sons could be killed while trying to force their doctrine on us, they'll back down. I should be gone no more than a few weeks, perhaps a month. Please, son. Won't you stay and help your mother manage the plantation?"

Josh knew his father was a skilled orator, a statesman, and a salesman, and, reluctantly, he knew his dad had also just sold Josh on staying a few more days by using his mother as bait. "Okay, Dad. I'll stay as long as I'm the boss. Make that perfectly clear to Trevor. If he mistreats the slaves one more time, I'll kick his butt off this land."

Rachel smiled, as did Elijah. Richard nodded his understanding. "No problem. I'll speak with him this very morning. I'm sure you'll do a good job. Mother has told me of your plans to go west on a field trip from school. I think that's a splendid idea. I'll help with a horse or two for your journey when I get back." Josh wasn't fooled. His father just said that once he won the war for his beloved South, he would return home and kick his son's butt off the plantation once more. However, for the love of his mother, he kept his anger in check and said nothing.

Richard stood up, leaned over and kissed Rachel on the top of her hair, then leaned down and patted Elijah's blond head and then walked around the table and stuck out his hand to Josh. "You're the man of the house now, and I expect you to act like one. I know you can do it. I'm counting on you." Richard then turned and left the room to prepare for his journey.

Josh had shaken his father's hand as firmly as he could. He wanted him to know that he wasn't a sissy because he loved Zeke. He was very much a man, no matter what.

Josh had thought of asking Samson to post a telegraph to Zeke, but thought better of it. He didn't want word to leak out that he was sending a note to his friend. So far, he managed not to tell anyone about his lover. He never mentioned his name, or the name of any other cadets. He spent the next several days making his way around the plantation. So far, Trevor had been cold but cooperative. Josh learned that the plantation now supported almost three hundred slaves. It was like a living breathing economical catastrophe. They needed more slaves to plant and harvest more crops, but it took more and more food and money to feed, house, and clothe the slaves they were buying. It didn't take Josh long to realize that the treatment of the slaves had deteriorated quite a bit since he left. He hoped it wasn't intentional, but rather a matter of money. His grandfather would not have been pleased.

He set about finding ways to improve the situation. He got his mother out of the house where she had been spending the past several months taking care of poor Mary. He asked her opinion on planting more farm crops to feed everyone. He then stopped the work crew from working on the swamps. He sent them to clear and plow the land near the house, a chore they could accomplish much faster. They soon were planting a variety of farm vegetables. With good spring weather in 45 to 60 days, he hoped to alleviate the need to buy any further food staples.

It was five days later by the time he broke away and trotted his horse into town to visit the telegraph office. He was surprised to find the normally quiet office abuzz with activity. There were all kinds of military soldiers waiting on messages.

Josh walked over to the counter and printed a note to Zeke. "Zeke. Family needs my help for a few weeks. If school closes, go to Ike's. I'll meet you there soon. Josh."

He wished he could say what he really felt, but the risk was too great. He waited his turn and then handed the message to the telegraph operator.

"Where's this going?" asked the clerk.

"Petersburg," replied Josh.

"I'll try to get it there. Things are a little hectic in Virginia. The CSA is quickly building up supplies and troops. We're swamped with military messages."

"Thanks," replied a hopeful Josh as he climbed back on his horse. He picked up another newspaper and left Charleston. That evening, while sitting in the study, he began reading his newspaper. He read about how the CSA, the Confederate States of America, was trying to overthrow the arsenal at Harpers Ferry, Virginia. Lieutenant Jones, a Union soldier, decided to blow the damned place up rather than let it fall into CSA's hands. That very same day, four hundred men from the great state of Pennsylvania arrived in Washington to help in the defense of the capital. The capital city was ideally set halfway between the north and south, but in this war, it was really sitting almost in hot southern territory. If the rebels take Washington, it might just put the Union at such a disadvantage, that the war may be called off. At worst, it would put Lincoln and his blue soldiers on a hasty retreat to Pennsylvania.

Josh knew that Harper's Ferry was on the Potomac River between the intersection of Virginia, Maryland, Washington, and West Virginia. It was several hundred miles north of Petersburg, which meant that the academy was south of perhaps the war line as Virginia joined the Southern States while Pennsylvania stayed with the Union. Using what he had learned in his strategy battle classes, it didn't take him long to understand that Virginia was going to be in the heart of the war.

He wondered what Zeke was doing. He wondered if the school had closed and if so, had he gone to Ike and Sarah's. Was he safe as a Yankee below Southern lines?

Then just as he thought he had read all of the newspaper, he noted a small article near the bottom of the page that stated the Union War Department had asked Robert E. Lee to take command of Federal armies. He knew Lee was a Virginian, and he wondered what his commandant of the academy, Colonel Augustus Lee, thought of the offer. He left the study for his bedroom hoping Lee wouldn't help the North because if he did, it would be far harder for the South to win. Obviously, Lee was well respected on both sides.

A few days after Josh left for South Carolina, Colonel Lee wisely closed the school and urged the boys to head to their homes quickly as he suspected the rail lines would be brought to a halt. Zeke quickly packed his gear and the rest of Josh's stuff, and moved in with Ike and Sarah who had a spare room available in their little place above the restaurant. It took Zeke two trips to get everything there. He then made a crucial decision. Although he and Josh agreed to leave the money they saved in the cottage floorboard, he no longer felt it was safe at the school, as the war could overwhelm the academy, and the cottage could be burned. He took out all the money and hid it in the wall of the spare room above Ike's. It worried him that only he knew the whereabouts of their small treasure.

Zeke helped Ike and Sarah where he could. He cleared tables, washed dishes in the restaurant, and soon learned to keep his mouth shut so that the Southerners in the town would not notice his Maine accent. For the first time in his life, he knew how Josh must have felt when he visited the North. He got a telegram off to his family explaining that he and Josh were heading west on a school expedition. It hurt him to lie to his parents, but he felt he had no choice and did it anyhow.

He received a reply the next day from his father urging him to come straight home as Maine's own Professor Chamberlain was forming a company of soldiers and engineers to help the war effort. He felt Zeke could advance quickly in rank if he came home and joined the Maine Volunteers. The family knew and respected Chamberlain, and knew he was a big supporter in the effort to begin a college there called Bowdoin.

This troubled Zeke a great deal. If he went home, he would be farther away from Josh, and worst, he could end up fighting the South. Josh had promised to come to Ike's in a few weeks, so he decided to stick it out.

The next day, he picked up a newspaper while sweeping the barber shop floor and saw that a group of Maryland Confederates had blasted several rail bridges along the Pennsylvania Railroad, cutting rail traffic to the North, and primarily keeping the railroads from bringing Union troops to Washington. He also read of General Robert E. Lee's resignation from the Federal Army, and the paper speculated the Lee would soon become a general in the Confederate Army. Having withdrawn from the Union even a non-betting Zeke would have taken the bet that Lee would now lead the CSA.

Slowly, the days and hours ticked by. Josh had yet to appear in Virginia, and he longed for a word from him. Zeke spent all his spare time worrying. He fired off a telegram to Josh.

"J. I'm worried. Are you all right? There's lots of activity around Petersburg. Railroad to the north is closed. I'm still waiting at Ike's for you. Please respond. Zeke."

Normal communications had been overwhelmed in Charleston. When Zeke's cable arrived, it was placed in a box labeled 'local'. There were two other boxes labeled 'urgent' and 'extreme'. The families and friends whose messages landed in the local box didn't usually get their messages until almost a week passed. The usual messenger runners were busy taking orders to the officers or notes to the politicians.

On the same day that Josh received Zeke's telegram, Rachel received another message from her husband, telling her the struggle was going to take a little while longer, but that he was safe and well. Rachel told Josh about his father's situation and urged him to stay on and help her. He still couldn't refuse his mother, but he worried night and day about Zeke.

He prepared a note back to Zeke and rode in to town the next day to send it. Charleston was crazy with excitement. Troops were marching up and down the streets. Banners proclaiming states' rights were hung over the balconies along the streets. So far, only a few mothers lost their sons in skirmishes, so public spirits were still high, and people remained ecstatic over their simple accomplishments. Josh's time at the academy told him that soon the public would realize that war is a bloody, dark, and dreary business and many sons would soon perish.

He sent the telegram and then bought a newspaper and rode back to the plantation.

Zeke received the telegram immediately as the office was just a few blocks away from Ike's. He read it aloud outside the office. "Zeke. Dad is helping the politicians in Virginia. I must stay to help family for a while longer. Please stay in Virginia, as I may never see you again if you head north. If things get too hot, buy a horse and head west to St. Louis and then telegram me from there. I'll then get a horse and join you before we head west. Take treasure with you. Josh."

Zeke sat down on the boardwalk and reread the message several times. He now knew Josh was safe, but it didn't sound like he hoped to get out of South Carolina soon. He decided Virginia was a whole lot closer to Josh than St. Louis, so he decided he would stay put as long as he could, hoping Josh would soon join him.

Zeke tried to cable his parents, but communications to the North had been halted fearing spies were at work. He tried to post a letter, but was told it would not leave the state of Virginia. He was now cut off from his family and they from him.

Zeke spent a restless night wishing he could see and hold Josh. He feared he might never see him again.

TWELVE

Days turned into weeks, and the weeks all too soon turned into months. Every time Josh had a chance to go to town, he took it, as it afforded him an opportunity to send Zeke a telegram. It also gave him a chance to buy a newspaper and catch up on the war. He kept hoping to read of a truce, an end to the turmoil, a resolution of conflict, but all he read about was how fast the war machine was building. It appeared that all the politicians could really do was to find fault and blame while never seeking a permanent solution. From the Northern view, saving the blessed Union seemed to be far more important than saving thousands of lives. From the Southern view, retaining the rights to own slaves outweighed the lives of their fathers, husbands, brothers, and sons.

Even to a young idealist Josh, the idea of war against your fellow countrymen was just too idiotic to imagine. To not be able to hold on to the one you love, and kiss them daily was far more painful than the South giving up their rights to own slaves. He was constantly tormented as memories of Zeke drifted through his mind, and he fought with himself to try to understand why he was following the wishes of a man who had forced him out of the house. Why did he feel such loyalty? Why was he following orders from people who had abandoned him? Why had he forsaken poor Zeke, the man he loved, and the very man he loved more than anyone else? There were no solid answers to his questions, only hope that tomorrow's newspaper would announce the end of the war and thus, the beginning of his and Zeke's life together. Hope was all he had, but the flame of that hope was dwindling with each passing day. He almost felt he was doomed to live an unhappy life, but no matter how low he felt, one daydream of Zeke holding him, kissing him, making love to him, and the flame brightened again just enough for him to once again see a glimmer of hope.

At dawn's light, he and five slaves drove five wagonloads of cotton to town. As they approached Market Street, they saw several other wagons of cotton parked in a line. He ordered his men to pull in behind them. He leaped down and went to investigate the purpose of their wait in line. He heard the sounds of the auctioneer as he cut through the crowds at the slave market. The auctioneer was screaming for the crowd to bid higher, but it seemed as if everyone was afraid to expand their lot of slaves now that the war had broken out.

Josh recalled reading an article by the editor of Charleston's **News and Courier** asking if when the bottom fell out of the market for slaves, would the last load of slaves get shipped back to Africa? On the other hand, were they to be left to roam free, perhaps robbing, and harming the plantations just as they did in the jungle? Josh knew the ship owners were too tight to send them back and too stingy to let them go free. He feared they would be killed, but doubted it for as long as they still took a breath of air, there was still hope the captains would find a market for their slaves even if they marched them all the way to Texas.

There was even talk of sending any freed slaves back to Africa as well. For most slaves, that was even a greater fear, as they no longer spoke the tongue of the tribal ancestors. They had lost their hunting skills and the abilities to survive in the jungle. They were like tamed animals. The survival instinct had left them. They would probably starve. The tribal spirits that had helped them survive centuries in the jungle were all but gone. All the slaves possessed were strong doubts they would be allowed to stay in the South, and many had already lost all hope of a future.

When he got to the dock, he realized there were no ships taking on supplies. As a matter of fact, there was no cargo going or coming in Charleston's harbor. He had never seen anything like it, and he had been coming to the docks to watch the ships since he was five years old. Except for the lap of the waves against the hulls, the harbor was completely quiet and everything associated with harbor life had come to a complete stand still.

"What's going on?" asked Josh of a sailor stitching a shrimp net while sitting on a barrel on the edge of the big dock.

"The Monkey has ordered a blockade of all Southern ports. We can't get a ship in or out. The Federals have boats sailing up and down the coastline with threats of blowing us out of the water."

It took Josh a moment to realize that 'monkey' was the man's term for Lincoln. "What am I to do with my cotton?"

"No one is buying it since they can't ship it out."

"Damn," replied Josh as he moved along. He found another man and asked him the same questions, and he became greatly agitated when he got the same replies. He rushed across the street, made his way to the telegraph office, and sent Zeke a wire. "Zeke. Working hard. Dad still away. As soon as he arrives here, I'll head there if I have to ride a horse, or even walk the whole way. Take care. Josh."

Josh reluctantly returned to the plantation with the loads of cotton still in tow. The slave village was abuzz with activity as the wagon drivers explained that Lincoln had blocked all shipments to and from Charleston. Josh went up to the house to explain to his mother what had happened.

"What'll we do for money?" she asked as she sat down at the kitchen table and nervously sipped on her coffee.

"It can't last long. I propose that we proceed as usual. Let's store our cotton on the second floor of the barn where it'll stay good and dry. When this stupid war is over, then we can ship the lot of it and make a ton of money."

Josh's mother could not think of any other solution and thus agreed to the plan. Yet she worried that the war might just last longer than their cash reserves did. She wrote her husband a long letter, seeking his guidance, as well as urging him to come home. Her worry for his safety and the safety of their family grew with each passing day.

Josh ate his supper while reading the newspaper he had bought in Charleston. He read one particular article over and over. He was sure it had to be written by someone that perhaps attended a strategy class such as his at the academy.

The article compared the resources of the North and the South. It was all just a matter of basic math, stated the writer. The North had twenty-four states while the South had just eleven. The North's population was almost two and half that of the South, and a third of the South's ten million people were slaves. Excluding the slaves, the North had almost twice as much wealth as the South. The North had become a manufacturing giant while the South remained primarily agriculturally oriented.

However, the biggest difference of all was that the North had twice as many miles of railroads as the South. This war, the author predicted, would show how rails could move equipment, supplies, and legions of soldiers to new positions in less than a day's journey. The North was at a great advantage in that they owned and possessed more railroads, and to make matters worse, they also had more ships on the ocean. Josh nervously chewed his lip as the realization of the author's story took hold. He knew the South was the underdog, and it would take great leadership for her to win. He was thrilled when Robert E. Lee was appointed commander of the army of the Confederate States of America.

Later that summer, the first major battle took place at Bull Run. Josh read intently about the war. It scared him to think that Bull Run was once again in Virginia where Zeke was still holding up. It was an important victory for the South. The Union army led by General Irvin McDowell had grown pompous and overconfident. CSA's Generals Beauregard and Johnson effectively clobbered them. The losses were heavy. Lincoln now knew the war was going to take longer than even he expected. The Union had thought they would whip the South in easy victories, and they got their noses bloodied instead. The telegram offices were busy all over the North as the short notes announcing the death of someone's son had to be sent.

A draft was set up in the North and the South. Young men were recruited into the war effort and thrust into battle. Confederate troops had taken over the facilities at the academy. This frightened the locals fearing that they would become like Manassas and have a major battle take place all around them. Many of the Petersburg locals moved out of town, taking all their possessions with them.

Zeke watched the Confederate troops move up and down the streets of Petersburg. He heard talk from some of the customers that Lee intended to march his armies all the way to Maine if necessary until the sting of war was far greater than the North imagined. He hoped that the North would back down and allow not only states' rights, but slavery as well and that all could go on as before.

Zeke thought the man an idiot, but it worried him nonetheless. He had many long talks with Ike and Sarah, and after a large force of CSA soldiers moved into Petersburg, they urged him to leave. Petersburg was a very important rail junction, and there were officers and soldiers everywhere. They feared Zeke could be harmed if discovered that he was from Maine. It was possible the soldiers might mistake him for a Yankee spy and hang him.

Zeke sent Josh a telegram. "Josh. Can't stay here any longer. It's no longer safe for me to stay. Must move west to Saint Louis. Will telegram from there."

Zeke took Ike's advice, bought a very good horse while there were still horses to buy, stocked up some supplies including some of Sarah's cooking, and left the next day on his journey to the West. Ike also urged him to stay out of the towns, except to purchase what supplies he needed and move on. He was pressured to keep his mouth shut, hiding his Maine accent, pretending to have a cold and sore throat to help disguise his voice. He gave Sarah and Ike a hug, thanked them for their help, and left before dawn the next morning.

After a week of riding, he began to feel more relaxed on the trail than he did in the busy war town of Petersburg. His confidence bolstered during the day, but would soften at night when he was alone and could see Josh in his dreams. He always fell asleep longing for him. He missed holding Josh. He ached for him.

He kept their treasure hidden in the bottom of his saddlebags in a bag he had marked 'salt' and he always slept propped against the saddlebags. One night after a long day's journey in the pouring rain, he came upon an overhanging rock. Chilled to the bone, he decided to get out of the rain for a while by camping beneath the rock. He unsaddled his horse, and set up camp. He managed to get a small fire going so he heated up some beans and jerky for his supper. Not long after he had fallen asleep, his horse neighed loudly.

Zeke woke instantly while pulling the new pistol Ike helped him buy from his holster. He quietly shook the sleep from his eyes. He saw something move out of the corner of his eye. Slowly he turned his head and found a man attempting to steal his horse. Zeke's heart skipped a beat. His breathing labored as he tried to figure out what he should say or do.

"Halt!" yelled Zeke suddenly.

The man glanced up at Zeke. From Zeke's right, a pistol fired from behind a tree. Zeke hadn't spotted a second person. The round hit Zeke in the leg. He screamed out as he glanced to his right, grimaced at the pain, then gritted his teeth, and fired back at the man rushing toward him from behind the tree. Zeke shot him in the chest, dropping him harshly to the ground on his chin much like the buffalo hunters of the west dropped a big bull.

He then turned back to the man untying his horse. The man, realizing his friend was dead, quickly swung on to Zeke's horse and attempted to gallop away by suddenly kicking the poor horse hard.

"Stop! Stop or I'll shoot!" yelled Zeke as he tried to stand and then as his wounded leg gave way, he fell face first into the mud. He propped himself up on his elbows as they mired deep in the oozing mud. "Stop!" he yelled once more, but the man didn't. He kicked the horse even harder, trying to rapidly move away from Zeke.

Zeke quickly wiped the mud from his eyes with his left hand. The rain poured down his face, but he ignored it, took steady aim as he had been taught at the academy repeatedly, and squeezed the trigger and fired. His bullet caught the man in the center of the back, sending the robber careening off the horse. The uncontrolled downward fall put his body in the line of a rapidly approaching tree. His head snapped against the trunk of a tree, and then the thief tumbled like a poor limp rag doll down a ravine. The horse turned and trotted back to Zeke.

Zeke struggled to his feet, and hopped his way over to the first man, leaned down and nudged him with the barrel of his pistol. The tip of the hot barrel hissed like a branding iron as it came in contact with the man's rain soaked shirt. The robber didn't move. He then hobbled past his horse and looked down the hill. It was very dark, but he was sure the man he had shot was dead as well. He picked up the reins of the horse, led it back to his campfire, and tied it off. He was losing some blood and feeling faint. He had never been shot before. He sat down by his fire, and threw on the dry wood he had gathered for his breakfast. As the flames built up, and the light got a bit brighter, he inspected his leg, and was pleased to find that the bullet had gone through the flesh of his upper thigh and out the other side. He tore a piece of cloth from his shirt, and made a bandage to stop the bleeding.

He began to wonder who these two men were, and more importantly, he began to fear that perhaps the crooks had friends that would soon find them dead and come after their killer. He recalled hearing stories of people being tracked for thousands of miles and killed over revenge. He knew he couldn't sleep, so he decided to pack up his gear, saddled his horse and, though it hurt like hell, he managed to climb into the saddle, and head off to the West, trying to put as much distance between him and the dead men as possible. The rain quickly washed away his tracks, however, it was several hours later before he realized he had just killed not one person but two. It bothered him a lot, but he kept riding alone in the dark, reminding himself that he must be more careful if he were to make it to Saint Louis alive, savings intact, and wait for Josh to join him.

In the fall, Josh received a note from the South Carolina war board. He had been drafted. He did not know it was possible to be drafted, but it seemed that the newly formed Confederacy was forming new laws and rules as fast as possible. He wrote his father about it. His father said in spite of the fact that he needed him to be there to run the plantation, that he should serve the state he was born in, and make its people proud. He added he would return home at the end of the month to take care of the plantation. Josh had been instructed to join the CSA Army in Charleston on the twenty-eighth of the month. As far as Richard Johnson was concerned, the decision for Josh to serve had already been made.

Nevertheless, if Josh had learned anything during his two years away from the plantation it was that he was capable of making decisions on his own. He did not want to join the CSA. He didn't like the North telling the South what to do, but he didn't think it was worth risking his life for, and he certainly didn't want to kill anyone over it. Then he made the crucial mistake of telling his mother that his friend Zeke was waiting on him to head west with the school group and that he had to join them in St. Louis as soon as possible. She saw the longing in her son's eyes, and instantly, she knew something was up. Deep in her soul, she suddenly realized it was what she had feared the most. Her anger began to swell up inside her. She stayed silent for a moment or two, to allow the anger to pass or for her to regain some control before she replied to his pleas.

"You have lost our respect once, and now you are going to lose it again! Won't you fight to preserve our home? Where is your honor? Don't you have any loyalty? Any allegiance? Where's your manhood? Don't you care about anything but yourself?" She then slapped him hard across the face and left the room.

The sting of her slap shook him all the way down to his boots, but though it hurt, it was not felt as harshly as her fiery words. He was ashamed, and he hated her for being able to do that to him. He found himself caught in a quandary. Did he rush to St. Louis, or did he stay and fight? His mother's words echoed over and over in his brain, “Where's your manhood? Don't you care about anything but yourself?”

Josh knew he should never have told her about Zeke or St. Louis. He should have just faked going to Charleston one day and rode west, and then all would be well.

His mother did not speak to him when she saw him. She assumed correctly that he had made his decision to go west and desert the family, the state, and the Confederacy. His father was scheduled to come home in a day or two, so Josh felt he should leave right away, and avoid the impending confrontation with him. He knew his father would be even harsher on him for deciding to desert the South. Except for seeing his sister one last time before she died, he wished he had not returned. His family made him feel small and worthless, while the academy and Zeke made him feel like a leader and loved. He packed his stuff and planned to get to bed early and leave at daylight for St. Louis.

However, long before sunrise, a carriage rushing up the road to the plantation awakened him. Josh leaped out of the bed and rushed to the window just as the carriage attempted to stop, but it had been going so fast, it bounced up and over the white rock curb, leaving the horse nowhere to go but up the front steps of the house. Thankfully, the horse stopped before entering the house.

Josh would have thought the accident comical, but there was something about the urgency in the man's voice that had climbed off the top of the carriage and came running to the door, waking every one up, by yelling over and over, "Mrs. Johnson! Mrs. Johnson! Help! Help me!"

Josh rushed down the stairs and lit a lamp by the door before stepping outside. He shielded the lamp's flame from the early morning breeze. "What is it?" he asked of the Negro driver.

"I have a wounded man inside. He told me to bring him here with all haste!"

Josh ran to the carriage and as the light of lamp shone in, he found his father crumpled over in a heap in the floorboard.

"Oh my God!" Josh sat the lamp down and began trying to pull his father to his feet. "Help me get him into the house," ordered Josh. "Get Sally. Hurry," he yelled at Samson who had come up from the slave quarters to investigate as well.

Josh lifted his dad out of the carriage, pulled him over his shoulder, and carried him inside.

"Richard!" screamed Rachel as she ran down the steps. "Is he dead?"

"No, Mother. I think he's been shot. How'd this happen?" he asked the driver who was following him into the house.

"We were attacked by assassins on our journey from Richmond. I bandaged him up, but he insisted that he be brought here."

Josh asked, "Assassins? What assassins?"

"Yankees. They are trying to pick off all the Confederate government leaders and the generals. Richmond is a boiling pot. It's dangerous there."

Sally came in and inspected the wound in Richard's chest. "It's bad, but I think I can get the bullet out. Let's get him to the kitchen table. There's more light there, and I need some hot water and clean rags," she added to a servant girl who had come up behind her. The girl took off running. Sally started telling everyone what to do, and they all obeyed even if Sally was a slave.

By late morning, the bullet now removed, Richard was resting comfortably in his own bed. He had lost a lot of blood, but with luck, he would live. Sally had done a great job. Josh vowed he would remember her kindness.

Richard slept for two days. Josh had put off his leaving, waiting to see if his father would be all right. Josh had just finished his lunch when Sally came to get him in the kitchen.

"Child, your father's awake, but I'm sorry. He doesn't look so good. He's spitting up blood, running a fever, and well..." she glanced out the window.

"He's going to die, isn't he?" asked Josh.

She didn't reply so he put his sandwich down, stood up, and walked over to her, took his index finger and placed it under her chin, and turned her face toward him so he could see her eyes. "Sally, you've never lied to me in your life. Is he going to die?"

Tears slid out her white eyes. "Yes," she whispered.

He hugged her tightly as tears began flowing from his own eyes. Moments later, she pulled away, and urged him to go see his father.

Josh climbed the stairs slowly, counting off each step as he had done so all his life. He glanced around at the big plantation house, and knew instantly it would never be the same without his father. In just a short while, he had lost his sister and now his father. He didn't know if he could handle the grief. He wished Zeke were with him. He desperately needed his support and his love.

Josh pushed the big white door with the brass handle back and stepped into his father's room, and knew that his eyes no longer fell on his parents' bed, but rather his father's deathbed.

He slowly walked over to the edge of the bed where his mother sat beside her husband, and was every now and then replacing a wet cold cloth on Richard's hot, sweating forehead. She glanced up at her oldest son and then stepped away from the bed. Josh walked a bit closer to his father, half afraid to get too close, fearing death might just snap him up as well.

Richard spotted his son through weary eyes. "Joshua. I don't have much longer. The Yankees are trying to force us to give up our home, our very way of life. We can't, no we..." He coughed deeply and struggled to continue, "We must not let them tell us what to do. We would lose our home and our plantation if you don't stop them from taking it from us. Fight, dear boy. Don't be a..." He coughed again, more deeply than before and then coughed once more and suddenly, his eyes went blank, drool slipped out of his lips to his chin, his neck muscles relaxed, and Josh knew that he had just seen his father die.

Zeke spent two days in Lynchburg after sending a telegraph to Charleston upon his arrival. He wanted to wait as long as possible for Josh to get the telegram and reply, but Colonel Baker of the CSA had set up camp just outside of town, and thus fearing he would be wrongly accused of espionage, he reluctantly left Lynchburg, heading west to Roanoke. Half afraid he might get lost, he decided to stick to the main roads, riding mostly by himself, but from time to time, he would pull off the road when he heard a group of wagons heading towards him, or a band of cavalry coming up the road. At least twice a day he came upon a group of CSA soldiers. He did his best to stay hidden away, and beginning to feel like a mute as he used his voice as little as possible.

He was more careful about where he camped and cut down stalks of briars to place around his campsite to give himself a bit more warning if would-be robbers decided to try to make him a victim. He always camped a good distance from the road in a hollow so the light of his fire could not be seen very far.

Not long after saddling up on his third day of riding for Roanoke, he heard a gunshot up ahead. He pulled his horse to an immediate stop. He listened and again the sound of a second gunshot came over the ridge. He chewed his lip while he searched his mind for a plan. He could not simply retreat, as he needed to keep moving west. Hesitantly, he urged his horse forward until he stood tall on top of the ridge.

He spotted something moving along the trail near the bottom of the hill. He undid his saddlebag and retrieved a pair of field glasses his grandfather had given him on his twelfth birthday. He peered down through them, adjusted the focus ring, and discovered two old mountain men chasing a woman round and round a wagon while a little girl and boy sat on top of the wagon screaming and crying for help.

One man caught her dress and tore it, but she got away. Zeke dropped the glasses from his eyes. What should he do? He wondered. He lifted the glasses once more and saw a man get close enough for her to slap his face. He backhanded her to the ground. Zeke put the glasses back in his saddlebag while thinking.

"Damn!" he cursed as he kicked his horse and began racing down the hill. The horse responded with a hefty gallop and in seconds, they were at the bottom. Zeke drew his pistol as he came up to a sudden halt, and leaped behind a tree. He spotted a man chasing the woman around a big oak tree. The kids were screaming. The men were laughing and taunting. They had been so busy tormenting her they had not heard Zeke ride up. Zeke fired a shot directly into the center of the tree. He was not as good a shot as Josh, but he was pretty fair competition nonetheless.

The men froze in their tracks at the sound of the gun, and immediately turned to see where the shot had come from. The woman wisely took the surprised misdirection, and made a quick break for her wagon. One of the men quickly turned to chase her. Zeke fired a second shot at the ground just in front of the man. He instantly pulled up.

"Stop right there! If you get any closer to the wagon, the next shot will be right between your eyes!" Zeke yelled.

One of the men scoffed, "There's two of us and one of you, so just who in the hell do you think you are?"

He took a step forward. "Damn," whispered Zeke to himself. He had hoped they would just be scared off. Zeke sighed heavily and fired taking just the tip off the man's boot. Josh would have been proud, he thought.

"Ow!" yelled the man who had been spared the flesh of his foot, but not the pain of having it jerked out from under him as he fell to the ground.

His friend ran up to help him up. "Let's get out of here!"

Zeke watched as the two men saddled up and headed east down the trail passing the spot where he was hiding. He kept a very close eye on them until they were well over the hill. Slowly, he uncocked his pistol, fearing they were faking about leaving, and he immediately replaced the three spent shells. He saddled up, eased his horse from hiding, and moved down the trail.

Relieved, the woman climbed aboard her wagon, huddled her children close to her, and waited for him. The two children stopped crying. Zeke thought she was perhaps in her mid-twenties and yet he was surprised she already had two children, one girl about four and a boy about seven. It was unusual for a lady to be alone on the trail with two young children.

"I'm much obliged," she said as she straightened her bright red hair about her head and attempted to repair her dress.

"No problem," replied Zeke as he tipped his hat to her and her family. "I'm just sorry it happened."

"Me, too. I thought we were dead for sure," she added.

"I'm glad I could help, but what are you doing out here all alone? You're just inviting trouble. I'm a man with a gun, and I still find my share of trouble."

"My name is Betsy Hough. I'm from Richmond, but we were living in Washington. My husband, Daniel, well, he was killed at Fort Sumter."

"Fort Sumter?" said Zeke alarmingly. "I thought I read where no one died at the firing by the Citadel cadets."

"No one died during the battle, but my husband worked with the cannons, and there was an explosion amongst the cannons while saluting the downing of the Union flag. He was the first person killed in this stupid war. I'm a Southern girl, but I swear, fighting over whether to have slaves or not is just too stupid for me to understand. He had but six more weeks, and then we were heading west. My older brother has a place in Oklahoma. He said I should move there and get away from the war. That's where we're headed. You sound like you're from up North."

Zeke suddenly realized he had allowed himself to talk freely, forgetting to hide his accent. He blushed and confessed, sensing no harm would come of it, "Yes, ma'am. I'm from Maine. I was going to school in Petersburg. My best friend is from South Carolina and well, we just didn't want to end up fighting each other so we decided to head west."

"I see and I don't blame you. I guess we're both following the same dream. Where's your friend?"

"He's in South Carolina. His sister got the pox and well, she died. I hope he'll be joining me in St. Louis."

She sat down and picked up the reins. "Would you consider traveling along with us? It would be great to have some company. I'm a good cook," she added hopefully.

Zeke felt like he should say no. He knew he could move faster and more quietly without them, but on the other hand, it was the honorable thing to do, as this poor family would more than likely be robbed and killed before they made it there.

"I'd be pleased to," he replied. She smiled. He continued, "With one minor request."

She gave him a puzzled look, "What?"

"That if we run into anybody else, that'll you keep it a secret as to where I'm from. Technically, I'm behind enemy lines, and I don't want any trouble. I just want to head west."

She slowly nodded her head, "I see what you mean. Okay, it's a deal. If we meet anybody, I'll do all the talking because you're a dead giveaway."

Zeke smiled. She smiled back. "Giddy up," she called to her horses. The wagon pulled forward with Zeke riding alongside.

It had been a week since they buried his father in the family graveyard behind the plantation house. Josh had visited the grave daily afterwards. For the first time in their two-and-a-half-year relationship, Josh didn't think of Zeke. He kept thinking of his father, and his grandparents as he stared down at their headstones.

He knew it was impossible to know who assassinated his father, but if he had, he would have ridden to Richmond, killed him, and then would have headed straight to St. Louis.

He rode his horse silently across the great open pastures of the Johnson Plantation. He recalled the many stories his grandfather had told him about the early days of the plantation. How he had chopped nearly every tree down himself, and then he and the slaves hauled away thousands of stumps.

Josh was proud of his father's and his grandfather's long hard work in building the plantation. It was indeed a thing of beauty.

He also thought about what his father had said about protecting it and defending their way of life. He thought about his mother's plea for him not to be selfish, and for the first time, he felt he was being selfish. Thinking of heading west instead of helping his family and his state weighed down heavily upon him.

After many days of soul searching, he saddled up one day and headed in to Charleston. The slave market had become a recruiting station. A sergeant sat at a small wooden desk and was busily writing the name down of each recruit as they stepped up.

The man ahead of Josh stood proudly in front of the sergeant. "Any experience?" asked the sergeant without looking up.

"None," replied the man.

"Infantry. Third Division. Follow the private. He'll get you outfitted. Next," said the sergeant as he hastily finished making his notes. Josh stepped up. "Name?"

"Joshua Jeremiah Johnson," he replied boldly.

"Any experience?"

"Two years at the academy in Petersburg," replied Josh.

The sergeant looked up from his book where he had been writing. He gave Josh a hard look over. Josh felt like he was back in Washington at the bar. "Are you trained in weaponry?"

"I'm the best shot in the school, second best at fencing, and by far the best horseman," replied Josh, trained to answer quickly and accurately.

"Not bragging, I assume," replied the sergeant.

"Sir?" quizzed Josh.

"Just hold your water. I'll be back." The sergeant left his desk, stepped into a small building that had become an office of CSA. Josh stood silently. Not moving, but wondering what would happen next.

Directly, the sergeant returned with a captain at his side. "Sir, this is Johnson. He trained at the academy in Petersburg, which makes him one of Lee's students. That makes him lucky, huh? He says he is good with a gun, a blade, and a horse."

Like the sergeant, the captain gave Josh the once over. He then nodded at the sergeant. "Son, come with me," said the captain as he led Josh away from the other men. Once out of earshot of the rest of the recruits he sized up Josh once more. Satisfied, he spoke carefully and clearly, "Son, if you can do what you say you can, I need you in my outfit."

"What outfit is that, sir?"

The captain was pleased to find a man with military training and manners to boot. He grinned, "Well, there are soldiers who approach the enemy from the front, firing cannons and muskets directly at them, but I plan to fight them from the rear."

"I've had strategy classes, sir. I'm not sure I understand, but are you forming a scouting party?"

"Good boy. That's precisely what I'm doing except we're going to do more than just scout the enemy, we're going to scout and destroy. Would you like to join us? Our squad could make the difference between victory and defeat. We could be instrumental in ending this war much more quickly. It'll be dangerous. Very dangerous."

Josh didn't hesitate. The adventure had already overwhelmed him. Perhaps, his work in his squad could avenge his father's assassins, perhaps it would save his family plantation, and if he was really lucky, his work might just end the war sooner so he could join Zeke. He nodded affirmatively.

"Good. Come with me. We'll get you a uniform and ride out to my camp. Let's go."

"Sir, I'm sorry. I don't know your name."

"It's Captain Robert Bell. Let's go."

THIRTEEN

Captain Robert Bell rode ahead of the open-air wagon of eight new recruits as they headed north out of hot, muggy Charleston. Josh felt happy to leave out of the city as everyone was hustling about either going to somewhere, or hurrying off somewhere. Nerves were on edge. The heat and the war were getting to everyone. Tension was at an all time high. Tempers were lost and fights among fellow Charlestonians happened all too frequently. There was talk of the war everywhere he went. He only had a moment to check the telegraph office, and find Zeke's telegram explaining he was heading west to Saint Louis. The news stunned him, as now Zeke was farther away, but at the same time, he felt better knowing that Zeke was moving away from the war zone. Josh knew it was the right call on Zeke's part, but it also meant that it would be even harder for the two of them to finally get together. He wanted to send a reply, but did not know which town Zeke would arrive in next. He stuck Zeke's telegram inside his coat pocket, and climbed aboard the wagon with the rest of the recruits.

A few miles out of town, the wagon turned down a winding road, and pulled up at a makeshift campsite. Josh spotted six or more army tents, a temporary corral of horses, the cook's wagon, and the rifles leaning into each other in front of the tents. His life was changing so quickly. He was no longer in school, he was far from the man he loved, his sister and father had died, he had once again left his beloved plantation, and now he was a member of the army of the Confederate States of America. Nothing had gone right in their simple plan.

"All right, gentlemen, out and on your feet. Stand in a straight line, and let's get you sworn in and outfitted properly. Hustle now. There's a war going on, and the sooner we get in there and fight, the sooner it'll be over," ordered Captain Bell.

Josh hoped the captain's words were true. He hoped he would only have to fight a few weeks, perhaps a month or two, and then he could join up with Zeke. He joined the others as they took the oath, swearing their allegiance to the Confederacy, and he soon found his uniform to be even scratchier than his old academy woollies. At least this time he knew how to dress. He had brought along his long johns and wore two pairs of socks to keep the new boots from blistering his feet.

After the brief enlistment ceremony, the captain gave them a simple order, "Very good, fellows. Now go pick out a horse and choose carefully, because you'll die behind enemy lines if your horse doesn't work with you and for you. Then saddle up and meet me over by that oak tree."

The men quickly moved to the corral. Josh leaped over the fence and carefully checked the legs of each horse. He felt their leg muscles and checked their teeth, just as his grandfather had taught him many years before. He finally settled on a chestnut horse with long, but strong legs. Josh redid the saddle several times until the girth was just about right, then he took even more care in making sure the bridle was adjusted correctly, and he finally adjusted the stirrups. He scratched her ears and patted her side. He was making friends with his mount, and giving the horse time to get to know him as well.

Satisfied his setup was perfect, he swung himself onto the horse. The horse was not fully broken, and she immediately began bucking about trying to throw Josh to the dirt. She bounded hard to the left and threw Josh into the fence, and then kicked and snarled her way around the corral before finally settling down.

The other recruits made jokes about Josh's riding ability, but Josh paid them no mind at all. The captain stopped a hundred feet from the corral, and sat on his horse beneath the shade of a moss-covered tree to watch. Josh got to his feet, brushed the dust from his new uniform, and slowly began walking across the rink toward his horse.

"Better watch out! She's liable to stomp your brains in," warned one man.

"You got to have brains to stomp out first," laughed another.

Josh never let his eyes leave the horse. Slowly he stuck out his hand as he continued walking softly toward the horse. He began to speak to the horse gently. "Whoa, now girl. I'm not going to hurt you, but you see, I have to be able to ride you so that you and I can work together. I'll feed you well if you work hard for me. Now doesn't that sound like a fair deal? Whoa, now. Be calm. You're okay."

The horse watched Josh carefully as he leaned down and pulled up the reins, readjusting the length. He then reached up and began rubbing the horse's snout very slowly and gently. The horse instantly began to relax. Josh continued whispering to the horse until finally, he felt a bit more confident and suddenly, he swung into the saddle. The horse stirred a bit, but Josh leaned forward, patted her neck, and talked gently to her once more.

He then took up the reins, squeezed her sides just a bit, and she instantly began trotting around the rink. Moments later he picked up the pace, and then he began working the horse from left to right and right to left, teaching her how to react to his legs. He was pleased at how well she responded and how quickly she learned. He knew he had made an excellent choice.

"Better watch out!" called a man as he spit some tobacco. "She's just fooling you into relaxing, and then she's going to throw you into the next county!"

The men laughed, but Josh never looked over toward them. To their surprise, he alarmingly dropped his reins across the saddle, and held his hands high over his head. The men instantly hushed and watched in amazement. Even the captain was stunned by Josh's courage and bravery. The horse still went left or right, stopped or started, and even broke into a gallop, all based on the simple signals Josh sent the horse through his legs. His exhibition complete, he reached down, grabbed the reins, charged her toward the soldiers sitting on the fence, and then pulled the horse to a sudden halt just in front of the other men. They all scattered over the fence. Josh laughed.

"Let's go!" called the captain grinning at the talents of his new recruit.

Josh looked over the fence in the captain's direction, suddenly smiled at the challenge, took a hard swallow, and kicked his horse hard as he raced toward the fence, and then leaped over the corral's single post fence. The men really chuckled and hollered at this final display of horsemanship.

"You weren't kidding," said the captain.

"Kidding about what, sir?" asked Josh as he pulled up to a trot beside the captain's horse.

"Your ability to ride. Are you as good a shot as you are a horseman?" asked the captain.

"Yes, sir!" replied Josh with a grin.

"Very well. I hope you don't mind teaching your fellow soldiers all you can. After all, if they learn what you know, they might just save your life."

"No problem, sir."

"You can cut the 'sir' stuff when we're in the field or alone. My name's Robert, okay?"

"Yes, s__." Josh caught himself and grinned.

"Let's ride!" The captain kicked his horse as he led his men into the open field.

For the next two weeks, Captain Bell devised every possible training technique and drill he could muster. Every scout learned to mount and dismount on the run. They learned how to shoot from the saddle. They carried a rifle, a pistol, a hunting knife, and Josh added his father's sword. They also practiced shooting and horsemanship all day long. They were only allowed to rest while the captain taught them about troop movements, and how to properly estimate an enemy's strength by counting heads in a small square and then quickly determining how many squares of men there were and multiplying it out. They learned the difference in the types of cannons the Yankees were using, they learned the difference in a supply wagon of food and a wagon carrying more gunpowder, and, finally, they saw pictures of the expected field generals and leaders of the Union army.

After just two brief weeks of training, they packed up their tents and supplies, and began a secret journey to the North. The captain forbade any man from writing letters or messages to anyone as their mission was to be kept secret. They were also not allowed to call him captain, only Robert. He knew that while under cover in a Yankee town, calling him captain could bring a hanging to all of them. The sooner the habit stopped, the better, he thought.

They rode northwest until they made it to Columbia South Carolina. The next morning they turned north to Charlotte North Carolina, and then on to Lynchburg, Virginia. They spent their days in the saddle starting before sun up and camping just before dark. Their spirits were high, their butts sore, and their anticipation great. Captain Bell explained that it would be several days before they were behind enemy lines, but they were still ordered to keep their weapons clean and ready every day.

Josh slept soundly each night, especially after the long hard rides. His horse became 'Chess' which was short for chestnut, the color of her coat. Unlike the other scouts, Chess was able to follow word commands given by Josh. But Josh wasn't completely satisfied with her training, so he began using hand motions and nods of his head, or even a quiet whistle to send commands to Chess.

The days of riding soon turned into long hard weeks. Each night Josh drifted off to sleep thinking of Zeke. He also went to sleep with a full erection and woke up the same way. There was little privacy in the camp, but more than once, he slipped off in the woods to relieve his sexual build up. By the time they rode into Lynchburg, Virginia, Josh had been in the CSA six full weeks. He hoped the war would not last too much longer. They restocked their supplies, and avoided all reporters and civilian questions about who they were, and why there were only ten of them in their unit.

The captain sent a telegram to headquarters and waited in the lobby for a reply. Josh wished he knew where Zeke was so that he could send a message, but he did not know where Zeke was just yet, only that he was on the way to St. Louis and then again, he had orders not to communicate with anyone.

When the captain returned to the squad he announced he had received orders, they were to meet a Colonel Harry Ashley just east of Roanoke. They saddled up immediately and began the journey west.

Zeke and the Hough family continued their journey to Roanoke. The primitive road was rough and full of potholes, and the recent rains made the ruts even softer. Zeke should have made the journey in three days. They were on their third day and still ten miles from Roanoke when suddenly, the left front wheel of the wagon went down hard in a mud puddle, and the wheel simply collapsed, dumping Betsy and her children into the floorboard, and nearly tumbling the wagon over.

Zeke quickly dismounted and grabbed the reins to steady the horses, while Betsy and the kids scampered out of the wagon to safety.

"Damn!" she cursed as she looked at the broken wheel.

Surprised by her remark, yet thinking she summed up the situation quite well, Zeke chuckled.

"What are you laughing at?" she yelled at him.

"I'm sorry. I was laughing at you. I know it's a bit of bad luck, but it's not the end of the world. Come on, let's unhitch the horses before they turn the wagon over, and then we'll figure out what to do. It could have been worse," he added with a smile.

Her cheeks were still puffed out from anger, but finally they relaxed a bit as she shook her head and smiled, "I don't see how. Are you always so agreeable?"

"I'll try to practice my mean side," he added with a grin. "Come on now. We can handle this. Let's get to it. I see a rain cloud coming. We're going to get wet."

Zeke tied off his horse, then unhitched the horses, and then went over to inspect the wheel. "Three rungs are broken clean through, and the steel rim has slipped off. We'll need a blacksmith."

"How far to Roanoke?" she asked.

"I'd say ten miles or less."

"Me and the kids will set up camp. Will you ride ahead, and get someone to help us?"

"Yes, of course, I will. Do you think you'll be all right, staying behind?"

"I've got a rifle in the wagon."

"Can you shoot it?"

"Yep, Daniel taught me. I can hit a rabbit at forty yards."

Zeke chuckled again, "I don't doubt that for a minute. Okay, I'll rush on to Roanoke and get us some help. Get that tarp up or you'll soon get pretty wet."

"Just hurry, will ya?" she smiled.

"I will. Bye kids!"

"Bye," they echoed.

Zeke remounted and headed out at a faster pace. After just a few miles, he came upon a stranger wearing a black hat and faded tan shirt. He carried pistols on both sides of his belt, and displayed a handle bar mustache. Zeke thought he was handsome from the get-go, but that did not mean he was a nice guy. He was still leery of running into anyone. Zeke pulled up to a stop as the man approached, and slid his coat back from his pistol in case he needed to draw it. However, he didn't think he would have to. There was just something about the man that intrigued him.

"Howdy," said the man as he pulled his horse up to a slow walk to avoid spooking Zeke's horse.

Zeke decided to try to hide his accent. "Howdy yourself," he replied with a slight smile, and a bit of a Southern sound. "How far to Roanoke?"

"'Two miles or less I guess," replied the stranger.

"That's good. My wagon broke down back there and..." he paused to think, and then added, "my wife and kids are back a ways. We broke a wagon wheel, and I've got to get some help."

"Can you and I fix it?" asked the polite stranger.

"No, it'll take a blacksmith or wheelwright, I'm afraid, but I'm much obliged. Would you mind telling them I'm close to town, and I'll be back soon?"

"Don't mind at all. My name is Ashley. Harry Ashley." He suddenly thrust his ungloved hand forward.

Zeke shook it and smiled again. "I'm Daniel Hough. We're heading west to do some farming."

"Well, good luck to you Daniel. With this civil war upon us, heading west would be the right thing to do. I'll tell your family you're on your way."

Then Zeke worried that Harry might harm Betsy as did the other men. "By the way, my wife's name is Betsy. She's got a rifle and can hit a rabbit at seventy five yards," he stretched. "Might give her a shout 'fore you ride up too fast," he warned.

Harry nodded, "I'll do just that. I have no intention of getting shot today."

"She's just a little nervous. We had some trouble a few days ago with a couple of men on the road."

"I understand. I'll see you."

Zeke couldn't help staring into Harry's eyes. He was indeed handsome, and yet his gentle face had a mystery about it. Zeke thought he might be homosexual. It was the first time he had ever seen another man that he was really attracted to. Before this encounter, Josh consumed all his sexual thoughts. He tried to shake the stranger's looks from his mind by kicking his horse and riding off quickly to Roanoke.

Ashley topped a hill and immediately spotted the broken down wagon. He pulled his trotting horse up to a walk. "Mrs. Hough!" he called. "I'm Harry Ashley. I mean you no harm. I met your husband a few miles back. Can I come ahead?"

Betsy was startled by the booming voice, but even more alarmed and confused by the statement, 'I met your husband', when everyone knew he had been killed at Fort Sumter. Then just as suddenly, it dawned on her that Zeke had lied to protect them. "Sure, come ahead." Then she turned to the kids and urged them to stay under the tarp.

She realized immediately Mister Ashley was a handsome man, and seemed to be safe, but she still carried the rifle in her arm as she stepped out of the tarp, and waited on him to approach.

Harry pulled his horse up alongside the broken wagon wheel and gave it a hard look. "Daniel was right. This is going to be a job for a blacksmith. I'm sorry I couldn't help. Do you need anything?" he asked as he tipped his hat toward her.

"No thanks, we're fine."

"I met him about a mile or two out from Roanoke. I imagine by now he's found a blacksmith and heading this way. I'm sure they'll probably have to bring a wheel back in a wagon so it may be nightfall by the time they get here. Looks like rain. Perhaps you should gather some wood, and keep it dry so you can build a fire if darkness falls before they get back."

She smiled and nodded. "Good idea. Thank you, Mister..."

"Ashley. Harry Ashley. Well, I have an appointment to keep, so I'll be on my way. I wish you better luck on your journey. It was a pleasure meeting you, Ma'am."

"Same here," she added with just the hint of a smile.

"Bye, kids," he said with a wink.

Betsy turned to find the kids peeking out the edge of the tarp.

"Bye," they called.

She stood there and watched him ride off before setting the gun down. "Come on. Let's gather wood for a fire. Zeke will be back soon. Can you smell the rain? It'll be here soon. Hurry up, now," she prodded.

Zeke found the blacksmith who was reluctant to ride out with a storm coming, but Zeke pleaded with him that his family was out there all alone, and that he would pay him double for the wheel. The man finally agreed and hitched up a small wagon, then threw in his tools and the spare wheel, hitched up a single horse, and followed Zeke quickly out of town.

Ashley had ridden but a few miles when he came upon Bell's men riding fast in his direction. He pulled his horse up to stop and waited for them. Ashley hoped they were the squad he was looking for. He knew he had to be careful. He cleared his coat from his pistol handles. Bell lifted his hand to signal for the troop to stop, and then slowly they walked their horses a bit closer to the stranger.

"I'm Harry Ashley. The sky is gray today," he added. Josh thought the added sentence a puzzler but said nothing.

"I'm Captain Robert Bell. The sun will be out tomorrow." Josh gave his captain an even more confused look as if the two men were the dumbest weather forecasters he had ever heard. Anyone could see the sky getting gray with a thunderstorm coming, but by tomorrow, the storm would be gone, and the sun would be out. He thought, what gives?

Harry suddenly broke into a grin. "I just love this spy stuff, don't you?" Josh noted how handsome the stranger was, and of course, he caught on that the sentences were like passwords or code to make sure they were talking to the right person and not the enemy.

Captain Bell dismounted and smiled, "How are you Harry?" He gave him a hug. That surprised Josh all the more, as he climbed off his horse and walked a bit closer.

"Robert, old friend, I'm fine. I've been way up north for weeks. I headed west before turning back south, and finally to the east to avoid the enemy troops. It feels so good to be in the South again. Is this scraggy-looking bunch your new outfit?" he teased.

Bell chuckled, "Yep. Good recruit pickings are getting pretty darned slim. What's up?"

"Davis wants you to head immediately north into Pennsylvania. Your job is to work your way eastward at that point, and then cause the Union army as much trouble, agony, and confusion as possible. Blow up bridges, rob trains, destroy supplies, you know, have a good old time," laughed Harry. "Just don't get your ass shot off in the process!"

"No problem there, unless of course, we get caught."

"I suggest you get rid of those new fancy uniforms as soon as possible. You should look like a band of outlaws perhaps—anything but soldiers."

"I see, but how do we get back across to our side without getting our butts shot off by our guys?"

"I've got paperwork from Davis for you." Harry undid his coat pocket, pulled ten slips out one at a time, and handed them to Bell who passed them around. "Put these passes in your boot, and if you're captured, do your best to keep your boots on no matter what. If you spot troop movement, or artillery build up, then send a man south to the nearest military post and give a report. Stay in the North as long as possible. Whenever possible, do your best to slow them up. Every delay could save thousands of Southern lives. Do you understand?"

"Yes, we do. We'll do our best, Harry."

"I know you will. Well, I hate to run, but I have to get to Richmond, and there's a downpour coming. I have a meeting with Lee shortly. Oh yeah, there's a woman and two kids back up the road with a broken wagon. Don't worry about her as her husband has gone to Roanoke for a blacksmith. She's a good shot, so don't spook her."

Bell chuckled, "I understand. I guess it would be kind of embarrassing getting shot on our side of the line by a pretty little Southern lady, now wouldn't it?"

"You just stay on your toes from now on. War means people die. Don't you become one of them. We need your eyes and ears. We need to know where the troops are moving, and what they're hauling. I have to go. Bye." He swung up and into his saddle, adjusted his hat, and pulled in on his reins.

"Bye, old friend. Godspeed."

"Adios!" Ashley called as he kicked his horse and headed for Lynchburg.

"Well, you heard him, boys. Get out of those uniforms and back into your street clothes. Hurry up, now. Rain's coming," he ordered.

The men climbed off their horses and soon the new uniforms were packed away in saddlebags, and their old clothes were put back on. Just as Josh climbed back on his horse, it began to rain harshly. The squad followed Bell down the trail at a slow trot as they could hardly see through the sheets of rains.

Zeke and the blacksmith hurriedly set about jacking the wagon up, then took the broken wheel off the axle, and put the new one back on. Just as they removed the jack, the downpour caught up with them. The blacksmith immediately threw the old wheel in his wagon, accepted Zeke's cash for the job, climbed aboard his wagon, and headed for home. Betsy and the kids quickly climbed aboard, while Zeke gathered up the tarp and pushed it into the back of the wagon.

"What shall we do?" asked Betsy loudly over the noise of the rain.

"I don't see any point in trying to make camp. We can be in town in a few hours. Why don't we just push forward, and stay in a hotel tonight where's it dry."

"Do you think we can make it in this storm?"

"It's better than staying here. The road levels out shortly, and then it's a pretty good road to Roanoke," called Zeke as he went to fetch the wagon horses.

"Need some help?" she called.

"Nope, I can do it, and I'm already soaked. Just stay put, and I'll have you ready to roll shortly."

Betsy sighed as she huddled with the kids in the center of the wagon as the rain began pouring down. Zeke worked as fast as he could to hitch up the horses. He then tied his horse to the rear of the wagon. Just as he was about to climb onto the wagon, a cold chill went up his back. It felt like someone was watching him. He slowly let his hand slide down to the pistol he wore at his waist. His fingers curved around the handle as he gingerly turned around.

He found nothing behind him and was greatly relieved. However, just as he relaxed his grip on his holstered pistol, he spotted a group of men riding toward them in the rain. They spotted him at just about the same time, and pulled up to a halt. Zeke gave them a steady gaze, but they were too far off to recognize any faces, and the rain made visibility a wet blur.

He turned to climb aboard the wagon, anxious to get out of the weather, away from these strange riders, and into a dry place in town. He reached up and took hold of the edge of the wagon seat to climb aboard. Instantly, he felt a chill run down his spine once more. He turned to see if the riders were coming, but they were not. A lone single rider stood off to the right on a tall chestnut horse. In the semidarkness, Zeke gave that rider a hard stare, and then shook his head as if trying to steady his nerves, slapped the reins, and the horses began pulling them toward town.

Josh moved away from the other riders as he gazed down the hill at the wagon. The hair on the back of his neck stood up. His pulse increased, and he didn't know why. At first, he thought he was going to be sick, but then as he watched the man walk to the wagon, there was just something about his gait...

"Impossible," he whispered to himself.

Bell asked, "What?"

Startled at being heard aloud, "Huh, nothing, sir."

"Let's get moving. We head north from here. Perhaps we'll outride this monsoon. Move out!" yelled the captain.

Josh took one last look at the wagon as it moved down the hill. It had been an eerie feeling he would not soon forget. He wondered what it was about the stranger that piqued his curiosity.

They had come so close to finding each other, but it was not meant to be. In the midst of a storm, they had been only fifty yards apart and did not know it.

FOURTEEN

They camped at White Sulfur Springs, which was just across the border from Virginia into West Virginia territory. The rain finally stopped, and for the first time in days, the men had been allowed to build a fire, and eat a hot meal before bedtime. Bell posted a sentry who grumbled just slightly at having to stand watch while the rest of the squad instantly drifted off to sleep.

Josh's bedroll was not very comfortable, and the ground he chose turned out to be harder than it had looked. As he always did, he pulled the blanket up to his chin, then reached down and unbuckled his pants so he could more easily reach inside. He shifted and adjusted his position several times before weariness overcame him and he fell asleep. He had been asleep for only an hour or so when a dream about Zeke, and the first time they had shared a bath together crept into his brain.

Beneath the woolen blanket, he allowed his hand to encircle and pull at his erection, as he continued to study Zeke's naked body in his dream. Zeke said something smart when Josh was climbing out of the tub. Josh reached back and grabbed Zeke by the hair, and pushed him beneath the water, then playfully pulled him back up. The dream had changed since the last time his unconscious mind explored this sensual memory. When Zeke came up this time, his head was bloody, bruised, and a tooth was missing. Josh woke up with a horrifying start. His breath was labored while sweat dripped from his face. It had been an awful dream, a real nightmare.

"You all right?" asked Skeeter, as he spat some tobacco juice into the fire.

"Huh?" asked a dazed Josh.

"You were talking in your sleep," replied Skeeter.

Worried that he might have said something he shouldn't have, he stretched and yawned, "Oh, it was just a weird dream. I'm wide-awake now. I'll take your post for you," offered Josh.

"Gee, thanks. Are you sure?"

"No problem. I doubt if I could sleep after that dream anyhow. Get some shut-eye," added Josh as he buttoned his pants, pulled on his boots, slid into his jacket, buckled the holster around his waist, and tied the leg string.

Josh stayed awake the rest of the night standing watch, and thinking over and over about the nightmare and about Zeke. He wondered where Zeke was, and when they would meet again. The dream had shaken him, and though it was just a dream, he hoped and prayed that Zeke was safe and well.

At dawn, they saddled up and headed north to Elkins, a distance that would take most of the day to travel. By late afternoon, the men were very saddle sore and weary from the weeks of riding. Complaining about anything and everything became the main topic of conversation. The captain knew they were also bored, but to him boredom meant they were all still alive and well. Days filled with action meant days where someone could be injured or killed. He dreaded those days, and yet he knew they would come, just as the cold weather comes in winter.

"Just another mile," urged Captain Bell.

"That's what you've been saying for the past three miles," grinned Josh.

"Well, these maps ain't all that accurate," replied Bell slyly, as he spit tobacco juice to the ground. He had been caught lying, but done to keep the morale up and the men moving forward.

They galloped over the crest of a hill and instantly Bell's hand went up. The sudden stop so startled the squad that a couple of their horses bumped into Bell's mount and nearly knocked him off his saddle.

The captain circled his horse until he could get a better view of what made him stop. He exclaimed as he pointed to the far side of the next meadow. "Look!"

"It's Union soldiers!" exclaimed Skeeter.

"Right you are," replied Bell, as mentally he quickly counted the troops. "A whole bunch of them. I estimate about a thousand men."

"What do we do?" asked Josh.

"Our mission, gentlemen, is to report this troop movement, and then do all we can to slow them down so our boys can be ready for them," replied Bell.

"How are we going to do that? There's a thousand of them, and just eight of us," replied a skeptical Skeeter.

The captain pulled his field glasses up to his eyes to study the long column of soldiers. Slowly a smile came over his face. "I think we'll hit them where it will hurt the most!"

"I beg your pardon?" asked a slightly bewildered Josh, half-assuming the captain meant kicking them in the crotch.

"Do you see that line of wagons at the rear of the column?" he pointed off to the left. "Well, that's their food, supplies, and ammo, and there are only a handful of men protecting it. They think they're safe this far above enemy lines."

"If we wait until dark, we could sneak up on them," suggested Josh.

"But then the chow wagons would be in the center of a thousand men. No, we'll circle around to the rear of the column, and camp tonight.

Tomorrow morning, the troops will march out right away, leaving the wagons to pack up and catch up with them. After the troops are over the next hill, we'll burn the wagons to the ground, and then ride like the wind out of there," laughed Bell.

"All right, Robert!" added Josh as the other men whooped and hollered at the excitement of the plan. Finally, adventure was coming their way. Without even thinking about it, Josh had found himself caught up in the excitement of going into battle.

"Let's get moving. We need a good night's rest so that we can ride hard and fast in the morning. Let's go," yelled the captain. The weary squad's energy had suddenly been restored, as they bolted after their trusted leader.

The troop of Pennsylvania blue coats had been trained in the basics but little else. Like most troops, North and South alike, they had been rushed into service, and there just wasn't time to teach a recruit everything he needed to know. Most learned daily, if they weren't killed before gaining valuable experience. There were sentries posted all about the camp. Bell awakened his men at four in the morning, and then carefully they rode their horses as close to the camp as they could without being detected. Skeeter was ordered to move up where the captain figured the soldiers would march in the morning. Skeeter had also been told to carry a shaving mirror.

The element of surprise was the key to their success. Bell drilled this into his squad over and over the night before. They were to hide in a thicket of bushes just a half-mile from the camp. At precisely five in the morning, the cooks stoked the fires, and began heating pots of hot coffee. At half past the hour, the bugles sounded revile and the exhausted soldiers were aroused from their warm bedrolls. They quickly dressed, relieved themselves in the woods, and then assembled for a quick cup of coffee and a cold biscuit.

Six o'clock saw sunrise and they were already moving out. Led by their commander, they marched out of the camp, and in the direction of the briar thicket where Skeeter was hidden. The remaining soldiers began striking the tents and packing them away in wagons while the cooks began putting away their gear. Josh was surprised to find a number of Negro men serving in the work detail. They looked and acted no differently than the slaves he saw down south. A rope line had been placed between two trees where the wagon horses had been tied off. The sentries guarding them had marched off with the rest of the troops. Josh and Bell crept slowly through the brush, and then cautiously they cut the restraining line, flapping their hats silently through the air to encourage the horses to simply wander off. Not one of the busy workers noticed what was quietly happening around them.

When Bell and Josh reached their hiding place, Bell lifted his field glasses and studied the column leaving the camp, and then moved his glasses off to the left until he spotted Skeeter's head in the briar thicket. He could not tell through the field glasses, but Skeeter's position was very close to where the troops were heading, and his heart was thumping hard. It was still a cool morning, but drops of nervous sweat trickled down his face. It took nearly a half hour before the last of the soldiers moved past Skeeter, and began climbing up and over a small hill. Bell watched Skeeter intently. When the last man disappeared over the hill, Skeeter took the mirror, caught a bit of the sun, and flashed it toward Bell and their squad. Their "all clear" signal had now been transmitted. Skeeter retrieved his mirror and began working his way back to his horse.

Bell studied the camp once more with his field glasses, and noted that not one single person appeared to be armed. However, he did note the stack of rifles leaning against the second wagon. "Josh, you're the fastest rider of the bunch. I want you to set fire to the first two wagons and then be sure to scatter the rifles leaning against that second one. If a soldier makes a move for those guns, you'll have to stop him. Keep your pistol handy. I don't think we'll have to kill anybody, but don't take any chances. Better them than us. Now you two men take the next group of wagons. I'll take these..." Bell continued giving them their instructions. Each man carried a torch they prepared the night before.

"Remember, we're not Indians. No whooping and yelling to try and frighten off any evil spirits," he warned with a grin. "Ride fast and silent. If we're lucky, a few wagons will be burning before anyone knows we're here. Then scatter in every direction as you leave the camp. Don't stick around to watch them burn. Meet up on top of that hill," he added as he pointed to a ridge to the north of the camp. He continued whispering, "Okay, men, this is important. All our training and riding skills will be used in our first real skirmish. Our lives depend on the actions of our fellow soldiers. We can do this. I know we can. I'm counting on you. Let's go!"

The men quickly saddled up, holding the unlit torches in their right hands, and the reins of their horse in their left. They stowed their rifles and pistols away in preparation for a fast escape. The rookie soldiers were risking their lives, and counting on the surprise of the attack to save them. The captain waited for Skeeter to catch up, and then he nodded as he led off on a trot toward the camp with the rest of the squad fanning out left and right.

The camp workers were still busily packing and stowing the gear when the CSA squad topped the hill. Not one of the Yankees spotted Josh as he leaned down towards a campfire, and allowed his torch to burst into a blaze. A few seconds later, Josh set fire to the canvas of the first wagon with his torch. He spotted the rifles leaning against the second. He kicked his horse hard, causing Chess to bump into the rifles scattering them to the ground. Then the horse stepped on the guns bending and breaking wooden parts with her hooves while Josh tossed his torch into the second wagon.

"Hey!" yelled a Negro soldier off to Josh's right. The alarm spread through the camp, but it was too late. In a matter of seconds, every single wagon had been set on fire.

Josh spun his horse around and spotted the man running toward him. The morning light reflected on the knife the man held in his hand as he ran toward Josh. Josh pulled a pistol from his belt, took aim, and fired, shattering the man's wrist. The knife fell harmlessly to the ground. The man screamed out in pain. Josh turned back to see how the rest of his squad was coming. The mission had been a success. He kicked his horse and began sprinting for the trees.

Skeeter galloped alongside of him. "That was fun, huh?"

But before Josh could reply, a sudden crack pierced the air, the sound of a bullet whizzing through the air, and then abruptly they heard a harsh thump as the ball hit Skeeter in his right shoulder sending him sprawling from his horse to the ground. "Josh!" he screamed as he fell.

Josh turned back and caught a glimpse of Skeeter as his chin hit the ground. He tossed and rolled over into a heap. Josh jerked Chess around. He looked back at the camp and spotted a soldier with his smoking gun still aimed at them. Another soldier took aim beside him and fired. Josh hunkered down low behind Chess's head as he galloped back to Skeeter.

"Skeeter!" he called.

Skeeter was slightly dazed, but he was scared enough to get to his feet as Josh circled, and then leaned down to grab Skeeter's good arm. The soldier fired. The bullet screamed through the air just over Josh's head. Josh pulled hard, swung Skeeter up behind him, then kicked Chess fiercely, and guided her toward the tree line. Skeeter hung on as best as he could with his good left arm. Blood trickled down from the right one. His frightened horse trailed after them.

Josh pulled up to a halt once they were safely in the trees. He swung a leg over Chess's head and slid off the saddle. He helped Skeeter down. "Are you all right?" He looked up at the blood oozing from his friend's arm.

"Damn. Shot on the first engagement. What kind of luck is that?" bellowed Skeeter as he grimaced with pain.

"Let's take a look," said Josh as he unbuttoned Skeeter's shirt, and carefully pulled it away from the bloody wound.

"Well, I'll be. It went clean through the muscle and out the other side," said Skeeter.

"What muscle? I'd say it went through the fat of your arm," teased Josh. "Let me tie a bandage around it, then we'd better saddle up, and get the hell out of here. The Yankees are surely coming after us."

Josh tore off a piece of his shirt, and folded it over the wound. Then he tore another strip and tied it around the bandage tightly. He then walked over to Skeeter's horse, and walked her over to him.

"Can you ride?" asked Josh.

"I ain't staying' here!" laughed Skeeter. "Just get me on my horse, and I'll do the rest."

Josh helped him up, and then brought the reins to him. "I'll lead so that all your horse will have to do is follow. Okay?" asked Josh as he swung into the saddle, and glanced back at the Yankee soldiers running toward the tree line.

"I've been better. Let's go. I can smell 'em coming!"

Josh kicked his horse as they rode deeper and deeper into the woods, and then headed north to join up with the others.

Three days later, they were camping on the outskirts of Keyser, West Virginia. Josh had been sent alone into town to scout it out, and check for soldiers. He trotted Chess into town just like he was some field hand coming into town on a routine trip. He pulled up at the first storefront, a general merchandise store, and tied off his horse. He then shook the trail dust from his clothes, and began walking down the old wooden boardwalks. They creaked when he walked as if announcing his arrival.

The town seemed innocent enough with a few stray dogs wandering through the streets, some children chasing a ball in front of the town's barbershop, and there was even a church at the far end of town. Josh walked toward the train station. So far, he had not spotted a single soldier in the town, but as he stepped around the corner of the rail station, he almost ran into two of them going over some shipping papers. The two men stopped what they were doing, and gave him the once over.

"Excuse me," said Josh, doing his best to talk like Zeke instead of himself. "When's the next train?"

The sergeant listened, but said nothing at first, and then asked, "Heading north or south?"

"North, to Pittsburgh," replied Josh quickly. "I'm going to work with my uncle. He's got a job for me," he lied with hopeful gleam to his face.

"Oh, where you from?" asked the sergeant a bit skeptical.

"Charleston," replied Josh as he watched their eyes enlarge just a bit. He always liked playing with folk's minds. "Charleston, West Virginia."

The two soldiers let out an almost silent sigh of relief, as they believed what Josh was saying, and assumed he was a Northerner.

"The next train through here is heading east at about six o'clock. There won't be a northern train until eight tomorrow morning."

"That long? Well, guess I had better find something to eat," replied Josh in his charming good old boy voice. "Thanks for the help," replied Josh with a friendly nod and a tip of his hat.

The soldiers nodded back. "Try Rose's diner," called the younger man.

"Much obliged," grinned Josh as he threw a half salute to the soldier, and walked around the corner of the rail station. He pulled out his pocket watch, and checked the time. He had taken it after his father's death without asking his mother. It had once belonged to his grandfather. It was just eleven in the morning. He had plenty of time. He put the watch back in his inside coat pocket, spotted the sign for Rose's, and headed directly to it. He had not eaten a good, solid hot meal in weeks, and trail rations were not that good, even when they were hot. He was already sick of beans.

He had just about eaten half of a fried chicken when two banker types came into the restaurant for lunch. They sat down behind Josh and continued their conversation.

The first banker was short and fat with a tiny blond goatee on his chin. His head was bald and shiny. His head was so polished that Josh thought he could see his reflection. Their clothes were like the kind he used to wear to church on Sunday. They were clean and well pressed. They obviously had become rich and were proud of it.

"Alfred, everything is all set. Washington is sending the gold to Pittsburgh to pay for the cannons. I've made a bundle off this deal, and all I did was introduce the buyer to the seller, and then prepare shipment. I made a hundred thousand dollars in commission. What a day!"

"Harry, you're really something. I congratulate you, my friend. You're a smart one!"

Josh ate his last bites quickly, laid a coin down on the table, and immediately left the restaurant, heading for his horse. However, when he turned the corner, he discovered Chess was gone. His heart skipped a beat. He turned his head left and right, then to the rear, and still there was no sign of his horse. Had she been stolen?

He walked to where he had tied her off and began scratching his head. Just then, a boy of about twelve came around the corner. "Oh, hi, sir. Are you the owner of the red horse?"

"Yes. Have you seen her?" asked Josh quickly.

"Of course, I have. She was just standing there in the hot sun and seemed a bit thirsty, so I moved her around back. Come, I'll show you." The boy led Josh toward the back of the building.

Josh had begun to relax, assuming the nice boy had just meant to take care of his horse. "Son, you shouldn't mess with another man's horse without his permission. Some folks could call you a horse thief and hang you. However, don't worry. I know you didn't mean any harm, but you did scare me to..."

Josh turned the corner of the building while blindly looking down at the boy. He did not see the piece of board coming at him as it hit him on the side of his head. Josh was knocked to the ground in a daze, but still conscious. The board did not connect squarely with his head, and he received only a glancing blow.

"Hurry, and see what he has on him. I'll check the saddle bags," urged the boy of fourteen who had hit Josh. He dropped the board and walked over to where he tied Chess off. He was just pulling out the collar of his CSA uniform when the younger boy tugged at the watch. Josh suddenly got his wits about him and angrily grabbed the boy's wrist. He then sat up, took his pistol from his holster, and cocked it.

"Hold it right there, kid!" said Josh to the boy twisting at the coat of his uniform as he tried to pull it free from the saddlebag. Josh rubbed his head, and felt for blood. He would have a huge knot there in a few more minutes.

The boy instantly let go of the uniform and took off running. Josh struggled to his feet. His head was pounding. He still had hold of the boy's arm as the boy jerked left and right, trying to free himself.

"I ought to shoot you where you stand, you little thief!" he threatened.

"Please, sir. We meant no harm. We're just hungry."

"Stealing is not your answer. Work is." Josh holstered his gun, took two bits from his pocket, and gave it to the boy. "Go get yourself a good meal, and no more stealing."

The boy took off running without even a mutter of thanks. Josh shook his head and tried to clear his eyesight. He was still dizzy and seeing stars. He then stuffed the CSA uniform back into the saddlebag, climbed aboard Chess, and led the horse out of town before he got into any more trouble.

He had begun to like this job of spying and scouting. If it was all as easy as the past few days, this war might just be over before winter, he thought. Then he could join Zeke in St. Louis.

Captain Bell and the rest of the squad marveled at Josh's tale in the local town. Bell made the decision that carrying their CSA uniforms in their saddlebags was too much of a risk, and so in the evening campfire, they burned their new gray and red uniforms until there was nothing left. They even buried the metal buttons with the CSA imprint on them. Then they set about preparing a plan of attack on the train rolling out of Keyser the next morning, knowing that it was to be fully loaded with a gold shipment that would pay for thousands of cannons for the Yankees. They decided they not only had to stop the train, but they had to steal and hide the gold from the Union.

"How are we going to stop a train?" asked Skeeter.

"We could undo the ties from the track and let the train derail," suggested a man.

"That would stop the train only temporarily," replied Josh.

"If we could find a trestle," began Bell, "then we could not only stop the train today, but many more trains for months to come. That would put this rail line out of service."

"Good idea," added Josh, "but what about the gold? If the rail cars spill down a gorge, how are we to get the gold and get out of there?"

"I don't know, but the trestle is the best idea. Let's saddle up, make our way to the railroad, and follow it away from town until we find the first trestle," ordered Bell as he threw the rest of his coffee into the fire.

"Saddle up?" complained a protesting Skeeter. "We just unsaddled. I just ate and..."

"Skeeter, the train leaves at eight in the morning," he interrupted. "We have little time left as it is. We'll sleep tomorrow night."

"Yeah, I've heard that before. Most likely it'll be two nights from now," Skeeter complained.

"They'll chase us tomorrow night, but we'll be long gone as usual," added Bell as he began saddling his horse. "Come on. Hurry it up. Let's get it over with!"

They rode for several miles until they were just a half-mile from town. Captain Bell lifted his hand to halt the squad when he saw the light of the town up ahead. "Josh, did you see any kind of supply store in that town?"

Josh thought hard for a second until he remembered the general mercantile store he had tied Chess in front of. "Yes. You think they might have explosives."

"It's possible. There are a lot of mines in West Virginia."

"I'll go and see what we can borrow," grinned Josh.

"Good idea. Take one of the spare horses. I'll take the rest of the men and make our way down the tracks until we find a trestle. Join us there as soon as possible. In addition, Josh don't you get caught, okay? They'd hang you," warned Bell.

Skeeter reacted by putting his hand to his throat and gulping.

Josh grinned at Skeeter, "I'll be fine, Robert. Don't worry."

Josh rode down the road until he was just a hundred yards from the town. Carefully they walked their horses into town and pulled them around to the back of the supply store. Josh spotted a few soldiers hanging around the rail station, but other than that the town was deserted.

Josh gave the back door of the store a swift kick. Nothing happened. The door was stronger than he thought. He backed up a step or two, and then lunged forward, hitting the door hard with his right shoulder. The door instantly gave way. Josh and the door collided with the floor. Josh thought for sure the noise would have awakened a neighbor, but thankfully, no one stirred.

"Way to go, Johnson. You nearly woke the whole town up," whispered a chuckling Josh. He got to his feet and dusted himself off.

Josh stepped over the broken door into the darkened store. Josh checked every shelf but found nothing. Then Josh made his way into a storage closet near the back of the store. He struck a match so that he could see.

"Oh, my gosh, gunpowder!" he said aloud to no one. He put the match out, afraid he would blow himself from here to kingdom come.

Josh picked up two small barrels of gunpowder and went outside to tie them on the spare horse. Josh found a coil of timing fuse, and then brought out two more kegs of powder and tied them off as well.

Josh then propped the broken door up into the jamb so the break-in would not easily be discovered. The damage would be obvious in daylight, but in the dark, it looked like a closed door.

He quietly led Chess out of town, then saddled up, and rode down the railroad track pulling the supply horse.

The first trestle was farther than they had hoped. Josh did not reach the trestle until almost daybreak. Josh had ridden just under twenty miles when he found Captain Bell inspecting the trestle and the gorge below. It was not as deep as he hoped, but he was rather confident that if they blew the crossing up correctly, the engine and several more cars would make the trip to the bottom. The trestle would be destroyed.

Quickly, the captain busied himself with setting the charges. He was the only one experienced with explosives. Josh had watched his dad blow up a stump when he was little, and thought it was kind of fun though his ears had rung for hours afterwards. The captain had the men tie the small barrels around four key supports, and if their luck held, the loss of these supports plus the added weight of the engine would cause the whole trestle to collapse.

He then carefully measured thirty-second fuses, and forced the end of the fuse into the small slit he had made in the top of each barrel. Satisfied, he sent Josh and the rest of the men to the top of the ridge about a hundred yards away. He sent Skeeter and his mirror down the tracks to signal him when the train was coming. The captain took out three matches and waited beneath the trestle for the signal.

Josh and the rest of the men hid down behind some rocks on a hill overlooking both the track from town and the trestle. He retrieved his rifle and pulled out his watch to check the time. It was just after six. He estimated that if the train left on time, it would be at the trestle in just twenty-five minutes or so. The same trip had taken him nearly all night to complete on horseback. Trains were changing the world very rapidly, he thought.

It was six thirty the next time he checked his watch and still no sign of the train. Josh caught himself nodding off as the early morning sun began to evaporate the dew from his clothes.

Chess and the rest of the horses were tied up behind them in a heavy thicket of pine trees. Chess whinnied. Josh turned to see what she was upset about. He then heard a faint whistle. He turned back to the trestle and almost yelled out when the sparkle of Skeeter's mirror nearly blinded him. Skeeter kept flashing the mirror until the captain waved at him. Then Skeeter hustled back to his horse and began working his way to where Josh and the squad were hiding. From their hideaway, they could easily see the smoke billowing upwards from the rapidly approaching steam locomotive.

Josh had the captain's field glasses out as he stared intently at the bend in the tracks where the engine would soon appear. When he saw the engine, he quickly moved the glasses to the trestle. He expected to find the captain lighting the fuses, but to his astonishment, the captain had his hands in the air. What appeared to be a West Virginia farmer had a hunting rifle aimed at the captain's back.

"Someone's down there," exclaimed Josh.

"What we do? The train's coming!" said Skeeter as he ran up beside Josh.

Josh turned the glasses back to the train, and he noted the engine was covered with armed soldiers. This indeed had to be the gold shipment. "Hold this," said Josh as he handed the field glasses to Skeeter.

Josh took his rifle and carefully aimed at the man holding the gun on the captain. While squinting, he said to Skeeter, "Cock your rifle, and hand it to me as soon as I fire this one."

Skeeter did as requested, working slowly but carefully with only one good arm, but didn't understand why. Josh watched as the hunter led the captain from beneath the trestle. They were going to climb the bank to the railroad. Josh could hear the whistle of the train and the roar of the engine. The locomotive was but a few seconds from the railroad trestle.

Josh carefully timed his shot. The captain dipped a bit to climb the hill, and at that very second Josh pulled the trigger. The bullet raced by the captain's ear and struck the hunter's forehead. The man fell backwards, dead instantly. Josh regretted having to kill the hunter, but he knew he had no choice. The poor man's body tumbled backwards down the hill. The captain looked back in horror.

Josh leaned up and yelled, "Run, Robert! Run!"

Captain Bell turned back around and saw Josh waving at him. At that very same moment, several of the Yankee guards on the engine spotted Josh. They didn't know what to do so they sent word back to their lieutenant. Captain Bell began sprinting away from the trestle. Josh saw that the engine was now only fifty yards from the trestle.

He snatched Skeeter's rifle and took aim at the only exposed powder keg on the trestle, held his breath, and fired. The bullet hit the keg dead center, and instantly it exploded. Just as quickly, the barrel just to the other side of it exploded. Then the third barrel exploded, and blasted and broken timbers started falling into the water below. Josh and Skeeter stood up to watch the impending crash.

A soldier on the train pointed at Josh and Skeeter, but before they could take aim at them, the engine reached the trestle. Many timbers immediately cracked and popped. The captain was scrambling up the hill to get away. Suddenly, the trestle gave way like a stack of cards. The final charge exploded as the force of the engine hit it. Bodies flew from the descending engine and hit the ground in sickening, horrifying thuds. The engine plummeted down into the gorge, taking the rest of the cars with it. The engine plowed right through the remaining timbers. In less than a few seconds, the entire six-car train had careened over the side of the hill. The noise of the crash and explosions had been deafening, but almost as quickly as it had begun, it was over. A billow of smoke and dust silently rose up from the gorge. Josh and the rest of his soldiers stood there in near disbelief of what they had just witnessed.

The captain reached the hiding spot before turning and sitting down on a rock to rest while staring at the scene below. Not one of them had ever seen a train wreck, nor had they envisioned such an event. Surely there were no survivors, they thought. They had killed them all. Josh had killed them.

Josh handed Skeeter his rifle, and then turned away from the scene, doing his best to fight back an urge to vomit.

"Good shot, Josh," laughed Skeeter.

"You nearly took my ear off," said the captain.

"No, sir," replied Josh quickly and with a grin. "I deliberately aimed at least a half an inch away from your ear."

The entire squad stood there silently, until the captain started laughing. "Well, thank you for giving me at least that half inch! Well done, men. Let's go get the gold and get the hell out of here. This place will be swarming with troops like bees around a hive, and I'm afraid that swarm will be hunting us for quite a while."

They saddled up and rode down into the gorge. No one spoke as they worked their way from car to car and body to body. They searched every box or bag looking for the gold. When Josh got to the center car, he struggled to pull some broken timbers aside until he could get inside. He found a man with a broken neck lying over a large crate. He pulled the man aside and pried up a splintered section of the crate. A bag of gold spilled over and gold coins began rolling out of the crate.

"In here!" Josh yelled. "I found it!"

The other men quickly gathered at the window as Josh handed out bag after bag of the gold until they were all gone.

"Let's get out of here before someone spots us," ordered the captain as Josh leaped from the car to his horse. The men meandered their way down the gorge and then turned north. By evening, they were at least twenty miles away and planned to be up very early the next morning to put even more distance between them and the train wreck.

"What do we do with the gold?" asked Skeeter.

"I think we should bury it," replied the captain.

"Bury it?" asked Josh. "Why?"

"If any of us are caught, this is evidence they would need to tie the train wreck to us. They'd hang us for killing all those people. Also, if we're caught, they'd get the gold back, and that means more cannons and more of our people will die."

"Where?" asked Skeeter?

"Let's dig a fake grave," replied Josh quickly.

"A what?" laughed Skeeter?

"You're crazy," added another.

"No, wait a minute. I get it, Josh. Good thinking. No one would dig up a grave. People are too superstitious. Okay, let's get busy and get some shut-eye. We're riding at four," he warned. Collectively the entire squad sighed, and mumbled their disapproval at the early riding hour.

They dug the grave near a huge oak tree and as a special added touch, Josh carved a piece of wood to put up as a makeshift grave marker. The sign read, "D.G. Goldblum. Born 1822. Died 1862." They put stones over the freshly dug dirt and then raked the ground with branches, hoping to make the grave appear to have been there for quite a while. Then without even a look back at their work, they headed to the north.

FIFTEEN

Zeke spent a full week in Roanoke looking after the Hough family. He had grown quite fond of Betsy and her two children, but still it was not the same as his love for Josh. When he was alone he began to wonder if what happened between him and Josh was perhaps a schoolboy thing, something he had already outgrown, and perhaps, he hoped, he was not as different as his friends in Washington. Maybe he should just tag along with the Hough family, and perhaps even marry Betsy and move west with them.

He allowed the thoughts to run wildly through his head, but a decision like this could not be made in just a few days. No matter how hard he tried to force Josh from his mind, the memory of Josh would always return the very moment he closed his eyes. He dreamed about him during the night, and daydreamed about him when riding or walking alone.

He finally made a decision not to make a decision. They rested in Roanoke while the blacksmith checked all their horses and wagons very carefully. The rest had done them well. Satisfied, they were as prepared as they could be, they set out early the next morning for Radford, Virginia, a small mining town just a hundred and twenty-five miles southwest of Roanoke. The weather finally cleared, and the sun was shining brightly before they made even a mile from town. Zeke had an odd feeling coming over him as he pulled out of Roanoke. It was as if each step his horse took was taking him farther and farther away from Josh. Even though the sun was shining down on his back, a cold chill crept up his spine. He thought of Josh, and only Josh for the next ten miles.

Bell and his men had crossed over into Pennsylvania several days before, doing their best to stay out of sight of anyone, including civilians. They spotted several other small troop movements, but managed to avoid any conflict.

They had orders to head toward Chambersburg where there was a large encampment of Union soldiers. Bell decided to camp about ten miles West of Chambersburg and then he, Josh, and Skeeter took a ride closer to town.

When they spotted the town, Skeeter began to get a little nervous, as they were traveling directly into enemy territory in the middle of the day. His arm was stiff from his wound, but he had been lucky. The injury was not as bad as it could have been, and Josh had done a good job keeping it clean and well bandaged. Skeeter mentally tried to practice losing his Southern accent, but he knew it was next to impossible, and so he kept reminding himself to say as little as possible.

They pulled their horses up to the first hitching post they came to. "Josh, you head south down this street and keep your ears and eyes open for news of the troops. Skeeter, you head in the opposite direction. Meet back here in an hour," added Bell as he turned to head across town.

Josh scouted the southern part of town, but found no signs of Union soldiers. He then spotted a restaurant and remembered his good fortune the last time he had eaten in a restaurant, and recalled how good the food had been. He took off his hat as he stepped in from the dusty boardwalk, and nodded politely at an older woman who stood at a counter.

"One?" she asked.

"Yes please," smiled Josh. "By the window if I may," he added, hoping he could eat, listen, and watch all at the same time.

"By all means," replied the lady cordially. "Our special is roast beef today," she added with a smile.

Josh grinned. Beef was beyond his wildest dreams. "That sounds perfect."

"Roast beef it is," she replied and started to turn away, but added, "You don't sound like you're from around here."

Josh's heart skipped a beat as two men a couple of tables away turned to see who the waitress was talking to. "I'm not. I'm from Philadelphia," he lied. "I work for the railroad. I travel a good deal inspecting the rails and the trestles."

"Oh, that sounds interesting," she smiled.

"It's not. It's pretty boring following the tracks while constantly looking for problems."

"I see," she replied politely. "Well, I'll get your dinner. It'll be just a moment."

"Thank you, ma'am," he added, now quite relieved she was leaving without any more questions.

Josh turned back to the street and to his surprise a Union cavalry troop of twenty-five men was heading east into the town. They rode right past Josh as he counted them. He wondered where they were going and what they were up to. They looked like they had been riding hard. Their horses were drenched in sweat, and a thick layer of dust covered their boots.

"Here you go," said the waitress as she placed Josh's lunch in front of him.

Startled, Josh almost pulled his pistol, but seeing the food and her smile, he chuckled at himself. "Thank you. It looks very good."

"It is. I'm also the cook," she winked at him. "I see those darn Union troops are back."

Josh said to her, "Oh, they've been here before?"

"Yes, they're looking for some Rebel boys that are rumored to be in the area. I don't know why some Confederate trash would want to come way up here, but they say they spotted their campsite a few days ago, so I guess it's true. I shouldn't complain too much, though, as they eat dinner here a couple of times a week. Well, I'd better go and let you eat in peace."

"Thank you," added Josh between bites of food. He had almost left the table right then to run out to find Captain Bell, but he knew if he left a plate of uneaten beef on the table it would look suspicious. He ate as quickly as he could, then dropped a silver dollar on the table, and headed for the door.

He glanced down the street to the right and saw one of the Union soldiers coming his way, but the soldier had not seen him, as he was too busy tipping his hat to some of the town's prettier ladies. Josh stepped quickly down the street to the left. He spotted the captain on the far side of the street. Josh tilted his head toward their horses, the captain nodded, and then turned away. Josh kept walking while searching the area for Skeeter.

Josh was adjusting his saddle when the captain came up beside him pretending to check his horse as well.

"Did you see the soldiers?" asked Josh.

"Twenty-five, I reckon," replied the captain, "Wonder what they're up to?"

"They're looking for some Rebels who have been causing trouble in these parts. I understand they found a campsite a few days ago."

"Damn. We have to be more careful, and we sure as hell need to get out of here. Where's Skeeter?"

"He should be here shortly. The hour's almost up," replied Josh.

"I'll head back to the camp. You wait for Skeeter and then join us there. Stay out of trouble," ordered the captain.

"Will do," added Josh as he pulled at the tangles in his horse's mane, and watched the captain ride out.

The captain had been gone only about five minutes when Skeeter came around the corner looking pale as a ghost.

"You okay?" asked Josh as he swung into his saddle.

"There's a Yankee following me," replied Skeeter as he quickly saddled up.

"Let's get out of here, but don't gallop, just slowly trot out of town. Let's go," urged Josh as he pulled his horse's reins to the left.

Skeeter followed. The Yankee soldier came around the corner and saw Skeeter riding off. "Hey, wait! I want to ask you something."

Skeeter started to look back, but Josh spoke through his teeth to him. "Don't look back. Pretend you didn't hear him and just keep riding."

The soldier began running toward them. "Hey, wait, I said!"

Josh and Skeeter kept riding. The edge of town was but another hundred yards or so.

The soldier had to momentarily stop his pursuit as a wagon full of corn cut across the street. "Hey, wait!" he yelled once more.

"There's another one," nodded Skeeter to his left.

"It's a sergeant. Keep moving. We're almost out of here." Josh was praying with his eyes open, and at the same time watching carefully as they continued their way out of town.

The sergeant heard his soldier's voice and glanced down the street. He then looked at the two men who were leaving town. A frown crept over his face. He stepped into the street just twenty feet from Josh and Skeeter, and held up his hand as if directing traffic.

"Hold on, boys," said the sergeant, a man in his mid forties with a hint of gray over his ears and sharp blue eyes. He did not carry a rifle, but rather a pistol fastened to his waist, and a tarnished sword sheathed at his waist.

Josh surmised the man would never pass an inspection at his school, but as quickly as that thought flew through his mind, a second more terrifying one pushed its way deep into his brain. Were they about to be captured?

They could not pretend they didn't hear, so Josh just stared at the sergeant and tipped his hat, while forcing a slight smile. "How goes it?" he asked.

"I'm fine. One of my men seems to be chasing you," replied the sergeant.

"Oh?" replied Josh innocently.

"Where are you from?" asked the sergeant as he stepped in front of the two horses forcing Josh and Skeeter to come to a halt.

"We're from Philadelphia."

"That's a great city. I've stayed there before. What brings you to these parts?"

"The railroad," replied Josh while Skeeter's heart skipped another beat, as he could not think fast enough to come up with a good lie. "My partner and I are in charge of inspecting the rails and trestles."

The soldier who had been trailing Skeeter came up to the sergeant. "Sir, I just wanted to ask the man where he was from. He looked familiar to me."

"Well," replied the Sergeant. "Where are you from?" he asked of Skeeter.

Before Skeeter could reply, Josh broke in, "I told you. We're from Philadelphia."

"I want to hear him speak. Where you from, boy?" asked the now suspicious sergeant.

"Philadelphia," replied Skeeter quietly.

"Is that where you were born?" asked the sergeant not yet satisfied.

"Yep, my daddy was a blacksmith there for as far back as I can remember."

Josh almost grinned at the huge lie. "May we go now? We have..."

"Just hold your horses. Do you have any papers to identify yourself?" asked the sergeant.

Josh thought for a second and then replied with a smirk, "No, do you?"

The sergeant was taken aback by the question. He did not need papers. He was wearing a uniform that identified who he was. "Fair enough, you may go, but may I ask you one last question?"

"Sure, Sergeant, what is it?" asked Josh as he began adjusting his reins, preparing to ride on.

"If you work for the railroad, then why are you heading south, when the railroad is on the other side of town?"

Skeeter's heart stopped. Josh spit on the ground, giving him a moment to compose another whopper of a lie, "That's simple enough, Sergeant. The waitress in the restaurant, who served me the most wonderful roast beef, I might add, told me of a small lake about two miles north of here. She said the fish in that lake was as long as my arm. Sir, we've been working about twenty straight days, and I decided it was time for us to take an afternoon off and do a little fishing."

"I can't say I blame you for that," replied the sergeant swallowing the lie just like an unsuspecting fish might swallow a worm on a hook.

"You guys want to join us? She said the fish were plentiful."

"Naw, we've got work to do, too. Go along now. Hope you catch a bunch," added the sergeant.

Josh tipped his hat at the sergeant then kicked his horse just slightly, and soon he and Skeeter were out of sight of the town.

"Josh, you've got balls of steel. I couldn't believe you stood right there in front of the Yankees and told them some huge lies," chuckled Skeeter.

"You expected me to tell them the truth?"

"No, but when you told them we were going fishing, I just about choked when you asked them to join us. I nearly pissed in my pants!" laughed Skeeter.

"That, my friend, was a close one. You did well by telling them your daddy was a blacksmith. That added fact gave you some credibility."

"I wasn't lying about what he did, just where he did it," grinned Skeeter.

Josh chuckled, "Come on, let's ride." He kicked his horse a bit harder, and soon they were galloping at full speed toward their hidden campsite.

By nightfall, they were twenty miles closer to Harrisburg and twenty miles away from the sergeant and his men.

It had taken Zeke and the Hough family several days to make it to Radford, and another week to make it to Marion, Virginia. The countryside was beautiful, but the hilly and steep roads were nearly impossible. The wheels sunk deep into the mud holes, and the horses were forced to struggle to pull them upward and out of the large holes. By the time they reached Norton, they were tired and exhausted. They rested a few days, did a few repairs to the wagon, and let the horses rest and regain their strength. The locals told Zeke the ride to Hazard Kentucky would not be as bad, and from there, they could follow the Cumberland trail to Saint Louis.

However, Zeke's heart sank when they told him Saint Louis was still a good three-week ride away. He made it to the telegraph office and sent word to his folks that he was okay, and asked if they had heard from Josh. A reply came the next morning that they were fine, but no word from Josh. He was also shocked to learn that his middle brother, James, had run off and joined the army after fighting with his parents about it. Zeke was deeply saddened that his brother had now entered the war.

Zeke also sent a wire to Charleston, but there was no reply, and the telegraph operator told Zeke he had heard nothing from the South in quite a while.

Zeke returned to his hotel room and lay on the bed in the dark thinking and dreaming about Josh. He was not surprised to feel an erection swelling in his pants. He longed for Josh. He was worried for Josh, and now he worried about his brother James. He wondered just how long it would be before Josh made it to Saint Louis.

The ride to Saint Louis had taken more than a month. The weather had been awful most of the way. It had rained most days, and their journey seemed to be plagued with problems. One horse got sick, and they almost lost him. Zeke had to use his horse to help pull the wagon. By the time they got there, they were muddy, tired, weary, and exhausted.

They rested for about a week before Betsy was able to arrange to join a wagon train heading for Oklahoma. Zeke did all he could to help prepare them for their journey by replenishing their supplies, and repairing the wagon and tack for the horses.

The entire Hough family begged him to join them, and he was very tempted to say yes. He developed special feelings for the family and Betsy, but they were not the same feelings he had for Josh. He felt it was his duty to stay in Saint Louis and wait for a telegraph to come, or better yet, for Josh to show up. What a reunion that would be, he thought to himself as he stood in the dusty Saint Louis street waving a tearful farewell to Betsy and her children.

That night, for the first time in a long, long while, he felt completely alone in this strange western city. He did not know what to do. Will Josh ever come? He wondered. His dreams were of him and Josh running through the fields of Maine and making love in his bed.

By morning, he was the first into the telegraph office to attempt to send a wire to Charleston. He did so for the next several mornings, but always, there was no confirmation that the messages were getting through.

He marveled at the rapid taps the operator gave the big black key. "Is it hard learning to operate that?" asked Zeke of the telegraph operator.

John was in his late fifties, medium height, blue eyes that seemed even brighter by contrasting of John's solid white hair and white fluffy beard. John ate too much and got far too little exercise. He had a big stomach and fat cheeks. He was a friendly sort that liked most people he met.

"I'm sorry, we haven't really met, have we?" asked John. "I'm John Sebastian." He stuck his big hand across the counter.

"I'm Zeke Robertson," replied Zeke with a smile as he took hold of John's firm hand. "I'm pleased to meet you."

"Likewise, I'm sure, and to answer your question, no, it isn't hard to learn the key, but you must have an ear for it. Some people have it and some don't. It's almost like listening to music. Come around the counter. I'll show you," urged John as he motioned for Zeke to step through the swinging counter door.

John sat back down at his desk. "Do you see this chart? It has all the letters of the alphabet on it. Each letter is made up of dashes and dots. When you're first learning, you try to listen to each dash and dot separately, but if you keep doing that, you'll never get the speed up. What you listen for is the sound of a letter so that when you hear dashes and dots, you know in your brain what the letter is, and you can write it down quickly. Would you like to learn?"

"Me?" shrugged Zeke.

"Why not, what else have you got to do?" teased John.

"I guess you're right. Until I hear from my friend, I'm sort of stuck here."

"Saint Louis is a nice place to be stuck in. You'll like it here. Now let's see. Let's start with a few simple words. This is the word for stop. That's how people end a sentence. Let's practice it."

John and Zeke practiced far longer than both thought they might, but Zeke had a ear for music, and picked up words very quickly. John was impressed, and pleased with his new protégé.

Zeke and John soon became good friends. Zeke spent his next few days in John's office learning to operate the key. John offered to let Zeke stay in a spare room at his house. Zeke agreed, but only if he paid some rent. The rent John charged was far less than the hotel Zeke had been staying in, so he gladly moved in. It felt good to both of them to have some company. Zeke found a loose wallboard in the room behind his bed, and hid the bundle of cash he and Josh put together for their journey west.

It was only after staying in John's house a few days that Zeke realized that John was not married, and furthermore, there was nothing in the house that suggested he ever was. He then caught John staring at him after he had pulled his shirt off while preparing to take a bath.

That night while eating their dinner, Zeke suddenly blurted out an unexpected question, "John, we're friends right?"

"Of course we are. I wouldn't let just anyone stay here, you know." John finished devouring a chicken leg while reaching for another.

"There's something I've noticed about you. Are you a homosexual?"

John nearly swallowed the second chicken leg whole. He choked and started coughing. His face flushed red. Zeke quickly patted his back. "Are you all right? I'm sorry. I didn't mean to startle you. Here drink some water."

"Forget the water. Give me a shot of whiskey," replied John, his eyes watery and sweat dripping down his cheeks.

Zeke chuckled as he poured John another drink.

"What makes you think I'm a homo... homo...?"

Zeke sat back down, "Homosexual."

"Yeah, that's the word. What makes you..." began John, but Zeke cut him off.

"I've seen the way you look at me when I bend over, or when I pull my shirt off."

John's face flushed much like it did when he was child, and he was caught stealing cookies from the kitchen. "I see..." he replied, but still did not answer the question.

If Zeke and Josh hadn't visited the homosexual pub in Washington, and met so many other gay friends, Zeke would never had been so bold as to ask such a question of a new friend, and he might not have picked up on another man looking at his ass. However, if he was going to live here in John's house, he wanted no secrets kept between them.

"It's okay, if you are. I'm a homosexual. In fact, I'm in love with the Josh Johnson we keep sending the telegrams to. He is supposed to meet me here in Saint Louis. Are you okay?"

John eyes went wide as he took in just what Zeke announced, and then quickly took another gulp of the whiskey, wiped his face with his napkin, and stared intently at Zeke. "My dear boy, you have discovered what no else in this town has ever guessed. Yes, you're right. I am a homosexual. I just don't do anything about it."

"Good. I thought so. I am getting better at spotting one. I'm glad that's out of the way. So now we can talk freely from now on. So what do you mean when you say you don't do anything about it?"

"I mean, I've known since I was a teen that I was different, that I liked music, and that I liked boys. But I have always been and still am afraid to let anyone know."

"But what about love? Whom do you love?" asked Zeke.

"I have a tougher question: who loves me?" replied John sadly. "I'm fat, gray haired, and basically ugly. Who would love me?"

"You're being very critical of yourself," replied Zeke.

"You're very kind, but the truth is we must accept who we are and what we look like, if we're to have any peace in this world."

"I agree. Josh and I went to a homosexual pub in Washington and we learned..."

"Hold on. Hold on!" interrupted John. You went to a what?"

"A homosexual pub, a bar...a secret bar where guys from all over the city come together to socialize."

"My word, my word, I've never heard of such a thing."

"John, you must go some time. Perhaps you can take a vacation or something."

"You forget there's a war going on back there," nodded John while lifting his eyes at Zeke.

"Oh, yeah. I guess you're right. Anyhow, we met many male couples that had been together forever. It was so inspiring. Josh and I want to marry, and live happily ever after out west somewhere where we can be free."

"It sounds romantic. You really love Josh, don't you?"

"Yes I do, and it feels so good to say that out loud. I haven't been able to say it to him in many, many months. If he doesn't come soon, or I don't hear from him soon, I just don't know what I'll do."

"He'll come. I'm sure of it. I think this night is the perfect time for me to ask you a question that I've been thinking about for the past few days."

"What's that?" replied Zeke as he took another bite of his dinner.

"How would you like to work at the telegraph office?"

"You mean, run the key?"

"Precisely. You're learning very fast, and you certainly have the ear for it. I could stand getting out of the office now and then. With the war on, we need to run the office from sun up to sun down, seven days a week. I could pay you five dollars a day. Will you do it?"

"Yes, if you think I can do it," replied Zeke with a grin.

"Yes, I know you can do it. Now finish your supper before it gets cold. You can start first thing in the morning."

By the end of 1861, the first year of the war, Zeke had become very proficient in Morse code, and John felt he was even better at it than he was. However, he wasn't resentful, but rather as proud of Zeke's accomplishment as if he had been his own son. Zeke enlightened John quite a bit on homosexual life in Washington as their friendship developed.

During 1862, Zeke had taken the reports of the war that came over the wire to the local newspaper or to the fort just outside the edge of town. He hoped the war wouldn't last long, but to his dismay, it was continuing. He had been working late when the key began to clack and crackle with news of Grant's victory at Shiloh, and Farragut's capturing of New Orleans. Nevertheless, he was deeply saddened at McClellan's defeat in the Seven Day Battle, and was dumbfounded at the huge number of fatalities he had written down.

Zeke constantly feared his brother would be killed, and he hoped and prayed that both James and Josh would be safe. Twice a month he sent a wire to his parents asking about James, and asking if they heard from Josh. They always begged him to come home, but he refused to give up his wait for Josh in Saint Louis.

The war had dragged on for Josh as well. At first, it had been fun spying on the enemy, destroying supplies, and weapons, but increasingly they were forced to kill or be killed, and the number of men he had killed was soon forgotten. He had nightmares of being shot. His face had become lean and drawn. They didn't always eat well, and when they had good food, his appetite diminished. He had dropped twenty pounds and could not really afford to. His clothes hung loosely on his frame. He had grown a beard, as shaving in the forest had become too difficult and too time consuming. The weather had been harsh, especially the winter, but he had managed to take great care of his horse, his rifle, his pistol, and his sword. He felt that these four things were the tools that kept him alive. He guarded them carefully, never once letting another soldier hold his weapons or ride his horse. He always fed his horse before he fed himself.

Over the months, he and his friends traveled hundreds of miles. They carefully avoided contact with the enemy whenever possible. They destroyed what they could. In a recent skirmish, Josh had taken a bullet in his upper leg, but the new pointed bullet had gone completely through the flesh. However, it hurt like hell to ride, he was half afraid he might be left behind. So far, he had spent almost the entire war behind enemy lines. They read newspapers when they could get one, and did their best to keep up with all the battles and the politics.

Spies and couriers had not been able to get through, and so Captain Bell was forced to come up with his own orders. His first order was survival. He attempted nothing he did not feel would be a success. Even still, they had lost four men in the past year. Three were wounded in battle, and the fourth was thrown from his horse, and impaled on a fallen tree limb when a snake spooked his horse.

The three men received a fitting burial though it was north of the Mason Dixon line and their grave sign bore only their name. The last man had fallen from his horse while they were on the run from a Union cavalry troop, and they could not stop and retrieve his body. It haunted the men to leave a friend like that behind, but they had no choice if they, too, were to survive.

Josh sat in a restaurant and read a four day old newspaper account of how fellow Confederate ranger, John Mosby, attacked the Fairfax Court House, just a few miles from Washington and seized several important documents. Their biggest discovery had been the capture of Union General Edward Stoughton, who had been asleep when the attack occurred. The garrison general had been taken prisoner and sent far south.

For Josh, the few minutes of reading the newspaper were the last few minutes of peace he would experience for the next month. Captain Bell received reports of the Union army building their strength and stockpiling supplies near Chancellorsville. Bell and his men spent every night attacking and destroying every possible supply wagon going that way. By the time the actual battle began, Bell's group had killed over a hundred Yankees, and burned over twice that number of wagons.

Zeke had the shift on the telegraph key when the news of a battle came chattering in over the wire. Jackson had led his army in a successful defeat over the Union forces, but at a very heavy price. Over 12,000 Confederate boys had been killed, but the biggest loss for the Rebels was the loss of Jackson himself, killed not by a Yankee bullet, but a stray bullet fired accidentally by one of his own men. The triumphant victory could not have been celebrated as the war weary Southern soldiers were stung by the loss of such a respected general.

It was three days later that Zeke got the telegram that would change his life forever. He had been working all morning, handling all sorts of transactions, when a telegram from his father came over the wire.

"Son, please come home. Stop. Your brother James was killed at Chancellorsville. Stop. Will you come to his funeral? Stop. Your loving father. Stop."

The tears fell from Zeke's eyes to the pad he was writing on. It was a gut wrenching telegram that he had had no time to prepare for.

"What's the matter?" asked John as he turned from his desk to find Zeke sobbing at the key.

"My..." he choked, "my...brother is dead. He died at Chancellorsville."

"Oh, dear, I'm so sorry," added John as he walked over and put his arms around Zeke's shoulders and comforted him.

"I must head home for the funeral. My family needs me."

"Of course you must. There's a train today, as a matter of fact." John slipped his pocket watch from vest. "Oh, dear me, it leaves in a half hour. You'd better run and pack."

"But what about your office? Who will help you?" asked Zeke as he stood up to leave.

"I'll be fine. I ran this office before you arrived, and I'll run it again. You take care of your family. Will you come back?" asked John quite hopeful.

"I suppose so. I fear that Josh will be killed too, but what else can I do." Zeke walked to the door dumbfounded, and then ran back to John and hugged him. "Thank you, John. Thank you for allowing me to stay and to work and, most of all, for being my friend."

"And I am grateful, too. You've inspired me. After the war, I'll vacation in Washington and look up your little pub. I'll have a hoot and a holler in that town!" he laughed.

Zeke laughed as well. "I'll wire you from home."

"I'll expect your wire. Be safe and be well. Goodbye."

"Goodbye, John. I'll miss you."

They hugged again, and then Zeke sprinted down the street to John's house to pack his things. He took a little money from the stash in the wall for his journey home. He then ran to the stable to pay the man to take care of his horse for a month, and raced to the train station to get a ticket. He had no sooner purchased the ticket than the usually late train came rolling into the rail station two minutes early.

Twenty minutes later, Zeke felt the train pick up speed as it began heading east, taking him far from Saint Louis, and perhaps even farther from Josh. He was, at least, heading closer to home.

SIXTEEN

Bell and his men knew their enemies were hunting them for a while after each successful mission, but Josh's news that there were cavalry soldiers specifically assigned to tracking the Rebel scouts, scared the living daylights out of his men. Bell knew he couldn't forget the purpose of their mission, but he reminded the men they killed soldiers that were trying to kill them, and yes, sometimes they had to take innocent lives. He prayed the killings saved the lives of thousands of Confederate soldiers, and perhaps even the lives of Union soldiers, too. He felt if the Yankees had no weapons, ammunition, or food to fight with, that they wouldn't fight, thus saving their own lives, too. While a bit idealistic wishing the Yankees wouldn't continue fighting without proper supplies, he still wanted to hope it was true. He knew the North possessed far more materials in storage that the South, and in time they would replace everything his men destroyed.

He always explained their objectives with many precautions in mind. Every planned attack included evasion routes, and other alternatives if required. They traveled mostly at night, and did their best to stay out of sight where possible. If they prevented the soldiers and civilians from seeing the scouts, it resulted in less chance of capture. When they grumbled and complained about constantly traveling at night, he reminded his men traveling in the dark kept them safe and alive. He forbade the use of their weapons unless absolutely essential, which meant if they stumbled upon a rattlesnake they couldn't shoot it, but were supposed to charm it to death, or so Josh teased.

Tonight's ride had been one of the hardest as the temperature hovered just above freezing, while a constant rain poured down on them. Josh was wet to the bone, and shivering constantly. He was sure ice was forming on the brim of his hat. He knew they didn't have to worry about snakes when the weather was this cold. No one said a word, as the exhausted, freezing soldiers trailed one another like the animals in a circus parade. The captain led them over hill after hill, across cold creeks and icy streams, until they climbed up and over the next mountain. By dawn, they were within sight of Harrisburg. They saw the lights of the city just before sunlight. Quickly they searched the terrain for a good place to hide, eat, rest, and sleep.

The team's new mission was an unusual one. They could take no credit for the success of their missions, as secrecy remained essential to their survival. For the past year and half, they attacked troops and supply trains as they headed south to join the war. They were fortunate as their guerilla tactics allowed the soldiers to sting the Yankees when and where they least expected it, and then, just as quickly, vanish in the dark. Targets were always at least fifty miles apart, sometimes hundreds of miles away, so traveling took most of their idle time. Now a habit, they watched their backs constantly, expecting the enemy to one day catch up with them. Even a cat only had nine lives, Josh reminded Skeeter one night around the fire.

They learned to hate the moon, although a partial moon provided enough light to see a trail, it also meant the enemy might see this far from home squad and come after them. A full moon made them feel like they were on stage in a theater. Sometimes, they stayed in the same place for three nights waiting on clouds to cover those big full moons. Though no moon meant safe travel from enemy binoculars, it required the men to totally trust their horses to stay on the trail, never knowing if the trail led directly to an enemy camp. Nevertheless, they preferred darkness to a full moon.

They always stole food, supplies, and ammunition usually just hours before an attack, so that once they hit the trail they stopped for nothing. So far, most of the attacks happen in out of the way areas with little or no civilian population, and limited army protection.

However, this time their orders called for the men to attack an iron foundry in the heart of Harrisburg, Pennsylvania. This place was far from what had become their home turf, almost two hundred miles farther north into the heart of Yankee country, and the chance of capture worried everyone. Bell and his men unsaddled just before dawn in a thicket just south of town. He posted two guards, instead of the usual one, hoping at least would remain alert. He sat down beside his men as they passed the heated coffee pot around. Breakfast became boringly simple. It was the very same thing they ate for the past two months. The hard dry biscuits were tough to chew, and even tougher to swallow, but if successful, the stomach rarely growled. Even a snarling stomach could give them away when they were crawling up close to the enemy just before an attack.

"This is going to be a tough one," began the captain, "as we'll lose the advantage of good tree cover, while attacking a factory inside that town." He pointed to Harrisburg. "I imagine this foundry will be well guarded, although I doubt they'd expect to find a Rebel soldier this far north."

"What in the hell are we doing this far north anyhow?" asked Skeeter, as he sipped on his hot cup of coffee and grimaced as he tried to swallow the bitter, sugarless brew.

"Good question," replied Bell, temporarily ignoring Skeeter's tone of voice. "One of the South's weakest points is the lack of ironworks to build cannons, muskets, rifles, pistols, or even swords. We'll soon run out of iron for shoes for our horses, and rims for our wagon wheels. We now have to buy them abroad, and ship them in at a much higher cost."

"If they can get by the blockades," added Josh.

"Right. We have to pay a high price to get these goods into the South while the Yankees simply pour more and more iron into their molds and make them far cheaper. They have several of these factories. This is one of their busiest. We must destroy it, or at least slow them down for a while. This mission, while a bit risky, could save hundreds of thousands of lives. Now do you understand the importance of our success?" asked Bell in such a way that not a single soldier dared dispute him. Skeeter caught Bell's look, and knew he had been out of line. He nodded approvingly.

"Let's rest a while, and then Josh and I will sneak into town and scout out the foundry. The rest of you must be on high alert and keep a careful eye out. If we're spotted, then the Yanks trailing us could close in quickly. If we alert the townspeople, they could either come after us, or set up a trap for us when we attack. I purposely traveled a long way in various streams these past few nights preventing an easy trail. I'm hoping the bloodhounds trailing us will think we've turned back south. They'd expect us to do so. Only a fool would head north like this, right?" he grinned. "So rest, stay out of sight, and when you wake, prepare your weapons for tonight's raid. We'll have a hard ride heading south after this is over. Be ready and take good care of your horses. Your lives depend on them."

They had heard his "be prepared" speech a hundred times, but not one of them failed to notice the intensity in Bell's eyes as he spoke this time. Josh swallowed hard at the thought of a possible trap being set for them. He had seen what a musket ball could do to a man's shoulder, and he wanted no part of the horrible pain that followed such wounds.

The captain and Josh slept but a few hours before rising and riding the final half-mile into the city of Harrisburg. Almost immediately upon leaving the woods and using the road, the traffic picked up. Farmers were hauling handpicked crops to town to sell. Traders hauled wagonloads of pots and pans, chairs and stools, wooden buckets and utensils, and a wide variety of other household items. Their wagons jingled and clinked in an almost musical fashion, Josh thought. They had spent their time traveling as silently as possible, as their lives depended on silence. They both thought these wagons seemed terribly loud.

Josh had grown a bit taller over the past twenty months. He was six feet three inches tall. His shoulders had broadened, and he had outgrown his boots at least twice. Had he been able to eat and rest regularly, he would easily have been the best escort at the debutante ball in Charleston in May. He was strong, but there was no bulk on his body. More than a hundred times, he had gone to bed hungry, with his body steadily burning up what little fat he had left. His face was lean and almost hollow. His eyes sunk inward hiding the sparkling blue that so captured Zeke's attention. He had also grown a beard out of necessity. Shaving and traveling at night didn't mix. His hair was longer too. He often doubted that his own mother would have recognized him. He was a soldier, a dirty one, he thought as he attempted to brush himself off and straighten his clothes up a bit.

"What are you doing?" asked the captain with a grin.

"I don't want to stick out in town. I want to blend in, and I can't do that if I look like a muskrat," replied Josh as he brushed out his beard with his fingers.

Bell chuckled, "That ain't going to change the smell on you."

"I know. I'll just stay down wind, as I used to do when I was hunting deer back home. Boy, I sure miss hunting game."

"I know what you mean. Maybe this little mission will help speed the war to an end."

"I hope so. Heads up!" He suddenly spoke a bit louder as he nodded ahead.

The captain glanced down the road and spotted three Union soldiers coming toward them. "Keep a cool head."

"No problem. I just hope to keep my head attached to my body," he added with a wink at the captain.

Bell smiled but his eyes remained focused on the soldiers. As they approached, he realized that two of them were very young, just seventeen, maybe eighteen. The leader was just the opposite. He was an old man—perhaps a retired officer. Josh took a deep breath as the threesome rode the last twenty-five yards toward them.

The captain reached up and tipped his hat at the soldiers while nodding at them. Josh nodded as well. He also prayed silently. They glanced in their direction, but only for a brief moment, and then kicked their horses and hurried on past. They obviously had other things on their minds. Josh looked back and soon the soldiers were around a bend and out of sight.

"That still makes me nervous," he said.

The captain sighed. "We were lucky. Let's hope our luck holds."

They topped a small incline in the road and suddenly, right below them, lay the town of Harrisburg. There were several large streets and on the far side, they could easily tell where the foundry was located due to the black smoke billowing from the huge coal fed furnaces that melted the iron.

"Bigger than I thought," remarked Josh.

"Bigger than I hoped," replied the captain. "Let's meet back here in an hour. Scout the town as usual, but be on your toes. Don't do anything that would draw attention. In addition, do your best to stay out of trouble. See if you can find out how many soldiers guard the town, and the security surrounding the foundry. Okay, let's go," urged the captain, his hands almost trembling with nervous anticipation.

Josh led his horse up to the very first hitching post in town, which was in front of a barbershop. He saw a Union soldier getting a shave, and he wished he, too, could slow down enough to shave. He attempted once more to brush the dust and dirt from his clothes before slowly walking down the street. Josh stepped around two kids playing Jacks, and then tipped his hat at a young lady carrying a newborn baby. He looked in the window of the general store, spotted two ladies looking at a bolt of cloth, and immediately thought of his mother. He knew she loved to design dresses, picking out everything herself. He glanced at an old man sitting by the potbelly stove chewing tobacco and shucking corn, and it remained him of his visit to Portland Maine.

The shelves of supplies brought back hundreds of memories leaving him in an almost dream-like state. As he turned to leave the store, he took a step without looking where he was going and bumped into a Union officer.

"What the hell!" said the officer, his folder of papers falling to the boardwalk?

"Oh, geez!" exclaimed Josh, and then quickly doing his best to control both his temper and his accent. "I'm so sorry, sir. Please, let me help you." Josh quickly bent down and began helping the man pick up his papers. Josh scanned the paperwork quickly, noting they looked very similar to the boat he and Zeke had worked on a few summers back during school break.

"You're not forgiven," replied the officer tersely, as he attempted to straighten the papers up. "Too bad you're not in the army. I would have you flogged for this." The officer paused, "Why aren't you in the army?"

Josh's mind raced for an answer. "I was going to sign up, but my father took sick and died, and my older brothers are already in the army. I was the only one left to care for my three sisters and my poor mother. I still hope to join the army, sir," added Josh for flattery.

"Very well, now get out of my way," ordered the officer as he took the papers Josh collected, stuffed them into the folder, and then stomped down the street.

Josh watched him long and hard while contemplating what he had just seen. He surmised the Union was about to build more boats that are ironclad, and apparently, this foundry was going to do the work. If they could blow up the place, the Yankees would not have cannons and muskets for a long while, and they wouldn't have any of the new metal boats to take on the South's navy. He assumed his old boss John Ericsson did the designs as they looked like his work.

Before heading down the street, he quickly turned to make sure he knew where he was heading, then winked at a little boy waiting for his mother to come out of the store, before hustling down the street.

He stopped into a restaurant and immediately ordered the lunch special, hoping for quick service. Josh spotted Yankee soldiers everywhere, and felt terrified of capture. He assumed he would shot by a firing squad or worst, hanged.

He ate silently, trying to listen intently to the conversations around him, but he heard nothing of use. He finished his meal, paid the nice lady that waited on him, and then meandered toward the foundry.

As he came closer to big plant, the traffic seemed to pick up. Wagons were rapidly coming or going, and civilians moved about briskly. He saw the workers as they left the foundry for their lunch. Black soot covered their faces and hands as if they were coal miners. He did not envy them at all. He was surprised to see many youngsters working in the foundry just like the adults. It made sense, since Lincoln drafted most of the labor force, leaving only younger boys and older men to work in the factories.

A six-foot high wall surrounded the foundry, but other than that, there were no guards, no troops patrolling, just workers scurrying about like ants after fallen breadcrumbs.

Josh wandered through the huge open gates along with the other workers and began making his way around the foundry. He saw huge rooms, the walls of which reflected a bright orange-red glow from the hot furnaces that melted the ore. He saw an area housing the big molds for the various cannon sizes, as well molds for rifle bores, and even steel bars perhaps for prison cells.

He wandered freely for nearly an hour before deciding to head back to the meet the captain. He began making his way to the gate. He quickly stepped to the side of the path as a wagonload of coal came towards him. The two horses were straining to pull the dead weight, and the driver angrily snapped his whip on their backs.

Suddenly, one of the horses attempted to rear, by side-stepping into a stack of wooden barrels. The barrels fell to the ground like cans of beans off a shelf. A large rolling barrel forced Josh onto the boardwalk. The driver cursed his horses and whipped them again.

The reeling horse broke free from the harness, and began to gallop down the crowded road. Pedestrians tried to scatter, but the horse bumped into one man sending him sprawling to the ground. The terrified horse stepped on another man, and still the frightened horse continued his attempt to run away.

The road ahead remained blocked with wagons and people, so the confused horse turned around and began running back toward his abandoned wagon, and in Josh's direction. The congested lunchtime crowd of civilians and workers tried to scatter quickly. Panic became chaos as everyone bumped into each other, and no one knew which way to run. Many were knocked to the ground. Josh saw the horse sprinting toward them as they quickly scrambled out of the way. He looked across the street and spotted a small boy carrying a mail pouch. The bewildered boy could not decide which way to run.

Josh called to him, "Run this way! Run!"

Just as the boy glanced up at Josh, a man tripped and bumped into the kid knocking him to the ground and into the path of the horse. The horse was but seconds from galloping right over the boy. Josh leaped over a fallen man, side stepped a spinning barrel, and snatched the kid out of the way just as the horse charged past. Josh and the boy crashed into the dirt, and into the feet of others who were desperately trying to get out of the way.

In less than a second, Josh went from being anonymous to the focal point of all who witnessed his feat of bravery. A cheer went up from the crowd. Josh lifted the grateful boy to his feet. He smiled and thanked Josh. Josh smiled at him as a man stepped up beside him.

"Let me help you up," said the man as he stretched out his hand to Josh.

Josh took the man's hand and pulled himself to his feet. Their eyes met. Josh instantly knew he had seen the man before. He glanced back to the boy, and patted him on the head, hoping the man did not recognize him.

"My name is John Ericsson. That was a fine feat, sir. You saved that boy's life," he said as he offered his hand to Josh to shake.

To Josh's astonishment, this was the very same man that Zeke and Josh met and worked for on the docks in Washington. If he had not recognized Josh then the accent would certainly give him away. Josh reluctantly stuck out his hand while hoping the shipbuilder did not recognize him.

The crowd swarmed around him patting him on the back. Another man lifted the little boy into the air, and, given the chance, the crowd would have lifted Josh up as well, but he politely smiled, nodded at everyone, and quickly began working his way through the crowd and towards the gate.

Just as he rounded the bend and spotted the gate, he also noticed a Union group of about twenty-five soldiers marching in. Their clean, well-shaven faces and tidy uniforms made it obvious they were fresh from training and had not yet seen battle.

Josh turned away, afraid that he would be spotted and shot on the spot. As soon as they passed, he joined the waiting line of people trying to head out of the foundry area. He worked his way down the busy streets, and soon found the captain waiting near his horse. Together, they rode out of town. He told the captain about the plans he saw for the ironclads, and running into the man that designed the first one. He surmised they were making molds to build more of these new boats. The captain looked at him in total amazement as to how Josh found all this out in less than an hour while all he found was the location of a small attachment of soldiers.

By two o'clock, the captain and Josh had explained all they saw to the rest of the men. Josh had drawn a map of the foundry buildings in the dirt by the fire. The captain gave them details of the city streets.

"Sir, I know we have to stop this foundry from building cannons and muskets, but they're planning to build more ironclads. I wish I could have stolen the plans. Then we'd have a chance to see what kind of boats they are going to build."

"Very good, Josh. This is all the more reason for us to blow this place up," he paused for a moment and looked at each of his men. "All right we'll break up into pairs and climb over the wall at two this morning. By then everyone in town will be asleep, especially the guards. At precisely two thirty, we'll set off the dynamite with a long fuse. We'll escape over the wall before it explodes, and then ride as fast as we can to the south. I learned from a shopkeeper that there is an inn about ten miles south of the town. It's called the King Charles. If anyone is lost or separated, then meet us there. If they suspect it a rebel scouting squad, they will come after us with a large force. We'll immediately head south, galloping as hard as we can, and in a week or so, we'll reach Richmond and wait for further orders. Be careful, lads. This won't be easy, but we can do it. We can do it because we have to. Our families and fellow soldiers are counting on us."

They slept until midnight and then carefully packed up, checked their weapons, and silently followed the captain out of the thicket and onto the road. They walked their horses hoping to stay as quiet as possible. On the edge of town, they split up. The men could find their way by the glow of the big furnaces on the far side of the town.

Josh and Skeeter leaned against the wall while carefully watching the two sentries at the front gate. The bored men paced awkwardly back and forth, rubbing their eyes, yawning, and stretching, desperately fighting off sleep. Josh checked his pocket watch, and silently motioned for Skeeter to climb up and over the wall. Josh followed him as well with a satchel of dynamite.

Once on the ground, Josh made his way back to the biggest furnace room of all, not far from where he saved the little boy's life. The once crowded streets were now empty. He glanced left and right and together, they ran to the shadows on the far side.

Josh leaned out from the alley and spotted a single man walking down the foundry street in their direction.

"Get down," he whispered as he and Skeeter crouched down in the shadows next to the building hoping the man didn't spot them.

However, the man appeared to be a civilian night watchman who could not care less about looking for Rebels. He walked by, never once glancing in their direction.

"Let's go," motioned Josh as they made their way down the street, pried open a window, and crawled in.

The size of the huge furnace left Skeeter standing in awe. Josh grabbed him.

"Hurry up. Let's go. We don't want to be standing here when the other charges go off."

Skeeter nodded and together they carefully took the dynamite out of the sack Skeeter carried over his shoulder. They silently made their way closer and closer to the furnace.

Even though there was no one tending the furnace, the fire continued burning inside, and the heat of the big fire made them sweat.

"Set 'em up here," urged Josh as he pointed at a big flat wall section of the furnace near the bottom.

Skeeter set the dynamite, while Josh prepared a fuse and pushed the end of it into the center of one of the sticks of dynamite, then pushed that stick into the center of the others.

"This place is so hot, I'm afraid this powder will go off before we get outside," complained Skeeter.

Josh pulled his father's watch from his pocket and checked the time. It was 2:27 a.m. They had three minutes to make it to the wall, and he knew the fuse was just about three minutes long. He struck a match on the wall of the big furnace.

"Let's get out of here!" urged Josh as he pushed Skeeter toward the window.

They trotted quickly toward the window. Skeeter leaned up to climb out and immediately ducked his head back down.

"What's the matter?" whispered Josh.

"The guard is just across the street," replied Skeeter quietly, his face flushed with excitement.

"What's he doing?"

Skeeter leaned up carefully and took another peek. "Damn! He's taking a leak."

Josh glanced back at the furnace. He could see the smoke billowing up from the burning fuse. He checked his watch. "We've got two minutes before this place is going to explode."

Josh leaned up cautiously. The man was just finishing his pee and now adjusting his pants. The man suddenly turned in their direction as if he had heard them. Josh ducked down quickly while putting his finger to his lips.

The guard felt sure that he saw something, and walked toward the window. The seconds ticked by. Josh's mind began searching for solutions. Skeeter's heart was racing as he looked back at the furnace and gulped.

The guard walked up the boardwalk just outside the window where they were hiding. They could hear his boots scuffle on the rough flooring. Josh checked his watch. They had less than a minute.

The man turned around with his back to the window as he glanced up and down the street, listening carefully. Josh carefully leaned up and saw the man outside the window. He placed the watch back in his pocket. He then rolled his eyes at Skeeter as if to say, "Here goes nothing," and then took a step or two back, pulled his knife from his waist belt, and then ran and dove through the window, crashing into the man as he turned toward him. The two men went sprawling to the ground with Skeeter coming out of the window right behind Josh.

"What the hell?" protested the guard?

But Josh could not let him talk as he suddenly stuck the knife five inches under the man's heart and pulled upwards, silencing him instantly.

"Let's go!" whispered Skeeter, but as Josh turned to get up, the dynamite went off, knocking them both to the ground as debris and wood splinters exploded all around them. A huge fire erupted, sending flames a hundred or more feet into the air.

"Run!" yelled Josh as he struggled to his feet.

Josh and Skeeter sheltered their heads from the falling debris as they cut down the alleyways, making their way back to the wall as other similar explosions went off all around the foundry. Josh got to the wall first and leaped up to the top of it.

"Hurry, Skeeter," he called as he reached down to help him up.

One of the guards at the gate spotted them. "Halt," he yelled before he fired at them. Just as Skeeter took Josh's hand, still needing assistance because of the wound to his shoulder, a bullet entered the back of Skeeter's skull and exploded out the front. Flying blood, bone, and brain matter speckled Josh's face as he let go of Skeeter's hand.

Skeeter fell back to the ground dead. If Josh did not know who it was, he never would have been able to determine it. He no longer had an identifiable face.

"Skeeter!" screamed Josh. The other guard fired, but missed Josh as the bullet ricocheted off the wall. Josh knew his friend was dead. Josh angrily pulled his pistol and fired back at the guard, killing the man that had shot Skeeter. He then rolled off the wall to the ground on the outside of the foundry.

Josh leaped to his feet as the townspeople began throwing open their windows to see what the commotion was all about. Josh ran to where he and Skeeter tied their horses. He swung his legs over his saddle while kicking his horse at the same time.

He darted out of the alley and headed directly toward a Union soldier running towards him carrying a rifle. The man tried to lift his gun to fire, but Josh kicked Chess into him, and knocked the man into a wall, knocking the breath from him. Josh did not look back, but quickly pulled his horse hard to the right heading south for freedom.

Another man came out of a storefront carrying a gun. Josh did not fire at him though he had his pistol his hand. He knew the man was probably a civilian, and so he kicked his horse once more as hard as he could and rode on.

Behind him, the succeeding explosions brightly illuminated the night sky. The fires quickly became out of control as the entire foundry began burning from the intense heat. Everything in the city appeared as bright as day, leaving very few places the captain and his men could hide. The soldiers killed two more Rebels trying to leave the foundry. The captain made it over the wall, but his was the longest ride of all, as he was on the north side of town. They shot his partner in the back as they climbed aboard their horses. Union soldiers were in a complete panic, firing at anything that moved. Someone yelled, "Rebels!" and even more volleys of bullets hit the walls and windows around the captain as he galloped through town.

Two other men made it to the south road first. Josh could see the edge of town, and did his best to avoid the pedestrians now scurrying about town trying to see what had happen. He reached the last row of buildings and immediately spotted a squad of Union soldiers running toward him. He had no time to change course. There was nowhere else to go. He was galloping far too fast to even think of stopping. He had already committed himself. There was no turning back. The lead man stuck up his hand and shouted, "Halt!" Josh ignored the Yankee. He pushed his pistol into his belt, ducked down low over his horse's head, and kicked him hard. "Hee-yah!" he yelled into Chess's ear.

The men had to dive out of the way to avoid a collision with Josh and his fleeing horse. Josh was fifty yards away by the time they got to their feet. The sergeant yelled for them to fire at Josh. They snatched up their guns and quickly took aim at the rapidly moving target. The first shot went high over Josh's head. The second grazed his arm, tearing his jacket.

However, the third shot caught him in the upper right shoulder, nearly knocking him to the ground. Josh gasped as the pain hit his brain. He fought with all his strength to stay mounted, knowing they would capture him if he fell. His heart was racing as fast as his horse galloped. Blood splattered off his shirt onto his saddle. His right arm felt useless and numb. He clung to the horse's mane with a tightly clenched fist, determined to stay on his horse. He also gripped her tightly with his legs to guide her.

He galloped out of town and away from melee that now overwhelmed the once sleepy town of Harrisburg. Bell's squad had been successful in their mission, but they paid a very heavy price. They killed all but four of the men.

Josh made it to the inn where he found the other two soldiers waiting. He stopped his horse successfully, but when he tried to climb off, he collapsed into the men's arms and passed out.

SEVENTEEN

They delayed Zeke's train in Columbus Ohio as a Rebel cavalry force had broken through the line and destroyed part of the railroad just east of there. In every town, he quickly purchased a newspaper, and began anxiously reading the accounts of the war. He read off the names of the Confederate generals and wondered if one day he would find Josh's name set in type. On the long layover in Columbus, he talked the railroad telegraph operator into personally allowing him to key a note to John about his journey. He sent a second message to his parents to let them know the reason for his delay, and his current location. Finally, he attempted once more to send a wire to Charleston, but again told that nothing was getting through.

When he reached Harrisburg, Pennsylvania, he was appalled to find the town in complete disarray. He learned that just that before dawn that morning a small Rebel force attacked the local foundry, destroying all but one of the furnaces. The remaining furnace received heavily damaged and mostly likely out of commission for months.

Zeke took a seat in the restaurant just a block from the rail station and ordered supper. He refolded his newspaper so that he could read while he ate. The reporter called the loss of the foundry a major blow to the war effort. Thousands of orders for cannons and muskets would move west to another foundry. This would be a huge loss to the economy of Harrisburg, and to the war effort.

Zeke stopped reading and took a bite of out of his large biscuit while glancing around the room at the other dinner guests. There was a man standing in the foyer that caught his eye. He put the biscuit back on his plate and continued staring at the man. Zeke wasn't completely sure, but he was pretty sure he knew the man. He stood up, wiped his face with his napkin, and began walking toward the stranger.

"Excuse me, sir, but aren't you John Ericsson?" asked Zeke, now sure, he was John, but not quite believing Ericsson was in Harrisburg.

"Why, yes, I am," replied John as he stuck out his hand to the stranger. Zeke instantly recognized his voice.

"I'm Zeke Robertson. Josh and I worked for you during a summer break on the docks in Washington."

Recognition came over John's face as he broke into a huge grin. "Oh my, yes. Yes, I remember now. You've grown a lot since then," replied John as he gave Zeke's shoulder a slight pat.

"Yes, sir, I have. Would you care to join me for dinner?" asked Zeke politely.

"There don't seem to be any more tables. The food must be good here."

"Yes, sir, I can testify to that. Come on. Sit at my table," urged Zeke extending his hand as a gesture for John to walk in front of him.

"I'd be happy to, my young friend. You're most kind."

After they sat down and John ordered his dinner, the talk immediately turned to what had happened in Harrisburg.

"This is confidential, Zeke, but I was here to help design a large quantity of metal plates to build more ironclads for the war effort. We were to cast the first of my new designs this very morning, but somehow the Rebels got wind of our plans, and they attacked and destroyed almost the entire foundry. Tomorrow, I head for Pittsburgh and will attempt to do the same there. The really bad news is that even if I can get the metal that I need, getting the finished iron back by rail to Washington will be quite a task."

"I know what you mean. I was just coming from Saint Louis, via Columbus Ohio. The railroads are in bad shape. The Rebels seem to know that if they can slow the North's industry, they can win the war," added Zeke.

"Yes, I'm afraid that's true. You know, I haven't really been in your country long enough to form an opinion or even to choose sides. I think slavery is unfair, but killing your fellow countrymen over such a thing is even more terrible. There must be a better way. There has to be. My goal in this war is to simply stay focused on building my designs."

"I wish for a better way and end to the war, too. There's been talk of abolishing slavery for as long as I can remember. It just never seems to happen and now this war," Zeke paused and swallowed hard, holding back tears, "My brother was killed recently. He was a Union soldier."

"Oh, I am so very sorry," began John. "Where are you going?"

"I've been in Saint Louis since the school closed waiting on Josh. He went back to South Carolina after the school closed to visit his family, and then he was supposed to meet me in Saint Louis. That was almost two years ago, and he never showed. I'm afraid the war caught up with him. I'm heading home to Maine. I'll be too late for my brother's funeral, but it was time for me to see the family anyway. I've been gone a long time."

"Ah, yes, you should. Family is most important. I have my dear wife with me in Washington, but I miss my family and friends in Sweden very much. However, I have such amazing opportunities to work, build, and develop my ideas in your country. You should come to work for me once again."

"Work? What are you doing?" asked Zeke.

"I've designed several new boats and the Union is paying me to build them. I get whatever materials and supplies I want. I have a hundred men working right this very minute in Washington. Go home. See your family, and then come to Washington and work for me. You'll be doing your country a favor, and you'll be doing me a great honor."

Zeke blushed at the flattery, "I don't know. It would be a great honor to work with you again, and I do want to be an engineer some day."

"There you go then. You shall work alongside me and learn the trade. Engineering is the future of civilization. We must build these boats, not just for war, but also for commerce and safe travel for all of America, and the world. Will you say yes?"

"I'll say, I'll think about it after I see my family, but more than likely, I will say yes."

John grinned and stuck out his hand to complete the deal. He shook Zeke's hand vigorously. "Very good—very good, indeed." He paused for a second, and said, "It is odd that we stumbled into each other at this exact time. Just yesterday, I thought I saw Josh at the foundry, only the man I saw was taller, skinny, and wore a thick beard. My eye sight must be failing me. Now eat your supper. It's getting cold. Enjoy, enjoy!" laughed John as he made his lunch order with the waitress.

Zeke didn't take another bite for almost a minute as the realization that John might have seen Josh finally sunk in. He wondered if Josh had anything to do with the foundry explosion, and if Josh might try to contact his family, if he was this far north. The possibilities consumed the rest of his journey.

"We must press onward," said the captain to his two men as they sat in a grove of trees not far from the inn where they met.

"Josh has lost a lot of blood. He's weak. He could die if we travel now," protested Billy.

Bell scanned his remaining men while thinking hard. He knew he made the right decision to blow up the foundry, at the cost of most of his men, but he also knew he had no choice but to keep moving. He spoke softly. "Soon this area will be swarming with soldiers looking for us. They've seen us. They know what most of us look like now. They are going to come after us with their hearts set on vicious reprisals and bloody vengeance. I don't think they would send us to a Union prison. I think they would string us up on the spot. I know Josh isn't doing very well, but if we stay, we could all die. We have to move on. Saddle up," he ordered.

"Shouldn't we at least wait for the sun to go down?" asked Henry.

"No time to waste. Let's get Josh in the saddle," ordered Bell as together they lifted Josh to his saddle. Josh grimaced with pain as they hoisted him to his saddle and put his boots into his stirrups for him. "Can you hold on, Josh?"

"I can hold on to the saddle horn with my left hand. Someone pull the reins for me. I'll stay on this horse if it's the last thing I do. Just get me out of here," stated Josh before gritting his teeth once more from the waves of pain shooting up his arm and through his shoulder.

"I'll pull your horse myself," replied the captain. "You just hang on. Think of other things. Doze if you must, try to dream, but please, stay on this horse."

"Billy, you ride ahead of us and watch for soldiers. If you see someone coming, take your hat off and stretch. That'll be the signal. They'll be looking for more than just one person. You can fake a Yankee accent better than the rest of us. You can fool them," ordered Bell.

"Yes, sir, no problem," replied Billy as he swung up into his saddle and took off.

"Henry, we'll follow Billy by about a couple of hundred yards. You keep your eyes on him and if you see him take that hat off, then we'll immediately dart off the road and hide in the woods until the soldiers pass. We have to head directly south, and get as far away from here as possible. Our mission is over. Home is now our only goal."

It had been another fast pep talk by the captain, but Henry had been too afraid to listen, and Billy had already ridden out of the camp. Josh was in too much pain to listen, but the sound of the captain's voice gave him encouragement. He had to hang on. That's all, he thought. Just hang on.

As the train rounded the final bend, Zeke knew the rail station would be just ahead. He suddenly realized that all his previous homecoming trips had been joyous occasions. Smiles and hugs would be waiting for him and he, too, would be smiling as well. Nevertheless, this time, his brother had died, and the family was still mourning their loss. Zeke did not know what to expect. He was very apprehensive.

The squeal of the train's brakes caused a shiver to go up his spine. He immediately spotted his father amongst the crowd waiting for passengers to arrive. He caught his father's eyes. The train came to a halt, so he jumped off, and began walking toward his father. Zeke stopped just a few feet from his father and looked intently at him.

"Welcome home, son. Welcome home." They were simple words and Zeke had heard them all very clearly. He interpreted them to mean,

"Welcome home, son. I love you." He knew his father had trouble saying he loved him, but nonetheless, he knew he did.

"It's good to be home, Dad. I missed you," replied Zeke, a bit bolder at showing his affection since meeting Josh.

His father gave him a slight smile, but no words would come. Finally, he muttered, "Let's go. Your mother is waiting."

They walked to the buggy. "How's she doing?" asked Zeke.

"She lost a son to this god-forsaken war. She's not doing well at all, but she'll recover."

Zeke noted the sudden harshness in his father's voice. "And how is Richard?"

"He'll be okay. He's young. He'll handle it. How was your trip?"

"It was long—very long. There were so many delays because of the war. The Rebels destroyed sections of rails and some bridges. However, when the tracks were good, we often had to be sidelined so that a supply train could get by. The war seems to consume everything and..."

"And everyone," finished his father, "I'm glad you're not in the war."

"People keep asking me if I'm going to join."

"Then tell them no, you're not. I've lost one son. I'll not lose another just to preserve Lincoln's blessed Union."

Zeke let the subject slip for now, but rather stared at the landscape surrounding his home as his father drove the buggy home. He had forgotten how beautiful Maine was. The rolling hills, the tall cliffs, but beyond the spectacular scenery, it was the smell of the salt air that lifted his spirits. He missed the sea far more than he had realized.

Richard spotted the buggy and leaped into the air with excitement. He ran into the house, called his mother, and then dashed out onto the porch. When the buggy rolled to a stop, Zeke jumped to the ground and leaped over the white fence. Richard scattered down the steps and into Zeke's arms. Zeke swung the little fellow around, and then put him down, while rubbing his knuckles playfully into his hair. Richard laughed and giggled—something he missed since the news of his brother's death reached them.

However, the moment of happiness came to a screeching halt the very second Zeke realized his mother was standing on the porch. He slowly set Richard down, and then one step at a time he began making his way to the porch. She tried to keep her pale face composed, but the eyes quickly filled with tears that now slid gently down her face.

"Oh, Zeke!" she exclaimed as she ran to his arms.

He held her tight. He did not know what to say. He did not know what to do. He squeezed her tightly and rested his chin on her neck. Allen came up beside his youngest son, reached down, took his hand, slowly they turned away and walked toward the buggy to retrieve Zeke's luggage.

"Oh, Mom, I'm sorry I missed the..." Zeke had begun to apologize for having missed the funeral.

However, Elizabeth would hear none of it, so she cut him off, "There's nothing for you to be sorry about. I'm so glad you're here. So very glad and thankful you are here. Come on inside. I've held dinner for you on the stove."

Zeke wanted to say he wasn't hungry, but he did not want to disappoint her. "Yes, ma'am," was all he could reply.

Captain Bell sat atop his horse overlooking a big valley below. He pulled his maps from his knapsack and studied them carefully. "Looks like Gettysburg is a few miles to our west and that means York is over there," he added while pointing southeast. "We'll camp outside York. I'll get us some supplies."

Billy and Henry were too weary to complain. They had been riding all but a few hours of the past forty-eight hours. Throughout their flight from Harrisburg, the captain only stopped when he thought the horses might die where they stood. Josh had grown weaker, and Bell noted how pale Josh's face had become. He hated himself for thinking it, but he knew that more than likely Josh would die.

After dark, Bell rode silently into town. York was a small town compared to Harrisburg and Baltimore. By ten o'clock most of the town's lights were off, and most of the residents were fast asleep.

Bell tied his horse up at the edge of town and walked down the back alleys until he found a mercantile shop. He pried off the lock on the back door and slipped in. He quickly found everything he needed, loaded it into a sack, and slipped out the back door.

As he turned to close the door, he heard a pistol hammer click and felt the cold steel barrel push into the back of his neck.

"Don't move. Don't move even a muscle or I'll blow your head off, mister," replied the voice.

Bell's mind searched for solutions. He guessed the person holding the pistol was probably a youngster because the voice had not fully changed its pitch. Nevertheless, it could have been a woman or a girl. He was shorter than Bell as the barrel poked him in an upward direction.

"I just needed some supplies. My wife's sick..." lied Bell. "I left cash on the counter and..."

"Shut your yapping. I'm taking you to the sheriff."

Bell determined it was indeed a teenage boy that held the gun on him. He tried once again to avoid the sheriff. "I can pay extra, but when I got to town they were closed and, well, I need this stuff badly. Here, let me get my wallet and pay you a bonus." Bell opened his coat, but instantly, he felt the barrel poke him a bit harder.

"Don't move, I said. I'll shoot you!" warned the stranger.

"But I didn't steal. The cash is over there. I just didn't know who to pay," protested Bell as stretched out his arm in the direction of the counter.

"Move to the alley. We're going to the jail," ordered the boy.

Bell took a step or two toward the alley, then ducked as he brought his left hand up to deflect the pistol from his direction, and then swung the bag of supplies around with his right knocking the boy's feet out from under him. The boy gasped, and pulled the trigger. The bullet whizzed just over Bell's left ear but missed him.

Bell grabbed the gun and tried to jerk it free from the boy's hand, but the boy pulled the trigger again slamming another bullet into the wooden wall behind them. Then Bell suddenly tripped on the bag of supplies, and fell face down onto the boy. The gun instantly fired.

Bell jumped back in horror. The boy's eyes went wide. His fingers fell from the pistol. His last breath escaped into the night. Bell had not meant to kill the boy. He just desperately needed to get away. This poor man was nothing more than a young boy, and he had killed him. Sorrow overwhelmed him. He heard footsteps coming his way. He snatched up his bag, took another last look at the innocent face of the teenage boy, and then darted down the alley and out to the edge of town.

By the time he reached his horse, he could hear screams and wailing as someone came upon the stricken boy. He bit his lip and kicked his horse.

"There he goes!" yelled a shopkeeper armed with a shotgun as he spotted Bell's horse fleeing from town.

The man fired. "I missed him!"

Another man ran up and fired, and then another until Bell topped a hill and was out of sight.

Bell gave a shout and galloped into their hiding place."Get Josh up and on his horse. We have to ride now. I was spotted in town, and had to kill a man," he lied. He had reluctantly killed a boy. "There will be a posse after us. We've got to hurry!" ordered frantic Bell.

Billy and Henry were very drowsy with sleep, but orders were orders and they were used to doing what the captain told them to do. They saddled up, put out the fire, and carefully lifted Josh to his horse.

The captain rummaged through his sack and found a loaf of bread. He broke off several hunks, and gave them to Billy and Henry. Then he rode up alongside Josh and pushed the bread into Josh's face. Josh took a few bites and then coughed. Bell gave him water. Josh took another bite and another sip. Bell ate the rest of the hunk of bread, took the reins for Josh's horse, and led them due south.

They rode all night and by dawn, they were on the opposite side of York than where the townspeople had seen Bell flee. They were now searching in the wrong direction for him. Confident now that there were twenty miles separating them and York, Bell made his way back out onto the road heading south, sending Billy up ahead to keep an eye out for trouble.

Two days later, they reached Reisterstown Maryland. Bell bought a few supplies in the town shops, not wishing to risk capture for stealing. He asked for directions and found out that Baltimore was due south, so he headed a bit west toward Frederick Maryland. From there, he felt he could cross the Potomac and be back in the South, and better yet, only about hundred miles from Richmond.

Outside Frederick, they camped at dawn preferring to travel by night again. Billy spotted troop movements up ahead, and Bell feared they would be caught up in a great battle. Henry and Billy counted the wagons and the troops as taught, but this time, Bell planned no more attacks.

Josh dreamed throughout the day. He dreamed of his journey to Maine and holding Zeke in his arms for the very first time. He dreamed of their first kiss. In his mind, he could see his hands caressing Zeke's soft flesh. Bell woke every hour or so and poured water down Josh's throat. Once a day, he checked the wound. Luckily, the bullet went completely through, but the nasty hole it left behind had torn tendons, and damaged nerves that would be hard to heal. Josh still could not move his right arm. His fingers felt like they rested on pine needles.

Bell cleaned the wound as best he could with what he had, but he feared gangrene would set in and if so, Josh would die. When a limb was infected, they generally amputate it, but if Josh's chest and shoulder became infected, there would be no hope.

Two days later, at four in the morning, Bell carefully walked his way to edge of the Potomac. The area was swarming with Yankee patrols. He walked up and down the river, searching for a good place to cross until finally he picked out what he felt was the best spot.

He had left Josh, Billy, and Henry in a stand of trees with his horse. Bell stepped on a twig that snapped as he approached their hideaway. Henry snapped his pistol toward Bell and nearly fired, but Billy recognized Bell in the shadows and pushed Henry's gun back down.

"Easy, Henry," whispered Bell. "We're almost home. The Potomac is just a few hundreds yards that way. However, we have to be careful. There's Yankees everywhere, but we can't wait for dawn, or they'll surely spot us. Our only chance is to cross under the cover of darkness. We'll walk our horses carefully and cross the river in silence. Not a word from anyone."

Bell leaned into Josh as he sat on his horse. "Can you make it, Josh? Virginia is just on the other side. We're almost home. Hang on," he urged.

Bell took the reins of Josh's horse in his left hand and his horse in his right, and began leading them to the river. On two occasions, they had to stop and wait while a group of five or more Yankees came down the road, but failed to see them.

Bell's horse smelled the river and neighed. Bell rubbed the horse's nose and tried to calm him down. They heard voices to their right. Billy's heart was pounding. Henry nearly wet his pants. Josh's eyes were open, but he could not move.

When they reached the water, Bell turned north until he found a longer section of riverbank he thought they could easily get down. He could not see the other side so he hoped they would be able to get out okay. They started down the hill.

"Halt!" exclaimed a sudden deep voice from a stand of bushes nearby. "Halt, I said!"

Bell pulled his pistol. Billy and Henry froze. Bell looked at the river then up at Josh. Josh winked at him. Bell took quick aim and fired, hitting the Yankee in the chest, knocking him to the ground.

"Let's go!" said Bell as he swung into his saddle. Billy and Henry saddled up as well.

Bell heard men rushing toward them through the trees. They were just seconds from a swarm of Yankees surrounding the exhausted men. He kicked his horse just as a second soldier standing over the sentry's dead body fired a shot. Bell swung around and fired, hitting the second man as well, then rapidly he turned back and darted into the water pulling Josh's horse behind him.

The river was swifter than he had hoped, and they had not gone far when the horses could no longer reach the bottom and began swimming. The horse instinctively started to turn and go back to shore, but Bell holstered his pistol, and pulled the reins harshly to steer his horse into the deeper water without letting go of Josh's reins. He then squeezed hard with his legs and forced the horse to cross. While swimming, their height lowered to just the chest out of the water, making a shot towards them far tougher.

Another shot fired. Bell turned to see Henry fall from his horse and into the river. Even in the darkness, Bell could see the pool of blood rapidly mixing with the water. Henry was gone.

The frightened Billy kicked his horse harder while drawing his pistol, turning, and firing at the man on shore who was trying to reload his rifle after killing Henry. Billy shot him in the right eye. It pleased him to get his revenge as the soldier fell into a heap.

"Hee-yah!" yelled Bell to his horse.

Other soldiers began firing at them. Bullets struck the water all around them, but the terrified horses continued swimming. Bell turned and fired several more shots, killing two more Yankees, and then turned back hoping they would soon reach the other side. Twenty more feet—just twenty more, he thought.

His horse's hoofs caught the mud and he rapidly began trying to struggle his way to shore. Bell felt the change in the horse's movement and kicked him onward, but the horse did not need any coaxing. The frightened animal was as anxious as its rider to get to shore.

More bullets flew all around them. They struck trees with a thud and sent showers of leaves. They shot Billy's hat from his head but he was unharmed. Josh, still slumped over on his horse, looked dead so no one seemed to take aim at him.

When they reached the shore, Bell let out a yell and charged up the bank, into the woods, and out of sight from the Yankees. Josh and Billy were right behind him, and for a brief moment, they all thought they were free and safe.

Bell's horse pushed through the bushes at a hard gallop not quite ready to stop as the Yankee bullets continued to zip their way through the trees around them.

"Halt!" yelled a sudden voice to his right.

Instinctively, Bell turned to face what he thought might be more Yankees and drew his pistol. The voice in the woods pulled the trigger. The lead ball screamed through the dark air like a missile. Billy saw the red fire ball leave the man's smoking gun and in a flash, it plummeted into Bell's left cheek just as Bell was yelling, "No!" The ball continued through bone before lodging into his brain. He instantly fell limp and flipped over the back of his horse to the ground never to move again. The reins of Josh's horse remained wound tightly around his fist. Seconds later, Bell died.

Billy did not know what to do. Soldiers aimed their rifles directly at him, and quickly surrounded him and Josh. Josh was still slumped over and unconscious.

"Drop your weapon and get off the horse," ordered a bearded man Billy could just barely see as the sun's glow began to change the sky from night to day.

A mist surrounded the soldier's head. Billy was terrified. Were they Yankees or Rebels? The sky grew a bit brighter as the bearded man checked to make sure Bell was dead.

Suddenly, Billy realized the man wore a Confederate uniform. "You're Rebels?" he exclaimed.

"Yes, of course, we are. You're in the South," replied the man as he stood back up to face Billy.

"Sir," replied Billy as he came to a weary attention. "I'm Billy Decker, sir—a proud member of the Confederate Army. That man, sir, is, I mean, was Captain Bell. We have fought behind the lines for almost two years, sir. We were heading back to Richmond. We've been on the run. There are only two of us left, sir. That's Josh Johnson. He's wounded in his shoulder."

"Rebels, you say? Do you have any proof that says you are who you say you are?"

"None, sir. We couldn't wear uniforms. We mixed in with the locals and then attacked at night. I'm sure there are some records of us somewhere. Nevertheless, sir, please help us. We're starving, and Josh may die if we don't get some help soon."

The bearded man was skeptical, but then again, the tale was too preposterous not to be true. "Get these men to our camp and get them fed. Get the surgeon up here on the double. There must be some truth to what you say because I watched you charge across the river and take out several Yankees at the same time."

EIGHTEEN

Zeke, home for almost three weeks, became restless as to what to do with his life, and more importantly, what to do about Josh. He felt sure that if Josh were alive, that somehow he would manage a word to him or his parents. In the two years since he last heard from him, he had not had one glimmer of hope, but still he did not want to give up. He sat atop the cliff overlooking the water on the very same rock that he and Josh sat on during Josh's last visit. He fixed his eyes towards the sea, while his mind replayed the vision of Josh's blond hair blowing in the stiff breeze.

It still amazed him that after only a few seconds of daydreaming about Josh, he would become aroused. It both delighted and angered him. He longed for Josh, but was also worried, frustrated, and confused. He blinked his eyes twice, trying desperately to force Josh from his mind, and focus on the problems that lay before him. He did not want to join the army, although many of his friends thought he should go and avenge his brother's death. Their pastor had said it was his duty to help free the slaves from their terrible bondage, but to fight would be to fight against Josh and his beliefs, and he just could not bear the thought of one day having to face Josh in battle. He also did not want to stay home as his mother encouraged him to do. He knew she would have him married off by Christmas. Although his father often alluded to what he expected of a Robertson boy, Zeke also did not want to go into the family shipyard business. His father had lost a son, but he still had Richard if he needed a son to run the family business.

It took another hour before he made his decision, and then abruptly he stood, threw a rock into the ocean, and then hiked back to town. Throwing the rock was a symbol of freedom, of taking a chance, of moving on, and, most importantly, a symbol of hope of a future.

At supper that night, he told his parents of his decision. "Mom? Dad? I have an announcement to make. I'm leaving tomorrow for Annapolis?"

His mother gasped. She brought her hands to her face. Tears began to swell up in her eyes. Her brow immediately wrinkled with worry lines, "You're joining the navy?"

"You're going where?" asked his father, putting down his fork and pushing his plate away from him, his appetite instantly gone.

"No. I'm not joining the navy. Do you remember that Josh and I worked for a ship engineer one summer in Washington? Well, I met him on the way home from Saint Louis, and he's designing and building many new boats for the Union. He's asked me to join him in Annapolis at a shipyard, and learn the engineering trade at his side. I'll be his apprentice. He's famous. It's the chance of a lifetime," continued Zeke with as much enthusiasm as he could muster, all the while knowing his parents were disappointed.

"I've already lost one son..." began his mother, but his father squeezed her hand gently, and pulled it towards him.

"Honey, Zeke's a man now and deserves to be treated with respect. I don't want him to go either, but he's like a bird that's grown too big for the nest. There comes a time when all birds must leave the nest or they won't survive. We can't keep a grown man cooped up like our chickens. At least he won't be in a uniform right, son?" His father winked at him.

It was the biggest sign of approval he had ever received from his father. Zeke beamed. He had not counted on his dad as an ally. "Right, Dad. Mom, I'll be safe. I'll be building boats, new ironclads. I won't be sailing away in them or fighting any battles. Heck, I don't even need a gun. I'll come away from the experience with a good trade, and practical experience that goes way beyond education."

His mother began sobbing, but smiled approvingly. "I guess you're right. You'll be missed."

"I know, Mom, but it's the right thing for me to do. I'll be able to come home from time to time. Let's see, I know I'll come home Christmas, and if you want, you can come see me in Washington."

"I don't think we'll be going anywhere near the war, son, but we'll certainly look forward to seeing you at Christmas," added his father.

"I can send you a wire from time to time to let you know how I'm doing. I'm a good telegraph operator."

"Then it's settled. When do you plan to leave?" asked his father.

Zeke grinned sheepishly, "On the morning train." He felt relieved he survived the announcement of his plans.

"Then you'd better finish your supper and get packing. Just let me know if there's anything you need."

"Thanks, Dad. Thanks, Mom. I love you both."

Billy had eaten everything the soldiers would give him, but soon felt it was time to get some sleep. Feeling safe, he pulled his boots off for the first time in over a month. His eyes focused on the piece of paper that fell out. His eyes lit up as he unfolded their orders. He gave it to the sentry watching him. The orders confirmed Josh and Billy's story, and immediately ordered them to come to Richmond as soon as Josh's condition stabilized.

Billy met General Lee on their second day there when Lee himself visited Josh's hospital bed. Everyone in the hospital was impressed that Lee had come to see Josh, but no one knew why or what he had done to deserve such attention. They probably never would. After a week's stay in Richmond, they allowed Billy to return home.

Josh's immense blood loss meant a lengthy recovery. He would continue to be weak until he began to eat more. A nurse by the name of Annie, a short red haired girl with a few tiny little freckles, which Josh had secretly counted while she fed him some chicken soup, was determined that the handsome Josh was going to get better. She had a bit of an Irish temper in her, but she had a huge dose of patience that kept it in check.

She had cut Josh's hair, and managed to shave his beard off though he protested throughout the entire ordeal. She fell in love with his blue eyes, and was ashamed that her heart pounded when she bathed him. He was just skin and bones as he lay there, but she knew there was potential behind those remarkable blue eyes.

She had taken care of him for more than a week before he finally spoke a few words. Until that time, he only grunted at her. The sound of his voice startled them both.

"How's my shoulder?" he asked boldly.

"'Tis good you're finally talking...you had some infection and the doctor was forced to cut away a bit more tissue, but it's doing much better. It's clean and healing," she replied.

"Why can't I move my arm?" he asked.

"The doctor says that several nerves and tendons were heavily damaged or scarred. He doesn't think you'll ever be able to...," she couldn't continue.

Josh chewed his lip at the news, and then he tightened the fist of his left hand before angrily slamming it into the bed sheets. "No!" he screamed and then passed out once more after the exertion. She knew he was still too weak and not alarmed. She hoped he slept well and healed quickly. He was much too handsome to just be lying around in the ward.

Washington was a maze of people, horses, wagons, and buggies all trying to get somewhere in a hurry, and there was absolutely no orderly way for them to do so. Chaos and confusion prevailed everywhere. On one corner, you'd find a pair of men selling guns to defend Washington from the Rebels, and on another corner, a man selling flowers, or a woman selling woven baskets. Zeke passed by a man with a big Bible standing on a box preaching as loudly as possible. Newspaper boys hawked their papers. Manufacturing salesmen from all over the world filled the city trying desperately to get the government to buy their products. There were shipping agents trying to fight their way through the crowds so the supplies purchased made it to the correct regiment on the front.

The soldiers reinforced the troops protecting the capital many times to prevent the city from falling into the hands of the Confederate armies. Windows on the south side remained boarded up, and everyone was encouraged to take precautions in case the Rebels attacked the capital. At the beginning of this War Between the States, whole families dressed up in their Sunday best clothes, packed a lunch, and rode out to enjoy a picnic overlooking a battlefield. It was a spectacle that soon turned ugly and personal, as families lost sons, brothers, fathers, or husbands. In time, what the public thought was a great adventure that would be over quickly, became the horror of defeat and death as wounded men roamed the streets of Washington with missing limbs, blinded eyes, and horrible ugly scars. Washington had lost the beauty that Josh and Zeke first experienced in their school days. She was now a city under pressure with Lincoln demanding it must survive at all costs. The cost of war had been much too high in blood and money, and so far, there was no end in sight.

Zeke wired Ericsson he would be coming to Washington, but he had deliberately allowed himself a night's visit with his old friends in Washington. He reached the tavern about ten o'clock, and pushed the door open. Immediately, heads turned his way, as Zeke was as handsome as ever, perhaps more so now that he had become an adult.

It took big Al a moment to recognize him, and then Al hurriedly made his way around the bar and gave Zeke a big hug. "How in the hell are you, my boy?"

"I'm fine, I guess. How are you?" asked Zeke while noting how good a manly hug felt, even from big old Al.

"I'm fine, but we've missed you and Josh. Where is Josh? Is he with you?"

"No, I'm afraid he's caught up in the war. We were trying to move west, but he never made it. I haven't seen him in two years now."

"I'm sorry to hear that. You were such a good couple. You two really loved each other, didn't you?"

Zeke choked and could not respond. The loss of Josh's love split him open like a sword. His eyes watered. Memories of their happy times in Washington flooded his brain. He politely nodded.

"Now where are my manners," began Al as he pushed Zeke to a table. "Let me get you something to eat, a cold beer, and we'll sit down and have a long chat."

In spite of the war, the homosexual bar filled up by midnight with many faces that Zeke had never seen before. Surprisingly, there were several soldiers now attending the evening festivities, and Zeke could not help but notice how good looking they were in their blue uniforms. One of the soldiers bought Zeke a beer, and asked Al to deliver it.

"It seems like you still have the charm, old friend. His name is Travis."

Zeke blushed but took a sip from the beer, and smiled as he nodded in Travis' direction. Not long after Al returned to the bar, Travis wandered over to Zeke's table. Zeke looked up and took a closer look at the soldier. He was handsome. He was about five feet eight inches tall with dark brown eyes, brown hair, and a few tiny freckles on a small nose. He had an infectious smile that made him even more attractive. He had dimples in his cheeks when he laughed, and a small, barely noticeable dimple in his chin.

"Hi, I'm Travis Lamsel."

Zeke stuck out his hand, "I'm Zeke Robertson. Thanks for the beer. Would you like to sit down?"

"I was hoping you'd ask." He sat down and then leaned across the table toward Zeke and lowered his voice, "Did I tell you that you are the most handsome man in this bar tonight?"

"No you didn't, but thanks anyhow," grinned Zeke. He didn't realize he missed Josh's compliments. No other man but Josh had ever talked that way to him before.

"Well, you are. What are you doing in Washington? I see you're not wearing a uniform. So, you're not in the army.

"No, I'm working over at Annapolis, building ironclads, or least I will be tomorrow. I start work there tomorrow."

"Wow, ironclads! I've read about them, but never seen one. I can't imagine how a boat made of iron floats," quizzed Travis.

Zeke grinned, "It's called displacement, but I've already had too many beers to explain it. I barely understand it myself."

"Did I tell you that your blue eyes are the most sparkling I've ever seen?" grinned Travis almost wickedly as he gazed directly into Zeke's eyes.

Josh awoke just after midnight. He had been dreaming about Zeke once more. He reached down with his left arm and felt his erection. It was hard and tall. He determined he would immediately ask Annie in the morning if she could send a wire to Saint Louis, and another to Maine. He had to find Zeke. He had to. He was sorry he had waited so long to do so. He could not believe how the time had flown by. There was no way he could send a wire from up North as he had been behind the enemy lines until wounded.

Nevertheless, for now, as far as he was concerned, the war was over. He had lost almost all of his friends, and there was nothing left that he was willing to die for except Zeke.

He fell back to the bed, preferring to drift off once more and begin dreaming of Zeke.

By two o'clock, Zeke and Travis were giddy and very drunk. Travis helped Zeke to the door, and led him down the alley to a room he rented. Before Zeke even caught on to what was happening, Travis pulled his clothes off, and was busy pulling at Zeke's.

Zeke had never been with another man, and the erection that bounced in front of his face as he sat down on the bed captured his full attention. He gingerly reached up and felt it, realizing he had not felt Josh's tool in more than two years.

Before long, Travis had all of Zeke's clothes off, was instantly on top of Zeke, and kissing him passionately. By dawn, they had worn each other out. Travis awoke, dressed quickly, kissed Zeke, and said he would be back at Al's on the weekend and hoped to see him then.

Zeke dressed, walked outside into the morning air, and replayed what he had done the night before. He almost threw up. He knew he should not have felt so guilty. Josh was the one who failed to arrive in Saint Louis. However, on the wagon ride to Annapolis, he felt he betrayed Josh and yet, more than likely, Josh was dead. He had not heard from him or seen him in over two years. Josh had promised he would meet him there, but he didn't. It was time to move on, he assured himself, but in the end, he was still in love with Josh. He just did not know how to find him. He knew he could not rest until they were reunited, or he found out what had happened to him.

Less than a hundred miles away, Josh managed to prop himself up as Annie came to his bedside. "Annie, you're looking so pretty today," he said with as much Southern charm as he could muster though laying flat on his back in the hospital bed.

She saw right through his flattery. "Now what pray tell do you want from me?"

"I need a favor..." he began, "an important one." He leaned up on his left elbow.

She was pleased to see him sitting up and happy to hear him say more than a few words. "Sure. Anything if you promise to eat today," she teased.

"All right, I promise," he replied.

"That was too easy. I should have asked for more," she added as she gave him a sip of the milk she had brought on a tray along with some grits and eggs.

"I need for you to send a telegram for me. Three messages actually. I want you to send one to Saint Louis to a Zeke Robertson. He's my best friend, and he's waiting on me there. Tell him I will be there as soon as possible. And then send a message to the Robertson family in Maine, and tell them I'm okay, and ask if they have heard from Zeke. Ask them to please respond with how to get in touch with him. Finally, the third message is to my mother in Charleston. Tell her I'm fine, and hope to see her soon. Will you do this for me, Annie? Will you?" he begged with his eyes.

"Sure, but I don't think I'll be able to get through with the one to the North. I've heard that nothing gets through the front lines."

"I did, so please try, Annie. It's important. I was supposed to meet him...," he couldn't remember how long ago. It seemed like a lifetime.

"Calm down. I'll send them. Now you keep your promise and eat this breakfast. If you want to travel, you've got to get your strength back."

Annie's words struck a chord. She was right. He could not just lie here and feel sorry for himself. If he was going to see Zeke, he had to get well and strong, and head off to Saint Louis to meet him. He had wasted enough time as it was. He had fought in a war that no longer meant anything to him. He had killed total strangers and watched friends die beside him. He wanted no more. He wanted only Zeke.

She lifted the spoon, expecting him to take a tiny little bite as he always did, but this time he opened wide, and took in the whole spoonful and swallowed hard.

"More," he ordered as he rapidly chewed and she complied.

The next month was the hardest that Zeke had ever worked in his life. From dawn to dusk, seven days a week, the crews worked feverishly building the next ironclad. Ericsson made several important design changes during construction, and Zeke was fascinated with the man's free hand drawings, his expertise at making things work on paper, and then on the docks.

By the end of the month, the boat was ready to test. It was a joyous time as they moved the boat to the water, and an even greater joy in finding out that she did indeed float. Even Zeke had his doubts after stowing all the cannons and supplies onboard.

"Shall we take her out?" asked Ericsson of his young apprentice.

Zeke laughed, wiping the sweat from his brow, "I think that would be marvelous!"

"Great, let's do it. Tell the men I'll be right down and we'll cruise around the Potomac a bit."

Zeke scampered down the bank to give the men their orders to prepare for sailing. John went into his office to clean up. He heard a knock at his open door and turned to find a Union officer standing there.

"May I help you?" asked John as he wiped a wet cloth over his face.

"Yes, sir. I'm Major Morgan. General Grant has sent for you, sir. We've received some disturbing reports of the enemy's plans for countering your vessels. Will you come with me, please?"

John recognized an order when he heard one. "Of course, but let me give an order or two to my assistant. I'll be but a moment."

"Very well," replied the major, extending every courtesy possible though he knew Grant was an impatient man.

John crossed the street and walked down to the dock.

"Let's go, John. She's ready!" called an excited Zeke.

"You take her out. I've been summoned to the War office. Stay within sight and get back here before dark. Put her through her paces, and I want a full report when I get back. Even fire a cannon shot or two on that knoll across the river. She's got to be in her in best shape."

"What?" asked Zeke not quite understanding the last sentence?

"Oh, never mind. Go. Set sail!" he said with a shout before turning to follow the major to his carriage.

Zeke stood there looking a bit dumbfounded at being given command of the vessel, but at the prodding of his friends, he jumped aboard and gave the orders to cast off. As the boat drifted from the dock, the crowd of onlookers cheered. The sailors aboard gleefully waved their hats back and forth in celebration of their work.

They had been out about an hour and sailed down to the furthermost point when Zeke gave the order to turn back. As the boat was coming about a loud scraping noise could be heard up top and below they felt something scraping along the hull. No one knew what it might have been.

Puzzled, Zeke dashed below to check to see if the boat was holding together, and was pleased to find that it was. Then a minute later, they heard yet another scraping noise against the hull. The crew began checking every piece of equipment in an attempt to determine the cause of the noise.

Before Zeke could return above deck, a third scraping noise could be heard, and then just as suddenly, it stopped. Seconds later, a loud thud could be heard from inside the boat, and then there was a large explosion. Water shot up into the air and several men were blown off the deck.

Below, the men were knocked all about, and a sailor died when a cannon fell off its support and crashed down his chest.

Zeke had been knocked off his feet and lay amongst kegs of black powder. His face was black from the smoke as he lay against the cold, iron hull. He probably would have been stunned for quite a while, but the water that was seeping in from every joint splashed across his face and woke him.

He struggled to his feet and felt like he was in a bad dream. The crew was abandoning the ship. Water was pouring in. They had apparently hit some kind of a floating bomb or a mine. The ship was quickly sinking. Zeke's attention turned to a man that was screaming near the bow. A cannon wheel had rolled over the poor man's leg, pinning him to the deck. Zeke rushed to help him, but the big weapon was much too heavy for him to move by himself.

He ran to the hatch and called out for another man to help. He was surprised to find several men still there. He later learned that very few of the crew could swim, and several of the first few jumping overboard drowned. He had learned to swim from an early age, growing up near the ocean.

He ordered two men below to help him. They struggled and grunted as the water kept pouring in. The man's head would soon be under the water if they did not move it quickly enough.

"Rig a winch!" yelled Zeke.

The men quickly untangled the ropes and put together the winch. The water rose to the man's neck. The man's face reflected the terror of drowning helplessly in what could become an iron casket.

"Hurry!" Zeke yelled.

The men threaded the ropes through the winches and pulled hard. Zeke joined them. The cannon moved just a bit, giving them a glimmer of hope. The man struggled to keep his mouth above the rising water line.

"Hurry! Pull!" yelled Zeke.

They took a deep breath and pulled with all their might. Suddenly, the hull cracked and popped from the shifting weight of the sinking boat. Water poured in twice as fast, knocking the men to the deck. Some fell into the river. Zeke was knocked against the wall. The men got up from the water quickly and scampered back onto the deck, their faces displaying their fear.

"No, wait. We must help him!" cried Zeke aloud.

"It's sinking. Run for your life!" yelled one of the men as he and the others jumped overboard and grabbed a floating log.

"But..." Zeke started to protest but the water was already to his chest.

He turned to the pinned man and his head could no longer be seen above the water. Zeke dove under and found the man, his eyes bulging wide, bubbles streaming from his face. Eventually, the man could hold his breath no longer and he drowned.

Horrified at being helpless and terrified of knowing that he, too, could drown if he did not hastily retreat, Zeke climbed up the hatch, took a quick look left and right to get his bearings and then dove off the boat and began swimming for the nearest shore.

The sting of cold water made him gasp when he came to the surface. The current was strong, but he had swum in ocean currents all his life, and he did not fear them. He kept a steady stroke until he reached the riverbank in darkness. The ironclad made its way to the bottom. He glanced up and down the shore, and, though hard to see, he spotted not one man from the crew.

He got to his feet and could see the lights of Annapolis upstream. He took but a few steps when two men came out of the woods.

"Halt!" yelled the first one.

"Just shoot the Yankee," yelled the other one.

"He might be important. Maybe he was the captain of that stupid boat."

"Okay, let's take him."

Zeke put his hands up when he saw the two rifles aiming squarely at his chest. "I'm not a soldier," he protested as he realized the men were wearing Confederate uniforms.

"Yeah, right. You were on a Yankee ironclad but you're not a soldier? I personally think we ought to shoot you, but Ralph here, thinks you might be worth something. We'll see. March!" ordered the man.

Zeke started to protest and dropped his hands. "I'm an engineer and I'm..."

The soldier swung the barrel of his gun around and hit Zeke across the back, damaging some ribs and knocking the breath from him. Zeke fell to his knees.

"Now if you want to keep yapping out here, then I'm going to keep hitting you with this gun until there's nothing left for us to take in. What's it going to be, Blue Boy?"

Zeke struggled to his feet and began following one of the men. The second man's rifle continually poked him in the back. They walked nearly a mile before they came to a camp.

"Whatcha got, Ralph?" called a soldier near a campfire.

"I got me a Yankee. We fished him out of the river. Where's the captain?"

"He's on patrol."

"Well, tie him up to that tree, and we'll wait right here for him to return."

The private took Zeke to the big oak tree in the center of their camp. He pushed his back to the tree and then began winding the rope around Zeke and the tree over and over again. Then he tied off Zeke's hands and checked his knots to be sure they would hold. A few others joined the three soldiers as they sat down to eat their supper, offering Zeke nothing.

Hours later, Ralph had to pee. He walked over to the tree and urinated on Zeke's legs. The rest of the soldiers laughed and taunted Zeke, throwing left over scraps of food at him, but never quite close enough to where he could catch something to eat.

By dawn, Zeke had been bitten dozens of times by mosquitoes and was weary and miserable. He had not slept all night. He was terrified of the predicament, but he hoped that he would be given a chance to talk to an officer. He wanted them to realize that he was not a soldier and release him.

His only solace through the night was his dreams of Josh. He knew that if Josh knew where he was and the mess he was in, he would come and rescue him like a knight in shining armor. It was the thought of Josh galloping in, his blond hair blowing in the breeze, his smile radiating from his soul that lifted Zeke's spirits through the night.

The sunlight brought on an even more harrowing ordeal for Zeke. The captain rode in at dawn, bleary eyed and exhausted from an all night scouting party. Eight men rode with him and they were all carrying food and supplies stolen from farmhouses near Washington.

"Where's Samuel?" asked Ralph.

The captain gave him a hard stare, swallowed slowly, and then answered coldly, "A Yankee shot him just a mile down the main road. There were two Yankees on lookout duty, I guess. We nailed both of them. Sam took one in the chest, and he died minutes later. We couldn't stop the bleeding." His voice turned angry and he kicked a bucket of water near the fire. Ashes and smoke billowed upward. "The bullet cut a hole in him as big as my fist. He died calling his wife's name. There's nothing we could do."

Then he paused as he stared at the men opening up the supplies they had stolen. Zeke had heard the Rebels were having trouble getting money for supplies and even if they did manage to get supplies, they had more trouble getting those supplies to the men on the front. Desperate and hungry, Zeke could tell these men had resorted to stealing to survive. The captain refused to call it stealing, always leaving Confederate money for the things he took. However, in his heart, he knew it was against what he had been taught. The years and months of battle had changed him. He was not the man he once saw in the mirror when he shaved.

"Eat those provisions with care, boys, they come with the price of Sam's life."

The men stopped and silently thought about the sacrifice that had been made, and only the growls in their stomachs allowed them the courage to continue to prepare breakfast for the squad.

The captain walked over to the tree, "Where'd you get him?"

Zeke realized that he must not have been the first sailor caught, as the captain didn't act surprised or even pleased. "Sir, I'm not a soldier. I'm an engineer, an apprentice," he confessed, "I'm just learning a trade. I was just testing the new boat, and huh, it just went down. There was some kind of an explosion. Everyone drowned but I'm just an engineer!" repeated Zeke almost begging.

"Shut your yap, Yank. I should hang you. Those boats have killed friends of mine. Maybe I'll just shoot you."

The captain suddenly pulled his revolver and aimed it directly at Zeke's head. The men stopped their foraging and watched. No one dared to interfere. Zeke thought his life was about to end.

The captain cocked the gun. "You people should stay north of the Mason Dixon Line and just leave us alone. We didn't do you any harm. You have all the industrial wealth. All we've got is our farms and the freedom to grow what we want!" His voice got louder and more deliberate. He took a step closer to Zeke, still pointing the gun at his head.

"You people just think you're so high and mighty, but you're not. You're just like us only we have slaves, and you have people who work in factories for nothing. What the hell is the difference?"

Zeke broke in, hoping for a chance to beg for his life by refusing to argue with the man in charge, but rather pretending to be on his side. He was desperately trying to save his life. "I agree, sir. I go to school not to far from here. Maybe you're heard of it, it's called Pine Ridge Military academy. It's over near..."

The captain took another step closer. The barrel of the dirty pistol was but four feet from Zeke's forehead. Sweat poured from Zeke's face. The captain interrupted Zeke, "I know where it is. It's in Petersburg. I went there myself. I graduated in 1860. And you?"

I was a sophomore when the war broke out. I didn't enlist. As a matter of fact, my best friend is from Charleston, South Carolina. Their plantation is near Moncks Corner. Perhaps you've heard of the Johnson family?" Zeke asked hoping conversation would calm the captain down and prevent him from killing him.

"Johnson? I knew a Johnson that was a horse trainer and a breeder. An old man, let's see what was his name..."

"Samuel!" blurted out Zeke and then the very instant he had said the name he regretted it.

"That's right. Samuel Johnson. He was a good man. We buried another good man today named Samuel." The captain's voice lost its fire. He grew quiet, so quiet that only Zeke could hear him. "Samuel was indeed a good man. I don't relish the idea of writing his wife of her loss."

There was a long moment of silence. Zeke could think of nothing to say. No words would come to his lips. He silently held his breath and hoped.

The captain gave Zeke a very hard long stare then aimed his gun upward, slowly un-cocked the hammer, and placed the gun back in its holster. "We'll take you to headquarters after breakfast. I hear they're sending prisoners to Georgia. After a few months in there, you may wish I had shot you right here and now."

The captain turned and walked over to the fire, sat down, poured himself a cup of coffee, and joined his men in eating some of the ham they confiscated.

Zeke slumped against the tree. The ordeal, the tension, and the possibility of death had all drained him of his remaining strength.

NINETEEN

Josh couldn't wait for Annie to arrive with the breakfast cart each morning. He knew she stopped off at the telegraph office on her way to work seeking a message for him. Every day he prayed she would come with a message from Zeke, or Zeke's parents, or from his mother. A week had gone by since he sent the three telegrams. Each day since then, he was a little stronger. He forced his sore and bed-weary body to sit up on the edge of the bed a few days ago, and was now able to walk the hallway with a little help from Annie. He was determined he would get his strength back, redevelop his muscles, and soon be able to ride a horse while regaining the use of his right arm.

Josh shut his eyes. He could tell Annie's footsteps from all the rest of the hospital staff. He knew her rhythm, and listened as intensely just as he used to listen for a deer walk in the edge of the swamps back home in South Carolina. He kept his eyes shut until he picked out her walk from all the others. He knew she would stop for his breakfast then make her way to him. He was always her first patient, and as she had assured him, her favorite patient as well. Her care and concern touched him deeply, and he couldn't thank her enough for all she did on his behalf. He was afraid she was falling in love with him, though he gave no sign of his intentions or desires. His only desire was to keep her as a good friend.

She turned the corner, and he opened his eyes to see her push through the doorway. He smiled and she smiled back at him. He propped himself up in the bed and she sat the tray down on his lap.

"Looks like bacon today," she said. "How are you?"

"Fine, thank you," he said politely and then more urgently, "Any news?"

"Yes!" she beamed. "You got a letter today from Charleston. It's from a Mrs. Elizabeth Johnson."

"That's her all right. Would you read it to me?" he said between bites of food. He could feed himself as long as someone cut up some of the food which she always did before she entered the room to avoid embarrassing him.

"Sure, if you promise to clean your plate."

"No problem. Thanks," he replied between gulps.

"Dearest Joshua. How good it was to hear from you and to know that you're still alive. We thought sure you were dead, as we hadn't heard from you since you went off to war. I hope you are healthy and coming home soon. Things have been rough around here. Trevor has done the best he could, but I really don't trust the man. Some of our slaves have disappeared, or run off, most likely because he beats them all the time. I've threatened to fire him, but who else is going to run the place? Most of the able men have left to join the fight. I hope this war ends soon. I just don't see the good in it. Please write and tell us what you've been doing and, yes, we do want you to come home. The past is all forgotten. Knobby was shot trying to escape. We need you. Hurry home. Love, Mother."

Annie let the words of the letter sink in a while before she spoke. "It sounds like she misses you."

"Yes, I guess she does. So much news in such a few words."

"Do you want to send a reply?" she asked.

"Yes, but for now I have to think a while on what she wrote. Thanks."

"You did a good job cleaning your plate. I guess you deserve a reward," she teased.

He hardly looked up from the tray, his mind already deep in thought. Poor Knobby. He deserved better.

"Yes, a reward you shall have. You got a telegram today as well."

Josh's eyes went wide. Where from? Maine or Saint..."

She laughed, "Saint Louis! Shall I read it?"

"Yes, yes, please do!" Josh could hardly contain himself as he sat up even straighter and hoped the words on the paper were from Zeke.

She unfolded the telegraph and began, "Josh. My name is John Sebastian. Zeke worked for me in my telegraph office before returning to Maine a few months ago. I heard from him there. All was well, he said. He's joining Ericsson in Annapolis to build boats. He waited forever for you. Zeke loves you dearly. I hope you are well. If I can be of more help, please call on me. Your friend through Zeke, John Sebastian."

Her voice stopped. She reread the telegram silently. She did not understand the sentence, "Zeke loves you dearly." What did he mean "dearly," she wondered.

Josh's face flushed. He was embarrassed at John's frankness in the telegram, but that did not concern him right now. The words that "Zeke loves you dearly" burned into his mind. His heart had stopped beating and then thundered loudly in his chest. He could hardly contain his excitement, his joy. He had to get to Zeke. He just had to.

Annie had watched his face as the emotion of the moment overwhelmed Josh. His eyes watered and then slowly tears ran down his cheeks, and bouncing off the corners of his mouth as he broke into a huge grin. She read the telegram again, and then looked intently into Josh's now beaming, exuberant blue eyes, and the realization hit her as hard and as fast as the bullet that had damaged Josh's shoulder.

"You... two... are..." she could not find the words, any words. Her voice failed her. She felt betrayed, stupid, and then angry. She ran from the room, tears streaming down her face, the telegram flung on the bed.

"Annie! Annie! Wait! Please don't. Please. I need you!" Josh yelled, but his words were ignored. He felt frustrated and abandoned, but as his left hand reached for the telegram, it was as if for the first time since the war began, Joshua Jeremiah Johnson was now reaching for a little light of hope. He could not believe that Zeke was in Washington and not in Saint Louis. He didn't have a clue how he could get to him, but vowed he would. He swore he would never again allow anything to keep him from Zeke.

Zeke had spent but a few hours at the field headquarters of General Sam Morgan. From there, he was transferred to Richmond, where he was questioned intensively about his work with the ironclads. Notes were taken and Zeke had been cooperative, hoping they would release him and send him home. To his dismay, once the officers obtained the information they wanted, they left the room without a single comment. Moments later he was marched out to a wagon and transported across town. Four blocks later, they made a turn and went by the army hospital. Inside the building sat Josh, but Zeke how no way of knowing it. He sensed release was not going to happen. They sent him to an old warehouse that had been converted into a stockade for Yankee prisoners. The prison was called Libby.

Zeke was horrified at being behind bars and was amazed at how many soldiers were being held. He had read newspaper accounts of reports of over five thousands soldiers being held captive. He suspected there were over five hundred in this warehouse alone. The men were dirty, hungry, and ill tempered as well. The stench hit his nostrils almost causing him to vomit. Pools of urine and fly infested feces were everywhere.

The guards frequently beat the prisoners, and surprising to Zeke, the prisoners often fought one another. Men fought over food, a place to sleep, someone's boots when the owner died or was nearly dead, and even the bugs that tried to cross the room. Zeke ate little and did his best to stay in a corner of the overly crowded cell he had been placed in.

His first night there, he knelt down in that corner and did his best to stay away from any others, very much afraid he would be killed. He overheard the men wearing Yankee uniforms and learned that they feared this stranger in civilian clothes might be a spy. Others doubted a spy would come to a prison, and they openly discussed what they thought would be Zeke's fate just a few feet from where he sat, as if he did not actually exist.

Zeke's biggest problem was the fact that even though he had not had a bath in a few days, and he had survived a shipwreck and near drowning, he was still cleaner and smelled better than any other man in the cell.

A tall, big man cautiously made his way over to Zeke's corner. He made Zeke nervous at first, but then the man began to talk to him and Zeke began to relax.

"Where you from?" asked the man.

"Maine," replied Zeke. "You?"

"Pennsylvania. I'm Jim," he stuck out his hand.

Zeke gave the man a careful look and then shook his hand, "I'm Zeke."

The man looked at Zeke's cleaner hand, and he held onto Zeke's hand a moment longer than Zeke thought he should. Zeke quickly pulled his hand back.

"What division you in?" asked Jim.

"I'm not in the army. I am an apprentice engineer. I was working on a boat in Annapolis."

"Good, lord. The Rebs done took Annapolis?"

"No, we were testing a new boat, and were sunk by what I've been told was a mine. I had to swim ashore then was captured. I don't know why they're holding me. I'm not a soldier." Zeke had been dying to protest to someone, even a total stranger who could probably do him no good, but he spoke on anyway.

Jim didn't say anything for a while, but Zeke could feel Jim's eyes looking him over. It made him very uncomfortable and very nervous. The sun set in the west, leaving the warehouse almost completely dark. There were no lanterns or fires for light or warmth. Most of the men quickly settled down to sleep. There were minor squabbles from time to time, as to who was taking another's sleeping place. Someone would pass gas and others would hit him. When one man happened to roll into another, sometimes a fistfight would break out.

Zeke was determined to stay awake. He relaxed after he heard Jim snoring. Suddenly a scream went out from a younger man in the cell across the hall. The men stirred a bit, but most did not even bother to look.

Jim opened his eyes and spotted Zeke staring at him.

"You worry too much. We're prisoners, and we must help each other survive."

"But why's that man screaming?" asked Zeke in a whisper.

"It's probably his first time. He'll get used to it, if he wants to survive."

"Used to..."

The young man screamed again, and then Zeke heard the thumping sound of flesh against flesh. The realization shocked him. He suddenly felt scared and more nervous than ever.

"You'll get used to it, too, my friend. If not, you could be dead before dawn. Think about it. Sweet dreams," said Jim coldly as he turned over to return to sleep.

Zeke pushed himself deep into the corner and counted the minutes until dawn. However, Jim was a patient man. He figured he wasn't going anywhere. Zeke's body was still strong, and he would wait a day or so for him to weaken.

Zeke watched the prisoners carefully. Jim seemed to be the boss of the cell. Twice a day the men were marched to an outhouse. Fights often broke out as the men with diarrhea tried to push their way to the front of the long line. Zeke always relieved himself quickly, and then hurried back to the cell and his corner.

It was now his second morning in Libby Prison. When he returned from the yard and entered his cell, Jim had been waiting for him. Jim grabbed his arm, swung him against the wall, and before Zeke could respond, Jim jumped against him, jammed his hand inside his pants, grabbed Zeke by the balls, and squeezed. The breath flew from Zeke's lungs as he gasped at the pain. Jim suddenly let go, and then massaged Zeke's sore genitals a bit.

Jim leaned in close to Zeke's face and stared him in the eyes, "If you want to keep these soft balls of yours, you'll do what I say when I say. Do you understand? Do you?"

Zeke could not reply. Words failed him. He nodded yes.

"Good boy." Jim slid his hand out of Zeke's pants, then slowly rubbed his hand up Zeke's chest, and then kissed him quickly on the mouth. Zeke did not respond to the kiss and tightened his lips. Jim pulled back and smiled, "You can do better, but we're going to get along just fine."

Jim turned and left the cell for his turn in the outhouse. Zeke turned to the corner and threw up. Some other cellmates, who had been watching, laughed and sneered at Zeke's dilemma. Some of them hoped they would be allowed a turn with him as well.

Zeke returned to his corner and began to search the room for a solution to his problem. He spent all day thinking, and all day dreading the night. When the lights dimmed, Jim moved beside Zeke and settled down to sleep. He snored while Zeke did his best to stay awake.

Zeke thought of Josh, and he knew that if Josh were in his place he would beat the shit out of this man. Zeke knew that he could not allow any man to own him like one of Josh's slaves. He would be a slave to no man, but he feared that if he lost a fight with this man and died, what good would it have done? He pondered this over and over again. His thoughts troubled him until he fell asleep and began to dream of Josh and their first wonderful night together in Washington.

After midnight, Zeke was deep asleep. He sported an erection as he always did when he dreamed of Josh. He felt a warm hand massaging his penis, and he dreamed of Josh's soft hand moving up and down on him. It felt wonderful to him and his tool began to swell more. He felt the hand undo his pants and push them down, and then suddenly he was turned over onto his stomach. He bumped his head into the concrete wall, which awakened him instantly. He felt his balls being crushed on the hard floor. His eyes popped wide as he knew it was no longer a dream. Jim was on top of him, and he could feel the man's hard penis probing in the dark for his hole.

"Where is it, lad?" whispered Jim as he bit the back of Zeke's ear lobe.

Zeke did not respond as he searched for solutions and his mind raced for a decision. He felt Jim's finger slide down his butt until he found his hole. He felt the finger push in. Zeke chewed his lip. His eyes darted around to the cell door. He spotted a bucket full of urine just inside the door.

Jim pulled his finger out, grabbed his tool, and pushed toward Zeke. Zeke felt the tip of the flesh as it touched his tender anus. He took a deep breath. Jim pushed a bit and the head entered Zeke. Zeke took another breath. Jim pushed just as Zeke swung around with all his might slamming his elbow hard into Jim's nose, breaking it instantly. All the nearby prisoners heard the loud pop. The blow knocked Jim against the wall. Zeke swung his elbow again, and popped Jim hard in the mouth, breaking a tooth.

Then Zeke jumped up, pulled up his pants, and kicked Jim hard in the groin. To his surprise, Jim clung to Zeke's boot as he pulled back, and even though Jim had to be in pain, he did not let go. Zeke tried to jerk free, but fell hard to floor nearly knocking the breath from him. Jim clawed his way on top of Zeke and began pounding his head on the floor. Zeke's left eye was cut and blood splattered the floor. Zeke struggled to get free, but Jim's weight was too great.

Zeke spotted the bucket near the door. He took another deep breath, and as Jim leaned down near him, Zeke swung his head back and popped Jim hard in the mouth. Jim fell off him. Zeke dove for the door, but Jim caught him by the leg and started pulling him toward him. Jim slammed a fist down hard onto Zeke's knee. Zeke screamed out from the sudden pain while desperately struggling to free himself from Jim's death grip. Jim hit him again hard.

Zeke leaned back and tried to reach the bucket with his hand but couldn't. He extended his fingers, but he still couldn't reach it. Jim hit him again. Zeke tried to kick, but Jim shifted and slammed another fist into Zeke's leg.

Desperately, Zeke rocked forward and then flung himself backwards as hard as he could. He moved but a few inches, but it was just enough. Jim reared back for another pounding on Zeke's knee, but Zeke had grabbed the bucket by the handle and swung it at Jim's head as hard as he could. He knew he had but one chance, and he put all his strength into the blow.

The bucket exploded on impact with Jim's face, tearing flesh and fracturing bones, knocking Jim backward. Zeke thought it would be over, but Jim turned toward him, his face now a bloody heap of flesh and bone now dripping with the urine from the bucket. He roared like a bull and spat blood on the floor. Zeke grabbed a sharp piece of the broken bucket. Jim dove toward Zeke. Zeke stuck out the stick like a small wooden sword, and Jim fell hard onto him, impaling himself through the heart with his own weight.

Jim's body immediately went limp. Zeke rolled him off his body. Everyone in the room could see the bloody mess Jim's body was now in. Blood formed puddles around him. Zeke struggled to his feet, walked to his corner, sat down, covered his face, and rubbed his swelling knee.

For the rest of his stay at Libby, no one bothered him again. He was now feared and respected.

Annie never came to Josh's bedside again. She also quit coming to the hospital. Josh was told that she had taken leave and no one knew just why. Josh was saddened at the loss of his friend. He knew now that he must work even harder to gain his strength so that he never again had to depend on anyone.

He spent every waking hour working his muscles, walking farther and farther, eating heartily, and walking some more. He was soon able to run again, and he had managed to swing his right arm as he ran. Then one day, he was resting from his run, and watched two boys nearby playing with a ball. They were playing catch and the taller boy threw the ball a bit too hard. The younger boy missed catching the ball and it rolled right up to Josh who was leaning against a tree.

"Throw it, mister. Please," begged the younger boy.

Out of reflex, Josh reached for the ball with his right hand. He had not been able to move it before. It hurt like hell, but it moved. He tried to pick up the ball, but the fingers just would not close. He grabbed the ball with his left hand.

"Throw it!" called the little boy.

Josh stood up. He pushed the ball into his right hand and tried to close the fingers. They moved a bit. Tears dropped from his eyes. A huge smile overcame him. The two boys walked up to him, dumbfounded as to why he was crying with a smile on his face.

"I can move my arm!" he exclaimed as he tossed them the ball. "I can move it!"

The two boys scratched their heads and went back to playing. Josh laughed aloud, then walked immediately to the general mercantile store in town, and bought a small rubber ball. He squeezed the ball every second of every day. Three weeks later, he could grip a sword, and a few weeks after that he could grip a gun. When he could hold a pen, he finally wrote his mother a long letter, explaining his duty in the army and the ordeals he had survived. He asked her if she had heard from Zeke. He said he would come home just as soon as he found his friend. He did not mention his plans to still head west with Zeke.

While he was retraining his body, he sent another telegram to John Sebastian in Saint Louis to see if John had heard from Zeke. John replied instantly, but with no news about Zeke.

After Josh was released from the hospital, he was ordered to the local commander's office. He had hoping to be relieved since he had already served so well and was now wounded. His request had been declined. When asked why, the sergeant replied that General Lee had been defeated at Gettysburg and thousands of Rebels had been killed. Every hand was needed now more than ever and that no man was being discharged.

He was ordered to help escort eight hundred Yankee prisoners from the Libby and Castle Thunder warehouses in Richmond to Columbia, South Carolina. Josh was angry at not being discharged, but if he was heading south, he might just have a chance to visit his plantation. He still hoped to be relieved soon, so he could continue his search for Zeke.

He reached the Castle Thunder Prison as the men were being led out of their cells to be marched south. Josh was overcome at how badly the men looked, and he was sorry for their condition. He had been put in charge of over a hundred armed guards, and so he went about doing his duty and began moving the men south of town.

Another four hundred prisoners from Libby joined them just before dusk. Rumor had it that the generals were afraid that Richmond might fall, and so they were preparing for that possibility by moving the prisoners farther south. The newspapers related accounts that although Lee had been defeated, another five thousand Yankee soldiers had been taken prisoner. Perhaps they were just making room for more, thought Josh.

The prisoners lost hope as the weary soldiers began walking south, mile after mile. They wore rags for clothes, and their hair and beards were unkempt. They were all weak. Their stench made the armed Confederate escorts gag.

Josh led the way as they avoided towns and marched the men south. It continued for weeks. He never knew that Zeke was one of the prisoners. He never noticed the limping man that had been injured in a fight during an attempted rape. He trained his eyes not to focus on the pathetic soldiers as he tried hard not to feel sorry for them.

Zeke's emotional state had been broken like so many of his fellow Yankees. Every step of every mile was more painful than the previous one. He did not notice the faces of his guards, or even the scenery along the way. He simply counted the days until he would be free to find Josh so that they would never have to sleep a single day apart. He had to find Josh, or at least find out what happened to Josh. He would not be able to go on with his own life until he knew something. One night he dreamed Josh had died, but the following night his spirits soared as he dreamed they walked hand in hand along the seashore.

The confusing dreams wearied him. His hope was like a candle burning slowly down. He wondered how long he could hold on to that flickering flame of hope. He feared he wouldn't survive the march to find out.

Day by day, emaciated and weakened men died on the march. Their graves were never marked. Their names were never noted. They were lost and forgotten. Josh silently grieved for their families. Their families would never have closure, making their losses even more painful to bear.

Zeke longed for Josh, and it was that hope of finding him that made him take one agonizing step after another. Hope was his determination and it would be the thing that would help him take the steps he needed to survive.

Josh spent his days as commander of his unit, leading the men who marched the huge group of prisoners south, mile after mile, day after day. He did not like the duty, but at least he was not forced to kill, and no one was shooting at him. He also did not like the idea of heading so far away from Zeke, but he hoped with each assignment that he would soon be discharged. He wanted to be free from the Confederacy, and free from his family so that he could find Zeke, head west, and live forever in each other's arms. He made an alternate plan that if he couldn't get through to Washington from the south, then he would take a train to the west, and make his way to Saint Louis, and get John to send Zeke a telegraph to meet him in Saint Louis, or he would catch a train to Washington from there. He would find a way to unite them. He knew he had to.

By night, he dreamed of Zeke and cherished his regained ability to relieve himself with his right hand. He was determined more than ever to use his legs, his injured arm and hand, his mind, and his very soul if necessary to find his beloved and to protect him. He wanted no more of the rest of the world and its problems. His world was Zeke, and he needed nothing else. He did everything he could to make his body stronger so that he could find Zeke and get them both to freedom and a life together.

War had indeed been hell. He wanted no more of hell. He knew that life with Zeke would be heaven on earth and more. Josh just knew it. He only had to find Zeke and he vowed he would.

TWENTY

Josh rode Chess to the top of a knoll overlooking the South Carolina valley below. He preferred to ride ahead of the column as the sight of the dying prisoners made him sick to his stomach. Mile after mile they marched. They were dying at an average of a man a mile. The burial teams gathered the dead bodies in a wagon until the wagon was too full. They then stopped to dig a large mass grave where they dropped the pathetic bodies one on top of another and moved on to collect more bodies.

Josh found himself quite frustrated that he could not keep more men alive, but his rations were short even for his own men, and the prisoners were lucky if they got a bite of hard tack for breakfast and some hard bread for supper. The march to Columbia, South Carolina was a bitter hard one. Over four hundred men died. Zeke had lost twenty pounds since being in prison, and saw no hope of gaining it back. His knee never had a chance to heal, and thus the swelling never came down. He limped and skipped the whole way to Columbia. He also never saw the face of the man in charge of the march. He concentrated on simply keeping his feet moving, pushing forward, afraid to fall, and more afraid to die.

When the prisoners saw the gates of Camp Sorghum, they were relieved that they had made it, and actually pleased to be locked up in one place again. This prison did not have but a few jail cells for incorrigible prisoners, and so most of the Yankees were placed in an open courtyard surrounded by a wooden fence. There were armed guards day and night. Prisoners attempting to escape were shot immediately. It took five executions before the prisoners stopped trying to climb the fence. The Union soldiers were over five thousand strong and the guards numbered less than a thousand. The Rebels were outnumbered, but they did not fear the unarmed Yankees, as they were far too weak to even think of rioting.

Smallpox had entered the camp and within two weeks, another eight hundred prisoners and over seventy-five guards died from the disease. Dysentery was rampant. There was little fresh water, no fresh food, and morale was at its lowest. When the temperatures dipped late into the night, there were no blankets and no wood for fires. Everyone was forced to endure or die.

After a month, Josh was ordered to take half the prisoners to Camp Sumter in Andersonville, Georgia. Prisoners were chosen at random and Zeke was among those selected. Josh's men did the picking as he checked the preparations for the wagons of supplies to follow them on the trail to Georgia.

The trail was once again harsh, but Zeke's knee had gained strength during the rest, and he managed much better on this trek. His stomach growled. He was always hungry. He caught a fever, and he thought he had caught smallpox, but after a few nights with a fever, his temperature returned to normal and he was thankful he had been spared.

His only time of comfort was when he went to sleep at night and dreamed of Josh. He did not know if he could hold on much longer, and he wondered what the next camp would be like.

It took a bit more than two weeks for the prisoners to make the march to Andersonville. On the last day of marching, Josh rode ahead to ask the Camp Sumter commander to prepare for his prisoners. He was hoping they would have food and supplies to help them.

He was shocked at what he found. Camp Sumter was one of the South's worst prison camps. It was the counterpart to the Union's notorious Elmira Prison Camp in southwestern New York State. Camp Sumter housed 45,613 federal prisoners. Men stood shoulder to shoulder and tempers flared easily. Men were choked to death simply due to a lost temper for something as minor as someone accidentally stepping on a tender, infected foot. No one had the strength to care or the energy to stop the senseless acts of violence against their fellow soldiers.

Like the Rebels, the Yankees had many young boys in uniform. At first, these boys were attacked nightly, and some eventually learned to relax, take the penetration, and to beg for food in return for the favor. Sometimes, the screams of the boys being raped were silenced only by their deaths.

Zeke was horrified at what he saw when he entered the gates. He was not prepared for things to be worse. There was one filthy stream running through the camp, very few shelters to get out of the rain, no additional clothing or blankets, and even less food than in Columbia.

After entering the gates, the prisoners collapsed from exhaustion and desperation. Josh was racked with guilt for having brought his men there. Camp Sumter's commander, a Colonel Henry Wiggins, cared nothing for the prisoners. Any supplies were first picked over by him and his closest guards, and if they were lucky, the prisoners got a few days rations.

Josh had been assigned to secure the perimeter. He set up rotating shifts of four hundred men protecting the gates and the fences surrounding the camp. He spent most of his time in his office or his barracks, or taking long walks in the woods. He did his best to avoid going inside the prison or even walking where he might see them. He did his job and nothing more. On his long walks, he daydreamed of Zeke.

He sent another message to John Sebastian in Saint Louis and even tried once more to get through to Maine with no success. This time he did not hear from John and feared he had lost contact with him as well.

Many of Josh's guards had begun to hate the prisoners. These were men who had lost brothers, fathers, and friends to Union bullets, and they showed no compassion. They actually hoped a man would charge the gate, as they would immediately open fire. It did not happen often, but when it did, the rest of the prisoners fell silent as they watched the dying escapee writhe in pain in the mud.

A month later, a new man was assigned to Josh's garrison. He entered the office and waited for an appointment with Josh. Josh had let his beard grow back as shaving it here was just as impossible as it had been while behind the lines. His hair had grown longer as well. Without Zeke, he cared nothing about his looks.

He was busy preparing a report on the prisoner count when the new man came to his desk and stood at attention. Josh returned the man's salute without looking up.

"Welcome aboard. My name is Lieutenant Josh Johnson. I'm in charge of the camp guards. You'll work the night shift until further notice. You are to report to Sam Evans. He'll be your squad leader. You are to protect the perimeter. There's no need to shoot anyone. These men are too starved and weak to even think of escaping. You're there just to keep them from trying anything stupid. Any questions?"

"Don't you recognize me, Lieutenant Johnson?" asked the man sarcastically.

Josh looked up from his paperwork and stared at the soldier standing before him. The man wore sergeant's stripes, had a full black beard, and Josh didn't instantly recognize him. There was still something about the man's face that made Josh uneasy. "I can't say that I do."

"My name is Daniel Carpon. Sergeant Daniel Carpon."

Daniel enjoyed the change in Josh's expression. He liked the idea that his name seemed to strike something in him. Josh felt his blood run cold. His pulse could be seen at his temples. An inner alarm went off deep inside him. Daniel Carpon had left the academy in shame. He was not supposed to even see or speak to him ever again, and that would have been fine. Josh had hoped he would never see the student that had been kicked out of their school after attempting to frame Josh for cheating. Josh had every reason to hate Carpon for what he had tried to do. Nevertheless, he was older now. War changes everyone. It had changed him. Perhaps it had changed Carpon, he hoped.

Josh thought long and hard about the situation and then responded professionally, "The past is behind us. We're in this war together, and we're on the same side. We have a job to do. I suggest you be on your toes, as I'll be watching you very carefully. I don't put up with any irregularities. Don't get in any trouble here, or the penalty could be very severe," he added coldly while staring at Carpon.

Carpon smiled and sighed, "Any time, any place you want to take me on, just let me know. This war will be over one day and when it's done, I will settle the score between you and me. You can count on that. Good day, sir," he added with a sneer.

Carpon left and once the door was closed, Josh sighed heavily. His mind searched for ways to get Carpon transferred, but he knew that the men stationed here were transferred here primarily because no one wanted them. He felt sure he himself had been stationed here because they did not think he could handle a gun in battle. He knew better, but he did not let on. He still hoped to be discharged. He had enough of war and enough of the Daniel Carpons of this world.

Eighteen sixty-four came in the form of a snowstorm that was very rare for this far south. Overnight, fifteen hundred prisoners, and over fifty guards froze to death. The next day, Josh had the bodies hauled out to a field. They tried to bury them but the ground was frozen solid. The stacked bodies were soon covered in more falling snow. Over the next few days, another thousand men died.

So many trees had been cut to build the fences for the prison camp, that his guards had to spend their off duty time riding far out from the camp to cut more firewood to keep themselves from freezing. Prisoners huddled tightly together during the storm. Everyone thought they were going to die. The storm refused to let up. Night after night, the snow fell and the temperatures dropped. Everyone moved closer together, desperately trying to pool their body heat, but by morning, the men closest to the wind were usually dead.

The winter was long and hard, and the war was not getting any closer to an end. Josh read all the newspaper accounts he could get his hands on. By spring, he read of the battles at Lookout Mountain, in Chattanooga Tennessee. He could not believe the Yankees were so far south, but then he remembered how far he had been in the North. His group, though, was but a squad of soldiers. The entire Yankee Army was cutting a path right through the South. General William Tecumseh Sherman had begun his march to Atlanta, and fear began to run rampantly throughout all the Southern towns. Civilians were leaving Atlanta by every means possible. Sherman had vowed to burn Atlanta to the ground. He was determined to bring an element of fear into the entire South, making his march even more terrifying and successful.

His nickname was Tecumseh after the vicious Shawnee warrior of Ohio. He was a fierce man and demanded much from his officers and his men. He found an equally determined foe in General Johnson of the Confederate States of America. Sherman left Chattanooga on May 6, 1864, but his march to Atlanta was met with skirmish after skirmish, brilliantly planned, and executed by General Johnson. Johnson's men attacked and counter attacked much like the mosquitoes that constantly bit at the ears and necks of the men in blue as they marched into the South during a very hot, muggy summer. The Yankees were not used to the heat and humidity. The strength of his soldiers seemed to wither, but Sherman was a determined man and drove his troops onward, never letting up and never giving in. It took Sherman four months to make it to Atlanta. He arrived there September 2nd never doubting that he would, only when. The success of taking Atlanta revived his troops, and now they felt invincible, as everyone in the South feared them. The tide was changing.

Josh's men were wild with rumors of what to do should Sherman's army turn in their direction. Sherman had told reporters he planned to march to Savannah and then on to Charleston. Josh thought that if Sherman marched to Savannah then he could easily come through Andersonville and take the prison camp. After the accounts Josh had read in the newspaper, he knew taking the camp would be like a Sunday picnic to Sherman's troops. They had the best the North could provide, and Josh had the worst the South had no use for.

Josh threatened his men not to let word out that Sherman had survived Lookout Mountain in Tennessee and taken Atlanta. He told them to be alert and be ready, but keep a cool head. He knew that if word spread of Sherman's successes, it would be very tough to keep the prisoners in line if they thought they were about to be rescued by Sherman. His men would be forced to open fire on those Yanks that tried to break free. He reinforced his guards and hoped the prisoners would not find out about Sherman's march to Savannah, and suddenly decide to make a charge for the gate. Josh and his men would be forced to shoot them and yet, the thought of doing so made him sick. With bribes of free beer and special food supplies, Carpon had already won over some of the really rough prison guards who would welcome any excuse to kill a prisoner. In short time he had a gang of loyal thugs.

Zeke had survived one of the coldest Southern winters ever, but now the hot spring brought on swarms of mosquitoes. There was not a day that went by that the burial team did not have a body to put in the ground. It was a good day when there was only one prisoner to bury.

Josh's men did not fare much better. Death had reduced his guards by over a hundred men since his arrival. With the news of Sherman taking Atlanta, he knew that the end of the war must come soon. He felt like the South was going to lose, and if so, then he felt it should just go ahead and surrender, and be done with it. Why must more men die?

Many prisoners died quickly during the harsh winter. Josh decided to record all the names of those still alive. When the war ended, family members could be notified. He assembled his guards, told them to make such a list, and then asked the prisoners for the names of the men who had died. Carpon and his squad of six moved inside the camp. Daniel sat at a table in the shade of a building as his guards stood around him, fully armed, and ready to kill any prisoner who stepped out of line. One by one, the prisoners stood in line to record their names and then to give Carpon the names of any known dead and where they were from.

It took several weeks to question the entire prison camp. On the very last day, Zeke stood in line. He listened carefully to the man ahead of him while he went over and over in his mind what he wanted to say when his turn came. He kept repeating the names of some of his comrades who had died. He did not want to forget a single one of them. He knew it would be important to their families.

As he stepped forward for his turn, Carpon asked without looking up, "What is your full name and where are you from?"

"My name is Zeke Allen Robertson, from Portland, Maine. I know the names of four men who died..."

Carpon didn't hear a single name that Zeke had repeated since mentioning his own name. He glanced up intently from his paperwork and began studying the underweight, bearded and dirty ex-Yankee soldier that stood before him. A strong wind could have easily blown Zeke to the ground. He was weak, frail, and weighed just one hundred ten pounds. He looked very little like his former self, but Carpon recognized the eyes, the nose, and the face of the man who had turned the entire school on him. His chance for real revenge stood helplessly in front of him, and he had the means to accomplish the task.

To everyone's surprise, Carpon suddenly let out a huge bellowing laugh. The realization that the two men he hated most in the world now were within a hundred yards of each other and did not know it was suddenly too much for him. It would be easy for him to get his revenge, he thought as he continued to laugh heartily.

Carpon stood up suddenly and upholstered his pistol. "Perhaps, Mister Robertson, you will remember the name Carpon, Daniel Carpon. I'm he. Revenge is mine, sayeth the Lord. Don't you just love the Scriptures?" he mocked with a huge grin and a slight shaking of his head back and forth.

Zeke was aghast that Carpon was standing before him, but before he could jump back, Carpon swung his pistol through the air and smashed the barrel across Zeke's face, splitting the skin just above the ear and sending the astonished and defenseless Zeke crashing to the ground.

Blood oozed from his scalp. Zeke was dazed and weak, but he heard Carpon loud and clear.

"I've waited a long time to get even with you and Johnson, and now I have you both here in the same place." He turned back to his table, "Guards, take this man to the cell."

"But, he didn't do anything..." protested a fellow prisoner. His words went unheeded as two guards snatched Zeke harshly under the armpits then drove a wooden club into his stomach to take the fire out of him. They half dragged him to a group of cells that had been put up in the middle of the camp for the unruly prisoners.

Zeke was tossed inside the second overcrowded cell by kicking him in the buttocks. He fell hard to the cement floor gasping for breath with blood still dripping from his head wound.

Carpon quickly finished interviewing the remainder of the prisoners, tidied up his paperwork, then marched out of the camp and over to headquarters.

"Carpon to see Johnson," he said to the secretary.

The young secretary, a boy of only eighteen, quickly entered Josh's office and announced Carpon. Josh sighed, already dreading whatever it was that Carpon wanted to talk about. "Show him in," he ordered.

"I've completed the listing of the camp. There's 38,000 men still here, and I hear there are more coming," he said as he set the list on Johnson's desk.

"Be sure and list each man as he comes to us from now on so that we don't ever have to do this again. I want you to also list the names of the dead before you bury them. Don't leave a single name out. It'll be important to their families."

"Why are you being so helpful to the Yankee families?" questioned Carpon.

"I hope they'll do the same for our families. I had to bury friends in the wilderness as we fought in Virginia and Pennsylvania. I hope their families know how and when they died. It's the least we can do. That's all," he added quickly, hoping to be rid of Carpon.

Carpon turned to leave, but as he reached the door he took hold of the knob and only slowly opened it. Josh had already begun looking over the hundred or more pages of names. "Sir, have you heard from your friend at the academy, let's see, what was his name, was it Robert? No, perhaps Richard," he taunted. "No, maybe it was Randall..."

Josh looked up from his paperwork and shook his head, "No, it was Robertson. Zeke Robertson."

"Yes, that's it!" Carpon grinned slyly, now fully convinced he had the right man. Perhaps, with a bit of luck, he might be able to get revenge on Josh and Zeke at the same time. "Have you heard from him?"

"No, I haven't."

"Perhaps, he was killed," teased Carpon and then anxiously watched the pain sweep over Josh's face. He grinned, very much enjoying the verbal attack he was inflicting on his lieutenant.

"I don't think so. He wasn't in the army. He was making boats in Annapolis. Is there anything more?" Josh asked in such a way that Carpon knew it was time for him to exit. Carpon was more afraid that in his haste for revenge that he would reveal what he knew about Zeke. It was too soon for that.

Carpon turned toward the door once more and then suddenly came back around. "Are you and Zeke still close friends?"

Josh was taken aback by the sudden question. He dropped his pen to his desk, gave Carpon a hard look, and then answered proudly, "He's still my best friend. Yes, my very best friend."

Carpon smiled wickedly, "Very good. Very good, sir." He stepped from the room and deliberately slammed the door a bit too hard. Josh flinched at the noise. Then Carpon opened the door once more and stuck his head in, "Oh geez, I'm sorry. I sometimes forget my own strength. So sorry." He chuckled to himself as he closed the door once more and headed for his barracks in a rush. He had things to do and plans to make. He was feeling powerful. He would enjoy torturing Zeke physically while doing the same to Josh, though only verbally for now.

After celebrating his victory in Atlanta, Sherman announced his plans to leave Atlanta and begin his march to the sea. He was heading for Savannah and promising to pillage and burn everything in his path. This announcement sent shock waves through Georgia and South Carolina. Word spread as if Paul Revere had been riding his horse once more. Families packed up and began heading to Florida or the mountains of North Carolina. Plantations and homes in Sherman's path were abandoned. Slaves went hungry with no masters to feed them. They could have run free, but where were they to go? Thousands of slaves were migrating to the North, but once there, they found they were not as welcome as they thought. Mister Lincoln may have saved them from slavery, but it was now up to them to save themselves from starvation.

Late in the night, Daniel and two of his men entered the cell area and removed Zeke. He was brought to a room and the door was closed. Carpon was in the room. He slipped on a pair of riding gloves, carefully smoothing them over his knuckles. Before Zeke could even ask what was going on, Daniel began beating him about the face and the abdomen. When Zeke fell to the floor, Carpon kicked his weakened legs, and then booted him again in the groin.

Zeke doubled up as the pain overwhelmed him. The guards held him up; Carpon spit in Zeke's face, and called him every name he could think of. He reminded Zeke of how he had lied and caused Carpon to be kicked out of school. He beat Zeke even more, but he had somewhere learned to do it skillfully. Carpon always knew exactly when to stop. He did not want to kill Zeke yet. He threw a bucket of cold water over Zeke's body, sending water down his nose and throat. Zeke coughed and sputtered while Carpon laughed.

"You're paying for your sins to the South and for your crimes against me, and you'll pay everyday from now on until you die. Take him back to his cell," ordered Carpon.

A week later, near the end of the nightly beatings, Carpon gave Zeke a bit of news. "I hear your old friend Josh was killed at Gettysburg. Too bad, he was such a nice guy," he added sarcastically then drove his right fist into Zeke's gut, sending him crashing to the floor. "Take him back!" he ordered once more.

The pain that wracked his body was nothing near the pain he felt in his heart that Josh had died. He did not want to believe it, but why would Carpon lie? He had heard so many stories of families who had heard their son was dead only to see him come walking up the road. Record keeping had been anything but exact during the war. More men had died in America than ever before. America was approaching her first centennial and the path to what should have been a joyful event was being paved with blood.

Near the end of July, scouts sent word to the prison that General George Stoneman and his Yankee Cavalry were planning to raid and liberate the Andersonville Prison. Josh's commander summoned his officers for a plan of defense.

"Sir," broke in Josh, "we can reinforce the walls as you suggested, but the wood is so far from us that if we go and cut it, and haul it back, that'll leave the camp even more defenseless. I say we don't wait until they arrive here to fight us, but rather we do just what they don't expect and we go after them!"

Josh's words caused alarm among the others.

Josh continued, "Sir, before I was wounded, my men and I raided hundreds of Yankee camps in the dead of night, catching them off guard, burning their supplies and scattering their horses. We did this far behind the enemy lines. It would be simple to do this here in Georgia. We know the territory much better."

"Will you take charge of such an outfit?" asked the Commander.

"Absolutely, sir. With pride," he replied, and then instantly reminded himself that he did not want any more war. This was his homeland, though, and his family lived not more than a few hundred miles away.

Josh quickly assembled his men and began preparing for the night's journey. Not long after dark, Josh got word that Stoneman's men were camping near Macon, Georgia. They quickly saddled up and reluctantly, Josh left Carpon in charge of the camp. Josh and a hundred guards rode hard and fast until just a few miles from Macon.

Meanwhile, Carpon entered the camp with some of his guards and once again set about beating Zeke. Zeke's eyes were swollen, his nose broken, and several of his ribs were fractured. He could hardly eat, but the men in his cell took care of him, saving him water and bread as best they could. He was alive, but only barely.

When finished with his last kick, Zeke's pulse quickened with Carpon's whisper, "Your friend Josh is alive. He's in charge of the guards. He's been here all along, you fool. He was right here in front of your nose and you didn't know it. He's alive, but not for long. I plan to kill him before the week is out and then bring his head here for you to see before I kill you as well. I'll piss on you both."

From somewhere deep within him, Zeke mustered up just enough strength to stand and charge Carpon. He managed to wrap his arms around Carpon's neck, knock him to the floor, and begin choking him. Zeke was still too weak for Carpon to fear him, but the stench of Zeke's body nearly made him vomit.

"Get him off of me!" screamed Carpon.

A guard quickly stepped over and using the butt of his rifle struck Zeke hard on the back of the head, knocking him unconscious.

"Haul him back. Not too many more nights before we turn his lights out forever."

While Carpon waited for his guards to return, he drew his sword and walked down the hallway of jail cells. The men were asleep. The blade of his sword had been honed until it was as sharp as his razor. He picked men at random and sliced their throats, leaving them bleeding to death. He killed over fifteen men before leaving the cell area. Then as he walked through the camp to the gate, he and his men killed another fifty or so men while they slept. He had become a blood thirsty killer and he delighted in every single murder.

Josh had sent a scout closer to Macon to find the camp. The scout discovered it was easy to find as the local citizens pointed out their positions to him. Stoneman's men had already plundered Macon and the remaining citizens were angry and ready for revenge as well.

Josh and his men walked their horses as they approached the Union camp. Josh walked with his scout up a hill overlooking the riverbed where Stoneman's men had set up camp. They counted over a hundred horses and dozens of wagons. Josh moved in closer until he could count the sentries on patrol and made mental notes of their location.

He crept back to his men and they made their plans. Josh checked his watch. It was half past midnight. He announced they would wait another two hours before attacking. Every man was ordered to prepare his weapons and to rest. At just past three, Josh mounted up. He had divided his troop into four equal parts. They silently and slowly circled the camp.

At precisely four in the morning, just as the last of the sentries had sat down to rest weary legs, Josh and his men attacked. Josh knew that this assault would be much different than his raids in the North. They were no longer attempting to just stop Stoneman and his men, or steal their horses and supplies. They were determined to stop them from ever making it to Andersonville, Savannah, and Charleston.

The Union camp was caught completely off guard. Though outnumbered, in less than fifteen minutes, the Rebels had won and the remaining Yankees were scrambling for the woods without their horses and without their burning wagons. Stoneman survived the battle. Josh lost fifteen men and the General lost over half his cavalry and almost all of his supplies.

The victory spared Andersonville, at least for now. Josh and his men returned to camp, not only victorious, but also delighting in the food and rations they were able to steal.

General Stoneman sent word of the raid to General Sherman. The next morning, Sherman announced plans of liberating Andersonville himself. Astonishingly enough, he told the traveling reporters of his plans knowing there was no way the Rebel force at the camp could defend itself from Sherman's army.

TWENTY-ONE

Sherman troops continued their advance from Macon, but before Sherman could respond to the attack on General Stoneman's cavalry, word arrived that General Wheeler of the Confederacy had cut Sherman's supply lines, and thus slowed his march to Savannah even further. Sherman was angry at this delay, but he continued pressing onward.

Josh then read of General Wade Hampton's cavalry charge across the Potomac. They attacked the Union cattle and horse pens, stole twenty five hundred head of cattle, three thousand horses, and captured another three hundred prisoners.

General Sterling Price of the CSA had begun an attack in Missouri. His guerrillas attacked twenty-one Yankee veterans who had been discharged after the takeover in Atlanta. His men killed the twenty-one and then horribly mutilated their bodies. Price's men sought revenge for the fall of Atlanta.

Josh began to realize that even though the war was now close to his location, and deep in the South, it was still not over. Every day he read the newspaper accounts with great earnest, but when he read of General P.H. Sheridan's successful raid on the Blue Ridge and the Shenandoah Valleys, his gut told him the war was lost. General Sheridan's mission was to cut off all supplies to the Rebels. However, he did more than that. He cut off all hope of supplies. His men burned over 2,000 barns filled with hay and grain. They burned over 70 mills filled with flour and wheat, and took over 3,400 head of cattle and sheep. His path had been wide, and the severity of his destruction had been as devastating as Sherman's March to Atlanta.

General Beauregard of the CSA urged the people of Atlanta to hide their food and themselves, and attack where possible. Soon, he promised, General Sherman and his men would be starved out of Georgia. Josh knew that it was a futile but gallant effort to encourage everyone to fight Sherman.

Carpon continued his nightly beatings of Zeke. Zeke knew he could not hold out much longer. He held on because Carpon told him Josh was nearby and alive. He desperately wanted to see Josh, but he could see little from his prison cell. He tried to get a glimpse of the Confederate commanders when they came into the cellblock, and constantly hoped he would see Josh's face. He did not trust Daniel to tell the truth, but hope was the only thing that kept him alive.

Early one morning, Josh received news that Sherman's men were on the move and would be there that afternoon. He quickly dressed and prepared himself for a battle he did not want to fight. He had placed a knife in the sheath in his left boot and a small derringer pistol in his right. He polished his sword, reloaded his pistol, and carefully cleaned his rifle.

He issued orders for all the men to stand their posts while he marched five hundred men out about a mile from camp to dig in and prepare for a fight. His commander had sent word to General Beauregard asking him for reinforcements. The General promised he would and so it appeared that by nightfall, the battle would take place.

Josh never doubted the outcome of the battle. The Yankees would clobber his men. He only hoped to survive. Sherman had thousands of men, and he had less than five hundred. He left only a hundred men protecting over 35,000 prisoners. A riot could happen at any time, and the prison would be lost. He feared being caught from the front by Sherman's army, and from the rear by a vengeful swarm of Yankee prisoners.

At just past three in the afternoon, Sherman's cavalry attacked. In less than an hour, their stand was lost. Josh and the remainder of his men beat a hasty retreat to the fort. The commander assured him Beauregard and his men were coming, so they once again dug in and prepared to hold off the enemy as long as possible.

Darkness fell. Josh moved all his men to the perimeter, including Carpon and his goons. At just past nine o'clock, a huge charge of Yankees began running from the tree line. Josh gave the order to fire. Cannon shot flew overhead, and musket balls filled the air. In the first hour, a thousand Yankees had been killed and a hundred Rebel soldiers. Josh checked once more with his commander, but there was still no sign of Beauregard.

Josh ordered his men to hold fast, assuming the reinforcements were coming. An hour later, a second charge began, and this time there were even more Yankees rushing toward them. Josh ordered his men to hold their fire until the Yanks were close enough. Josh waited patiently and then finally at the last possible moment, his men opened fire and killed hundreds with the first volley.

However, in twenty minutes they were overrun when the cavalry charged and Josh knew it was over. He screamed out orders to retreat. As he began his own run to the prison wall, he happened to catch sight of Carpon and his goons entering the gates ahead of him. He feared what they might do with the harmless prisoners so quickly he ran after them.

When Josh arrived at the fort, he ordered his remaining guards to run for their lives. Then he swung the gates open and yelled at the top of his lungs, "You're free! You're free! Run for your safety!" He hoped the prisoners would run towards the cavalry, giving his men time to escape. He also hoped the battle would stop, and that finally the prisoners could be taken care of properly.

However, as the ragged throng of weak prisoners in threadbare clothing quickly filed past him, he spotted Carpon and his men near the prison jail cells. He saw Carpon stab a helpless man with his sword and then shoot another. Josh began running to stop him, but the news of their freedom caused the prisoners to rush against the gate. Josh fought his way through the crowds, threatening everyone with his pistol and his sword.

Carpon entered the jail with two of his men. They stopped at each cell and began shooting the men inside. Josh heard the shots and even saw the gun smoke as it billowed out the windows. He realized that Carpon had also set the building on fire in an attempt to hide his crimes.

Every few feet, Josh fought prisoners trying to attack him. He fired a shot into the air to threaten them, and urged them to pull back and run for their freedom. He did not want to hurt them. One man jumped on his back, so he flung the weakened prisoner to the ground, and then put the sword to the man's chest.

"It's over. Run for your freedom. Don't waste your time on me. Run!" Josh yelled.

The man leaped to his feet, and did as Josh had suggested, running for the gate.

As the thousands of prisoners flooded the battlefield, the cavalry was forced to a stop. The few remaining Rebel soldiers made their way in the dark, hoping to escape the wrath of Sherman's army. Beauregard's troops never made it. Andersonville was lost.

Josh made it to the cells and stood just outside a window as he heard the screams of more men as Carpon and his goons fired and stabbed the helpless men one after the other. Josh worked his way through the door. Blood was everywhere. The stench stung his nostrils.

One of Carpon's men spotted Josh and immediately turned and fired. Josh dove to the right to avoid the shot, and without a second of hesitation, he came up with pistol in hand and shot the man between the eyes.

The other guard made a run for the door, but Josh shot him in the leg sending the man careening into a wall. He scrambled to his feet and turned to fire his gun at Josh, but Josh shot him in the heart. He was angry, but he was keeping his wits about him.

Carpon dived into the next cell to avoid being shot. There were but three men left in the cell. He could not believe his good luck. He stabbed one of the men and then swung the sword hard into the second man's neck, nearly severing the man's head.

He shoved his bloody sword into his scabbard, pushing bone and tissue away as it went back into the sheath. Holding the pistol in one hand, he grabbed the other prisoner by the back of the neck, stuck the pistol hard into the man's back, and then began inching him toward the hallway.

"Hold your fire, Johnson! I'm coming out, and I have a prisoner in front of me."

Josh took cover behind a wooden barrel, just twenty feet away. "Come on out, Carpon. It's over. The battle's lost. Why did you kill these poor men? Why?"

"Shut up, you fool. I'm coming out!" warned Carpon as he pushed the man ahead of him, and then stepped into the hallway, turning the man to use him as a shield.

"Let the man go. He's done nothing wrong," said Josh, his pistol aimed at Carpon.

"Nothing wrong? You're not serious. This man has done me great harm, and caused embarrassment for my family and me. He had me expelled from school. He had me kicked out of the place I was to graduate from. I was to become a career military officer. He has shamed me, and for that, he will die as will you."

Josh heard Carpon's words, but it did not make sense to him. "Let him go!" he said once more. "That's an order!"

"Not on your life. He'll die where he stands if you don't put your gun down. Put it down now."

"No, let him go!"

Carpon took the pistol and placed the tip of the barrel to the back of the man's head. He grabbed the man's hair and shook his head. "What's the matter, Josh?" he said sneeringly, delighting in the words he was about to say. "Don't you recognize your former roommate, your former friend, and now Yankee traitor?"

Zeke stared intently at the man behind the barrel as best he could through his swollen eyes. A second passed, and the sudden realization of who was behind the barrel struck him like a bolt of lightening. He could finally tell that the blue eyes he now saw, belonged to the man he had fallen in love with several years ago. They were those same sparkling eyes he had dreamed about for so many months. Zeke instinctively tried to break free from Carpon's hold on him, and for that Carpon struck his temple with the barrel of the gun.

Josh stared at the poor, powerless, ragged figure that Carpon held easily in front of him like a puppet. Zeke's body looked like that of a scarecrow, and it was tough for Josh to realize that the poor man before him was indeed Zeke. However, even in such a state, he knew it was his Zeke.

"Let him go. Don't harm him, or I'll kill you!" yelled Josh.

"I'm going to kill him, and I'm going to kill you, too. I just want you to suffer a bit," laughed Carpon.

Zeke desperately tried once more to struggle free, but he was too weak for Carpon's grasp. Carpon struck him again, and Zeke nearly went limp. Watching his beloved friend pistol whipped nearly drove Josh insane with rage.

Trying to keep a cool head, Josh said, "Hold on, Carpon, it's not Zeke you want. It's me. Zeke would never have been involved in your ouster had it not been for me. If you let him go, I'll lay down my pistol and we can fight it out like men, sword to sword. Are you afraid to fight me? Are you really as good as you think you are?" Josh taunted.

"I can whip your butt any day of the week. You're piss to me," relayed Carpon.

Josh slowly stood up. Zeke saw him and his heart soared. There before him was the man he had been waiting and searching so long for. There in front of him was his lover, a mere twenty steps away. For years, they had been divided by entire states, but now they were close.

Josh slowly laid his pistol down on the top of the barrel. "Let him go. Let's you and me go at it. Come on, Carpon. Are you a chicken? Are you afraid? Are you still a coward?"

Suddenly, Carpon hit Zeke hard across the back of the head sending Zeke unconscious to the floor. For a moment, Josh thought Carpon was going to kill Zeke with the pistol, but slowly Carpon holstered his pistol, and then drew his sword from his scabbard. He laughed a sickening laugh as he raised his bloody sword.

Josh answered the challenge by drawing his own sword. Carpon drew closer, waving the blade tauntingly at Josh. Josh held true to the form he had learned in school. He spread his feet to shoulder width apart, and then kicked rubble from his path and moved closer. The smoke from the burning building was billowing around them, but neither man seemed to notice or fear being caught in the fire.

Carpon drew back his arm quickly and swung hard, but Josh met the thrust, countered, and took a quick nip at Carpon's shoulder, ripping his jacket.

Carpon jumped back and swung again. Blades began to collide with such force and intensity, that both men were surprised the blades did not snap in two. Over and over, they parried. Zeke regained consciousness. He could hear the ping of the blades and slowly he opened his eyes. His vision was blurred. He desperately wanted to see Josh's face.

Josh pushed Carpon to a corner, but Carpon responded with another crushing blow, and then a swift kick to Josh's groin, dropping him to his knees. Sensing victory, Carpon reared back for a swipe at Josh's neck, but Josh dropped to the floor, rolled to his side, and instantly kicked Carpon's feet out from under him.

Daniel hit the floor so hard a tooth flew into the air. He came up chewing his bleeding lip. His face damaged. Josh dove on top of him, and the two began slugging it out. Zeke sat up and rubbed his eyes. He could see Josh. He turned to hold on to the prison bars, and gradually he pulled himself to his feet. He was dizzy from the blows to the head, but his desire for Josh gave him the strength he needed.

Carpon tried to pull his gun from his holster, but Josh knocked it free. It skidded across the concrete floor and spun out of Carpon's reach. Carpon hit Josh in the face. Josh countered, ducked, and came up hard with a right to Carpon's chin.

Daniel fell back and drew a knife from his boot. Josh responded by pulling his own knife, and they began swinging the smaller blades at each other.

Zeke took a staggered step, and then fell back against the wall. He tried to clear his head. Carpon cut Josh's upper right arm. Josh punched Carpon hard in the chest, and then sliced Carpon's cheek.

Carpon screamed as jolt of pain raced to his brain, but the bloody wound angered Carpon, and he charged Josh. Josh quickly sidestepped and hit Carpon hard in the back. Carpon swung around and sliced Josh across his chest.

"I've got you now, you bastard," proclaimed Carpon.

Zeke took another step, rested, and then another.

Josh gave Carpon's right hand a swift, hard kick. The knife flew into the air and clattered harmlessly to the ground. Now defenseless, Carpon dove for his pistol. Josh saw what he was attempting, and scrambled to pull his derringer from his boot.

However, as he frantically tried to find the gun in his boot, he spotted it on the floor just six feet away. Apparently, it had fallen out during the scuffle. He lunged for the gun, but he knew Carpon's gun was closer. Carpon snatched up his pistol, turned, and slowly took aim at Josh.

"Stop. I won. You're dead," laughed the bleeding Carpon as he held the pistol on Josh. Slowly and deliberately, he cocked the gun. Josh had no means of escape. No weapon to pull and no sword. It was over.

Just as Carpon's finger twitched, a loud boom sounded from behind Carpon. Carpon's hand turned slightly and he fired, just missing Josh's head. Josh flinched, but watched as Carpon's body shook oddly. Carpon's head cocked to the left at an odd angle. His eyes bulged. He swallowed hard, and once more, he desperately tried to lift his pistol and fire at Josh.

A second boom was heard. This one lifted Carpon onto his toes and then he fell harshly on his face to the floor, breaking facial bones and scattering teeth as he toppled to the concrete. Smoke circled in a cloud behind where Carpon had stood. Josh slowly rose to his feet. The heat and smoke were pouring in from the roof. His eyes watered from the smoke. He took a step forward and then another. Finally, he spotted Zeke still holding the smoking gun. He had made it to the barrel, picked up Josh's pistol, and killed Carpon. Josh ran to Zeke as Zeke sat the gun down and collapsed into Josh's arms.

"You're alive. You're alive!" screamed Josh. "Don't die on me now. Hang in there. I'll get us out of this. Hang in there!" The roof began to break apart, sending cascades of burning timbers down into the cells.

Zeke made a feeble attempt to smile as he stared intently into Josh's deep blue eyes. He passed out.

Josh shook him, "Zeke? Zeke?" Then fear that Zeke had just died overwhelmed him and he screamed, "Zeke!" Tears swelled up in his eyes and dripped off his cheek to Zeke's face. A single tear caused Zeke's face to flinch. Josh smiled while choking back the tears. He slammed his ear down to Zeke's chest, heard his heartbeat, and quickly took Zeke's weak, frail body tightly into his arms for a moment. He held Zeke with one arm, grabbed his weapons, then began making his way out of the burning jail, and immediately began searching for a way out of the prison camp.

The advancing Union army could not overtake the prison as the now freed prisoners were swarming out to meet them. Josh pushed his way out the gate, made his way to his horse, and swung Zeke into the saddle and climbed up behind him. Josh kicked his horse and made a run around the rear of the prison wall and far away from the Yankees.

He just turned the corner when he suddenly saw a squad of Union soldiers directly ahead. They yelled for Josh to stop, but he had experience in outrunning Yankees. He knew his best chance was to ignore them and gallop on.

"Stop!" They yelled once more. Then he heard one of them say, "Shoot the bastard!"

Josh kicked his horse even harder. The tree line was still a half-mile away. Zeke was like a rag doll in his arms. Josh hunched down over him, and prayed they'd make it.

The bullets raced over his head. He turned his horse a bit left and right, causing them to miss. They re-aimed, and he heard another rush of air as the bullets whizzed past him. A hundred yards to go, he thought. We can make it. We have to.

Josh kicked his horse hard and yelled, "Yee-ah!"

Chess was panting hard, but she had been trained well and responded quickly to Josh's legs. Josh spotted a good break in the trees, the horse leaped a bush, and they entered the safe haven of the woods. For a few more minutes, the bullets shattered limbs and scattered leaves around them. Josh made a sharp cut to the left and disappeared out of their sight. They were safe, at least for now, and they were together.

Josh pulled his horse up to a stop to allow Chess to catch her breath. He pulled Zeke up to him, and listened for his heart by putting his ear to his back. He could hear Zeke's heartbeat, and he could feel his lungs expand against his face. He pulled Zeke ever closer to him and kissed him on the cheek.

"Hang on, Zeke. Hang on. I'll take care of you. Just hang on." He paused. The words he wanted to say he had not said in several years. He had been afraid he would never be able to say them to Zeke again. He thought he had lost Zeke forever. He leaned in to Zeke's ear and whispered, "I love you. I love you, Zeke. Do you hear me? I love you."

The words were like music to Zeke's ears. He could not speak. He could not reply. He could not even open his eyes, but nonetheless, he heard the words, and the words alone made the difference in his determination to stay alive.

TWENTY-TWO

It did not take Josh too long to figure out what to do. He had spent the first hour just riding away from the melee at the prison camp. He did not relax until he was so far away that he could no longer hear the guns at Andersonville. He immediately began using the same evasive tactics he had learned from Captain Bell. He avoided the main roads and avoided all contact with anyone. He had read articles of disgruntled soldiers forming outlaw bands that were robbing and pillaging even their fellow Southerners. He trusted no one but Zeke.

He then steered Chess east. During the hour's ride, he also made another tough decision. His heart told him that he and Zeke had wasted too much time apart already, so perhaps they should just head west and begin their new life.

However, he knew that Zeke's wounded and weakened body might not make it. He could not bear the thought of losing Zeke, so reluctantly he turned east to head toward Charleston and his family's plantation. There were things he needed to settle there, but more importantly, they'd find a safe haven where Zeke could recuperate. Josh could gather supplies while helping to get his family squared away, and then when Zeke was strong enough they'd head west.

It all sounded simple enough as he thought it through, but he really had no other options to choose. Nevertheless, the war was still raging on, and the battles were moving eastward as well. With the prison camp now conquered, Sherman was pushing once again toward Savannah.

Josh stopped every few hours and forced Zeke to drink some water. They came upon an isolated farmhouse. Josh hid Zeke in the bushes, and then approached and bought some cold biscuits and hard tack from the old farmer. He refilled his canteen and moved on. He fed Zeke breadcrumbs by softening them in the water and pushing them into his mouth. Zeke remained barely conscious and silent, and it was that deathly silence that made Josh worry the most.

After riding two days and nights, Josh turned through the woods, crossed a small creek, and onto Johnson's land. He felt revived and free the moment his horse's hooves dug into the soft dirt of his family's plantation. He allowed himself a moment to grin. When he came into the first of the many open fields, he was surprised to see there were no crops growing, no slaves in sight, and no one working.

He crossed onto another field. He studied the soil and realized that the weeds that now covered the field meant the farm had not been worked in quite a while. He wondered what had happened, and he hoped his family was still safe and well. He rode as fast as he dared, trying his best not to bounce Zeke around too harshly.

He rode over a small hill and spotted the main house. He sighed heavily, relieved that it was still there, and undamaged from the war. He was home.

"Mrs. Johnson! Mrs. Johnson!" yelled an old Negro woman as she approached the big house.

Rachel came running to the door. "What is it, Sally?"

"A rider!" the Negro woman exclaimed as she leaned against the hitching post to catch her breath.

"Oh, my God! It could be Yankees or worse. Go find Elijah. Get the rest of the men. I'll get my rifle! Hurry now. Hurry, Sally!" she ordered.

"Yes'm," replied the woman as she made her way around the house to the slave cabins.

"What is it, Mother?" asked Elijah as he came running through the kitchen out of breath.

"A rider. Get your rifle. You know the stories we've been hearing. We can't trust anyone. There's many ex-Confederates robbing homes, raping women, and looting. I'll not have that here. I'll go out and face him. I want you to take aim out the front window and cover me. Keep your rifle aimed on the rider. If he pulls a gun, then you fire. Don't hesitate and don't wait. He might shoot me. Do you hear me, son?"

Elijah was wild-eyed with excitement. "Yes, ma'am. Don't you worry? I can knock him off that horse at a hundred yards. I'll use Grandpa's hunting rifle," he boasted as he ran to get the gun.

"Very well," she said as she cocked her rifle and stepped onto the porch. She had to shade her eyes so that she could see the rider more clearly.

The morning sun was climbing up through the trees and a mist was rising from the grass. She noted the rider was wearing some kind of a uniform. She squinted a bit and realized that the rider was a Rebel. It should have made her relax, but her church friend Sarah had been killed a few months ago by a band of former soldiers who burned Sarah's home to the ground. She was not about to let that happen to her place. She would fight an entire army, and then some if she had to. Since losing her husband, there was nothing more important to her than her family and their home.

Josh entered the circular drive leading to the house. He had never seen the yards and bushes in such a poorly maintained state. He wondered where everyone was. Why weren't the slaves in the field? What had happened? Was his family still here?

As he silently asked himself these questions, he spotted someone moving on the porch. He halted his horse and recognized his mother standing on the porch with a rifle aimed at him. He whispered at first, as the words just did not come out easily. He was overwhelmed with emotion. "Mother?" he yelled.

She did not say anything, but she lowered the rifle slightly.

He kicked his horse slightly, and they moved closer up the drive, just twenty-five yards away. He spoke again more loudly, "Mother?"

Rachel froze. She had pulled the rifle up to aim at Josh. Sally could see more clearly from the second floor where she had been spying. She realized sooner than anyone else who it was. She bolted from the room and ran down the stairs. She spotted Elijah aiming the rifle out the window.

"Hold your fire, Master Elijah. It's our Josh!" she exclaimed as she opened the door.

Josh moved closer.

"Stop where you are. That's close enough," a fearful Rachel warned, now raising the rifle at Josh.

Alarmed, Josh pulled his horse to a sudden halt. He started to climb out of the saddle.

"Stay where you are, I said," she warned again. Then hearing the door open behind her, she turned to see Sally coming toward her. "Sally, I told you to stay..."

"But, ma'am..." began Sally.

"Get back in the house!" Rachel harshly said.

"Ma'am, please. It's Master Josh!"

Sally turned Rachel back to face the rider. Josh recognized his mother, but the slave standing beside her would have been a mystery to him had he not recognized her voice. He urged his horse forward slowly and rode up to the hitching post. Elijah came out the door carrying his rifle and stood on the other side of his mother. Together, the three of them stared intently at the stranger on the horse.

Josh dismounted and carefully pulled Zeke from the horse and carrying him in his arms, he made his way up the steps until he was just a few feet from his mother.

"Mother, it's me. It's Joshua," he said.

At once, the rifle fell to her side. Elijah took the rifle from her. Her hands went to her face as she gasped. Tears rolled down her cheeks. Her heart pounded and then she whispered, as no voice would come, "Joshua?"

"Yes, Mother. It's me," he grinned.

She could not believe the dirty, bearded man that stood before her was her son, her boy, her beloved Joshua. She ran to him and attempted to hug him even though he still had Zeke in his arms.

"How are you?" asked Josh.

"I'm fine," she cried.

"And how's my little brother? I see you're not so little anymore," grinned Josh.

Elijah smiled. "I'm fine."

"And who is that pretty young lady?" winked Josh at Sally.

"Oh, Master Josh!" she exclaimed as he ran to him and hugged his neck.

"What are you doing with that man?" Elijah asked staring at the lifeless creature, he held in his arms.

"This is Zeke."

His mother gasped, "Oh, my word. He looks so bad."

"Mom, he's been beaten pretty badly. I need help. He's still alive. Can we stay here?"

Without even an ounce of hesitation, she replied, "Of course. Let's get him in the house. Sally, get some clean linens. Elijah, get some hot water. Take him up to your room. I'll get some soup. Hurry, he doesn't look good."

Josh and his mother had taken great care to strip Zeke out of his ragged bloody clothes, bathe him, and then carefully clean his numerous wounds. One by one, they bandaged cut after cut. Josh was horrified to find that Zeke had several broken ribs. His hair was covered with head lice. They cut his hair short, scrubbed him with harsh soap, and then Josh carefully shaved him.

Rachel stood by and watched with amazement as Josh carefully force fed Zeke some chicken soup. It did not take long before she realized that Zeke was more than a friend to Josh. She knew that her son loved the man lying there. There was a part of her that was horrified at the thought, but she was so glad to have her son home that right now nothing else mattered.

"Let him sleep now, Josh. He'll be okay. At least I hope he will. He's been beaten up pretty badly. Who did this to him" asked Rachel as she took the bowl of soup from Josh with one hand, took his arm with the other, and led him from the room.

"A Rebel guard by the name of Carpon," he replied. "He had gone to school with Zeke and I, and we caught him cheating. He was expelled from the academy because of it. He took his revenge out on Zeke when he was captured. He was just about to kill him when I found him. Sherman's men overtook us at Andersonville. All those Yankee soldiers are now free."

"Let's hope they head north," she added. "What about Sherman?"

"He's marching to Savannah. I guess Charleston will be next," said Josh.

"Oh, my Lord. We must take all our money out of the bank there and hide it. Things have been rough here."

"Where are the slaves? Why isn't anyone working the fields?" asked Josh.

"Honey, use the guest room, get a bath, and then come down for lunch, and I'll explain. I'm sorry there's no hot water. There's no water on the stove right now...just soup."

"That's okay. Even a cold bath will feel good right now," replied Josh as he turned to enter the guest room, and then turned back to his mother, "Thanks for helping me with Zeke. I thought he was going to die."

She looked into her son's face and saw her son's baby blue eyes water. "I know he's special to you. He's going to be fine. You'll see. Now get your bath. We have so much to catch up on. We'll talk later."

He watched her walk down the stairs, and he came to the realization that she knew that he loved Zeke. It scared him and yet made him feel so good that she knew.

Josh entered the kitchen carrying Zeke's tattered prison clothes he had taken from a dead prisoner to keep warm and his own Confederate uniform. The Negro woman at the stove heard his boots on the floor and turned to Josh. Sally dropped her spoon and hugged him, "Oh, my child. My precious Joshua! I'm so happy you're safe." Josh had not yet shaven, but it made no difference to Sally. She would have recognized him with a mask on. "Sally? How are you?"

"I'm fine, child. Fine, indeed. Whew! Where'd you get those smelly clothes? Shall I wash them?" she asked, fanning the air with her hands in an attempt to remove the assault to her nostrils.

"Do you have a soap fire going out back?" he asked.

"Why yes," she replied with a puzzled look on her face.

"Good, I'm going to burn these," he announced as he stepped out the back of the kitchen, walked over to the fire, and without hesitation, dropped the clothes into the fire.

Elijah walked up behind him, "You're burning your uniform? Why?"

"...Because I want nothing else to do with this war. I fought hard. I did my part. I was wounded and I watched many friends die. I've seen so many men die and all for what? It wasn't worth it, I can promise you that. I'm so glad you didn't join up."

"I wanted to when I turned fifteen, but mother wouldn't let me. Things were just too rough here."

"Come on, let's eat," called Rachel from the kitchen.

Josh entered the kitchen and found both his mother and Sally sitting at the slave's kitchen table. He had never sat with his family at this table. He had only taken meals in this room when he was a little boy and Sally fed him.

Rachel noted the look on his face, "It's all right. There are just a few of us here now, and it's just too hard for Sally to feed us in the main dining room. Besides, quite often this is the warmest room in the house. Sit down. Let's eat."

She then said a long blessing, thanking God for Josh's return and asking for Zeke's recovery.

After a few minutes of eating, Josh's curiosity piqued, "Mother, where is everyone? What's happened?"

Rachel took a bite of a biscuit, finished chewing, and replied, "Do you remember that foreman your father hired?"

"Trevor? I didn't like him much," replied Josh.

"Me neither," added Elijah.

"Well, none of us did, but help was hard to find. After your father died, Trevor got even surer of himself, and he started beating the slaves. He got so mean to them, that one night about a year ago we had an uprising. I thought the slaves were going to kill us all, but as it turned out, they knew it wasn't our doing. I never knew he was hurting anyone, or I would have tried to stop him. The slaves hunted down Trevor and hung him.

"But they were afraid the white plantation owners in the area would seek revenge and kill them all. Therefore, during the night they packed up their stuff, and scattered to the woods, heading north. Sally is the only one that stayed behind. I don't know what we would have done without Sally, bless her heart," Rachel winked at Sally and smiled.

"Sally's free, now!" added Elijah.

"That's right. I decided that I would not give the Yankees the pleasure of freeing my slaves. Sally decided to stay on her own, but they probably would not have believed that. She deserves to be free and so she is. She works for wages and room and board, but we've little money. Now Sally's family as far as we're concerned."

Josh winked at Sally. "Congratulations Sally, and thanks for staying and taking care of the family."

"Now that you're here maybe we can just put this plantation back in gear," added his mother.

"But how can you work a plantation without help?" asked Josh.

"We'll have to start small, like farmers. Work a few fields. Raise chickens and pigs. Perhaps buy some cattle." Then she stopped and the happy expression left her face. He took a shallow breath and added firmly,

"We'll do whatever it takes to save our home. If I have to plant vegetables to keep us alive, I will. We will survive."

"Mom, I can't stay. When Zeke recovers, we have to head west. He's a Yankee and won't be welcomed in the South. I'm a Rebel and won't be treated with kindness in the North either. There's a lot of bad blood between the North and South, and that's not going to change even if this war does end. I killed Yankees, and they killed my friends. I saw many Rebels mistreat Yankees, and I'm sure the same happened to our men. It'll never be the same. Zeke and I must head west and start over."

"You're leaving?" asked Elijah.

Josh reached over and squeezed his brother's shoulder, "Oh, not for a while just yet. From the looks of this place, Elijah and I have our work cut out for us. The war isn't over just yet. I won't leave you unprotected. We'll come up with a plan, find you some labor, and get this place going. Before long, the old plantation will look pretty good again."

None of them was happy with Josh's announcement of his plans to leave, but his enthusiasm for bringing the plantation back to life brought them the hope they had not heard for a long time.

Josh did not sleep in the guest room, but instead sat beside Zeke's bed in the very same rocker that Sally had sat in when he had been sick as a child. However, as the moon climbed high in the sky, the weary Josh climbed into the bed, slid his arm under Zeke's neck, and cuddled into him.

During the night he dreamed of the happier times, he and Zeke spent together. He reminisced about their first night together in Maine, and their fun times in Washington.

When the sun shined on his face through the open window, Josh stirred a bit and felt his erection rubbing against Zeke's bare back. He momentarily forgot where he was. He felt Zeke stir, and he leaned up just as Zeke opened his eyes. Josh's heart raced. Zeke's pulse quickened as he desperately tried to get his eyes to focus on the face before him.

The blue eyes took shape, then the nose, then the blond hair, and then Josh's smile. Zeke's began to smile as well.

"Zeke? Are you okay?"

"Josh? Is that really you? Am I dead? Is this a dream?" he whispered, his throat dry and his voice hoarse.

Josh laughed, "No, it's not a dream. You're not in heaven, and you're no longer in that hell of a place in Andersonville. You're in South Carolina. You're at my family's home. How are you?"

"Where?"

"South Carolina."

"Oh, my. I thought surely I was..."

"Not for a minute. I couldn't let the person I love the most in the world leave me. I love you." The tears slid down his cheeks and splashed on Zeke's bandaged chest.

"And I love you."

"Are you okay?" asked Josh.

"I hurt something awful."

"I know. You were beaten badly."

"By Carpon, right?" asked Zeke.

"Yes, but never again. You shot him. He's dead."

Zeke wasn't even a soldier, and now he had shot a Rebel. Even though Carpon had treated him badly, he had never killed a soldier before being captured, and forced into the hellish prisons.

"Are you hungry?" asked Josh as he began climbing off the bed.

Zeke struggled, but slowly reached and grabbed Josh's hand. He was so weak, Josh could easily have slipped his grasp, but the touch of Zeke's pale white hand on his flesh, instantly made his stop moving.

Zeke's bruised and swollen lips parted as he fought for the right words, "I'm hungry all right. I'm hungry for you to kiss me," he managed with a grin.

Josh's burst into a huge smile. Slowly he leaned into Zeke.

Just as their lips touched, Zeke let out yelp. "Ow!"

"I'm sorry, I hurt your lips," apologized Josh.

"No, you're squeezing my ribs. Are they broken?" asked Zeke.

"A few..."

Zeke interrupted, "But don't stop kissing me. Don't ever stop kissing me."

They embraced once again, with Josh propping himself up on an elbow to keep his weight from pressing in on Zeke's ribs. Zeke's weak hand managed to slide down and squeeze Josh's erection. It was the very moment he had been dreaming about for so long, and now that it had finally come, he was determined to make it last forever.

TWENTY-THREE

Josh came in from the plantation work to personally feed Zeke every meal, but while Zeke took his long recovery naps, Josh and Elijah made plans for the land. They also cut firewood, took care of the remaining livestock, and then sat down with Rachel to discuss a strategy.

"Mom, I don't think we'll ever be as big as we were without slave labor, but we've got a chance if we work smart and diversify."

"Diversify?" she asked.

"I learned it from Captain Bell. We never attacked head on, but rather scattered ourselves in twos and came in from different directions. We had men in our group who were sharpshooters at long range, and some were good at handling horses. A few were good with explosives. In other words, Mom, we can't just raise cotton anymore. We don't have the labor to do so."

"What do you propose?" she asked with apprehension.

"I think we should plant about five acres of cotton, and a few acres of corn and tobacco."

"Tobacco? I hate the stuff. I don't like men who smoke it either," Rachel stated strongly, holding her nose as if she could smell smoke at that moment.

"Mom, tobacco is becoming very popular. It's a cash crop and not too hard to grow. Our weather is perfect for it. We can grow it, dry it in the empty slave cabins, and sell it throughout the winter. It'll keep some money coming into this place when the corn and cotton won't."

"I see," she smiled a bit.

"The cotton will bring us in some money each summer and the corn will keep us alive. We need it for cornbread and grits, and our livestock will need it for feed. We should try to grow all we can and store it up in the lofts in the barns."

"That sounds good. What else?"

"I think we should plant a huge garden out back. It was your idea really, Mom, but the war has devastated the South already, and it's still not over. We must not be reliant on buying anything. We must grow or make it ourselves, if we're going to survive."

"I agree. I was thinking we need more chickens and pigs."

"You're right Mom, but we also need a few more hands. Elijah and I can't do this all by ourselves, and we must find a few good workers. When Zeke gets well, I need to move west, so we must work fast, and we must be prepared if the Yankees come our way. Let's take all the silver, china, and anything of value and bury it out back."

"I heard stories of plundering. Do you think it could happen here?" she asked.

"Yes, I do. We must make a plan. Mom, you, and Sally must have a place to hide if someone comes. We'll ring the bell three times if trouble comes, and you must hide quickly. Do you hear me? You must!" he said strongly.

"I think we'll hide in the spring cellar. The brush has just about grown over it. We'll check it out, but I think it'll do just fine. I'll put a gun or two in there."

"Good, Mom. That's the idea. Now, how much money do we have in the bank in Charleston?"

"Just over ten thousand dollars."

"Elijah and I will head out early in the morning to get it. We'll have to hide it with the silver, too. What else do you need from town? I don't plan to go back there for a long, long time."

"Just a few medical things."

"Make a list. If I can, I hope to hire someone to work with us, perhaps a former slave. Maybe they'll work for an acre of land."

"You'd give away part of our home?" she asked angrily.

"Mother, we have land on the other side of the swamp that we'll never use. I saw men's legs sawed off to save their lives. I think we need to amputate some of our holdings to survive," he paused to allow his gruesome point to settle in. "Mother, we need to hold on to our cash, but we need other ways to survive. We don't even know if our money is even worth anything anymore. All I've seen for the past couple of years are worthless Confederate script. We will survive. It'll be fine. You'll see."

She couldn't reply. Josh at that moment reminded her so much of her dead husband. He was strong, confident and she knew she trusted him. She simply nodded her head in understanding.

Josh curled in tightly to Zeke as they kissed as best as they could in Zeke's weakened state, but just holding each other, and kissing was more than enough for now. They would have plenty of time for other things as Zeke healed and became stronger.

At dawn, Elijah and Josh saddled up, checked their guns, and headed for town. They had gone about twelve miles, when suddenly four Negro men came running from the woods toward them.

"Run!" yelled Josh to Elijah as he kicked, drew a pistol, and fired a shot from his pistol just over the heads of the Negro men. They were carrying axes and hoes, and one had a large machete knife.

After they rounded a bend, Elijah pulled his horse up to a walk. "Is it like this everywhere?"

"It's going to get worse before it gets better. The slaves have freedom, but no work. They have no food and no place to go. When a man gets hungry, or when his family gets hungry, he'll do anything to keep them alive, even if it means stealing or murdering. Come on, we must hurry to town and back. Don't ever go away from the farm by yourself, and always carry your guns even on our own land. Do you hear me?"

"Yes, big brother," grinned Elijah. "Race you!"

"Hi-yah!" yelled Josh as he accepted the challenge, but never in his wildest dreams had he thought his brother would be such a natural in the saddle. Elijah rode tight in the saddle, barely moving his torso at all, and he placed his head low and almost against the neck of the horse. He rounded curves without the slightest hesitation. He was not afraid of falling, and he easily outran Josh.

"You must have inherited Grandfather's genes. You're a splendid rider," laughed Josh.

"I beat you," proclaimed Elijah as he threw his hands in the air.

"Yes, you did. Do you like horses?"

"I raised this one myself. Her name is Settie," replied Elijah as he petted his horse's neck.

"Very well, that gives me another idea. Come on, let's get moving."

Josh and Elijah were amazed to find Charleston in such panic and disarray. Homes had been abandoned and looted by thieves. Families were leaving the city by the thousands. They were told by retreating Rebel troops that Sherman was heading their way. News of the burning of Atlanta had brought panic to everyone.

Josh and Elijah carefully steered the horses to the side of the rode to avoid being trampled by the wagons and carts leaving the city one after the other.

The family's bank was downtown. They rode along the battery and discovered it was now a fortress, protecting Charleston from a naval assault, but the city lay virtually unprotected from a ground assault. Small garrisons of men had been stationed along the roads, but Josh saw nothing strong enough to stop Sherman's 65,000 veteran troops.

They found the bank. Josh decided it was not safe to leave their horses unwatched, so he put Elijah in charge of guarding them while he went inside. He had to wait for the manager before he was finally ushered inside.

"Mister Johnson. It is so nice to see you," said the bank manager as he shook Josh's hand and gestured to a vacant leather seat in front of his desk.

"Mr. Campbell, it's a pleasure to see you as well. Charleston seems to be in a total uproar."

"You're right about that. Everyone says Sherman is coming."

"Let's hope not," replied Josh, and then bit his tongue to avoid talking about his experience with Sherman's troops at Andersonville. "I'm here to withdraw my family's money from your bank. We have some planting and fixing up to do. I believe we have just over ten thousand in your bank."

"That's right, but your mother..."

Josh handed him a letter. "That's from Mother, giving me permission to pick up the money. Is there anything else you need?" It was his polite way of saying that that was all the man needed and was all he would get.

Mr. Campbell read over the brief note. "I see, no, I guess not, but there is a bit of problem."

"A problem?"

“All Union money was removed from the bank over a year ago. I can't pay you in United States currency. I can give you Confederate money."

Josh thought hard about that. "No, I prefer the money we put in your bank."

"I can't give you what I don’t have. When the war is over and everything settles down, then I'm sure I can pay."

Josh got angry. "You gave our family money to the Confederacy?"

"I gave them nothing. They needed cash to buy weapons abroad. They took it, gave me promissory notes, and Confederate bills."

"What about our safe deposit box?"

"It is still under lock and key."

"Let me see it."

"This way," said the manager as he led Josh from his office.

They walked down the hallway and into the huge safe. The manager took out a key and unlocked the little door, opened it and pulled out a long steel box and placed it on the table.

"I'll be back in a few moments to help you lock it up," said the manager as he left the room.

Josh took out his father's brass key and unlocked the box. It hadn't been opened in three years, but the lock turned and clicked. Josh opened it slowly, half expecting to find nothing in it.

Instead, he found several stacks of Yankee dollars. He quickly counted and was relieved to find at least five thousand dollars in cash. He then found another two thousand in gold coins, and the deed to their land.

Josh removed everything and stuffed it into his father's old money belt he had brought with him, lifted his shirt, and tied it around his waist and then adjusted his clothes to hide it.

When the manager returned, Josh had left the empty box on the table and vanished.

"Let's go," said Josh as he swung in the saddle.

"Trouble?" asked Elijah.

"No dollars, only Confederate money. We'll have to wait until the war's over to get our money, and then only if we're lucky. Let's get our supplies and get out of town. I don't have a good feeling about this town any more."

They went to the nearest mercantile and tied off the horses. Josh sent Elijah in to get the stuff for his mother. He found most of the shelves nearly bare, but managed to find most of the things she needed.

Josh bought a paper while he waited on Elijah. He immediately began catching up on the war. He read an editorial on Sherman, which indirectly praised the man's insightfulness. Sherman had long ago figured out that if he divided the South, then the South would fall. Marching through Tennessee and then burning Atlanta was all part of his plan. Conquering Savannah would be the icing on the cake, said the editor.

Then Josh read that Sherman had wisely sent a group of men back to Tennessee to head off General Hood, who was trying to cut off Sherman, and force him from Georgia. General Thomas, of the Union Army, managed to stop Hood, and thus allow Sherman to continue advancing toward Savannah.

Elijah came out of the store with saddlebags full, handed Josh a twenty pound sack of flour to throw over his saddle, and, together, they mounted up and headed for the stockyards. The last time he was here, the corrals were filled with animals. Now there were less than two hundred head of cattle and only a few horses.

"What are we doing here?" asked Elijah.

"We need some cows and a good stud horse."

Elijah asked, "A what?"

"You heard me. Come on."

Together they walked their horses through the muddy stockyards until Josh found a man selling dairy cattle. He bought two cows. Then after much searching, they found a man selling horses. Josh and Elijah went over the horses very carefully. Josh once again used the knowledge that his grandfather had taught him, and what he had learned with Captain Bell. Elijah used the natural abilities he had inherited, and together, they selected the horses.

"I think this mare will do nicely for Zeke. She has good feet for the long miles we have to ride and a strong back. I don't see a good stud horse," said Josh.

The man selling the horses spoke, "The Reb army has most of the horses. I just brought these up from Florida this week. That one will cost you a hundred dollars, and I don't want Confederate money."

"A hundred! That's robbery!" exclaimed Josh.

"Take it or leave it. It's all the same to me. I can sell that horse a hundred times over. You want her or not?"

"You'll have to throw in a saddle and bridle," replied Josh.

"I'll give you the bridle. Don't have any saddle. Take it or leave it," he said gruffly.

"Okay. Hold her for me. I'll be back in a minute," replied Josh as he suddenly turned to watch a rider move down the street.

Elijah turned to see what had caught Josh's eye.

"Come on, Elijah. That's the horse we want."

Josh and Elijah followed the rider until he pulled up at the barbershop. A tall thin man with a black mustache climbed off, and then two other men pulled up beside him. Josh had not even noticed the accompanying riders as he had been studying the horse's legs, and the way it walked.

"Excuse me, sir. My name is Josh Johnson." Josh shook the man's hand politely.

"I'm Sir Henry Clayborn," replied the man with a thick English accent.

"I must say you have a very nice horse there. It so happens that I'm in the need of a stud horse. I'd like to buy your horse."

"I'm sorry. It's not for sale. I just purchased it a few weeks ago. It runs like the wind. It suits me just fine."

"I see. You like fast horses, do you?" asked Josh with a grin.

"Yes, I like to ride fast. I'm a foxhunter in England. It's a great sport."

Josh thought for a second and asked, "How about this? You and my horse will race. If I win, you sell me the horse at a fair price."

"I see." The man thought a second, "And if I win, what do I get?"

Josh pondered the question for a moment, and then to Elijah's surprise, Josh laughed hard and deep, "Well, I could give you my sister, but she's ugly as an old mule!"

Henry and his companions laughed. Henry immediately liked Josh, and Josh had used his Grandfather's knack for misdirecting a buyer until he had him in the proper position.

"I'll be fair. If I lose, you can have my horse."

Henry looked over Josh's horse. "It's no race horse, but I like the other one. If I win, I'll take that horse," he said pointing to Elijah's horse.

Elijah started shaking his head no, but without even a blink, Josh replied, "A deal. Now where shall we race?"

A stranger had been listening. There's an open field at the end of the yard. There's at least a three hundred yard run there."

"Thanks, friend," grinned Josh.

"Henry, shall we give it a go in about fifteen minutes?" Josh asked with his hand outstretched.

Accepting the challenge, Henry shook it strongly, "Agreed!"

Elijah began immediately protesting to Josh, "Josh, you had no right to bet my horse. I raised this horse from birth. I'm the only one that's ever ridden her. I can't lose. I won't lose her!" he began yelling.

Josh cut him off suddenly and swiftly, "Precisely why she's the horse you're to ride to win the race!"

Elijah's eyes went wide. "I thought you said you were going to race Mister Clayborn."

"Nope, I never said me. I offered my horse but never said it was my horse that was going to do the riding, or that I was going to be the rider. You ride much faster than I do, and your horse runs like the wind. We need Henry's horse to raise more horses. When the war ends, the price of horses will go sky high. So many animals have been confiscated or killed that the South will almost be horseless. If we raise horses, we are diversifying. I think grandfather would approve of this race, don't you think." Josh grinned.

A worried Elijah couldn't help but smile. "Do you really think we can win?"

"I know we can. I never bet on nothing but a sure thing. I've seen you ride. The Yankees couldn't catch me. Very few men can beat me, but you did. You'll whip that English chap's butt! You have to."

Josh quickly scanned the terrain of the field where the race was to take place. Although mostly sand, it did have some loose granite stones that could cause a rider to stumble. He picked out a level spot, picked up a stick, drew a line across the sand with the stick, and pronounced it the finish line to a crowd of men who had already heard about the race and had gathered to watch.

Elijah nervously rubbed his horse's mane, trying to calm himself more than the horse. Henry Clayborn entered the field riding his mount and followed by another twenty-five or so well-wishers.

"I thought you were going to race me," protested Henry.

"No, I never said I was racing, but I wish I could. A Yankee bullet caught me in the shoulder, and I can hardly hold on to a pair of reins now. I can tell you this, I can sure hold on to my money and your money with my bum arm!" Josh chuckled.

Henry and the crowd laughed. "Very well then, who is the rider?"

"This is my younger brother and since it is his horse that is our end of the stake, well, I thought it fitting that he races you. He's young now, so don't you go beating up on him and making him look bad," grinned Josh.

"Yeah, right, somehow, I think I've been suckered, but no matter, my horse is still faster, and I'm the fastest man in all of Charleston to ride her to victory. Is this the finish line?" asked Henry.

"Yes, I propose the two of you ride from the far end of the field to here. When I fire my pistol in the air the race is on. First one across the line wins!" yelled Josh.

"Let's do it!" laughed Henry.

The crowd cheered as Henry rode his mount to the far end of the field. Josh walked over to Elijah and grabbed the bridle of his horse. "Now Elijah, it's just a race. There are other horses you could own, but this is not about winning a race, it's about building our lives and plantation back to what we once knew. If you concentrate on winning, then you'll not only have a great stud horse we can use for breeding, but you'll still own the mare to start the process. Don't be distracted by the other rider or the crowd. Do you see the finish line?"

"Yes, of course I do," replied Elijah nervously.

"Good, now look past the finish line about twenty-five yards. What do you see?"

"I see an old broken carriage."

"Good. In your mind, make that the finish line."

"I don't understand."

"If you ride just hard enough to the finish line, he might just beat you, but if you ride hard enough to make the farther finish line, you'll get to the first one sooner. So, concentrate on the carriage. Got it?"

"Yeah, I see."

"You can do it, Elijah. I know you can. Let's go!" Josh gave him a handshake like a gentleman to a gentleman. All their lives they had been big brother and little brother. Today, Elijah was a man. He suddenly sat taller in the saddle. Josh had learned how to treat boys who had to do adult jobs from Captain Bell. He immediately noted the change in Elijah's posture and his attitude.

Josh ran back to the finish line. The crowd formed two lines perpendicular to the finish line so they could all see the race. A few stragglers gathered just ten yards past the finish line, hoping to see a good race from a great view.

"Nice horse, son," said Henry without emotion.

"Yes, she is. I raised her myself."

"It'll be a shame to take her from you, but a bet's a bet. My horse is fast, very fast. You'd better hang on tight," warned Henry.

Elijah saw Josh raise his pistol in the air. He hunkered down behind his horse's head, whispering quietly to his horse. He shortened the reins a bit and pulled his feet forward. The moment the gun sounded, Elijah kicked his horse hard and yelled, "Yeooow!"

They both got off to a good start. Elijah was immediately a full length ahead of Henry. Josh was yelling with all his might. The crowd was yelling, but the two riders heard nothing more than the sounds of their voices mixed with the thump, thump of their horses' hooves as they pounded the hardened sand.

Elijah pulled a bit farther into the lead. He kept his eyes on the carriage, determined not to look anywhere else. Suddenly, his mount hit a patch of soft sand and he stumbled, breaking stride and struggling to keep from falling. Henry passed her. Elijah took his eyes off the carriage and fought to hang on. Josh's heart sank. The lead had been lost, and now Henry had a full length on Elijah.

Elijah kicked his horse hard and the mount did not seem to like the rear view of Henry's horse. There were but seventy-five yards to go to the finish line. Elijah focused on the carriage once more, kicked his horse again, and yelled, "Run! Run!"

Josh's eyes were gleaming with the excitement. Elijah pulled within a half-length with only fifty yards to go. Elijah yelled some more, the mare pushed a bit harder, and the new riders were now side by side. The crowd cheered. It was a magnificent race with just twenty yards to go.

Elijah's eyes were on the carriage. He kicked his horse and she nosed ahead just a half second ahead of Henry and slammed over the finished line. Henry pulled up immediately, but Elijah's mount kept running. The people at the end of the finish line dove out of the way. Elijah didn't stop until he reached the carriage, and then he turned around to a stunned crowd, threw up his hands, and shouted like an Indian brave who had just killed his first deer.

The crowd burst into applause and cheers. Henry tipped his hat to the boy who had ridden a good, hard, solid race. Then shook the grinning Josh's hand.

Elijah rode back to the waiting crowd who patted his horse and shook his hand in admiration.

"Good race, son. Very good race," said Henry as he shook Elijah's hand firmly and smiled. "I haven't been beaten in a long, long while. You're a good rider and apparently a good trainer as well."

"How much?" asked Josh?

"Two hundred dollars," replied Henry.

"Two hundred? That's way out of line. Your horse isn't worth two hundred dollars," protested Josh.

"To me she is. I tell you what. I'll make you a deal. You can have her for free as long as I get the first foal."

Josh grinned, "That's a deal, Henry. You're a fair man, and I have to admit, a good rider as well."

"I'm not finished, I get the first foal after she's been trained by Elijah. I want a horse faster than the one he rode today. Do we still have a deal?"

Elijah grinned. Josh shook Henry's hand once more. "We have a deal," Josh answered.

"Would you two join me for lunch?" asked Henry.

"We didn't bring proper clothes for a fancy lunch," said Josh.

"No need to. I have a cottage on the edge of town. Come, I'll show you."

Josh stopped by and finished the deal for the man selling the other horse. He paid him a small fee to look after the horses and the cow they had bought then they followed Henry home. They sat down to eat a picnic meal under a big moss covered oak tree. Although the calendar said it was November, the sun was still quite hot in the middle of the day in Charleston.

"I've decided to stay in Charleston," began Henry. "I like the town. I even saw a play the other night at the Dock Street Theater. There's a lot of culture in this town, but there's also the feeling of a pioneer spirit here as well. I've been lucky enough to inherit my fortune, but if I'm not careful, I could lose it just as I lost my horse today. I bought a plantation earlier this week. Perhaps you know it. It was the Chatsworth place."

"Yes, I do. Old man Chatsworth was in shipping. I didn't know he had it up for sale," added Josh.

"He died a few years ago, his oldest son was killed at Bull Run, and his wife and daughter wanted to move closer to the city."

The sudden reminder of the loss of friends immediately changed the expression on Josh's face. Henry noted the change and quickly moved on.

"I don't plan to continue to raise cotton there. I want to raise horses. I see a greater market potential in horses."

"You're right. That's why we wanted your stud. We plan to mix up our plantation as well. You should come over and see us."

"I will. Will you draw me a map as to how to get there? I get so lost in these lowlands," grinned Henry.

"Sure," replied Josh.

Henry had his servant bring pen and paper, and Josh quickly drew the map. "It's the Johnson plantation. Elijah and I manage it for my mother and my sister. My father's dead."

"I'm sorry to hear that. This war has caused your country such great harm, but I believe that it will emerge even stronger. I'm betting on it. I'll see you two very soon. I may have another deal for you."

"Yeah, what is it?" asked Josh as he stood up to leave.

"I'm working on it. I'll see you soon," grinned Henry, enjoying the tease.

Josh and Elijah collected their two new horses, the cows, and the supplies and began the ride back to the plantation about mid afternoon. Unlike their previous ride down the road to the plantation, they could not outrun any thieves. Cows were not known for their running speed.

"Keep your eyes peeled and your gun ready," warned Josh as if he was talking to one of Bell's riders.

Elijah's heart pounded. He had never shot a man. The palm of his hand rubbed nervously over the handle of his pistol. "There's a man and a woman up ahead. They're Darkies," added Elijah.

Josh had already seen them. They were carrying a few belongings in sacks on their shoulders and were walking north. They did not appear to be carrying any weapons, but nonetheless Josh took his pistol out of his holster and held it across his lap.

The couple turned as they approached but kept walking. Josh guessed the Negro man was in his early thirties and he looked strong. He had labored hard as a slave. The man smiled just slightly and tipped his hat to Josh and Elijah. The Johnsons responded politely as well, although they were not used to treating slaves in this fashion. Elijah and Josh rode on without a word being said.

They rounded a bend and immediately discovered an overturned wagon. A man lay beside the wagon. A horse was caught in the harness and remained motionless while waiting for help.

"Someone's had an accident!" exclaimed Elijah. "Come on. We'd better help!"

"Wait, Elijah!' called Josh, but it was too late. Elijah had kicked his horse, and was pulling one of the cows as fast as he could. Josh's eyes left the road as he began scanning the trees for any additional signs of trouble.

The man lay in the dirt with his eyes away from them. He could hear Elijah approaching but he did not move. The horse neighed and tried once more to pull the overturned wagon. The horse stomped her feet in the soil in frustration.

Elijah pulled up just a few feet from the man, leaped from his horse, and ran to turn the wounded man over. As the man turned over, he held a pistol cocked and aimed at Elijah. Josh saw the man's gun and instantly took aim with his own. The man quickly leaped to his feet and told Elijah to put his hands up and to turn around. The man used Elijah's body to shield him.

"Drop your weapon!" yelled the man to Josh.

Josh kept his aim at the man.

"You heard him! Drop the gun!" exclaimed another voice from behind a big oak tree off to the left.

Josh turned to his left and saw the man's rifle pointed squarely at him. He had no choice. He slowly un-cocked his pistol and dropped it to the dirt. The man with the rifle moved closer, and motioned for Josh to climb down and walk up beside Elijah.

Josh noted Elijah's eyes. They were dancing with anger and fear. He was afraid Elijah might try something stupid. "Be calm," he said.

The man with the rifle slammed the barrel over Josh's back, knocking him harshly to the ground. "You'll speak when and only when I tell you to. Now give us your valuables and give 'em up now, or I'll cut your ears off!" threatened the man.

Elijah took out his wallet and the man holding the gun on him snatched it from him, opened it up, and laughed, "There's only a few Confederate dollars here! Where's the rest?"

The man with the rifle poked Josh in the back. Josh moved up to his knees and turned to face the man. "May I speak, sir?" he mocked.

"Give me your wallet," demanded the man.

"You've caught us at the wrong time. We've just come from town where we bought these two horses and cows and some supplies. We spent almost all of our money. We've haven't much anyhow. I've got a few coins." Josh fetched the coins from his pocket.

"Come on!" demanded the man as he took the coins, and then pushed Josh to his feet and forced him off the road to the woods. Elijah was pushed along as well. They tied Elijah to a tree. Once tied the man began searching Elijah's clothes for more money. The man unbuckled Elijah's pants, pushed them to his ankles, and then laughed at the sight of his nakedness.

Suddenly the man quit laughing, holstered his pistol and took out a long, shiny, sharp knife. He placed the knife under Elijah's balls. Elijah's face went ashen white.

Josh saw the man place the knife and he took a step to stop the man. The man with the rifle hit him hard against the back of the neck and shoulder, hitting his old wound. Josh fell to the ground as the pain wracked his body.

"Where's the money, kid or I'm going to turn you into a bitch very quick!" threatened the man with the knife.

"In Charleston. We spent it," screamed Elijah.

The man nicked him just a bit on his thigh. Blood dripped down to his pants. Elijah screamed again. Josh turned his head quickly, while grabbing fistfuls of sand in each hand.

"Let him go. I will tell you where the money is," began Josh as he suddenly sprang up and threw the sand into the eyes of the man holding the rifle. The sand was temporarily blinded the man. Josh knocked the rifle from the man's hands and dove onto him. They began to roll over and over, slugging, kicking, and jabbing one another.

The man with the knife turned to watch, but the knife was kept in place at Elijah's genitals.

Josh hit the man hard in the jaw, but the man did not go down. He was a tough, mean street fighter. The man hit Josh back and then dove on him, and began slamming Josh's head in the dirt, bloodying Josh's nose, and splitting the skin just above his left eye.

Suddenly, the man stopped, pulled a hunting knife front the calf of his boot, and clenched his fist around it tightly. He reared back to drive the knife deep into Josh's back.

Josh managed to turn his head just slightly, though the wind had been knocked from him, and his eyes were blurry from the blows to the head, he managed to see the sharpened steel in the air above him and then he heard a sudden boom. The man's eyes froze. Blood oozed down the man's shirt. The knife fell useless to the ground. The man fell on his face just to the left of Josh.

It was only after the man fell that Josh saw the Negro man he had passed on the road holding the smoking pistol. The Negro man turned the gun to the man holding the knife on Elijah.

"Drop the knife!" ordered the Negro man.

"You drop the gun or I'll cut the kid's fucking balls off!" screamed the man, shaking at the sight of his friend's dead body.

"Hell, I doubt that young white buck has had a chance to use 'em anyhow. He don't know what he's missing'. So go ahead and cut his balls off, but the moment you do, I'm going to put a bullet through your stupid, ugly white head. You know something? I'm a free man now and at this very moment, I'm free to blow your nasty head to kingdom come. Now what's it going be, white boy?"

Josh had never heard any Negro man speak like that. The man spoke as if he was educated, but at the same time, he was menacing. He was tall—over six feet, with big arms and jet-black skin, white teeth and black eyes. The whites of his eyes were like looking at twin full moons. The Negro man didn't flinch, but began walking closer to Elijah.

The man reluctantly pulled the knife away from Elijah and suddenly took off running for the woods. The Negro man fired a shot at him but missed, and the man escaped into the swamps.

"Damn! I never was good at shooting one of these hand guns," protested the man as he lifted the knife from the dirt and cut the ropes, freeing from Elijah.

Elijah was too frightened to move.

"You okay, son?" asked the Negro man as he patted his shoulder to comfort him.

Elijah could only nod.

"Pull your pants up. Let's see about your friend, shall we?" added the man encouragingly.

Elijah did as he was told. The Negro man walked over to Josh who had pulled himself up to a sitting position. He turned the gun around and handed it handle first to Josh.

"I believe this is yours, sir. I saw you drop it in the road. That's when my wife and me headed for the bushes. Are you all right?"

"I've been worse. I'll manage." Josh holstered his gun, and made a move to stand up, though a bit dizzy. The Negro man extended his big hand. Josh took it and pulled himself up. "Thanks, and thanks for saving my life and my brother's."

"My pleasure and I'm sorry one of them got away. There ain't enough room in this world for the likes of these two. I never shot a pistol before. We're lucky I hit him," grinned the Negro man as he looked at the big hole in the back of the man's chest.

"I'd say you shot him pretty good, but if anyone asks I shot him. They'd lynch you, even if you are free," warned Josh.

"You're right. Well, if you're both okay, I'll get back to my wife. I left her hidden by the road. She's probably still scared to death."

"Wait," said Josh. "What's your name?"

The man took his hat from his head politely, "They call me Tubbs. Hezekiah Tubbs. Hezzi for short. My wife's name is Florence."

"I'm Josh Johnson. This is my brother Elijah." Then Josh surprised the Negro man by sticking his hand out to shake it. "I'm so grateful for your help. Where are you from?"

"Savannah. We were slaves for Albert Finson. He died a few weeks ago with no heirs. He gave us our freedom in his will, but his place was sold, and we had no place to go. We're heading north, looking for work."

The three of them stepped back onto the road. Hezzi waved to his wife, and she cautiously walked over to them.

"Ma'am, I'm Josh, and this is my brother Elijah Johnson. Your husband just saved both our lives and we are most grateful."

She beamed with pride as she slipped her arm around Hezzi's waist.

"Hezzi, you speak properly. Are you educated?" asked Josh.

"Yes, my master didn't follow the Southern rules of keeping slaves ignorant. He liked to talk to me and expected me to talk back intelligently. We became good friends, friends for twenty years. He bought me when I was but a boy. He was good to me. Never beat me."

"Are you afraid to work hard in the fields?" asked Josh.

"There's no work too tough for me."

"All but a few of our slaves took off, and we have a plantation to work. If you and your wife would come to work for us, I'll trade you an acre of land for a year's work, plus room and board. What do you say?"

Florence broke into a huge grin. Hezzi squeezed her hand and glanced into her eyes for silent approval. "We could own a piece of land?"

"Yep, an acre and then the second year, we'll pay you wages and help you build a house on your own land," added Josh.

"We'll take your offer, sir. And thank you."

Josh stuck out his hand once more. Florence had never seen her husband shake hands with a white man before. Hezzi met Josh's grip strong and sure, and they both grinned.

"No, it is still us who thank you for saving our lives. Now, the way I see it, since these robbers were so unkind to us, the least we can do is confiscate their wagon and horse. Do you think you'd like to own it, Hezzi?"

"Yes, sir. I sure would."

"It's yours, compliments of that dead man over there."

"Let's head home before dark. Hezzi and Florence have just got themselves a new wagon and horse, a new job, and before they know it, land of their own!" beamed Josh as the three men pushed and grunted until they righted the wagon, adjusted the harness, calmed the horse down, and then together, they all rode down the road toward home.

TWENTY-FOUR

Henry Clayborn visited the Johnson Plantation on several occasions after striking up his deal with Josh and Elijah. Josh's grandfather used to say that a deal was a good one when it was fair to both parties. Henry's promised deal was quite a surprise and more than fair. Henry would furnish over one hundred horses he had gathered from his recent travels to Florida and Georgia. The Johnson plantation would board and feed the horses, train them, and then the Johnsons and Henry would split the profits from the sale of the horses. If a horse became a runner, then they would also share in the winnings if their horse won. They were all counting on lots of winners.

Henry and the Johnsons instantly became good friends, and Josh's mother thought Mr. Clayborn to be a refined gentleman, that brought great pleasure and honor to her household.

Zeke had grown stronger but was still unable to ride or even walk too far as his broken ribs were taking much longer to heal. Sudden movements brought him to tears. However, with each passing day, improvements could be seen by everyone. However, even though the ribs still hurt, Zeke and Josh did manage to enjoy nightly lovemaking. Zeke told Josh the pain was a fair price to pay to sleep next to him after all these many months of just dreaming about him.

They were careful to remain quiet in Zeke's room, and though his mother knew of their love for each other, everyone else assumed Josh was still sleeping in the guest room. She didn't like the idea of her son sleeping with another man, but for now, the family needed Josh more than he needed the family. Therefore, she bit her tongue, said nothing, and tried hard not to blame poor Zeke.

She, too, had become fond of Zeke, and found him to be bright, intelligent, and most gracious. She delighted in his artful manners and hoped such attributes would rub off on Josh. Sally found him to be very handsome, and delighted in bringing his tray to him for his meals. Over the last few weeks, Zeke finally gained enough strength to make his way down the stairs and into the kitchen. He would arrive at the table with his brow wet with perspiration from the effort, but the family cheered him when he completed the long walk into the kitchen.

Hezzi and Florence became immediate members of the family as well and a big help almost everywhere. Working together, they soon put the house back in order. As Christmas approached, Rachel began to make plans for a big feast. Elijah shot a wild turkey, and so tomorrow's holiday dinner would be filled with excitement. It had been a long time since the Johnson household found any joy in Christmas. This year would be a special one for all, especially Josh and Zeke. In just a few months, Josh had restored hope to the family, and it was hope they needed the most.

Henry Clayborn arrived about noon for the big dinner, and thrilled to have an invitation to celebrate what he called a Colony Christmas. Sally and Florence secretly decided to set the family dining room table instead of the kitchen table. They brought in holly leaves and berries, and decorated the table without Rachel knowing it. This was no easy task as Rachel kept trying to check out all the dinner preparations. With Sally's coaxing, Rachel was encouraged to decorate the rest of the house, and leave the cooking to her and Florence.

Everyone was all decked out in their best clothing. Josh, Elijah, Zeke, and Henry had taken a walk down to the corral where the horses were kept. They toured the stable where the breeding mares were kept. Henry was most pleased with the hard work that Josh, Elijah, and Hezzi had done, and was far more than confident of his good fortune in having met the Johnson brothers—even if he did lose a good horse in the process! He never again bet against the Johnsons, but when Elijah was riding, he always bet on him to win.

When Sally rang the dinner bell, the family gathered in the foyer. Rachel was the last to arrive. As she descended the grand staircase, everyone was overjoyed to see Rachel dressed formally with her hair washed and arranged nicely. She was wearing her best evening gown, a gown she had not worn since her husband died. The family cheered her arrival and clapped for her as well. Rachel blushed, making her face glow a perfect pink. Josh thought his mother had never looked more beautiful than she did descending those stairs on Christmas night.

"Well, let's go eat. Everyone in the kitchen," she urged.

"No, ma'am," said Sally boldly. "We've a surprise for you."

"A surprise?" quizzed Rachel.

"Yes'm. This way please," urged Sally as she bowed with a hand to her indicating all should proceed to the dining room.

Sally pushed the huge double pocket doors open, and before them was the fully set dining room table. They had dug up all the family silver and china, had washed every piece, and polished everything until it gleamed. The chandeliers were lit and red ribbon streamers adorned the table. Sally even managed to find some pretty wild flowers that somehow survived the recent frost.

"Oh, it so beautiful!" gleamed Rachel. "Thank you. Thank you ever so much." She gave both Sally and Florence big hugs. "Let's all sit down and celebrate as one big family. This will certainly be the best Christmas ever."

After the jubilant dinner, the men retired to the library to smoke cigars and sip a bit of Father's brandy.

"I brought you a newspaper from Charleston," said Henry as he entered the room after retrieving the newspaper from his overcoat hung in the hallway.

"Thank you, Henry. I do enjoy catching up on the war, and other special events around the world," said Josh as he took the newspaper and opened it up.

"I'm afraid it is filled with both good and bad news. A few days ago, December 22, 1864 to be exact, Savannah fell. Sherman sent a telegram to Lincoln saying Savannah was his Christmas present. Sherman has both defeated and cut off the South. I'm sorry, that's the bad news. The good news is surely the war will end soon, and we can all get on with our lives."

Josh listened to what Henry was saying, but thoughts of Sherman's troops attacking Andersonville were playing over and over in his mind. Zeke came around the back of Josh's chair, knelt down, and began to read the paper over his shoulder.

"Oh, my!" exclaimed Josh. "It seems that General Hood's plan to cut off Sherman has caved in on him. He lost six thousand Confederates at the end of November at the hands of the Union Army led by General Schofield. They also lost five generals and fifty-three officers. I just don't see how the South can hang on much longer. And look at this," added Josh as he pointed to another article. "Two weeks after this stunning defeat, General Thomas of the Union destroyed the rest of Hood's army in Nashville."

"Sherman's strategy has worked," added Zeke. "All that is left of the Confederacy is Virginia, which is all but surrounded by Yankees, and the Carolinas. Surely, the war is close to being over. What's the point of going on? How many more must die?" Zeke surprised himself by saying the word Yankees as if he was not a Yankee himself. He really didn't feel like a Yankee, but rather just a person born in the state of Maine.

"Weren't you a Yankee?" asked Elijah of Zeke. "I saw your uniform before Josh burned it."

"It wasn't my uniform. I was working as a telegraph operator in Saint Louis, waiting on your slow poke of a brother to join me there so we could head west." Zeke nudged Josh at the tease. "When he didn't show, I was offered a job to work for a naval engineer, John Ericsson, building ironclads at Annapolis. I took the opportunity to learn engineering while I waited to hear from Josh. I was testing a new boat when it was hit by a Confederate mine and I was captured. They assumed I was a soldier and made me a prisoner. Later I was marched to Columbia, South Carolina and then on to Georgia. When winter came to Andersonville, I nearly froze to death. I was forced to take the clothes off a dead soldier in order to stay warm and survive. The uniform Josh burned belonged to an old man from Indiana." Zeke stopped. The pain of Andersonville crept over his face. He dropped his chin. His eyes had watered.

Henry took a sip of his brandy and cleared his throat as an attempt to change the subject, "The good news is also that once the war is done, trading will be back to normal, and horses will be a big commodity. Josh, I've taken your advice and bought many tobacco seed for spring planting at my new plantation. I think there are enough cotton farms. I want to be different and successful. Do you need to borrow some seed?"

Josh quickly grinned. Normally his strong Southern pride would have told him to say no, but Henry was a friend, and cleverly asked if Josh would like to borrow, knowing full well that Josh would never have asked to borrow. "Yes, that would be a big help. Thank you."

"I'll bring some next trip. By the way..."

Before Henry could finish his sentence, they all stopped as the sounds of approaching riders entered the room. The day had been cool. All the windows had been closed, and the thought of posting a sentry never entered Josh's mind. By the time they got to the door, a swarm of over fifty riders had entered the circled driveway.

"They're Confederates!" exclaimed Elijah.

A cold chill rushed up Josh's spine, but he stepped out onto the porch and waited for the riders to halt. The rest of the family gathered behind him. Josh noted the men had been riding hard. They were dirty and their uniforms soiled. Their horses' manes were white from foam. They snorted and panted hard as the riders pulled up to a halt. A colonel stepped from his horse and walked up to the gate.

"Can I help you?" asked Josh politely.

"Yes, you can. My troops, though they fought bravely, were defeated in Savannah. We're heading north to Virginia and we're out of supplies. We need to water our horses and borrow a few supplies."

"You're welcome to water your horses, but we have little supplies. We haven't been able to plant crops..." began Josh before being interrupted.

The man looked up and down at the family's fine clothes. He looked a little too long at Rachel and the two Negro women. "It seems you're doing pretty well anyhow, now doesn't it."

"Listen, I fought for three years. I was wounded. I was a Confederate soldier, but this is my home. You can water your horses, and I'll get some supplies together for your men, but after that you must be on your way. You can camp by the river tonight if you like. There's plenty of fish in the river."

Abruptly, the colonel pulled his pistol, cocked it, and aimed it at Josh's head. Suddenly, the rest of his men did the same. Josh and his family were immediately outnumbered and outgunned. "Now, sir, you are finished with telling me what you're going to do. I no longer take orders from anybody. I've followed orders from some pretty big idiots long enough. Now I'm going to tell you what we're going to do. You all are going to move to the left, put your hands up over your heads, and shut up. We'll take what we please, and if any of you try to stop us, we'll kill you. Now move!"

Josh and his family began moving to the perimeter of the porch. "Josh! Look!" whispered Sally as she nodded across the road.

Josh turned and saw the orange glow of a large fire. It was the Baldwin plantation, and he knew these men must have set fire to it. Several of the colonel's men guarded the family while the rest began ravaging through the house. They gobbled up the remaining food, dumped out pillows, made sacks of the cases, and loaded up the silver, the supplies, the brandy, and anything else that interested them. Josh knew these men weren't just defeated soldiers who were hungry, they had deserted and become robbers and thieves, and they were stealing from anyone and everyone. They had no honor, and he knew that made them all the more dangerous.

One of the soldiers reached out, grabbed Florence's hand, and pulled her to him. She screamed. Zeke was the closest to her.

"Stop, you're hurting her. Let her go," he said.

The man drew his pistol, cocked it, and aimed it at Zeke's head. Then the man turned his head as if sniffing Zeke. "You don't sound like a Southerner. Where are you from?"

Josh's heart stopped, but before Zeke could reply, Henry moved up beside Zeke. "We're from England, you fool. He's my manservant. He's from Liverpool, actually. Ever been there?" he added sarcastically.

"Nope, can't say that I have or want to, but I would like to taste the flesh of this pretty young thing." He pulled her off the porch. He yelled at one of his men guarding the family, "If one of them so much as moves a muscle, shoot 'em dead where they stand!"

The man quickly kneeled, pulled Florence over his shoulder, and carried her around to the back of the house like he was carrying a sack of flour. She kicked and screamed, and he just laughed all the more.

Rachel clutched her cheeks. She was nearly in shock. Sally huddled close to her. Josh was searching for solutions. Zeke had no plan and nothing would come to him. Henry was desperately trying to think of something. Hezzi was just looking for an opportunity.

Suddenly, Sally had an idea. "Oh my lord!" she exclaimed suddenly. "I clean forgot about the apple pies in the oven. They're going to burn!" She made a move from the family toward the door.

The nearest soldier stopped her. "Halt or I'll shoot you dead, darkie!"

"What? Don't you like hot apple pie? How long has it been since you had a fresh, hot, juicy apple pie?" She taunted.

Before he could answer, the guard nearest Josh turned to him. "Let her go get some. The rest of the men are having fun while we're standing guard. Let her go get us some..." He never finished his sentence.

Josh pulled his knife from his boot when the man diverted his eyes and in a flash, he stabbed him in the chest just under his heart, cutting rib, and bone in the process. Josh sliced upward, and the man fell instantly dead. Zeke dove toward the other guard nearest him, and knocked him to the ground, but was still too weak to fight. Henry came up quickly and kicked the man hard in the teeth, knocking him unconscious.

The guard near Sally lifted his pistol as he turned to fire, but Josh grabbed the gutted man's pistol as the man dropped to the ground. Josh rolled to his right, came up, and shot the man in the left eye. He fell to the ground as blood and brains splattered the grass. Sally screamed.

"Quick, run for the woods!" yelled Josh to his family. Zeke snatched up another gun. Henry grabbed the rifle from the man on the porch, and they all ran to the back of the house. Josh spotted Florence's petticoats pulled high over her head. The man stood before her, his pants around his knees. Josh aimed and shot him with no hesitation, but the man jerked in two different directions with the shot. Josh turned and realized that Hezzi had shot him from the corner of the house at the same time. The man fell forward into the chicken coop as Florence leaped out of the way at the last second. The chickens scattered and flew over the fence. Florence dropped her dress, screamed, and ran to Hezzi. He embraced his wife briefly, and then pushed her towards Rachel who led her off into the woods to hide. Hezzi ran back around toward the front of the house, firing at the escaping thieves.

"Come on!" yelled Josh as they circled the house, and entered the back door through the kitchen.

Josh shot the first man that tried to stop them. Zeke shot a man running around the back of the house. Another man ran through the family dining room carrying a sack of silver. Josh shot him in the back. Another took a shot at Josh and missed, the bullet hitting the door near him. It sent splinters into Josh's face, but Josh barely flinched, and coldly shot the man straight in the heart. The man's bag fell to the floor.

They're making a run for it," yelled Henry from the window as he spotted soldiers running to their horses.

Josh pushed in to the foyer. He shot a man on the staircase. Another was rifling through books looking for hidden cash. Josh shot him as well. A man ran in through the front door. Zeke shot him as the man took aim at Josh. Henry and Hezzi ran to the windows. Hezzi grabbed one of the fallen Rebel's rifles. They all began firing at the men on the horses. Several men fell to the dirt.

The colonel rode around to the back of the house and tossed a torch into the kitchen window. Josh saw him out the corner of his eye as he came around the house. Josh ran from room to room trying to get a shot, but the colonel was just a step ahead of him.

When the colonel disappeared around the back of the house, Josh angrily ran and dove through the hallway window, rolled over in the bushes, landed in a heap on the grass, but came up quickly to one knee. The colonel lit another torch. He came riding hard and fast around the back of the house, preparing to toss the torch through the front window.

Josh fired quickly. The first shot would have been enough as it caught the colonel dead between the eyes, but the second shot took out several teeth and exploded out the back of the man's head as he tumbled over the back of his terrified horse and fell to the ground. Josh walked up to him. The torch was still burning in the man's hand.

Someone came running from behind a tree, and took a shot at Josh that just tore the padding from the shoulder of his dinner jacket. He rolled to his left and shot the ex-Rebel. Then another came up and fired. Josh shot him as well. Then a man on horseback came charging toward him while firing. Zeke leaned out the window and fired twice, but missed the man. Josh dropped to a knee and fired, but he was out of bullets. The man fired twice at Josh while charging with his horse. Josh rolled and dove left and right to avoid the bullets. The soldier emptied his gun and then angrily holstered the empty gun, drew his sword, and kicked his horse even harder as he charged toward Josh. Josh rolled across the colonel's body, snatched up the torch, landed on his feet, and came up swinging the torch as hard as he could. The man swung downward as hard with his sword. The sharp blade caught the torch just below the wrapped rags that been soaked in oil. The stick severed, but the flaming end of the torch flipped over and into the soldier's face immediately catching his hair, cap, and shirt on fire. The man fell off the back off his horse to the ground screaming. Josh no longer had a gun. He grabbed the man's fallen sword, ran him through, and left his body burning in the grass.

The remaining soldiers quickly mounted and scattered. Hezzi and Henry had picked off a few of them, but in just a few minutes, the entire melee was over. In all, twenty of the soldiers had been killed including their leader. Henry had been grazed with a stray bullet just above his ear. Hezzi had killed several men, but taken a bullet in the arm. He would be all right. Zeke killed several men, something he had never done before. As Josh surveyed the mess, he suddenly realized Elijah was missing.

Josh spotted Zeke, "Where's Elijah?"

"I don't know. Are you okay?" asked Zeke.

"Yes, I'm fine, but find Elijah!" Zeke began searching the main floor. Josh dashed through the front of the house, jumping over dead bodies and ran up the staircase. He ran into room after room until he came to his mother's bedroom.

Her drawers had been snatched from the proper place, and their contents dumped into a pillow bag. Josh heard a groan. He turned and saw a pair of black boots, toes down on the other side of the bed. He still had the sword in his hand. He recognized the boots as standard Rebel issue.

With the sword in front of him, he moved around the bed carefully. He found that the boots belonged to a huge soldier who was laying face down to the floor. Josh just barely caught sight of his brother's right arm sticking out from under the man.

"Elijah! Elijah!" yelled Josh.

"I'm here!" he yelled back. "Get this fat ass off of me!"

Josh grinned, grabbed the man by the collar, and pulled him to the side. The dead man had his mother's scissors stuck in his chest. The man's blood had soaked Elijah's shirt.

"Are you hurt? Are you bleeding?" asked an alarmed Josh as he pulled his brother to his feet.

"Nope, he was stealing mom's stuff. I tried to stop him, but he was too big for me. He hit me hard. I fell over the bed, spotted the scissors and when he dove to finish me, he dove right onto the scissors. He died on top of me. It was awful! I couldn't get out from under him. He weighed twice what I do!"

Josh burst out laughing, and gave his brother a big hug. "Way to go, little brother. Way to go! Let's go find your mother and Sally."

Josh yelled, "Mom, Sally! It's okay. You can come in now."

It had been both a happy Christmas and sorrowful one. It took them two days to bury all the bodies. While they kept the abandoned horses and their weapons, they buried everything else. Part of their silver had been taken and would never be recovered, the kitchen was partially burned, but Henry had acted quickly by throwing a pot of soup onto the fire before he raced out the front door after the escaping thugs. Lamps and pictures had been broken all over the house. Most of the windows were destroyed along with a lot of their furniture.

However, they had fought as a family and they had won. Josh vowed they would never again be caught off guard. He would sell the soldier's horses, and use the money to hire more help, and from now on, a sentry would be posted as if the war was just outside his family's house. No one would ever take the Johnsons by surprise again.

TWENTY-FIVE

By February 1865, Zeke had rehabilitated enough that he could finally ride a horse around the corral. Josh was indeed proud of his hard work, and thankful he was recovering so well. His ribs were still sore, and he still limped a bit, but each day he was getting stronger and better. Zeke often said it was all due to Sally's fantastic Southern cooking. He wished he could send a telegram home, but with the war still raging—there was no wire service that got any farther north than Richmond. There also had not been any mail service for a long time.

Josh read Sunday's newspaper and discovered that Sherman had left Savannah, and though they feared he might come their way, he turned toward the northwest, and by February 12th, he had taken and secured Branchville, South Carolina. He had also sent part of his army to Charleston. The Yankees were prepared for a fierce, stubborn battle in Charleston, but to their surprise, upon their arrival, they were met with little resistance. They forced the Confederate soldiers to retreat from Charleston, and after evacuating; the Yankees just marched in and took over. The citizens of Charleston all feared their fine city would be burned like Atlanta, but General Gilmore did not wish any harm done to the city. However, in spite of his orders, the soldiers destroyed valuable property, including six thousand bales of cotton and five hundred head of horses. The newspaper story failed to make a determination as to how it happened as the instigator may have disappeared in the explosion, but when the ammunitions stored at a nearby rail yard exploded, many lives and property were also lost. It was General Gilmore's great pleasure once again to hoist the American flag over Fort Sumter. From the famous Battery, which still protected the city of Charleston from harbor waves, the Stars and Stripes could be seen. Word spread quickly, and the war was now over for all Charlestonians, but still the war continued elsewhere.

Upon hearing of the fall of Charleston, Josh ordered round-the-clock sentries for the plantation. Since Christmas, he had hired twenty-five Negro men, some with families, and all with the same deal, he had offered Hezzi. They were good men, carefully picked by Josh. He taught them how to fight, and how to shoot straight. They all learned his methods of taking care of horses, and Elijah soon had them all riding like experts.

In groups of six, they circled the plantation house about a half-mile out and hid just off the main roads, listening for signs of Yankee troop advancements or more renegades.

With Henry's help, they expanded their herd to over two hundred horses, and hoped to have many new foals by spring. Elijah was working as hard as any man, and Josh could not have been prouder. They now had several Negro ladies helping with the house, and Rachel took an active part in running the household and managing the books of the plantation.

Josh was still nervous as their cash reserves were rapidly depleting, and he knew it would still be May before they could expect to bring any corn in from the fields. Zeke used his engineering skills to help Josh plan the fields, looking carefully at the slope and drainage of the land. They abandoned some of the regular acres because of poor drainage and opened up several new ones. The Johnson plantation was once again beginning to take shape, and other plantation owners were stopping by for a tour.

Columbia, South Carolina had fallen and with great relief by South Carolinians, Sherman moved into North Carolina taking Fort Anderson and Fort Armstrong just two days apart. Shortly thereafter, he captured Fayetteville, North Carolina and just six days later Sherman withstood a heavy attack by General Johnson's army.

It became obvious to Josh that as the tide of the war turned so did Lincoln's popularity. Josh recalled all the hateful words he had heard the Yankee rail car passengers say about Mr. Lincoln. With the Rebels now on the run, Lincoln was re-elected for a second term on March 4, 1865 with Andrew Johnson as his Vice President.

Josh had not been in Charleston since early January, which was before Federal troops had occupied the city. However, they were getting low on several crucial supplies, including ammunition, which he was sure he would have trouble obtaining.

"Mom," began Josh, "I have to go. We need more supplies. We can't wait any longer. There is no more time," he argued.

"I'm afraid. The Yankees will shoot Rebels on the spot," she said.

"Mom, I was in the Confederacy, but I'm not any more. I don't wear a uniform. How will they know? Do I sound like a Rebel?" he teased.

"You sound like a spoiled brat, and I've a good mind to give you a good licking," she countered with a grin.

"You'd have to catch me first, Mom, and you know I'm too fast for you!" he laughed.

"I'm smarter. I'd wait until you came in for your supper. Lord knows you never miss a meal!" She took a playful swing at him.

"I'll go along, too, Mrs. Johnson. My accent alone will show them I trust Josh, and know him as a friend of the Union, so to speak," Zeke added with a grin.

"Oh, you two boys are hopeless. You both nearly lose your lives in the war, and here you are walking right back into it," she protested. She moved from room to room pretending to straighten things that did not need adjusting which Josh knew was her habit when she was upset or nervous.

"Sherman is in North Carolina. There's no fighting in Charleston and..."

"And you're going no matter what I say. Isn't that right, Joshua?" she suddenly asked, and before he could answer she added, "Then please be ever so careful. I love you both very much. I can't stand the thought of you being hurt again. Be careful. Come back to us." She gave them both a hug. It was the first time she had hugged Zeke although she had been most polite to him.

It was true, she had grown fond of him even though she did not approve of their love for one another, but watching Zeke fight for her family, her house, and her son last December while he was still so very weak made her admire him. That admiration had now turned to love.

She did not understand her son's love for Zeke, but neither could she deny it. Life was hard enough without the burden of being different, but it was not her cross to bear she reminded herself. Still, she couldn't help hoping they would one-day change. Change she could wait for, just as long as no harm came to either.

She knew Josh was safer with Zeke at his side because no man alive would fight harder to protect him than Zeke. She smiled when she realized that Zeke was as safe as he could be with Josh at his side. She subconsciously reconciled their relationship as protecting each other made more sense to her than the two of them loving each other.

Elijah and Hezzi protested that they should go along as well, but Josh felt that it would be easier for just him and Zeke to sneak in and out of town rather than the four of them. Besides, they were in charge of the plantation forces, and Josh felt better knowing that his family was safe here.

Josh and Zeke left late in the afternoon, each pulling two pack horses rather than a wagon. Josh led the way using many of his old hunting trails to work his way to town. Eventually, they were forced to ride on the main road, but they waited until long after dark.

They were surprised to find there were no guard posts surrounding the city and, as a matter of fact, they found very few Union soldiers patrolling the city. Most of the troops had retired for the evening. The city was quieter than usual with over half the population still in hiding in the lowlands of the Carolinas. Other than that, the city seemed to be back to normal.

Josh walked his horse down an alley just off King Street. He climbed off his horse behind a mercantile shop. He knew the owner. They would be safe here, he thought. He knocked on the door while Zeke kept a hand on his pistol. The manager lived above the store in a small apartment. Josh knocked again.

He heard footsteps and then the cocking of a gun. "Mr. Goldsmith? It's Joshua Johnson. Do you remember me?" whispered Josh.

"What did you say?" asked the old man from inside the locked door.

Josh spoke a little louder, "I'm Joshua Johnson, Richard's boy. Do you remember me?" asked Josh again, hoping he was not speaking too loudly. Zeke turned his head left and right, watching the alley carefully.

"Sure, I remember you." There was a long pause, but the door still didn't open.

"Well, will you let me in?" asked Josh.

"Huh?" the man replied.

"I said will you let me in?" replied Josh, exasperated.

"Oh, sure, I'm sorry." The old man turned the lock and opened the door. He was carrying an oil lamp.

"Thank you, Mr. Goldsmith. I have a friend in the alley. He'll stay there and guard the horses. I need your help. We need some supplies, flour, salt, beans, and we need some ammunition."

The old man shut the door after taking Josh's hand and pulling him inside, leaving Zeke alone to watch the street for trouble. A few minutes later, Zeke climbed off his horse just as he spotted two Union soldiers walking down the far end of the street. He drew his pistol, but soon realized the soldiers had been drinking, and were far too drunk to notice him.

"I can help you with the food supplies, but the Yankees took all our gunpowder and bullets. We have nothing," replied Mr. Goldsmith as he began walking through the store picking up the staples of food that Josh needed.

"Where can I get them?" asked Josh.

"Do you know a Sam Ferguson?" asked Mr. Goldsmith while studying Josh's face for a reaction.

"Wasn't he the man they suspected of killing the Mayor in a card game dispute several years ago? Goodness, I believe that was when I was still a boy," added Josh as he recalled his mother and father discussing it.

"No proof, but three men saw him do it. Only none of them would testify. Sam said he would kill them, too, and I guess they believed him. I don't blame them. He has a tavern just on the edge of town. The Anchor Inn, they call it. He deals in the black market, I've been told," he added as he shook his head in disbelief. "And he preys on those who can't afford things, and charges them four times the price. I despise him, but he might be able to help you."

"Thank you. I guess we'll stop off on the way back. Any news of the war ending soon?" asked Josh as he stuffed the food in the big sacks he had brought along with him.

"Here's this week's newspaper. The war is bound to end soon. Richmond will fall before the month is out, and then there will be nothing left. That darn Confederate Congress voted to allow Negroes to serve in the Rebel army. Can you imagine such a thing? I don't think so. I'd hate to be up on the front lines knowing the man behind me was a darkie, and he was holding a loaded gun. I don't know whom he'd shoot first, the Yankees or me! I'd be afraid to find out!"

Josh had already heard more than he wanted to. He checked his sacks to be sure he had everything on his list. "Thanks for the paper and thanks for helping us," said Josh as he handed Mr. Goldsmith the money.

"No problem, son. Now you be extra careful, and I hope you get home safely. There's lots of robbers and thieves out there, and I ain't just talking about the ones in the army either," he warned.

"Thank you. Good night," replied Josh in a whisper as he handed Zeke a couple of the bags. They tied them off carefully on the spare horses, and then began working their way quietly out of town, taking the alleyways and back roads.

"Shouldn't we turn northwest about here?" asked Zeke.

"I couldn't get ammunition at the store. The Yanks have confiscated it all. We have to get it on the black market. There's a tavern called Anchor Inn. We have to go there to buy it."

"Is it safe?" asked Zeke.

"I doubt it, but what choice do we have. I have my dad's Derringer in my left boot and my knife in my right. My pistol's loaded and so is my rifle. How about you?"

"Knife in the boot, my pistol and rifle are both loaded, and I bite like hell!" laughed Zeke.

"You're crazy!" Josh chuckled.

"I must be. I'm in love with you, and already following you to the end of the world!"

"I hope we can soon head west like we planned and live on our own."

Zeke thought a bit, "How long do you think?"

"We'll help them do the planting, then I'll help Elijah and Hezzi with a few horse trades, and perhaps by late spring we can go. I think Clayborn will be a big help. Hezzi will make a good foreman. I think they'll be all right. I wish I could stay and help longer, but I don't think it's safe to be too friendly with the neighbors with a Yankee living in your house. It probably won't be safe for a Yankee in the South for a long, long time."

"You're right. I've enjoyed my stay here. It helped me to understand you a bit more. Your family is terrific. It's hard to believe they once threw you out because you were..."

"Different?" Josh interrupted. "Well, times have changed. War changes people a lot. I don't know if they've really changed. They needed us a whole lot more because of the war, and if there had been no war then perhaps..."

Zeke cut him off, "If there had been no war, we'd have finished school and then headed west. We'd have never been separated like we were, and I wouldn't have gotten the crap beat out of me in Andersonville."

"Carpon. Who would have ever thought..." Josh stopped in mid sentence. "I hear music. We must be close. Let's approach slowly. I want to see who is coming and going from that place."

They reined the horses to a slow walk and eased down the street as quietly as they could. They tied off the horses in the alley across the street.

Josh and Zeke watched the door for a while, but so far, there seemed to be only locals coming and going. No uniforms, mostly just merchant sailors, and drunks.

"I'm going in. You watch the horses," said Josh in a tone that made it sound like an order.

Zeke rebelled, "I'm not letting you go in that place by yourself. Somebody has to watch your back. I'm going, too."

"Are you crazy? With your accent, the whole place would go nuts, and we'd be fighting Bull Run all over again, except the odds would be about thirty to one!"

"Thirty to two," corrected Zeke. "Who said I would say anything. You go in first, and make your way to the bar to ask for— what was his name?"

"Ferguson."

"Right. I'll wait a minute or two before coming in, and sort of hang out near the door. If anyone asks me anything, I'll motion that I can't talk," Zeke used his index finger to act like he was cutting his throat, a gesture to indicate he could not speak.

"You're hilarious. Yep, you're crazy, cute, but still very hilarious. Okay, but keep your hand close to your pistol and your mouth shut. Okay?"

Zeke squeezed his lips together like they were sealed and nodded yes.

"I'm in love with a lunatic!" Josh chuckled as he crossed the street.

Zeke watched Josh enter the swinging doors of the tavern, and then began counting to a hundred. He soon became too impatient and by the time he got to eighty, he just whispered, "Eighty, ninety, one hundred," and started walking.

He took a deep breath and pushed through the swinging doors. He saw an old stove to his right, which barely kept the frost out of the place. He sidestepped his way to it. He spotted Josh at the bar with a beer mug in his hand. Josh chugged down half of it without stopping.

An older lady with a dirty rag in her hand was wiping off the table in front of where Zeke was standing. She turned around quickly with the little tray she carried and nearly knocked Zeke down. It was all he could do to keep from saying, "Excuse me."

"I'm sorry, sonny. Can I get you a beer? My, you're a cute one, aren't you?" she added without even a pause for breath. Zeke guessed that she probably said the same to every man that came in, which was pretty smart, because the short statement already made him both blush and feel good at the same time.

Zeke motioned he could not talk.

She nodded her head. "You know, since the war, more and more men can't talk. Some got their ears shot off, a few got their balls shot off, and for some, well, they just can't talk. Hell, you'll be fine. At least you still got your balls, huh?" With that, she unexpectedly grabbed Zeke's crotch and gave them a little squeeze. "And from the size of them, I'd say you'll be having children in no time. How about a beer?"

Zeke nodded yes.

"Great, I'll be right back."

Zeke was relieved when she was gone. She had diverted his attention for less than a minute, but by the time she stepped out of the way, Zeke was in panic as Josh was nowhere in sight. Zeke stepped to his right and left trying to see through the smoke filled crowded room, but he knew Josh was not there.

Zeke decided to stand still for a few more minutes. He noted a curtain pulled over a doorway near the back, and thought maybe Josh had gone back there to get the ammunition. He could not follow him there, as that would have been too obvious, but the more Zeke searched his mind for what he should do, the more worried he became.

The lady brought the beer and Zeke gave her a coin. She smiled and he began drinking his beer. Zeke's eyes were diverted from the doorway when a rather larger patron took another man's hair in his hand, and slammed the poor man's face into the table, breaking his nose.

The man yelled, "If you beat me again, I'll kill you. You must have been cheating. I never lose." The man was drunk.

Zeke watched the bleeding man make his way to the door. He felt sorry for him, but knew he could not interfere. He checked the curtains once more. No, Josh. He was anxious to leave, and wished they did not need the ammunition. He leaned against the wall.

The loud drunk yelled at the man dealing cards. The man slammed his fists down on the table, and everybody in the bar began looking to see what the commotion was all about.

Josh came through the curtain carrying a large sack. A big man was following him. The man wore a black patch over one eye. Zeke thought he looked like pirate. The big man motioned for two other rough types to come to him. He huddled around them, and Zeke saw him point at Josh's back, as Josh was busy trying to get through the crowd.

Just as Josh went by the table with the loud drunk, the man suddenly flipped the table over, threw the man beside him out of the chair, and backed right into Josh. Josh dropped the sack.

"Whoops, beg your pardon," apologized Josh, hoping to keep things civil.

Zeke fingered his gun in his holster, anticipating trouble. He looked back, saw the two men still talking to Ferguson, and looking in Josh's direction. He guessed more trouble was on the way.

Josh reached to the floor for his bag. The drunk took the opportunity and kicked Josh in the butt, knocking him head first into the bar. Josh flinched at the pain. He came up with fists clenched, and then thought the better of it.

"Hang on, Mister. No harm done. It was just a..." began Josh.

The man spit on Josh's shirt and swung at him. Josh ducked the first punch, but the man had fought hard and dirty all his life and though drunk, he still managed a quick upper cut with his other hand that caught Josh squarely on the chin. The crowd parted and people immediately began chanting, “Fight! Fight! Fight!” while others started placing bets.

Zeke was bewildered as to what he should do. Should he help Josh, or lay low and watch the other two. He knew Josh could take care of himself, but it hurt him to see Josh be punched.

Though stunned from the upper cut and angry, Josh controlled his temper. He pretended to be dazed, but when the big guy reached to pull him up for another punch, Josh came up fast with his knee and kneed the man hard in the balls. When the man grabbed himself, Josh swung hard and fast, and hit the man squarely on the left side of his face. The man staggered and fell to the floor. The surprised crowd cheered.

Zeke hoped the fight was over. Josh prayed it was over. Josh reached for his bag, and started once again for the door. He took about two steps when the downed man suddenly came up with a pistol, and took aim at Josh's back.

The crowd shrieked and quickly moved away from Josh. The man was cursing Josh, but Josh ignored him and took another step toward the door. Josh did not turn around and was unaware that the drunk was armed. Zeke saw the drunken man cock the pistol and put his finger on the trigger. Zeke could not wait any longer.

Zeke drew his pistol and fired, hitting the man in the chest. People scattered even farther back as they stumbled over chairs and tables to get out of the way. The big man fell to the ground and then onto his side.

Josh ducked at the sound of gunfire, jerked his pistol from his holster, and turned to see the big man fall. Once he realized the big man had already been shot, his eyes turned to Zeke's smoking gun.

"Let's get the hell out of here!" Josh yelled.

Zeke spotted the two men with Ferguson. He was yelling something at them, and they began pushing their way through the crowd. Zeke held his gun on the crowd for another moment, and then dashed out the door. He found Josh already tying off the sack on the packhorse. They both swung into their saddles just as the two men came out of the door. Their guns were already drawn and they began firing.

"This way!" yelled Josh as he returned fire, and then darted with horses in tow down behind a row of houses. Zeke kicked his horse hard and followed Josh. Bullets whizzed over their heads. A clothesline nearly jerked Josh off his horse before it broke. He scrambled to pull himself free from the line and the hanging clothes.

The men ran down the length of the house just as Josh cut back across to the road, leaving a house between them and the gun shots. Zeke stayed right with him, yelling at his horse to run.

They didn’t slow down until they were a half-mile away, and the gunfire stopped. They had made it.

Josh pulled his panting horse up to a walk, "I thought you were going to remain silent."

"I didn't say a word," replied Zeke, out of breath, his stamina still not completely restored. "He was going to shoot you in the back. Why didn't you just knock the idiot out instead of playing with him?" asked Zeke as they walked the horses down the road.

"What? I hit that drunk with all my strength. He had a jaw made of steel. He wouldn't go down and stay down. I kneed him hard in the balls. Those testicles must be like cannon balls," laughed Josh.

"Well, do you think we're safe now?" asked Zeke.

"Yeah. It was self-defense. The man was going to kill me. What choice did we have? Let's go home. I'm hungry." Josh gave his horse a slight kick to make him trot.

Zeke told his horse, "Giddy up," and then to Josh, "Did you say horny?"

Josh took off his hat and swatted at Zeke. "Hungry, I said. You're impossible. You're supposed to be recovering. I wish you'd go back to keeping your mouth shut."

"Only after you kiss me," shot back Zeke.

Josh obliged by pulling his horse alongside Zeke and in the pale of the moon, he leaned over and kissed Zeke, not once but several times as they made their way home.

TWENTY-SIX

Josh and Zeke slept in the next morning after arriving home at just past three a.m. The late morning sun warmed up their room in spite of the windy March weather. Josh was in Zeke's arms, snuggled in tight and cozy beneath a quilt his grandmother had made for him when he was six years old. He opened his eyes and found his fingers intertwined in Zeke's. He kissed Zeke's wrist softly. Zeke stirred just slightly by flaring his nostrils, but otherwise, he did not move. Josh felt Zeke's flesh against his bare back and smiled. He had never felt better, more confident, more alive, and more in love.

His brow wrinkled at the sounds of a horse trotting quickly up the drive. He wondered who it could be. He knew the sentries were posted, but he was instantly awake.

He leaned up from Zeke's grasp to listen more carefully. The rider was not letting up. He was galloping hard for the house. Josh reluctantly climbed from the warm feather bed, and walked to the window while pulling his shirt over his naked body.

"What is it?" asked Zeke as he propped himself up on one elbow, disappointed to not still be holding Josh.

"A rider," replied Josh as he pulled on his pants, and then his boots.

"I'm up!" protested Zeke as he climbed from the bed.

Josh leaned closer to the window and pulled the curtain open. He spotted Hezzi as he ran to meet the rider. Josh leaned into the window until he realized the rider was James, one of the new men he had hired. He pushed open the window. Zeke was quickly dressing.

The rider pulled to a quick halt and swung out of the saddle.

"Rider's coming!" said the panting man.

"Who?" asked Hezzi?

"Two Yankees, the Sheriff, and three other men—one with a patch over his eye," exclaimed the man.

"Warn the others!" ordered Hezzi as Elijah rode up from the stable to see what was going on.

"Trouble?" he asked.

"Afraid so," replied Hezzi.

Josh yelled from the window. "If they're looking for me or Zeke, tell them we went to Florida to buy horses. Elijah, you meet them. Hezzi stand with him. They won't respect Elijah without some muscle. Sorry, Elijah. It'll come with age. Don't let them search the house. Tell them Mother is taking a bath. Got it?"

"Yes, I can handle it," replied Elijah, his pulse already rising while he was wondering why he was going to have to do all that lying. Then he thought perhaps Josh was protecting Zeke, but the man said some Yankees were coming, maybe he was protecting himself.

"Hezzi, go get our rifles," ordered Elijah.

Hezzi took off in a sprint as he headed for the kitchen.

"Zeke, they could be looking for you or me, or both of us. We can't trust the court judges during wartime, and certainly not a Yankee being tried in a Southern court. We'll have to hide out until we find out what they want. Let's head out back, grab our horses, and head for the woods."

Zeke grabbed his jacket, strapped on his pistol, and together than ran down the stairs.

"What's going on?" asked Rachel as she started up the stairs, carrying some spring wild flowers.

"I can't explain right now. Stay out of sight. You're supposed to be taking a bath," said Josh quickly.

"A bath? It's almost noon," she protested.

"If anyone asks, just tell them Zeke and I are gone to Florida, and we'll be back in a month," he said as he ran out the back hallway.

"Tell who?" she asked to no one as they both bolted out the door.

They saddled up and just made it to the woods when the riders galloped up the driveway. Josh and Zeke spun their horses around back and into a grove of thick trees and bushes, tied them off, and ran back to the bushes to watch.

Elijah stuck his hand up and waved as friendly as he could while keeping his right hand on his rifle. Hezzi scouted the perimeter and was pleased to see that his men had followed his orders and moved in silently behind the riders. They were hidden behind trees, bushes, and fences, but each man aimed his rifle at the one of the riders.

"Whoa," said the Sheriff, who seemed to be in charge.

"Hello, Mr. Johnson. I'm Sheriff Albertson. This is Colonel Parker. We need to speak to Josh. Where's he working today?"

Elijah thought the Sheriff sounded friendly enough, but he recalled Josh's words and yawned while he formed his words. He did not have much practice at lying, except to his mother when she asked if he had practiced reading today. "Josh is gone to Florida to buy some horses."

"I heard you were building a horse farm. How many head you got?"

"'Bout two hundred or so," bragged Elijah and then being fair, "They're part Henry Clayborn's, too. We raise and train them for him. We're breeding, too. From the looks of your horse, I'd say you'd better come see us for a new mount soon."

Josh poked Zeke in the ribs. "Can you believe my little brother? He's as cool as can be."

"Let's hope so."

"When did he leave?" asked the Sheriff.

Elijah eyes widened. Josh had not said how long he'd been gone. Shit! What to do! Elijah cleared his throat. "He left day before yesterday. Why?"

"He was seen at the Anchor Inn last night. He and a fellow killed a man," replied the man with the black patch over his eye.

Elijah gulped. He did not like the look of that man at all.

Josh frowned. "That's Sam Ferguson. I don't get it. I paid him for his stuff, what's he care about the drunk?" asked Josh to himself and to Zeke.

The Sheriff walked closer to Elijah, "Son, I have several witnesses that say Josh was there last night and not in Florida as you say. This man here is Sam Ferguson. The man they shot was his brother. Now where is Josh?"

Elijah chewed his lip. "Josh wouldn't shoot anybody that didn't first deserve it, and besides, like I said, he left for Florida. Don't worry, he'll be back at the end of the month, and then you can talk to him."

Elijah managed to stay in control. The Sheriff did not believe him but started walking back to his horse.

The Yankee colonel spoke up. "Search his house," he ordered the Sheriff.

"Now hold on. The Johnsons are good people. I know you Fed boys are in charge, but there's no need to search the house."

The colonel ignored the Sheriff's pleas and turned to his two men, "Search the house. Find them!"

The Sheriff bit his lip. "I'm sorry, Elijah. I have no choice. They're the bosses nowadays."

The Yankee soldiers unsaddled, took their rifles with them, and ran to the house. As they started up the stairway, Rachel came out of the room, her hair wet and wearing but a robe.

"Oh, my lord! I'm taking a bath and the Yankees have invaded my home!" she shrieked convincingly.

Sally came running from the library yelling, "Miss Johnson!" she saw the soldiers and quickly fell silent.

"We're looking for Josh Johnson," said the older man.

Rachel spoke up before Sally could reply, "Why, he's gone to Florida. May I be of help?"

The men were embarrassed for having invaded the woman's privacy. "We'll search down here. I'm sorry, ma'am. Orders," the older man mumbled as they ran from room to room.

When they came out the front door, they shrugged their shoulders. "Nothing in there, sir."

"Let's search the entire grounds. They must be somewhere," ordered the colonel.

"Begging your pardon, your highness," mocked the Sheriff, "but Josh knows these swamps better than an alligator. If he was here, he is now long gone. We've only a few men and no hope of catching him. I really don't think he did it anyhow."

"I didn't ask you what you thought, but you're right, we do need more men. Let's head back, and I'll bring twenty of my best riders back. We'll find him."

The Sheriff shook his head in disgust, but saddled up, tipped his hat to Elijah, and led the group back down the road.

Hezzi waited until they were out of sight before he yelled to his men, "Return to your posts. Be sure and let us know when you see these men again."

Elijah ran to the house. His mother, now dressed, came down the stairs. "What did they want with Josh?"

"They said he killed a man last night," replied Elijah.

"Preposterous! Not my Joshua," she said as if she needed to convince Elijah.

Josh entered the back door with Zeke.

"Did you hear them?" asked Elijah.

"Yes. We had to buy the ammunition from the man with the patch. A man sucker punched me. I tried to back down, but he was determined to fight, then he tried to shoot me in the back as I was leaving, and..."

"And I had to shoot him to stop him from killing Josh," said Zeke in Josh's defense.

"Oh, my! What are we going to do?" asked Rachel as she moved to the hall bench to sit down.

"I don't know, Mother. We must think quickly," replied Josh.

Sally checked to make sure the men were gone, and then entered the room to announce, "Lunch is ready."

The entire Johnson family and Zeke, along with Hezzi, Sally, and Florence, sat down to eat. The meal conversation was somber at first. Josh and Zeke should have been starved as they had missed supper and breakfast, but their appetites had left them. It was Josh who broke the long silence.

"I don't think Ferguson is going to let this go, and I don't know what that Yankee colonel is going to do. As for the Sheriff, I could handle him. What I fear most is that a court would never convene. They'd declare justice by hanging Zeke. I bought ammunition from a man who deals in the black market, and yet he was riding today with the colonel of the Federal forces and the local Sheriff."

"I see," broke in Zeke. "To make the black market work, as we studied in history at the academy, someone must be paying off someone."

"That's right. I think Sam has the Colonel and perhaps even the Sheriff in his pocket. We'd get no fair trial. You'd be dead before you got to Charleston's jail," surmised Josh.

"What are you going to do?" asked Elijah.

"We'll get a solicitor," suggested Rachel.

"Unless they're good shots, they can't help us. Lawyers right now can't stop bullets or hangings," protested Josh.

"Mother, I'm afraid my stay is over on the Johnson Plantation. I had hoped to stay and help with the spring planting, and to help Elijah with the trades, but I fear our time has already run out. Zeke and I must head west immediately. They'll be back, and they'll come back stronger."

"Leave? Now?" she protested.

"Mother, we must put a lot of ground between us and those troops. There's just two of us and there's no telling how many of them," replied Josh as he stood up from the table. His mind raced with the things they needed to do, and he began giving orders to everyone, "Sally, will you pack us as much grub as you can spare. Hezzi, get our horses ready. Elijah, check our weapons, and make sure we have ammunition. Zeke, get us packed. I'll meet you on the porch in ten minutes."

"But Josh," began Rachel once more, "how will we manage without you?"

Zeke ran past her and up the stairs. Josh walked around the table and gave her a big hug. "Mother, the same way you managed while I was fighting the war. Elijah's growing fast. He knows horses. I've prepped Henry Clayborn on looking after you. Hezzi can handle the men. You're in much better shape than when I arrived. I wish I could stay, but you knew all along that Zeke and I could never have stayed forever. There would have been too many embarrassing questions. In time of war, you forced yourself to handle it. In time of peace, it will become a burden once again. I'll write you, but I have to leave, and we have to leave quickly."

Josh ran from the kitchen and up the stairs. Zeke was busy packing when Josh entered the room and grabbed his knapsack and bedroll.

"Are you sure about this?" asked Zeke.

"What choice do we have?" shrugged Josh. "Besides, given the choice of staying here, seeing you hang, and me rotting in jail, or spending the rest of my life with you in the wilderness..." he began and then tried to lighten the situation, "I guess I'd rather sleep with you." Josh grinned broadly. "I hope you're in shape for this trip," replied Josh as he tossed Zeke a shirt.

"I'm in great shape, thanks to you and your family. I hate to leave them like this."

"We have no choice. Got everything?"

"Yes," replied Zeke as he turned in a circle to see if they had missed anything.

They descended the stairwell and found Rachel, Sally, and Florence waiting for them. They were all were dumbstruck at the speed at which they made this big decision to leave.

Josh spoke first, "I'll miss you, Mother. I love you."

"I love you too," she said then she grabbed Zeke while hugging Josh, "and I love you too, Zeke. Take good care of my boy."

"I will, ma'am, and thanks for...everything," Zeke swallowed hard. He had grown genuinely fond of Mrs. Johnson.

"Sally, how could I ever..." began Josh as stretched out his hands to her.

"Just hug me a good one," she encouraged, tears running down her cheeks as well. Then he hugged Florence, turned to look over the house once more, and then ran out into the front yard.

Hezzi had their mounts saddled up and ready. Josh and Zeke tied on their bedrolls and saddlebags. Elijah brought their rifles out. They tied on the sacks of food Sally fixed for them. They shoved the extra ammunition into their saddlebags.

Josh shook Elijah's hand, "You and Hezzi are head of the plantation now. You know my plans, and I know how smart you are. Henry will help, but in the end it will be your decisions that make or break the future. I know you can do it, just as I knew you could win that horse race. I'm proud of you. I love you."

Elijah could not think of anything to say as he shook Josh's hand as firmly as he could. Zeke leaned down from his saddle and shook his hand as well.

"Hezzi, I'm counting on you. Don't let my little brother step into trouble. My family needs you."

"I know. I'll take care of them."

Josh shook his big hand and smiled. "I know you will."

Josh swung himself into the saddle, and pulled his horse into a slow circle taking in what he knew would be his final look at the Johnson plantation. He had grown up here, and banished from here, but still it was his home, and the people standing on the porch were the family he loved. Only one love was strong enough to pull him away from his roots.

Half afraid he would begin crying, Josh took in a deep, slow breath. "Let's ride!" he suddenly exclaimed as he kicked his horse and trotted down the drive.

"Which way we headed?" called Zeke as he came up along him while waving back at the same time.

"We can't use the main roads. The word will already be out. Let's head through the swamps!"

"I was afraid you'd say that."

Josh kicked his horse in front of Zeke's, leaped over the fence along the drive, and began galloping across the open field. Zeke kicked his horse hard, and leaped over the fence and began chasing after Josh.

By the time, they reached Chattanooga, some three weeks later; Lee had surrendered at Appomattox Courthouse. President Davis had fled to Georgia to go into hiding with his key personnel and his family. Josh and Zeke did not stay in Chattanooga long—just long enough to replenish their supplies and get back out on the trail west. Josh managed to buy a paper while Zeke tried to send a telegram to Maine. He found out the lines were still down to the north.

It had been few years since Zeke had left Saint Louis in a rush to get to Maine for his brother's funeral, but he hoped his friend was still there. He stepped into the Chattanooga telegraph office. Zeke begged the operator to let him key his own message. The operator hesitated but after staring intently into Zeke's eyes, he felt the boy could do the job, and so he stepped away.

Zeke quickly sat down and began the wire to John. Zeke told him he had found Josh and all was well. He thanked him for all his help.

John quickly replied he was glad to have known Zeke and hoped to meet the boys again some day soon.

Zeke replied by telling John where to find his bundle of cash in the wall in his room. Astonished to hear from Zeke, John quickly found the money hidden in the spare room. John quickly wired back he had secured the funds. He proposed to ship it to Memphis by stagecoach. Zeke grinned and replied to send it in his name as soon as possible, and to keep the funds needed to pay for the shipment.

Josh was astonished that Zeke had left so much money in John's unknown care, and Zeke was greatly relieved John was still taking care of it, all though he did not know where it was hidden until today. The money would help them with the start in the west.

They boarded their horses with the blacksmith, took a much-needed bath in a bathroom, and then got a room and began making love on a mattress instead of the ground. They were sore by morning. A few days later, they sat on a bench waiting for Wells Fargo stagecoach to arrive. It was past due by an hour.

Josh had just flicked a fly away from his face when he spotted the coach coming down the street. He and Zeke stood as the dusty but thirsty passengers made a hasty retreat from the coach for a much need pee and then a long drink of water.

The driver unloaded the packages to the ground. Zeke walked over to him.

"Sir, I'm Zeke Robertson. Do you have a package for me from John Sebastian in Saint Louis?" Zeke smiled but kept a firm face of confidence.

The driver gave him a hard look and then smiled, "Yes, son, I do. John told me to make sure I gave it to the right person. He described you perfectly." He reached down and picked up a package labeled Truss. "I'm sorry to hear about your injury, but this here truss will fix you up good."

Zeke took the package and thanked him. The word truss confused him, but wisely, he said nothing. He had no idea what a truss was. Josh gave him a grin, and they headed to their room to open the package in private.

Josh held up the truss and busted out laughing. Zeke looked at the diagram showing how it should be worn, and soon realized it was device to help with a hernia. He laid it down and picked up the all the money John had sent and a note from John.

"Dear boy, I don't doubt that you and Josh have been working long and hard on making up for all those years of no sex, so I suspected you might need a truss! I'm sorry for the joke, but I suspected with the word truss on the package, no one would steal it. I trust you received the truss in excellent shape. Happy trails and send me a telegraph when you can. All the best. Your friend, John." Zeke ran to the telegraph office to send a note of thanks to John, and another note to his parents, hoping it would get through.

Josh bought a newspaper and discovered that Lincoln had been shot and killed, and the last battle of the war had been fought in Brownsville, Texas. The war was finally over. Over 349,000 Yankees had died and though records were scarce, about an equal number of Rebel soldiers had been killed as well. The news reporter wrote the war had been the worst catastrophe in America's short history. She almost failed to survive, but somehow, the Union was once more together.

Over a meal in a restaurant, Josh and Zeke discussed what they thought the future of the country might be. Neither boy had the answers to the insurmountable problems the country now faced.

By dawn, they were heading west across the Mississippi. Summer had arrived, and the sun was hot on their backs. They did not know what the future held for them, but they certainly knew the past. They had nearly lost each other more than once. Their love had stood the test of time. Through the challenges of separation and the fear that doubt feeds upon, they had not only managed to remain true and loyal to each other, but they had beaten the odds and found each other once more and survived.

With the love of the other, they each stood taller in the saddle, more confident, more assured, and they slept secure in the knowledge that this was indeed the love of their lives. Few would understand their love, but no one would be able to deny it existed. They were careful. They knew how the average person reacted to two men in love. They could never show affection in public, but longed for the nights by the fire where, alone, they could celebrate the pure joy of each other as well as the jubilation of having survived what were the most perilous of times.

If love truly conquers all, then there were no odds that Josh and Zeke could not conquer and overcome. With each step of their horses' hooves, they moved closer and closer to the freedom they had so wanted and planned for in their tiny cottage at the academy and in their dreams during the war.

They were finally living those dreams. They were finally together and could finally tell each other a hundred times a day how much they loved each other. In their hearts, they knew that each day their love would grow stronger and stronger.

Josh and Zeke reached the Rockies before fall. They worked quickly to build a cabin, and store up food and supplies before the rapidly approaching winter.

More than once when their funds were running low they discussed returning to the east to dig up the gold that Josh and his men had left in the false grave with the name of Goldblum. It had been a tempting idea, but even the bags of gold hidden there were just too great a risk. Never again did they wish to be dragged into the politics and problems that going east were sure to bring. Perhaps going back some day, but not for a long while.

They spent their spare time either panning for gold or digging in a tunnel for it. After the big snows fell, it was easier to work in the tunnel than the river. In late February, they experienced a cave in that nearly did them in. After removing the new pile of rocks from the tunnel path, they discovered a vein of gold. They were immediately overjoyed! Their stash of gold put their thoughts of the Goldblum grave in their past.

They hid the entrance to the tunnel and told no one about their good fortune, but secretly they bought up more land until their log cabin sat in the middle of four thousand acres. They bought only five hundred acres at a time saying they had inherited their money from their parents.

No one suspected they were rich, as they did nothing with their acreage. They built no corrals, not put up any fences. They did not even put an entrance to their land. They posted no signs and though they spotted hunters crossing over their land from time to time, they made no effort to stop them. Most folks just assumed the land to be part of the Rocky Mountain wilderness.

As Josh would often say, they lived in a place the Indians called the land of the angry gods because from time to time the ground would tremble like the beginnings of an earthquake. However, the gods were not angry with Josh and Zeke because it gave them wealth beyond their wildest dreams.

Zeke and Josh knew it was not angry gods that made the nearby geysers shoot hot water and steam high into the air at regular intervals, but they did not explain that to the Indians. The facts that the Indians feared the hot bursts of steam made them feel more secure and safe from the Indians and hopefully from others.

Reaching their cabin was intentionally difficult. The climb up the side of the mountain was as tough on a man as it was on a horse. No one would ever just wander in.

Zeke had dug out a pool not far from a geyser, allowing the bubbling water to make its way down a narrow canal into the pool. It had taken him six months to dig it out with all the rocks he kept finding, but the reward was worth it. The pool was not as big as Josh's old swimming hole back in the swamps of Charleston, but as long as Zeke was with him, the warm water pool would do just fine.

In the middle of winter, they would often run naked from the cabin to the pool and quickly jump in. They ran even faster on the return hoping to reach the cabin before they froze to death.

With the arrival of spring, Zeke and Josh sat in their natural spa as the hot water swirled around them. The sky was blue and the sun was bright. Eagles flew high over their heads probably wondering what the strange humans were doing. They had two dogs that watched the only trail leading to their cabin, but no one had bothered to make the climb since their arrival.

They had thousands of dollars in gold buried beneath their cabin, but they did not need much money, nor did they need cities or wars. They did not need a cause to die for, and they did not need to live the way people thought they should.

Josh rolled onto his stomach and slid over on top of Zeke while he lay on his back absorbing the hot, steamy water with his eyes closed. Josh squeezed Zeke's flesh, then cuddled up in Zeke's arms and kissed Zeke deeply. Slowly, they made love as they had so many times over the past year. Josh teased Zeke about making up for the lost time during the war, and often said they only had to do it another thousand times, and then they would finally caught up. Zeke responded that after a thousand more times they would have caught up for the first year they had been separated, and soon after they would have to begin working on the second thousand.

For them, it was not just the act of making love. It was their declaration to each other that they knew their love was special. No couples they had ever known had stayed so much in love. They grew comfortable in their relationship as most couples did, but the passion of their love never dimmed.

They had not given it all up for the love they shared. They simply gave their all to each other. They spent most of the war apart, but it didn't break them. They willed themselves to survive not just any war, but the worst war ever fought by America. Against all the world could throw at them, their love had overcome, and so their celebration of each other and their success continued.

"It still feels good, doesn't it?" smiled Zeke as he leaned up and kissed Josh deeply, his tongue flirting in and out. He studied the deep blue of Josh's eyes as he had done on so many occasions, and looked at the tiny dimples left and right of Josh's mouth. Zeke smiled contentedly, knowing he loved Josh with all his heart and Josh loved him the same.

Josh enjoyed the swirling of Zeke's tongue for a few moments and then pulled away and kissed Zeke softly over his eyelids. "If it didn't still feel good," he said between soft kisses, "I'd trot on over to the nearest Indian village, and pick out one of those handsome braves for these cold nights!"

Zeke started laughing. Josh got the giggles and soon they were rolling each other over and over in the hot shallow water before ending up on the edge of the bank. They kissed deeply and once more shared their love. They knew they would be together forever, and together they would make forever a long, long time.

TJ Johnson
November 2008

EPILOGUE

At the request of fans and bookstore owners, the author began writing the sequels to the story of Josh and Zeke. Their new journey, **A World Ahead – Part II,** begins in 1866 with the war in the east completed, and the war with the Indians exploding in the west. The tracks of the railroads continued to grow while the herds of buffalo begin to disappear. Gold seekers found nothing but frustration and despair. Some settlers continued moving west while others took up an easier life of crime.

Josh and Zeke's past catch up with the boys when a band of former Confederate soldiers, now looters, cross their paths. General Sherman takes command of the area, much to the frustration of General Custer.

The Indians, no longer congenial hosts, begin banding together to force the white men back to their ships and across the big sea. Against difficult odds, they win some battles, but already feel they are losing their war.

Josh and Zeke wish to remain neutral in a western land where neutral often means both sides are against you. Surviving in the Colorado Rockies is difficult for most frontiersmen, but survive they must while taking on the battles and wars repeatedly heading their way.

For updates on the publication of this new story, **The War Ahead – Part II**, plus part III **The World Beyond,** bookmark **www.ItsFiction.com**

Acknowledgements

I must give high praise to my editing team and their amazing patience to put up with my typos and mistakes, and I want to thank them for helping me.

TJ Johnson

Author TJ Johnson

TJ spent most of his early years hating to read, and thinking even less of his senior English class. Fortunately, a special teacher insisted he write a fictional short story, a two page tale about something he found interesting. Instantly, TJ became hooked on the fun of writing fiction. Thankfully, he now reads constantly, going from one book to the next, with several in queue waiting their turn. His favorite part of writing is the crafting of a rough draft. A period in the process when the words fly from the storage center deep in his brain like a movie stuck on fast-forward. The agonizing part begins with the painstaking restructuring, as TJ edits one sentence at a time until he is either happy, or exhausted into believing he is happy with his conclusion.

His new release is **The Raceboys** about a national champion forced to come out as a gay driver. Also available is **The Will** and **Stranded.**

Coming Soon: TJ is currently polishing "**A Writer's Fantasy**" about his favorite college sport basketball, as well as his favorite player. In the story he plays himself as he writes about the fictional Taylor University's historic basketball program, and the circumstances that led up to meeting their star player. The story tells how they fell in love, and TJ begins writing a book called "A Backstage Pass to Taylor University's Basketball Championship." It is meant to a be a funny, improbable, love story, but as TJ states in the beginning, "It's MY fantasy, and I'll write it anyway I please," which means in the story TJ is thinner, has more hair, and far better looking!

Currently TJ is editing **The Blackfeet Boys** set in the northwest in a time when two young warriors must abandon their home with the most feared and blood thirsty tribe in North America, and search for a safe and isolated world together. Followed by **Gay Grifters:** Chris Connors learns his new friends not only steal your wallet and gold, but also your heart and soul! With little honor among thieves, these young gay men take pleasure in robbing their tricks, while aiming for bigger scores. Will the biggest thief in America give up a life of crime for a lifetime of love? Only the tale will tell.

Fans of the War Series (**The War Apart - Part 1**, **The War Ahead - Part 2**) will be pleased to know that the research is finished, and the writing has begun on **The War Beyond - Part 3**.

Future works include several new stories: Followed by: **Forever Alone...Again** a funny sentimental tale about a man's countless attempts to find real love, only to watch his new perfect relationship self-destruct before he can move their love from third base to a home.

Requests for additional information and Inquiries can be obtain from **Hard Title Publishing,** at **Info@ItsFiction.com**

WWW.ItsFiction.Com

Contact TJ Johnson at:

Info@ItsFiction.com

1. I try to answer all my email myself; however please read "Bio & Info" before writing as your question – saving time for all! Many readers ask the same questions repeatedly.

2. Please do not add my email address to any group for jokes, thoughts, prayers, or riddles, etc. I always delete these without reading.

3. I do not open any emails with attachments as these may contain viruses or other nonsense!

4. Please do NOT write suggesting plot lines as I delete these quickly, too. I like to write my own stories. If your plot is good, write it yourself! Do not send your manuscript to me – I am a writer, not a publisher, and I do not have the time.

5. All characters and names are part of my imagination and indicate no one particular. If I like a person's name, I may use the first or the last name but never both at the same time. It is true some of the events in my books are historical in nature but many are not. Choosing which to believe is your job, but this is why fiction is fun.

6. If you do not receive a reply, perhaps "Bio & Info" contain the answer already, or your email address is not functioning correctly.

7. If you have read all the above, I cannot wait to hear from you!